The Bewitching

THE BEWITCHING

JILL DAWSON

SCEPTRE

First published in Great Britain in 2022 by Sceptre
An imprint of Hodder & Stoughton
An Hachette UK company

1

A CIP catalogue record for this title is available from the British Library

Hardback ISBN 9781473654662
Trade Paperback ISBN 9781473654679
eBook ISBN 9781473654648

Typeset in Janson Text by Hewer Text UK Ltd, Edinburgh
Printed and bound in Great Britain by Clays Ltd, Elcograf S.p.A.

Hodder & Stoughton policy is to use papers that are natural, renewable
and recyclable products and made from wood grown in sustainable
forests. The logging and manufacturing processes are expected to
conform to the environmental regulations of the country of origin.

Hodder & Stoughton Ltd
Carmelite House
50 Victoria Embankment
London EC4Y 0DZ

www.sceptrebooks.co.uk

For Thomas Cakebread

Author's Note

The events described here happened in the village of Warboys, near Huntingdon, England, over the period 1589–93. Many of the details are as described in a pamphlet published at the time, but I have shortened the time frame, so that events in the novel take place between autumn 1589 and 1591, and I have invented characters and incidents. For my main sources, please see the Acknowledgements.

Part One

The Accusation

Although now in her fiftieth year, Alice Samuel remembers that Plough Monday as if it were but a week ago. She hates to walk through the springing sprouting gravestones laced with bindweed, the angels marred with lichen, foul-faced and scowling. This churchyard is an ungodly place and she is the only one truly knows it.

Sixteen she'd been and newly flowering. The naughty part of it, the part that always made her blush remembering, was not the Plough Boys themselves, with their soot-blackened faces, and their eyes seeming to glow red inside the masks of dirt and ashes, but something else. It was the thoughts she'd been having. In that she felt shamed.

She had been dreaming, playing; she'd been *pleasing herself*. It was probably only the second time she'd ever been to Warboys, seven miles being a long morning's walk from her home in Chatteris. She'd come with the Plough Monday celebrations. A plough was dragged through the mud; boys with faces disguised by soot were behind it, crowds of young men, and a fiddler playing among them; the boys were shouting, threatening to plough up your land if you didn't 'Bestow us a ha'penny, whoa up!' and cracking their whips at each front door. They held out soup ladles for money and their legs and sleeves were tied with ribbons: alleygags, locals called them.

It had been late and she should have gone home but somehow she had followed the crowd and ended up here, in the churchyard at Warboys wandering from stone to stone, tracing the angels and their trumpets, their green tangled lichen, with her fingers. And then she'd looked up and the procession of dancers and fiddlers was long gone, back towards Chatteris and Ramsey via every nearby village where they might hope to beg some coins. She'd drifted around the church gardens, doing nothing at all. She could not remember ever being so idle before. It was cold; she hugged her woollen shawl closer. She'd been standing with ears cocked to the sounds of a wintry robin peeping and been in no hurry to make the long walk home to help Mother, who was sick. Worst, and most shameful of all, she had crept inside the church, shoved the heavy stone covering of the font aside and, standing on tiptoe, tried to stare into its dark water, to catch her own reflection.

So, in her heart, she felt punished by what happened next. The church door opened. Vanity, a sin: the pleasure she took in her big green eyes, her soft red-brown curls. It was only to be expected.

It's unfortunate that she has come through the churchyard and been so reminded, today. She had been gathering kindling over the other side of the manor where wood is plentiful. She takes the basket to her cottage door and sets it down, picking up a loaf from just inside, where her daughter Nessie has left it for her, still warm, wrapped in linen.

4

She has the feeling that someone is watching. That someone at the window of the Warboys manor has seen her, going back and forth, unlatching the gate of the churchyard, going to the door of her cottage, quickly inside and now back again, to the main door of the squire's house. Her behaviour, she fears, looks round about, inexplicable and ungodly. She hugs to her stomach the rye loaf she's baked, rapping the brass knocker of the manor house with one hand, remembering one nightmare from long ago, only to walk into another.

Elizabeth Throckmorton is all charm and ease as she opens the door to her. Alice was expecting Mother Caterill or another servant and is taken aback. But this lady of the manor is modern and kindness and wants you to know it of her: she is not what you would expect. Dark hair, big eyes, a sweeping emerald green dress with square neckline and puffed sleeves, such smiling and graciousness and then, yes, when Alice says how sorry she is to hear that the youngest daughter is so afflicted, Mistress Throckmorton is all gratitude and concern, saying sweetly, 'Oh, Jane is not the youngest – that's our Grace and Hob. Do come and meet the children.'

The room Alice is shown into smells strongly of the turves of peat burning in the fire and of damp clothing being warmed: hot and stifling. Perhaps the child is sitting too close to it. Daughter Jane Alice guesses to have nine years of age. A dark girl, like the mother, with a round face, plump, a pink spot on each cheek, like a doll. Jane is sitting next to the fire in the inglenook, sewing or pretending to, and she scowls on seeing Alice, with an expression that says she cares not for old women, least of all poor ones or neighbourly ones she has to greet and be sociable towards.

Alice is directed to a settle facing the fire at a little distance

– a rug between them – and refreshment is ordered. She has hardly noticed the soundless servant girl with the slow, fat face, standing as if turned to stone, for a good few moments until Mistress Throckmorton gently prompts her: 'Martha . . .' then says to Alice, 'Martha is deaf in one ear so if you get her bad side, the right ear, she misses things. She hears perfectly well in the left ear. She can understand you, though she rarely replies.' The servant girl at last seems to understand, gathers herself and disappears to fulfil the errand.

'It's such a strange kind of sickness and distemperature of body . . . Last night little Jane sneezed for almost an hour. And so loudly too!' Elizabeth Throckmorton begins. She glances at her daughter, who is listening keenly.

'And the other children, is it just this one who suffers?' Alice says, dimly remembering John coming back from his meeting with Master Throckmorton yesterday to report a gaggle of girls, worse than geese with the racket they made.

'We've been blessed with five daughters, two sons, too, and it is only Jane . . .'

The drinks are brought then. The moon-faced servant clomps between the inglenook and the settle with her tray. She still seems bewildered or mute or a simpleton as she stumbles over every task and cannot take her eyes from Alice, until Mistress Throckmorton almost scolds her in the fondest of ways.

There are the tray and the jug and the clattering spoon to be dealt with, and both women pause to navigate the ritual as gracefully as possible.

'The swamp fen so close to Warboys brings biting insects of all kinds,' Alice says, slurping her elderberry wine loudly. 'Oh, we're strangely handled by them.' She ignores a titter coming from somewhere, and continues, dunking a piece of almond cake in her cup, 'You grow accustomed to it, when you grow up in the fens,' here trying to recall where John said the family had lived before Warboys. 'You lived . . .?'

'Yes. We're from the village of Brampton. Do you know it?'

Alice shakes her head. She cannot help but notice that Mistress Throckmorton looks relieved by this.

'We . . . yes, my husband has some connections here, so when he was offered the position of squire, we were pleased. Sir Henry, of course, appointed him.'

'Your husband – is he a long-standing friend of Sir Henry?' Alice asks.

Elizabeth flushes and glances down at her own drink, a brief hesitation and then: 'Oh, not at all. It is a distant acquaintance but such an honour and we are truly grateful . . .'

Jane's big eyes widen and her mouth opens a little. The maid stares at the mistress in a way that Alice cannot read.

Alice bids her pattering heart to still, trying to focus attention on Elizabeth Throckmorton's chatter. And, after all, why *should* Alice be surprised at the mention of the name of Sir Henry Cromwell, the Golden Knight, or to hear – as Elizabeth prattles on – of how kindly he has given the manor and the position of squire to this woman's husband, Robert Throckmorton?

'And there was not enough space in the old house in Brampton for the children. They were crammed into one small bedchamber, and here the chambers are much larger . . .'

As she listens Alice considers the name Throckmorton: the man who was executed five years ago, was he a cousin or brother to the squire? Yes, there was much talk of him, of his role in a plot to put Scottish Queen Mary on the throne. Francis Throckmorton. Wasn't he beheaded? *That* was where she had heard the name before. Well, no wonder the family would like a fresh start here in Warboys and leaped at such a grand position. A sudden thought then: she hopes that her memory and connecting of the name Throckmorton to the traitor does not show in her eyes. She tries to concentrate on drinking the wine and enjoying the sweet biscuits on the silver plate beside her cup. She tries not to catch the eye of the little fat girl, Jane, with her insolent face and mocking manner.

After all, her husband John had said, only that morning (standing naked by the fire, as he loved to do, as if he were a glowing god, holding his eel spear aloft – after thirty-four years of a rackety marriage he can still make her laugh with his muscular body and his vanity), she would seem rude indeed if she didn't visit. 'And mind it's the pretty mistress and not the master you speak to.' The master, the new Squire of Warboys, well, John had heard that the man had been sent as some kind of spy to keep order and make sure nothing like the Muchwood riots ever happened again.

The Throckmortons had arrived at Warboys Manor weeks ago; it would have been neighbourly to visit, yet she had not done so, until now. An invitation had arrived, a formal one from the mistress, mentioning that the girl Jane was sick and she'd heard Alice had some gifts in healing.

'Find out about the womenfolk for me,' John had said, when she opened the letter.

Nessie had said, 'I heard the new squire is very handsome for a man of that great age!'

Alice had protested a little: she had enough to do with baking bread and brewing – hadn't she already sent them two loaves of rye bread – without making visits too? She didn't need to meet 'grand folk' but John had waved her aside with one of his customary barks of laughter and a loud fart. 'Grand! *We*'re grand, aren't we? We live in a house with two rooms and eat duck for dinner five times a week!'

This is true. The pond at Warboys, though it might look like the shiny bald head of an old man with tufts of hair – reeds – at the edges, is nonetheless as rich as any stew: a soup of fish and eels, geese and ducks, and guarded by a heron that the villagers would never touch because, with her piercing eye, she is the best indication of where the tastiest morsels hide. And so here Alice is, in response to an invitation that has not been mentioned at all.

Elizabeth is still speaking of their new location, the village of Warboys in this season being surrounded far and wide by water, by marshy lands full of will-o'-the-wisps and carrying the fen ague that is more evil than the plague for carrying folk off. (Alice's entire family had gone that way; well, no need to mention it now.)

'Aye! My own husband were knocked off a causeway into a bog only last week by John Chappel, who broke his patine . . .'

Mistress Throckmorton frowns.

'A wooden shoe, you know. They use it for skating out on the fens when the water freezes. It's not been cold enough this year,' Alice says.

'My husband Robert spent some boyhood years here, so he is not unfamiliar with its character, and his sister Rosemary is married to the vicar next door . . . Oh, here's Grace, come to join us!'

The younger child enters the room and squeezes into the nook beside her sister, pressing the cushion behind their backs to make them more comfortable. She is a slimmer version of the first chubby girl, with a dark foxy face and a mouth that has a little misshapen lump at the top lip. She makes no pretence at sewing or flicking through a book, only stares openly at Alice. Grace and Jane whisper to one another, touch their heads together and giggle: what an odd old lady and how they hate old women, how crinkly their skin and ugly their shapes, how watery their eyes!

And then a masculine sound, a cough, a door banging open. The father – Robert Throckmorton – enters the room and the light in the doorway darkens as he fills it. A big man. Tall, formally dressed, with a neat grey beard, finely trimmed, like the point of a pencil. Older than his wife by a good few years. Behind him, the half-wit maid Martha has returned and stands just a little to one side, her gaze resting on her master.

He is undoubtedly handsome, as Nessie had said, with a fine profile and a commanding figure. He stands very still, survey-ing the room. He has a small scar on his cheekbone, which looks as if the tip of a jousting lance once touched him. It only adds to the handsome effect. Alice finds herself staring into her cup of wine, unable to raise her eyes. The stillness of Robert Throckmorton is unnerving. The way a stag pauses, even after a chase, to stand and stare directly at you, just before the arrow flies, as if in rebuke or provocation. The squire is here to remind the people of Warboys that their landlord sees and hears all, has loyal men everywhere, so if they are thinking again of sedition they had better think twice. But while John ought to worry, *she* has no reason to. And yet the man, his great composure, makes her uneasy.

'Our neighbour, my dear, Alice Samuel,' Elizabeth Throckmorton says to her husband.

Alice lifts her eyes from her cup and he acknowledges her

with a nod; she murmurs a greeting in return. She returns her attention to the little cup in her hand, now almost empty.

The sisters' giggling converts to coughing, and soon, in Jane's case, to a great expulsion of sneezing. Yesking, as Alice thinks of it. Throckmorton is striding towards his wife but falters, unable to ignore Jane's sneezing. A sound like the wings of a swan, opening and closing with a swoosh. He makes a gesture as if shaking off something – someone – and turns towards his daughter.

As his gaze falls on Jane, something happens. Her face – none could be mistaken: something passes over it. A changed demeanour. Her eyes glaze over, unseeing. They fall first on her father and then, glassily, roll towards Alice.

The room holds its breath. A small crackle as one log snaps in the fire and then Jane's arm jerks out in the same direction as her eyes. Her plump face no longer looks like that of a nine-year-old child. Something else – some old story – has possession of her. The focus in her eyes has shifted and suddenly it is as if the child sees in the room something that no one else can, or will permit.

Jane's finger jerks out, pointing, and in a loud, deep voice, seemingly from elsewhere, from outside the room, perhaps, she says, 'Look where the old witch sits! Did you ever see one more like a witch than she is?'

The room contracts like a lung. Martha gives a shriek, and quickly puts her hand over her mouth. Elizabeth stiffens, and Robert Throckmorton stands still again, alert in every fibre. A trembling begins in Alice, from her toes upwards, and she feels her teeth chattering.

'Take off that black knitted cap!' the child demands.

Alice's hand goes to her bonnet. This old thing? The thrumbed cap? The girl can hardly be offended by that, though

11

the ribbons dangle at her chin and, yes, it would have been polite to remove it on entering the warm room. She wonders now why she forgot. What can it be – what has the child seen? At the same instant, Robert and Elizabeth both move, breaking the spell of stillness and embarrassment that has enveloped them all at this perplexing command from one so young. Alice dreads to bare her head now in front of the commanding Master Throckmorton, with his grand ways, and yet she knows she must. Her fading auburn hair, woven now with grey, her two plaits braided together on top of her head with a hair-lace: she feels shabby and exposed.

Elizabeth leaps up: 'Mother Samuel, I am sorry. You will understand – we don't know where these thoughts of hers . . . Perhaps your knitted bonnet, unfortunately . . .'

Alice has removed it, and the muffin-cap now lies unoffending in her lap, folded and without power, like the wings of a small creature, sleeping. A bat. The little foxy-faced one that lives in the eaves upstairs, that feels like a bundle of knitted twigs in your hand and that Nessie – Nessie, her daughter – has adopted for a pet and nicknamed Patch.

Jane lowers her hand and, like a puppet, topples sideways and begins shaking and jerking, the way an eel twitches, caught in the glaive.

'Oh!' the sister, Grace, cries.

'No need to apologise, ma'am,' Alice says. 'The poor child . . . Does she recover swiftly?'

Elizabeth rises. The spell cast over the master is broken and he strides forward to pick up his daughter. He bends and scoops her lightly into his arms, but the twisting and twitching of her little body continues, making it difficult for him to carry her.

'Grace, come with me.'

Robert Throckmorton, a curt bow to Alice, sweeps from the room, Grace running beside her father.

Elizabeth's face is pale, dark shadows under her eyes as she turns to her guest. 'You'll excuse me, Mother Samuel? Martha will see you out.'

'Of course.' Alice rises too, considers returning the muffin-cap to her head – which feels vulnerable, and her hair rather mussed without it – but thinks better of it, continues wringing it in her hands.

She is shown to the door. Why does the servant girl pause like that, as if she is about to say something? Why is her gaze so fixed?

In a room somewhere upstairs or along a corridor – she does not know the inside of this house and it is five times the size of her own – Alice can hear a man's voice, speaking calmly, then the deep growling voice of a younger man (there was a son mentioned, or was it two sons?) and the whimpering of a child, or perhaps the voice of Mistress Throckmorton.

Alice's teeth are still chattering and she wonders at the chill in her chest, the leaping heart and shaking hands in this house where the fire burns so brightly. What has just happened? As Martha opens the door for her she ponders the girl's face up close for the first time and sees that she is pretty and older than Alice thought. She is a woman of some thirty years, and surely the dumb manner is deceptive: her eyes are green, clever and watchful.

Alice hears the woodsman in the forest chopping logs with a regular strike. Since the new squire arrived all is chopping and breaking, she thinks, for no reason at all. A bird suddenly gives a shriek of dismay and shoots across the trees. It is hardly consoling. The maid is about to close the door behind her (still with that hard gaze) when Alice suddenly spies the loaf she had baked that morning and brought warm to give to her hostess, still wrapped in linen and now cold as stone on the visitors' table. She swipes it back – watching Martha's expression alter – as the door closes in her face.

***

'Was she play-acting? Where did the gruff voice come from if it wasn't Jane's?' Dottie says.

In the kitchen, they are preparing the evening meal, chopping and seasoning, running to keep the fire stoked and obey Mother Caterill's every command, but in between they prattle so persistently that my head spins.

'No, it *was* her own voice,' I say, struggling to remember. 'It just *seemed* to come from the devil himself. Jane was marvellous strange and tormented . . . yesking, very loud and thick, too, just like the first time it happened.'

'And what was it about Alice that so grieved Jane?' Mother Caterill asks, and I hear a warning in her voice. Didn't Popsie, who has lived in Warboys all her life, didn't she say that Mother Caterill knew Alice Samuel well, was she perhaps a *friend* of this strange old woman, this neighbour?

Popsie is stirring the stew. Barely five feet in height she has to stand on tiptoe to reach up to a shelf for some parsley and sweet herbs. 'Oh, it was her thrumbed hat! A black bonnet! Jane thought she looked exactly like a witch, and the moment she'd said it, her fits started.'

'But you weren't there,' Mother Caterill says, taking the

14

herbs from Popsie to fuss at the amount she's used and return them to the shelf. 'Was it Martha who told you so?'

Master Gabriel lopes into the kitchen to steal a peeled carrot to eat. His mood is downcast, but I can see he still prompts some fluster and excitement in Popsie, until Mother Caterill shoos him out, the better to resume our talk.

'You!' Mother Caterill turns angrily to Popsie. 'You need to stop dallying whenever that boy is around!'

Popsie's face reddens and she returns to her stew in silence, adding a slug of ale vinegar to the eels, and stirring more than is needed.

'I heard hard speeches from the master,' Dottie says. 'Gabriel is in disgrace.' Popsie jerks her head up, wanting to know more. But Dottie, like me, a maid from the old house in Brampton, is far keener to hear more detail of the scene that just took place, when this Alice Samuel visited. I am thinking of something else too, puzzling over my mistress's comment that Sir Henry was but a 'distant acquaintance'. Perhaps because Sir Henry is unpopular in many quarters and my mistress does not want our new life in Warboys to be tainted by association.

'Everyone says she's a scold – doesn't she have a daughter, far too pretty to be soberly made, and live in a naughty marriage?'

Mother Caterill makes as if to swipe Dottie with a cloth and laughs. 'Nessie. That's the daughter. Oh, I think the parson blessed it eventually – although after all these years, who can remember? I warrant Alice rues the day she married her John. He's a drinker, always up for a fight. But if you want my opinion,' and here she pulls herself up to her full size and gives all of us the benefit of her wise counsel, 'her trouble is not John or her naughty marriage, but her own short fuse and loose tongue. My, what a temper! She's never been able to hold it, about anything. Most of Warboys will remember her ill-wishing them over some slight, refusing them bread or beer when they knew she'd brewed or baked that day. She'd speak her mind no matter what cost, and in a woman that's lamentable. Her tongue runs away with her. She once told me a wicked secret, one she would have been better to keep to herself. A Plough Monday . . . long, long ago . . .'

'Oh! What? *What*?' Popsie asks. Dottie, too, stops what she's doing to stare at the housekeeper, weighted with secrets and seemingly a temptation to spill them. But as we wait, Mother Caterill's eyes fall on me. She seems to take note of me for the first time. What has she heard about me? I stiffen, pausing in my task of cleaning the silver, and wonder at her expression. Does she remember that I was raised by an old nun at Chatteris, or does she fear I will run to my mistress and master, report harshly their rude talk?

Mother Caterill passes me the sweet herbs and chopping knife as if in silent instruction and seems not to notice how ill at ease I am with taking her orders. My role in the household has always been difficult for outsiders to understand, and the old housekeeper is no exception. She looks at my face for a good long while, then takes the clay pipe from her pocket and puts it into her mouth, chewing it without lighting.

The little room swells with the warmth and smell of good eel stew. It mixes with the tansy and catnip strewn on the floor to keep the biting insects at bay. I wonder at the secrets of Mother Caterill but her mouth is firmly clamped and it seems I am the cause of it.

Popsie turns talk again to the tormented behaviour of poor

little Jane, what might be the cause of the mysterious disgrace that Gabriel is in, and our neighbour Alice Samuel with her naughty marriage and her pretty daughter, who is no better than she should be.

On the stairs, my master passes me. I try to summon the courage to ask after Jane but can't find the words so I stop, one stair below him, head bowed, unable to go up or down.

The master's mood is much recovered. 'Well, Martha, Jane is no longer in her fits and seems very merry,' he says, as if I had asked. He puts out a hand to lift my chin, smiling.

'Struck dumb again, are we, Martha? I hear you chattering in the kitchen with the other servants and yet with us . . .'

I feel his fingers beneath my chin, warm and firm, and I watch him smile inside his trimmed beard. I'm close enough to see the white scar under his eye, the shape of a crescent moon. I smell his breath: sweet wine, something salty. It feels too close. I would like to pass, but fear being thought rude. Not knowing what else to do, I close my eyes. When I open them again, I see Johanne, standing behind her father, glaring at me. Fifteen-year-old Johanne, in her plum-coloured dress, dark and glimmering, giving me – or perhaps her father – a disgusted glance. At last I feel able to move. The master lingers, says something to his daughter, and they continue down the stairs together.

I check myself. My arm, my shoulder, my waist, my neck and my face. Pressing my chin. Is something there? Every part of me is the same. I am the same girl with the broad face whom Sister Dorothy raised to be God-fearing and pure, a devoted servant to the Throckmortons since coming into their service at the age of thirteen. I am the same spinster woman who lived at Brampton in that crowded house and minded the children and my duties. Nothing in me has changed.

God sees all and knows our secret heart. But my master cannot do the same. He cannot know that he appeared to me. It was just a dream, and it must be put away. The different rooms, the newness, the strangeness of moving house and sleeping in a new bedchamber – and on a feather mattress – were to blame. Now that I have taken up sleeping on a straw mattress downstairs with Popsie in the kitchen by the fire, all will be as before and I am to dismiss it for ever from my mind and tell no one.

I go to the bedchamber carrying with me a little plate of pepperwort to burn for Jane's health. But the child is not in bed: she is upright in an armchair and fiddling with her bed-curtain.

'You look in fine fettle to *me*!' I say.

I put the pepperwort on the windowsill and stamp out, much vexed, to fetch a bowl of steaming water from the kitchen to place under Jane's feet to warm them. She lifts her chubby little soles for me and plays with a lock of my hair straying from my coif, curling it around her finger as I beck my head towards her. Of course, that makes me smile and all is forgiven.

'You mind that bowl now,' I say. Jane is a forgetful girl and nothing burns as bad as a steam scald.

It's on my tongue-tip to ask her, *What grieved you so about that funny old woman your mother invited, your neighbour? Why did you call her witch?* A witch in a thrumbed cap. Something so sudden had arrived in the room with us all. The master. Alice. Everyone seeming marvellous strange. I shudder to remember.

Jane is idling with a paddy-whack. She accepts my tendings

and my kind cautions with the water-heater, then says, 'I had such a dream, Martha.'

She takes my silence to mean I did not hear and shouts a little louder: 'Why is everyone fussing me so? I'm not an invalid!'

I sit back on my heels. 'You don't remember what you said in there?'

Jane shakes her head. She flicks the ball with the paddy-whack, catching it with her child's skill. 'Smack!' she says.

'You don't remember pointing at the neighbour and being in your fits and all those fast sneezes?' I say.

Do you remember you charged Alice Samuel a witch?

'I remember the loud church bell tolling horribly. Is it a new one? Ding-dong ding-dong . . . your nose is this long! Is it just that our house is so close to the church? It hurt my ears,' Jane says.

Her mother appears in the doorway, come to inspect her daughter.

'The fits have been coming on stronger each time. Your father says we should send a sample of your water to Cambridge to Doctor Barrough. Would you arrange that, Martha, and we will send a messenger?'

I stand up straight, rubbing at my creaky back. Mistress Elizabeth comes to say, 'Unless you have a better idea? Have we tried everything you know for fits?'

I shrug, then nod. We have. For violent shaking limbs, a fresh eel skin tied around it. Then there was the peat ash and horse urine.

'There's still fuzzballs,' I mutter. My mistress gives me a suspicious look. 'Puffball mushrooms. In a mouse-skin bag. Sister Dorothy . . .'

'I thought you'd tried that the first time?'

'They were old. I could make us some fresh.'

'Well, do you think it might offer a remedy? What did you tell me about bones crushed in milk?' she says, making a move to snatch the paddy-whack from Jane to put it to its original purpose as a cure. Jane wails and clutches the toy to her chest, and my mistress is so angered she looks for a moment as if she is about to strike her. Jane is our dearest beloved chubby little being but she is not admired for obedience.

I feel badly for my mistress, cast down with worry. I follow her out of the bedchamber and into the hallway, where Jane will not hear us.

'You have thought better of our plan to ask our neighbour?' I whisper. I don't know why I whisper, but something makes me sure Jane should not hear too much of this. My mistress closes her eyes for a second, sighs, then tugs her gold cross out of her bodie and kisses it.

'You saw what happened. It was ill advised. And Robert – he would be angry if he found out my intention,' my mistress replies.

'A prayer to Saint Valentine, then, if it be the falling sick-ness,' I say, keeping my voice low.

The mistress is mindful to address herself to my good ear and never forgets which ear it is. 'I have finished with Saint Valentine. He's not answering my prayers,' she says sharply. I glance about in shock at these ungodly words, quickly cross myself and murmur a silent prayer. We – my mistress and I – have tried to hide our adherence to the old ways, our candles to the saints, and our other practices, mindful of how times have changed, how the charge of papism would attach to us, with the name Throckmorton so recently sullied as a Catholic and traitor to the Crown. But it has never occurred to me that the saints were not listening. My mistress's change of tone, her mood, what can it be about? It feels to be more than Jane's illness. I cannot understand why she would say such a dreadful thing. This has been her tone since first we arrived in Warboys at Michaelmas. Little care for wifely duties, and with grim lines between her eyebrows. I feel anxious when I see her coldness. It is not logical, but an old habit from the nunnery means that I blame myself for things. For the misfortunes of others.

Crabbie appears then, creaking up the stairs to find us whispering in the hallway. He stands very stiffly. For a moment I think this strange young man is going to be able to contain himself, to stand still, but suddenly he becks his head to the side in the curious manner he has, and shouts, 'Horse, ma'am! Horses ready.' My mistress starts a little. But his mannerisms have become familiar in only a few weeks and we know that with the horses he is becalmed: the animals steady him.

'Why have you saddled the horses?' she begins, and then: 'Oh! Is it for Gabriel?' Tears fill her eyes. So it is true: Gabriel is in some disgrace, as Dottie said, and he is to be sent away.

'Gabriel is to go to his uncle in Titchmarsh,' my mistress murmurs. I had hoped Dottie was mistaken but my mistress's mood confirms it: it feels as though Gabriel is in disfavour; it is not a happy parting.

'How long will he be away for, Mistress?'

She shakes her head, not wanting Crabbie to see her tears. Crabbie returns downstairs and then, just as my mistress is about to speak, her other son, young Hob, hiding somewhere, springs out, making us both jump.

'Make a black cat spit on mutton fat!' he shouts, flinging pieces of fluff from his hair. He rolls and spins like a tumbler in the market square. Grace is never far behind him. The little ones disappear and reappear, like puppets being shaken one way then flipped upside down to reveal their double. In better times my mistress would tarry and embrace her youngest children but today she shoos them away. We are all rather cramped in the hallway; my mistress turns down the stairs without a glance behind.

I follow Grace and Hob into the bedchamber, calling, 'Stop running! Her feet – her feet. Mind the water-heater!'

Grace heeds me and the water stays untroubled.

'Oh! He's taken the paddy-whack!' Jane cries, stretching for her brother, who wriggles out of reach.

Hob sets up his own hue and cry, 'It's my turn!' knocking the ball to the other end of the bedchamber with an almighty great whack.

Then he's singing: 'Scrape it off within a week, then go outside a toad to seek . . . make it sweat into a pot, with wooden spoon mix the lot!'

Since it is I taught him I can hardly scold him. I go to fetch a tray of soup and rye bread and a glass of ale from downstairs. And with it a chamber pot.

On my route to the kitchen, I pass Gabriel, in the hallway, wearing his boots and outdoor cape, a travelling bag beside him. He cannot meet my eyes, but I step forward – there is no one else in the hall – and embrace him.

To my horror, his shoulders begin shaking, and he gives a sob. I seek something to say, anything at all, to comfort him. But since I do not know what he has done, when he might return, or what disgrace he is in, I find myself mute. I only pat his back, through the thick black wool, and say, 'Dear child, Titchmarsh is a fine place. You will— Your uncle will offer you a good home.'

'But I've done *nothing*, Martha!' he blurts, and his voice is full of anguish, and tears, and his huge boyish eyes seem to beg me to believe him. I continue my patting. The life of a servant is one of hidden traps, like the ones left in the woods for coneys. I must say nothing to question the master or mistress's wishes and intentions and good judgement but my heart aches, and the fine young man I've raised from boyhood is staring at me beseechingly. I can only kiss both cheeks, wish him well and murmur, 'God answers all prayers, Gabriel, and – why – you are almost a man and all men must leave home one day.' I try to smile, but he does not respond. His curly head on his long stalk of a body simply droops forward – a flower bending towards water – and his shoulders drop as he picks up the bag and heads towards the door, without a further word.

When I return to the bedchamber, much preoccupied, Mary is in the room, sitting close to her sister, and putting aside her Bible studies to say, 'I saw her as she left, that horrible old woman! How could Mother have asked her in? She was too fierce for someone so old! She was like one of the boys who catch rabbits. Smelt like them, too! Shouldn't she be quiet before us, and gentle like Mama? And the thumbed cap! She should surely have removed it sooner.'

I put down the tray and clap my hands. 'When you're ready, miss,' I say to Jane, shooing Mary away. She leaps from her seat, along with Grace, and flees. Jane stuffs a large piece of rye bread into one fat little cheek and allows me to hold the pot under her, to wait for the warm, wheaty stream of urine to cease.

***

The letter from Doctor Barrough flies back in no time. I take it upstairs to the mistress to read alone in her bedchamber.

Her mood has been anxious while we awaited the results, and there is still frost between her and Master Throckmorton, her eyes downcast whenever her husband is in the room. In my worst moments I wonder if it is not Gabriel but I who am the cause of this trouble. That night when I dreamed such strange things, dreaming my master mistook my room for his own and stood swaying and drunk before I guided him out. Something about the new arrangements in the house . . .

Since Gabriel's departure, my mistress's low spirits have fallen further. I have not yet uncovered how long his banishment is for, or any further detail as to the cause of the row that led to it. Sometimes, on entering the garden or hearing a horse outside the window neighing, I have a sudden picture of Gabriel as a boy: curly-haired, rosy-cheeked, his wriggling warm limbs, climbing on my lap to be cuddled and petted, the way Hob sometimes does now. And then I remember his habit of often hiding behind a door, and leaping out at me on my deaf side, just to see how high I might jump and laughing and kissing me afterwards in great delight. A teasing boy, but no cruelty in him.

My mistress has rued her wicked remark about Saint Valentine, and in penance we prayed over a silver ring and we pushed it upon Jane's fat thumb where we both hoped it might ward off the next fit. We are afraid of discovery, using the ways that Sister Dorothy taught me. The reverend from the church of Saint Mary Magdalene would be very angry. I know my mistress is not much reassured. I stand by while she tears open the letter.

I have not brought a candle, so she squints in the grey afternoon light, calling out, 'Johanne! Johanne! Come in here and read this for me.'

I chide myself then for I should have offered to read it, but it is too late: Johanne is already in the room. Plucked from her prayers, dark in her plum-coloured dress, she makes sure to be sulky and slow in manner, as if her mother has caused her a great disturbance to leave off her devotions.

Johanne snatches the letter, begins reading, then chuckles. '*Worms!* Not epilepsy, then. Jane has worms caused by "rude, raw, gross phlegmatic matter and through convenient rottenness, such as gathered especially in children and *other great eaters*"!'

Johanne laughs. A good description of her sister's appetite. But having a little more wit and seeing the expression on her mother's face, she quickly continues reading: 'The doctor writes, "This urine shows no such distemperature and as for the falling sickness, I warrant she is clear from that disease." She doesn't have epilepsy, or palsy either. "Those with round worms feel an incredible gnawing in their bowels and belly and issue thin and small coughs. In some cases yesking from the nose occurs."'

'The sneezes! Why, yes, that must be it!' My mistress moves closer, taking the letter from her daughter. I have found a candle and light it with a stick of kindling from the fire, holding it near as she reads.

'"Bitter herbs will kill the worms. Especially absinthium."' Mistress turns to me, bewildered.

'Wormwood,' says I, very knowledgeable. Sister Dorothy used that name for it.

'"Equal parts wormwood, marrubium" – what's that?'

'Horehound.' (I'm marvellous clever in this respect.)

' "And lupinum . . . and cook in honey water or spiced wine to drink and also to stroke it on the navel to kill her worms. Take a stalk of the plant and girdle the child's stomach with it. Its healing powers are astonishing." '

'Wormwood. The green fairy,' I tell her, folding my arms and trying not to make a 'hurrrmph' sound. So they sent Jane's water-sample all the way to Cambridge and no doubt paid this doctor a pretty penny too, and what had the learned man told them? Worms. The green fairy. I would have made that cure if they'd asked me. That would have been my first piece of wise counsel, had the mistress asked *me*. Worms! Worms don't lift you up and shake you like a doll in their arms – only the devil does that. Worms might make your belly heave up. Sometimes Jane's belly *did* swell as large as a penny loaf. That is *one* of her symptoms, but scarce the most tormenting one.

'You can drink it, Mistress, or if I cooked it in water and soaked a piece of linen in it, then wrapped it round her stomach . . .' I have some downstairs in the pantry.

Johanne disappears now that the song and dance is over and her sister's dreadful affliction named. The mistress sinks down upon the bed, flapping the letter against her face, like a fan, then folding it neat and small. 'Well, Martha, could you do that for me and quickly? Does it need to steep or might it be ready soon?'

'It should steep for a while, Mistress, because the wormwood is old, picked last year, dried. But I will make a start.'

I move to leave the room, placing the candle on its holder atop a blanket box. As I'm doing this, she says, more to herself than to me, 'Thank the Lord I didn't ask that old crone Mother Samuel. Robert would have been furious. To discuss Jane's most intimate . . . Is it the green sickness, then? Rather than worms? Is that the real reason Doctor Barrough suggests the green fairy?'

'She's young to have the green sickness. She's . . . a developed girl, isn't she, Mistress? A little fat one. She doesn't look pale and she eats plenty of red meat. The green fairy will cure all women's difficulties, it's true, but in a larger dose, it will . . .'

Here I cannot think how to put it delicately. What the green fairy might do for a woman with child who didn't want to be.

'They say the kiss of the green fairy gives a tremendous headache,' is all I add.

'Poor little Jane,' my mistress says, and in the light of the leaping candle her face is shadowy. I see again the trouble on it and ponder to myself how much older she looks and all of a sudden, too. We are but a few years apart, she thirty-eight to my thirty-four, but lately, she is all pinched brows and thoughts that are not in the room with us. Once, at Brampton, surveying our boxes, all packed and ready to leave, she had alarmed me by looking around at her daughters sitting in the hallway surrounded by their belongings and saying, 'If only a mother could speak truthfully to her daughters . . .'

'Of what, Mistress?' But she shook her head, as if speaking to herself.

Now she crosses herself once, feeling for her little necklace again, and then, seeing my look, straightens.

'The Reverend Doctor Dorrington will lock me up for a papist yet.' A confiding remark. In this matter, at least, I understand her. I was raised by nuns and my mistress had a secret Catholic heart. She hid it well as times changed and it became more dangerous to reveal it, but sometimes I thought of her heart as a secret chamber, a pocket or priest's hole in her inner self: as if a little person crouched there, beating differently.

She may have grown reckless, melancholy or faithless, but I have prayed to Saint Valentine devoutly, ever since Jane's fits began.

'Seven healthy children. I am truly blessed and must never forget it!' my mistress says.

I nod gravely. To cheer her, I add: 'At least there is no drink or food that Jane will refuse. For once we can be glad of her appetite.'

My mistress gratifies me with a smile, and we go down to the kitchen together.

Little Grace loves to watch me cook up my cures: she has hoisted herself onto a window-ledge to study me, dangling her skirts and wobbling dangerously close to the two candles I've stuck into bottle necks. She's the smallest, the sweetest in nature, well named for her grace. She and Hob are rarely separated: he's there beside her, though he is never still, and jumps on and off to shriek and stare into the pan and ask me what I'm doing.

Grace is like me, the watchfulness I learned from Sister Dorothy. The habit of quiet. Let the adults forget you're there and they'll reveal things. Grace has a pointed chin and a mouth that's a little split at the front, malformed. A hare lip when she was born but we stitched it quick and now it hardly troubles her. I feel tender whenever I glance at it, or when, as now, she pulls at her mouth, tucking her bottom lip under her tooth.

'If a person has a bad belly-ache after eating mushrooms from the woods when they shouldn't, this is what you give them,' I tell Grace. She nods her head to show she is listening. I always talk freely with the children, when my mistress isn't there. 'Equal parts wormwood, horehound and lupinium – wolf milk

– cooked in spiced wine. Worms. Your sister Jane. And if you're melancholy, in a bad way, the wormwood's good then, too.' Some green leaves were crushed last summer, and in the jar now it's just a powder, which I spoon into the sludge in the pan.

'Let me taste it!' Grace begs.

'It's bitter. You don't want to if you don't have to. It smells good because I'm masking the taste so that your sister won't refuse it.'

'Jane won't ever refuse anything!' Bessie laughs. Bessie is ever playful, her spirit quick and lively; an unruly girl, always with some curls escaping, or a trailing hem to her skirt. She and Mary are seated on stools near the fireplace, a good deal under my feet, a nuisance and a hindrance both. Mary, at eleven years a fast reader, sings her loud verses from the Bible, quick and musical. I stop to listen for a while.

'"And they brought him unto Him, and as soon as the spirit saw him he tore him. And he fell down on the ground wallowing and foaming . . ."'

The Gospel of Saint Mark, of Jesus casting the dumb spirit out of a boy with the falling sickness. I know she and Bessie, despite pasting a cheery face on it, feel much troubled by their sister's affliction.

I stand stirring and still for a moment, and Mary goes on, '"And Jesus said unto him: Ye, if thou couldst believe, all things are possible to him that believeth. And straightaway the father of the child cried out with tears, saying Lord, I believe; help thou mine unbelief! Thou dumb and deaf spirit, I charge thee, come out of him . . ."'

Hmm. I set my mouth, dangling some extra honey from a spoon into the foul green sludge. I've never liked those words together: *dumb and deaf*. Sister Dorothy did say many a time that 'A bit of deafness be no impediment to learning and no excuse for not studying either.' Oh, sometimes I know others – perhaps their uncle Francis, the Reverend Doctor Dorrington, is one of them – mistake my blank looks, believe me marvellous slow. Those cases when I easily startle, when I haven't heard them approach me – also that shriek of mine that flies up some-times, from nowhere. I'm slight in build and some can mistake me for a woman much younger than my thirty-four years, until they see the beginnings of the fine creases around my eyes, perhaps. But I'm not a fool and have never believed myself one. The mistress understands me. The children do. Maybe the menfolk are under some misapprehension.

It's a while since I was given the task of mixing good medi-cine like this. I can never do it without remembering. Those sad occasions when I learned healing were also the times when Sister Dorothy told me her stories. How Sir Henry's father just rode in one day – it was a long time before I was born, Sister Dorothy was a novice nun in those days – he rode into Ramsey the Golden, in service to the King, and offered the abbot a huge sum of money: a big purse with four thousand and six hundred pounds in it! And, yes, the abbot would receive this as well as a pension for ever more, and the abbot, of course, did not see that it was an idea inspired by the devil and simply agreed, with little heed that the nuns had nowhere to go.

Grace hops off the windowsill to open a jar and take a big sniff, breaking into my thoughts. 'Ugh! It stinks! ' Grace says, putting her finger in to take a pinch of the green powder inside it, rubbing it under her nose.

She believes it the wormwood but I snatch the jar away from her: so precious is the powder, it's not for a child to be touch-ing it. 'Vipers' gloss. That's what the abbot at Ramsey did use for polishing his gold and silver plate. It's valuable – put the lid on that jar!'

Grace and Hob are fascinated, of course, and crowd around the jar sniffing the filthy snaky smell.

'Does it really come from a snake?' she asks, in wonder, as I take the jar from her.

'When Sister Dorothy was a girl, that was her job. Collecting the vipers' gloss. She showed me how to collect it: little heaps on the ground where the snakes had been. Because they ate snails and the snails passed through them and it came out as this greeny-brown powder.'

I let them look at it – the older girls too – but then I screw the lid on tight and put the jar on a high shelf.

'Sister Dorothy said that Richard Cromwell – that was Sir Henry's father – traded it for coins and she cleaned their precious gold with it or the pewter tankards. That is the very last of the jars so mind you don't open it again.'

'Eating snails!' Hob opens his mouth as wide as he can – performing for the girls – and, pretending to be a snake, writhes on the ground, clutching his belly and saying, 'Oh, now the snail is passing through me!' writhing and twisting. 'Are they the sandy-coloured ones?'

The children are laughing now that Hob has caught a new antic, but I turn back to my pan and my stirring. I do not like them to know that I'm afraid of snakes. That I dream of vipers, and how Sister Dorothy never left off the subject. The sandy snakes in the uplands were one thing, she said, no cause to fear those. But watch out for the black ones that live in the water, disguised by their darkness. When they lay against the dark, peaty soil they might rear up and bite you, a bite that could kill you. I remember looking into the wide fens as a girl, the boggy lands near Chatteris, staring at the snails that floated there, trying to spy a snake who wanted to feed on them.

The children have set aside their bible, always happier to hear my Sister Dorothy stories.

'A witch knows she can slit open the snail's belly, remove the fat, and repair the opening with horsehair. The fat from the snakes' bellies makes a good ointment. Perfect for the cure of ulcers and running sores.'

'Fat from a snake's belly! Don't put it on me!' Hob shrieks.

I lean down to tickle him under the arms and whisper, 'Keep the snakes in a dark cupboard and they will appear the following spring, no worse for their operation. Their fangs have the power. You can preserve the venom in home-made wine. Unmarried girls can make good use of it.'

'How did she know all this? A nun, your Sister Dorothy?' Bessie asks, leaving off her stool and her embroidery and her sister Mary to stand by me, suddenly serious and wanting, as she often is, to learn things. I breathe in the deep, outdoor girlish scent of her. She has been playing with the hens and a feather clings to her skirt. There is a curious note in her voice. Just as I'm wondering how to answer, she says, 'When will Gabriel come home? Why did Father send him away?'

'It is not my place to question your father,' I say.

'They seem angry,' Bessie says. 'Mother, Father . . .'

'Now, Bessie, don't upset the others. We will find out more about Gabriel soon enough.'

The sky is darkening and outside a bat flits from its home close to the window, looping to the trees and back, appearing between the tiny lead frames: fast and irritating – *Now you see me, now you don't.*

'Must be strange to have a nun as a mother,' Bessie says

softly, standing close, watching me pour the liquid from the pan into a pewter mug. 'Is it not forbidden? A nun can't marry, can she?'

Bessie at thirteen is at an age where such questions tremble dangerously on the tip of her tongue at all times. Why can't a nun have a baby? Why does she need a husband to make one?

'Well, young lady, I have told you many times. Sister Dorothy *did* marry, for the shortest time. Lots of the nuns from Chatteris did. After Sir Henry's father came, and all the nuns were cast out from the nunnery, the sisters did not want to leave God but they had no money, and no homes, so they had no choice. Sister Dorothy married a young man who sadly drowned one night out on the fen when a causeway gave way. He and his horse sank into the water and were never seen again . . . and that was how she had me.'

I wonder if the children, now quiet, hovering, growing sleepy with the heat in the kitchen and the powerful wormwood smell, know that this is a story. In my mind there is no father drowning in the fen but only a great white stork stretching out its beak and dangling me over a ditch and dropping me at Sister Dorothy's feet and she, now old and ejected from the nunnery, does take me in as a blessing from God and that's an end to it. I wonder why I cannot say it: I was a foundling. I was given to Sister Dorothy to care for. I do not know my parents. It is foolish of me to persist in the story of Sister Dorothy's brief marriage when the true story of my beginnings follows me everywhere. I suspect Mother Caterill has already heard it, perhaps from Dottie. 'That's why Martha loves to cast herself as mother to the Throckmorton children,' Dottie would say. 'Because she had no family of her own, no one she belonged to.'

'Sister Dorothy knew a powerful witch,' I say. 'That's how she knew so much. She knew a cunning woman called Elizabeth Mortlock. She was – she was tried when I was ten, at Ely Cathedral, for giving women help in childbed. A magic girdle and prayers, a charm to the Five Wounds of Christ. Eel liver fried, if the labour was a difficult one. I was not supposed to know any of this.'

But as I tell them this, my old fears float to the surface. Such a long time since I've wondered this: Sister Dorothy. She *knew* a witch. She *knew* an awful lot about witches, their cures, the glamour they might cast. She taught me medicine, my letters, Latin, sewing, laundry, cooking, weaving and midwifery. What did I believe of the stories she told me? How quickly she began her tales with 'Elizabeth Mortlock says . . .' or 'An old witch, Elizabeth Mortlock, told me . . .'

Didn't I think just once, as a girl – *is Sister Dorothy a witch?*

I mutter a little prayer under my breath and give Grace the spoon with the honey on it to lick.

And so we have had our sighting of the ungodly neighbour – asked by the mistress to come and visit – and now the household is more troubled than ever, and how we all regret it so. Something wicked was stirred: vipers, smooth, matt, black, glistening up from the fen waters, the snails floating all around them. Marvellous strange, this Alice Samuel.

I put the tankard on a tray and fold a little linen cloth beside it. There's dinner to prepare and other servants back from their tasks in the yard with the sow and the hens and the cow. Dottie – loud and large – arrives in the kitchen dangling a goose in both hands, and laughing at the gift of it, she says, from the neighbour John Samuel, husband of the old biddy Alice, its sad beak dripping to the floor. Dottie tries to shoo the children out so that she can start her plucking.

'Bessie, will you take this green fairy to Jane and stay beside her until every drop is drunk?' I say.

She beams a smile at me and a quick kiss on my cheek. Bessie is the one who loves it best when I tell them things that the mistress or master would deem unfit for a child's ears. I might regret it – I always do – and wish myself buttoned up with the children, as I am elsewhere, but Bessie never fails to let me know her gratitude.

I'm sitting with a silver bodkin darning when Bessie comes bouncing downstairs in happy step, crying what a delicious smell of goose or is it ox-tongue pie?

Jane follows close behind still in her nightshift and felt slippers with a bodie tied loosely and stops, hearing the loud and rolling voice of her uncle Francis, the Reverend Doctor Dorrington.

'Why is there so much churching since we came to Warboys?' Jane, with folded arms and shoulders rising to her ears, stops.

'He'll hear you!' I hiss.

She drags her slippered feet over the red tiles. I go to the kitchen where Dottie hands me a plate of the pie to take into the dining room. The girls give each other a naughty look.

The dining room is already fixed in silence. All sit with heads bowed, awaiting Bessie and Jane. There is a commotion as chairs are scraped noisily and the sisters sit down.

'You survived the green fairy then,' Johanne mouths to Jane beside her. Then to Bessie: 'Did you try it?' The girls use this method of talking often, forgetting how well I can read their lips. The Reverend Doctor Dorrington has his eyes closed. Their aunt Rosemary, their father's sister, a tiny woman, pert and lively, gives them a bright smile. Jane sighs, then becks her head.

'O Lord, for what we are about to receive, may we be truly thankful and ever in thy service. Amen,' the vicar booms, addressing the tapestry on the opposite wall as if the whole village of Warboys might be in the room.

I give careful watch to Jane and am pleased to see some roses back in her plump cheeks and that her eyes light up on spying the wine poured into glasses (ale for her) and a plate piled high with the goose and a big piece of the ox-tongue pie with ale-gravy. My mistress is surely thinking the same thing, for she beams across the table to Jane and remarks, 'Doctor Barrough's cure was so speedy. Perhaps we need not have concerned ourselves with it.'

But it seems the vicar is not done with praying.

'Let us thank the Lord for that,' he says, and heads have to lower again (just as knives were about to be lifted, too!).

Dottie and I stand with our backs to the wall. Dottie has a long spoon in her hand, of the kind used to make a mash for babies, which she had thought little Jane might need if she could not face her food. She seems unsure whether to offer it, and at a fierce glance from the vicar we servants, too, lower our heads to pray.

Since coming to Warboys, this is the way. The vicar visits and prays with us night and day. The church of Saint Mary Magdalene being so close to the manor, and our master's sister, Rosemary, being married to the vicar, things here are very strict. Every man, woman and child in Warboys must attend church or face a fine. The Reverend Doctor

Dorrington's cook must be a poor one, unlike Mother Caterill, as he and his wife expect to eat at the Throckmorton table most evenings and to share in my master's new good fortune in being made the Squire of Warboys by Sir Henry, giving him the fine manor and the woods behind it.

We all know that Sir Henry's gift was a means to lift his old friend Robert from the shame that descended on us in Brampton, because the name Throckmorton became in time a sullied name in the village, after the bad business of his cousin Francis Throckmorton, executed for being a traitor to the Queen, in league with a Spaniard. I remember walking past the Black Bull and a drunkard there hissing, 'Papist!' at me, so that I had to pull the children close and stop up their ears. It was an unjust accusation, since the master was not a practising Catholic at all, and as I have said, my mistress was doing her best to be a faithful Protestant wife, but the master did long for a fresh start. We all believed that in Warboys tongues would not wag as much and the neighbours would be impressed by the title of squire, and the relationship to the vicar next door, who was of the proper religious hue, would stop them if they did. It seemed a good solution. We were grateful.

All the natural voices and laughter of the children are now snuffed. I peep out from behind my hands at the vicar and see that Johanne is doing the same, regarding with her cool dark eyes his pockmarked skin, the tell-tale sign of his brush with smallpox. The dining room is a place of trembling and silence, and growling stomachs.

The vicar leads the table in another prayer of thanks, then opens his eyes. 'A short lesson before we eat. Now, who will lead? Johanne?'

Is this her punishment for the fierce look she had been giving him?

'We will read from John, chapter one. Is that the part of the scriptures you've been studying today?'

Johanne, in silence, pushes back her chair to fetch the bible from its place on a shelf, to bring closer to her a candle. Jane looks longingly at the slices of goose, the glistening pie and jug of gravy. I'm aware of Dottie beside me, a little sweaty, slapping the long spoon lightly against her thigh as if beating time.

Johanne opens the pages, smoothing them down. The other sisters watch, hoping no doubt to escape their uncle's gaze and instruction. Dottie and I flatten ourselves against the wall, awaiting our instruction to serve. The goose slices begin to dry, the pie to cool. The mistress looks at her husband beseechingly and the children's eyes are down at their empty plates, until suddenly, the parson blasts, 'No, *Jane*! It should be Jane, of course.'

Jane leaps in her seat at her name. My mistress protests, 'But, Francis, poor Jane has been in bed all day. She is only just recovering. Mary is an excellent reader.'

Jane glances at her uncle from under her eyelashes; Johanne's shoulders rise. She is holding her breath.

'Nonsense! I'd like to hear from Jane – and the food will be becoming cold if we don't hear from her, the first chapter of St John.'

Our hearts grieve for little Jane but I see the pickle my mistress is in: my master grazes her arm with his hand, as if to still her. Dottie and I press ourselves against the wall, like moths. Oh, the pie we slaved over and the thrill of the goose: how nasty it would all be, cold!

Johanne passes Jane the bible and Jane stares down at the flimsy pages of the book in front of her. Her stomach rumbles loudly and her face reddens as Johanne barks a quick laugh, then falls to silence.

My master tries: 'Francis, it has been a long day for Jane. Let Mary read to you. She's the most devout.'

'Well, that's just it,' the vicar replies. 'If Mary is already devout, that is well and good. What about daughters who are behind her? What about your servants here, who need an example to be set? And the ladies, whose appetites are bird-like, won't mind a short wait while Jane soothes them with her reading . . .'

Beside me the tap-tap of Dottie and her long spoon, and the smell of the food and the sweat on Dottie and the terror in my breast for poor Jane start to make me nauseous, but I stand up straight, seeing only that the shoulders of little Hob in front of me are shaking and attracting the attention of his mother. The food! The wilting goose, the soup in the tureen gaining a skin.

Jane smooths the pages of the bible with one finger, her uncle's eyes on her. As she does, the church bell next door tolls so loudly that all the children, Elizabeth, too, jump, and tiny Aunt Rosemary squeaks out a scream as if somebody has stepped on her. Her hand flies to her heart. Seven loud bells clang around the dining room and the glass in the black frames of the windows trembles.

I am not looking at Jane. Where am I looking? My eyes are fixed on my hands, tightly clasped in my apron. So it is the loud bang of the wooden chair on the stone tiles that alerts us. Jane flailing backwards, the same gaze as before, the same stiffness in her body, but she is jerking and jerking, just as before, like an eel caught in the sharp prongs of the glaive.

'Oh, my goodness!' My mistress leaps up and crouches next to her daughter. 'Robert, Robert, can you lift her?'

All is chaos and confusion as servants and the men move swiftly to lift Jane, who tries to throw them off, twitching, leaping and springing in every limb, her eyes now rolling in her head showing the terrible whites, like a cow. A bubble of shame rises, too, in the room and we all wish for it to be dispersed.

My master carries Jane, her slippered feet dangling. Her mother goes after him and I trail behind them both.

Aunt Rosemary, in ringing tones, says, 'She has no foam at the mouth? If she did, I would say it was the sacred sickness for certain: I saw that look once in the eyes of an old nun at Chatteris in her fits.'

As I mount the stairs, the rhyme 'If a woman is as little as she is good, a peapod would make her a gown and a hood,' comes to me, as it did the first time I met Aunt Rosemary. She is so small and mouse-like compared to her loudly lamenting husband. But then, she did dare to give the falling sickness its papist name so perhaps she is bolder than I imagine.

We push aside the curtain and lay Jane on her parents' bed, removing the fine velvet coverlet, taking off Jane's slippers, unlacing her bodie and placing her on a linen sheet, shooing the other children out. She is still twisting so piteously, it grieves us to watch.

I clutch one hand, my mistress grasps the other, while my master tries to hold her feet. The room fills with a curious smell and a great fear, coming from the three of us. We know not where the other children are, although I glimpse Grace, once, in the doorway, pale and ghostly as a barn owl.

We sit like this a long time, not knowing what else to do,

simply watching her, her face, her eyes rolling back in her head, our hearts anguished in our breasts. Finally, Jane's face changes and she stills. Her palm in mine relaxes and I release it. Whatever it was has passed. As if a cloud has rolled past the sun. Her face appears calm, her eyes gently close and she seems to fall asleep, her breathing soft and no longer laboured.

'Martha, go down and bid the children eat,' my mistress says. And then to her husband, 'It's not polite to leave our guests.'

I do not want to leave poor Jane. I know that my master, kind-hearted and devoted as he is to his little daughter, feels the same. He stands up.

'Oh, why did you do nothing at the table to prevent this?' my mistress wails. The anger is back in her voice. I am shocked at her open complaint and hardly dare glance at my master to see how it is received. As I leave the bedchamber Grace comes running at me, burying her face in my skirts.

'What is wrong with her?' Grace asks. 'Will she die?'

'Sssh now, your sister's fits have passed. She's only sleeping,' I reply.

We return to the dining room together.

'How calm when the gaggle of children are silenced!' the vicar is saying. 'Now eat – what is everyone waiting for? Do we want the servants taking gossip to Warboys that we are wasteful of God's good food?'

The master appears then and joins the table. I cannot meet his eyes but go about my duties with Dottie and Popsie beside me, bringing rye bread and the plates that were taken back to the kitchen to keep warm on the stove. After murmuring grace my master puts a spoonful of food to his mouth. The children do the same. But all save the vicar and his wife have lost their appetite.

'Never have I been in a room with so many girlish voices and thoughts a-circling. I will need to preach on Sunday about drowsy female minds,' the vicar is saying to my master, as they stand in the study later that evening. The wives and children have departed to their bedchambers and the men remain cloaked in pipe smoke, musing on the day's events. I bring them a glass of brandy each.

My master's face is grave. He gives an account of Jane, and how worried he and the mistress are. Her fits seem to be becoming more severe and prolonged. I make up the fire in the corner for them, adding fresh turves and poking hard to bring some flickers of orange to the embers.

'A very shocking thing to witness,' the vicar muses.

And then he asks, 'I heard you had a visit from your neighbour, Alice Samuel.'

I feel a prickle along my spine. It is as if the air alters with the mention of Alice's name.

'The husband is a seditious man, Robert. I am sure you know that. I imagine that's why Sir Henry placed you in Warboys. To show the people some authority. John Samuel is lucky Sir Henry did not oust him from his tenancy, after what happened at Muchwood. But Sir Henry had no proof, and he could not find a local man who would testify on a jury, so he has to bide his time . . .'

'Yes, yes, I'm aware of that.'

'Still, I cannot imagine that Sir Henry, even if he knows John Samuel, has ever met or known the *wife*!' The vicar chuckles to himself. 'And the family do have some champions in Warboys. So, I'd advise caution. You need to establish a firm hand.'

'I've had much to attend to, business with Sir Henry Cromwell in Ramsey, as you know. I've hardly been here. Elizabeth has been settling the children. I did not imagine that the old woman and her brute of a husband were of any great import.'

Here the vicar takes on a confiding tone: 'Well, it's true Mother Samuel has a rough tongue and doesn't trouble to hold it. But that's exactly why you, as Sir Henry's deputy, as it were, have to establish your position in Warboys, stamp your—'

'It is a great shame my daughter said what she did and angered this Alice Samuel, then,' the master says, eyes blazing, mood worse than before. 'The woman gave me a look that would stun a rabbit. Jane's remark was . . . startling. I could scarcely understand what I had stepped into. Authority is one thing, unpopularity quite another. Heaven knows Elizabeth and I have no desire to make enemies in Warboys so early.'

'Quite.'

Here there is a lull, brimming with troubled thoughts unuttered. Straightening, I ask if anything more is needed.

'Bring me the brandy, Martha,' my master says. He has the controlled manner that signals to me he has drunk a great deal already.

I leave to fetch it, and re-enter with the tray and the decanter of brandy.

'And Gabriel has been sent to his uncle in Titchmarsh? Is that a permanent position for your young son?' the vicar now asks.

My master gives a fierce look, makes an odd shake of his head, as if to say that the matter is not to be discussed in front of me, and the vicar accepts this, purses his lips and changes the subject. 'Do not worry too much over Jane's accusation of Mother Samuel. I doubt that's the first occasion someone has called Alice Samuel a witch! She scolds her neighbours at every turn. And knowing the sorcery happening abroad – why, sorcery everywhere! – we must be ever vigilant, Robert, and if we find it, be not afraid to root it out.'

'I would rather not draw attention to ourselves,' my master says, very quietly, with great meaning.

But the vicar seems not to hear any warning in his voice and continues recklessly, 'You hope to gain respect in Warboys, to distance yourself from the Catholic side of the Throckmorton family. But your reluctance to consider any possibility that—'

My master gives a shrug of his shoulders, and sups his brandy. The vicar considers him for a moment, biting his lip and staring with bulbous eyes, as if to winkle out my master's secrets. Then he says airily, 'Your daughters – Jane. Have your children heard of the trials of the three Chelmsford witches only a few months ago?'

'I imagine so. Mary is a good reader, Johanne too. The halfpenny pamphlets find their way into the house.'

'Yes. Filth, they are. Making a sport of work that God and Queen have ordained us to undertake in all piety and seriousness.'

My master takes a deep breath. I hold mine, wondering when they will notice me again and find another task for me. In due course, the master turns towards me and says, 'Martha, is there a plate of cold meat or cheese or any fritters in the pantry?'

(My master's appetites are legendary. An evening meal rarely suffices. Many an evening my mistress would tease him that he would never fit in his doublet again. But in that threat she is quite wrong: he remains a sporting man.) Once again I am despatched to fetch something – 'And bring the pepper box!' – and on returning to the room, I discover the subject has turned again, to a discussion of witches and the question of whether my master's cousin, Francis Throckmorton, had resorted to consorting with them in his plot against Queen Elizabeth.

'With Jane, Elizabeth believes it's not witchcraft at all, but the green sickness,' my master says, in answer to something the vicar said but I did not hear.

The vicar colours at the master's mention of the female disease. 'Isn't she rather young for that?'

'Well, Elizabeth says that long before the actual . . . before the time of . . . girls' earthly bodies are in some sort of tumult . . .'

'Ah, well, a ship and a woman ever need repairing.' The vicar helps himself to some cheese, taking the linen napkin I hold out to him. 'But, after all, no sense in taking your *wife*'s diagnosis in place of a physician's. You need a second opinion. William Butler. A fellow at Clare. You've heard of him?'

My master laughs. 'Does he live with his old maid? Next door to an inn, where he's seen far more often than at his studies?'

The vicar gives a blast of laughter, a sound like a sudden dog bark. He nods to me to pour him more brandy.

'That's the fellow! She has to haul him out of there more often than not. But let us not hold that against him. He's neither a Galenist nor a Paracelsian, but bases his cure on empiricism and experiment.'

'I shouldn't like him to experiment on Jane.'

'No, not *experiment* – a poor word! He doesn't rely on theory, on the work of others. He is *original*. He makes his own judgements after close observation – he allows the patient to teach him. It's highly radical. I think you'd be impressed.'

'If it is only the green sickness or the mother fits, Jane will settle in time, surely,' my master says. 'I feel certain Jane needs *my* protection and good judgement more than she needs interference from another.'

'But you surely would not want the people of Warboys to discuss the Throckmortons any further. Sir Henry has been generous indeed in your new position. He will not want any . . . idle talk. And that my dear wife Rosemary is your sister will not have escaped the gossips in the White Hart. As well to have this business cleared up.'

Here the vicar is looking at me. Suddenly he booms, waving his glass, 'There are spies everywhere. But not your Martha. You were wise to bring her from Brampton with you – as good as deaf and dumb. The perfect servant!'

He is at last rising from his chair and promises my master he will write to Doctor Butler at an apothecary in Cambridge, and we must all visit and take along another bottle of Jane's urine. 'Martha, you will arrange this,' the vicar says, loudly, for my benefit. 'If anyone can propose a cure for Jane's fits, Butler is your man,' he announces, his voice thick with the brandy. His gait is good and wobbly as he finally fixes his hat on his head, rolling through the hall without troubling to be quiet.

Later, as I am falling asleep, smarting afresh at the vicar's description of me, I think again of my master and the curious dream I had, not long after our arrival at the house. It was in the confusion of the new arrangements of rooms. I had gone to sleep in the little side-chamber next to the children's room, the room that had briefly been Jane's until she decided she preferred to be with the others.

In the dream, I had perfect hearing. First I heard my master come stumbling up the stairs, unmistakably a man's step, much the worse for drink. And then, to my astonishment, the door to my chamber opened and there he stood, swaying, holding a candle. That was all. It was nothing. He stood for a moment, in that characteristic still way, then the candle he held went out or was snuffed, and he said nothing. In the dream I spoke some words but I did not know what they were.

Then the dream left, and I woke up, stirred and trembling. I tried to see the door in the darkness but it was firmly closed and no light came from under it. I lay sleepless for such a long time. And in the weeks that followed the dream floated up again even in daytime and I felt marvellous strange and almost expected the master to mention it – as if it had truly happened. But the master has been his friendly, playful self, teasing me, as of old, when he isn't worried and harried and vexed by his daughter's illness and the worldly concerns of a gentleman of his standing. So I chide myself. What is a dream in the mind of a servant woman like me? It was not sent by the devil or God. I'm not a saint or Joan of Arc. And such an inconsequential dream! Foolish and silly, a small thing.

Now I'm wide awake again. I feel like a parchment roll that has opened out flat and the dream is a map, symbols written on it, which I struggle to understand. Perhaps it is the fear I have about the master's drinking. At Brampton, when things became more troublesome, when he and the mistress seemed forever to be quarrelling, my master often drank alone in the evening, or sat eating the supper that Dottie would provide for him, or even sometimes went out on his horse and came back in the early hours. I feel sure the mistress hoped that on coming to Warboys he might change, perhaps spend less time drinking or away hunting boar with Sir Henry. She would never say it, but if she did, her hope has proved vain. And is his quarrelsome habit worsening? But my master has great skill and command of himself. He rarely seems drunk. In truth, the more he drinks, the more tightly contained he seems: like the skin on a barrel of water, trembling as it reaches the top, threatening to tip.

The noises in my bad ear – a high note that sounds like a woman crying – often worsen at night, making sport with me. I lift my head from the straw pallet to relieve it but I am all the more certain I do hear crying. Wailing. Sounds all around the house, as if there were a high wind and we travelling on a ship at sea.

I let my head fall to the pillow. My ear once squashed shut gives up the wailing sounds but with my good ear I think I hear angry voices and muffled thuds, falling and thumping, and other ungodly noises from who knows where. These watery sounds arrived when *we* did, in Warboys, and now I know not whether to trust them: are they within or without? They feel like a river of sound swimming through my dreams.

The morning of our visit to Cambridge brings news of Gabriel. He has swiftly been found a position, apprenticed to a local groundsman in Titchmarsh, by his uncle Gilbert. 'So he's gone for a good while,' Dottie says. Popsie is downcast. The mistress has red eyes.

The sky is stretched and empty, except for a lone marsh harrier pointedly going about her hunting as we travel with the three bundled-up girls, Jane, Mary and Bessie, me and my master, he on a horse, we with our driver, Crabbie, whipping up the horses, the girls covered with blankets and their feet wrapped in straw, inside the carriage.

There's a neat's tongue pie along with some rye bread, and I have them on a napkin on my knee, and Jane, greedy little Jane, snuggles beside me and picks crumbs from beneath the linen. Her brother teases her often about her fat cheeks and her great appetite, but today it seems pitiful, done out of fear and to comfort herself. Mary, as ever, is reading, and devout, and holds her book close to her eyes, which she has tired out with her efforts. Bessie, her big eyes wide and bright, sits alert as if embarking on a great adventure.

As we trundle down the driveway from the manor house with the big wheels shaking us, and a short distance through the village of Warboys, we see her. Alice Samuel. She is walking from her house with a young woman. She is not wearing the knitted cap of her visit to the manor, and yet you could not mistake her. The girl with her is slender, with long hair of a shocking colour, peeping out from her coif. That must be Nessie, Alice's daughter.

As I am craning to look at mother and daughter, I see that the master up ahead is doing the same. He almost falls from his horse. The animal rears to a halt, the master yanking at the rein and then – when brief greetings 'Well met, neighbour!' are made – he starts up again, and the horse is now almost at a gallop, as if my master is trying to escape. I lean out from the carriage window to watch his figure for a second, rising and falling in the saddle, his velvet coat flapping.

My heartbeat has quickened, for no good reason. Once again I'm thinking of Jane's voice, as she pointed at Alice and called her a witch. Why did I have the thought – did we all have it? – that it was not Jane's voice, but another's speaking out that day? And how could the old crone have a daughter so fresh and pretty? Did she herself once look like that? Her grey-streaked hair, wound up on her head, must once have been that shameful red colour. Perhaps that was the direction of my master's thinking and his wish to get away.

Alice and her daughter are walking in the direction of the pond, no doubt at this time in the morning to gather eels from the traps left overnight. They are carrying a heavy basket between them and squabbling. I am the one nearest the open window of the carriage. I pull back the curtain. The basket is swinging this way and that as first mother and then daughter grab it, like two naughty children. 'Give it here, you bitch!' Alice screams, and I drop the curtain, flattening my hands over Jane's ears, though I know it is too late. Jane snuggles closer to me.

As we leave Warboys, the watery expanse of the fens appears in the distance. Warboys is surrounded by fens. We must stay on the uplands. Twice Crabbie finds our way blocked by water. 'Plenty ducks, plenty ducks,' he mutters to himself. The mud on the causeway is thick and slows the wheels of the carriage. I am glad of his skill, his gentle coaxing of the horse, and how well he knows these drowned lands, the winter bog and marsh, and the reeds that spread for miles, the hoar frost icing their edges stark and white against the great murky depths where only the snails and vipers live, where white skeleton trees stretch their fingers to point out how deep it is, where the water rolls right up to the doors of the houses, and the men – the Slodgers – walk on long stilts to get through it.

After an hour or two of this rackety, painful journeying we rest to eat and to feed the horses, which the girls love to do. Crabbie is hopping from foot to foot. 'Fart once and you're over. Fart once and you're off,' he says, making Jane laugh. He is probably talking about guiding the horse on high ground, away from the fens. He straightens up then. ''Tis a long way, Cambridge,' he says soberly. He thinks a boat might have been better.

It is dusk as we reach this grand town of Cambridge. The sight of it makes the girls squeal first with delight and then fall to trembling. The golden buildings rearing up, the stone everywhere, so much of it, and the river with the lit boats upon it and scholars in their black cloaks, flapping. Our first glimpse of a chapel bigger than anything we've ever seen, as grand, the master tells us, as Ely Cathedral, which sits like a snail on the distant horizon for much of our journey. This wondrous spiked building looms as huge as Heaven itself and long-necked swans sweep over it, passing the lordly vastness, the river and the fancy bridges, the air alive with chatter and wheels rolling, horses and birdsong. We fall silent with awe and pull our heads in from the windows, because we are nearly at our destination.

So then we shake and rattle – our bottoms sore by now, our backs aching – down some narrow cobbled street, sloshing with rain water, dark and lit only by the candles in the windows of the little buildings lining it. There is a huge stink as we step out, worse than that of the sow in the pen, and we pull our cloaks up to our noses and mouths, for this is surely a place where the pestilence still lives. Glancing around we see piles of horse dung, strewn with straw. Jane clings to me and I feel her starting to sob. My master, dismounting his horse and joining us, is short-tempered with her and bids Bessie to straighten her out. We have come all this way and Doctor Butler is a very great man and we are not going to show ourselves to be silly in his company, are we?

A rough woman answers the door to us. She has a fat back-side and hands full of bottles and ointments. She uses her back-side to close the door behind us. She barely greets us but shows us a small room in which to take off our cloaks and bonnets.

And then a man appears, reeking of the sweet smell of sarsa-parilla and wearing a large apron, with a beard sticking out in every direction. I drop a curtsey and the three girls huddle in front of me, shaking. This man slaps my master on his back and is introduced to us as Doctor Butler. I set my mouth to say nothing, keeping one hand firmly on Jane's trembling shoul-der. He seems nothing like a doctor to me, more like a smithy or one of the tradesmen or our neighbour John Samuel, so coarse is his manner. If only Crabbie had come with us. He'd be sure to be muttering something amusing. *Fat backside fat backside*. It might comfort us some.

'Ah, Throckmorton – what a gaggle of beauties. Since women like a German clock never run true – they must be costing you a fortune!'

My master laughs. I dare not glance at him: the laugh strikes a false note to me. He puts a hand protectively around Bessie and ushers us all in. The fat housekeeper or wife or whatever she is bustles in (*not a sober wife, not a sober wife!* Crabbie would say), bringing a tray with tankards of ale on it. We stand around in the cold orange light of the apothecary shop, surrounded by the little labelled bottles and the dancing light of candles on the windowsills.

The ale is unlike anything I've ever tasted. I swallow, and the first gulp is aniseed, and delicious. But on downing it I taste senna, and can feel it snaking through me rather quickly. The doctor catches my look and laughs.

'Butler's Ale. My own special blend. Yes, it has *purging* properties – maidenhead, senna, agrimony. Would you like another, my dear?'

I shake my head. Doctor Butler turns to my master and says, 'Is she a mute? I have cures for that too.'

But Master Throckmorton smiles kindly and says, 'She speaks when she needs to,' and thankfully the doctor turns his attention to Jane.

'Let the child come into my examining room,' Doctor Butler says, nodding to his wife or housekeeper to take away the empty glasses. Jane bursts into quiet stifled little sobs, tears streaming down her cheeks.

'The woman – your maid – must accompany her. You stay here. And perhaps send me one of the sisters.' The doctor's eye falls on Bessie. Bessie is a bold girl, with a bright, open expression, and she does not drop her eyes when he glances at her. He nods his approval, so Jane, Bessie and I follow him, leaving Mary with her father, our skirts brushing the floors of a dusty corridor, with stale, strong-smelling air, into a small room with a bed and on it a stained coverlet.

Jane is instructed to lie down, whereupon her whimpering turns into uncontrollable shaking.

'Good, good, you are about to be in your fits in front of me? That is all to the good,' the loud Doctor Butler says, and his big eyes, the baggy pouches beneath them, glitter. I move forward to take hold of Jane's fat little hand, but he frowns at that and shoos me away.

'No, sir, these are not her fits,' Bessie ventures boldly, as Jane has been struck dumb. 'She is only frightened, sir. If she was in her fits she wouldn't know us, or be able to talk to us, and her arm jerks like so –' Bessie demonstrates '– and her eyes are unseeing and her countenance changes utterly and her belly heaves up with her head and heels touching as if she were a tumbler in a theatre show.'

The doctor smiles, showing yellow teeth behind his beard. He gently takes Jane's hand, cocking his head a little towards me, and saying, 'You see, my dears, I am not unkind, but we do need to examine her, don't we?'

He then turns to Bessie. 'Your sister is how old?'

'Nine years and three months,' Bessie says. She is not looking at her sister, but at the doctor, a habit she has of fixing her full and complete attention on a person as if no one else is in the room.

'Hmm. And you are?'

'Thirteen years, sir.'

'You look older,' Doctor Butler says, touching Bessie's hair. She preens a little.

'You have your monthly courses? At what age did they begin?'

Bessie – unused to being asked such a thing and not having the slightest idea what he means – shakes her head. I find myself flushing red. Bessie mumbles something.

'Hmm. So you are rather late. Well . . .' And here Doctor Butler, to the horror of all of us, whips up Jane's apron, skirt and petticoat. My poor little Jane squeals and I step forward with an instinct to protect her but am brusquely pushed back.

'Out of my way, woman! How else am I to examine her testicles?'

His back is now blocking my view. I reach for Bessie's hand to squeeze. The two of us stand as deer do when the hunter first spies them, frozen in foolish inaction.

Jane's cries are tiny. They break my heart. I put a hand over my good ear – a habit when I want to block something out – but to no avail. The doctor spends some moments on his ministrations. I can only see that he has one hand on her stomach and the other is somewhere else.

'Did you bring her urine sample?' he asks me. I did but had left it in a bag with Mary, who has remained in the parlour, reading her book beside her father. Mary's calm is a mystery to me: how does she achieve it, in the midst of her sister's agitations? Bessie goes in search of the urine bottle.

I am alone with the strange uncouth man, poor Jane on the bed and him bustling in front of me. His examination swiftly over, he washes his hands in a bowl with water and nods to me to pass him the linen towel. Would that I had dared to ask the filthy man why he did not think to do so before he touched my beloved Jane.

The doctor has not troubled himself to pull down Jane's skirt so I step forward to do so, smoothing it and trying with my eyes to convey reassurance to her, to let her know her ordeal is over. The affront and shame still cling to her – to both of us – and her teeth are chattering. She suddenly whimpers, 'Martha! I'm going to be—'

I look around and snatch up a bowl, just in time cupping it under her, holding her head as she spatters up the Butler's Ale.

Doctor Butler makes a sympathetic sound and offers her a grubby cloth to wipe her mouth.

He then turns his attention to me, with a remark so shocking that my mouth drops open. 'The child's testicles are intact. The mother – the womb – too. But she has lost her maidenhead. This happens sometimes – girls might ride a hobby horse or an actual one or even jump a gate and affect such an accident. No need to concern the family with such a delicate matter, but between ourselves, do you know something I do not?'

A man who could throw up a girl's skirts and touch her so ingloriously, there is no knowing what such a man might do. I tremble and shake my head. I do not know how to answer him.

'You're a strange one, aren't you? Why do they keep you? Are you a good cook? Are you deaf, perhaps?' Here he moves to touch my ears but I twitch my head angrily from him. 'You seem to be *reading* my lips rather than listening to me.'

'I hear you well enough,' I say at last. (He chuckles.) 'I am a good cook, yes, and I am loyal and have been with the family since I was a girl of thirteen. I'm a good midwife, too, and I can read and write my letters and make medicine.' Here I stop. What once seemed a skill and something to be proud of has taken on a different hue. My mistress believed Alice Samuel to have some healing skills, superior to mine. I do not want to be tarred with the same brush.

'And do your children share your affliction? Are you married?'

I shake my head.

'Some man might still have you, deafness or no – how old are you? More than twenty?'

'I'm thirty-four,' I manage to splutter.

'Ah, you seem much younger than you are, which is surely good fortune for a woman who is half deaf. Although some men would find your holding your tongue a distinct *advantage* . . .'

He takes a step towards me, as if to examine me, and I move back.

Thankfully, Bessie returns to the room and interrupts him. She holds out the bottle with Jane's urine in it.

The doctor takes it to the candle to examine it.

Jane is allowed to sit up. I sit beside her on the examining couch and put my arms around her to try to comfort her. She no longer cries but only stares ahead, her soft hair smelling so familiar under my nose. She is a little stunned. My bunny. I kiss her cheek. My heart aches for her. If only I had anticipated what he might do I might have prepared her, or even prevented it, but I know nothing of doctors, or the ways of learned men.

I glance at his hands as he flicks through the book, watch him writing something on a piece of paper. His hand is fat with warts aplenty. It reminds me of a toad I once nearly stepped on, mistaking it for a stone down by Warboys Pond. An ugly moment for my toe but the animal leaped free, unharmed. It had been gorging on fireflies, and in the twilight it glowed its warning to me, and this is what I am thinking of in that sad and strong-smelling room: a warning, an eerie light, something disgusting and not of this world.

'Do you want another glass of my ale, my dear? Doctor Butler's Ale is sought out for all ailments, you know.' Now he has turned his attention to me. His face seems congested with feeling, the face of a drunkard. I shudder.

He has added some kind of powder to the urine in a glass tube and is swilling it around. Despite myself, I am intrigued and leave the couch as he beckons me, to study it.

Bessie remains by the door, hands by her sides, her anxious eyes on her sister. Jane sits as if turned to stone. Doctor Butler continues his experiments. A fat ginger cat slides into the room. Bessie realises she has left the door ajar and softly closes it, mindful of her sister, I'm sure, and wondering what further indignities might be performed.

Finally, Doctor Butler says, 'Well, let us go and speak to your father. Hop down, my dear.'

Jane's legs will scarce hold her. She and Bessie are released, and I put my arm around Jane's shoulders, steering her into the room where her father and Mary wait.

Bessie, Jane and I squeeze onto a bench beside Mary, the crammed shelves towering above us, threatening to topple their contents of books and phials onto our heads. (Mary has no curiosity about her sister. Only the books and the shelves intrigue her.) Our shock and silence cloak us, and we keep our eyes downcast.

My master has his back to us, sharing a pipe with Doctor Butler.

'This began with Jane on first arriving at your new home in Warboys? She never had such fits before?'

'No,' my master says.

'None of the others suffer so?'

My master shakes his head. 'Just Jane.'

'And Doctor Barrough suggested worms?' the doctor asks.

'He did. And he twice said that I should no longer strive by physicians or spend any more money on them.'

Doctor Butler coughs and splutters a little on his pipe.

My master glances over his shoulder at the four of us, exactly at the moment I raise my eyes to his. He turns back quickly. 'Barrough asked me if anyone wished us harm. He wondered if witchcraft was behind Jane's torments,' my master says.

Butler moves around the cramped space, pouring more ale from a bottle. He no longer troubles to offer us any. Only my master.

'You have no such suspicions?' the doctor asks.

'I can think of no reason any person would wish us ill,' my master replies, with a casual air. 'We've only just moved to Warboys. Sir Henry has made me squire and given us the manor house. I'm very much hoping to inspire nothing but *respect* in our new neighbours.'

My master's back is to me again. The memory of a bent figure of a woman, swinging a basket and, with a loud voice, calling her daughter a bitch springs into my head. *Did you ever see one more like a witch than she?* I wonder if Jane is thinking the same thing: why does my master not mention Alice Samuel?

'Hmm. Well, I am not one of those who believe, as Aristotle did, that a woman is but an error of creation. Even so . . . one must concede that the passive nature of the female and her general weakness make her prone to many more diseases than the male. All of that notwithstanding, I find the child's body to be in good temper.'

Mary looks up from her reading, listening intently. She is the cleverest of the girls, no question of that, and is no doubt trying to follow his words. Jane's plump little body edges closer to me, so that I feel the heat of her, smell damp woollen clothes and childish sweat, a smell as dear to me as my own body. *Please, Lord,* I pray, *make her well again.*

'Her urine did not show any evidence of illness of any kind: the colour was true and there were no clouds or other warning signs. I felt inside for the female testicles and they are functioning well, though, of course, very small, and as I determined, she is too young to be in her mother fits. This monthly pollution is surely the cause of five hundred miseries, as we know. However, God has ordained that it should happen around thirteen or fourteen years of age – about the age of your daughter Bessie – so Jane is too young for this to be the reason for the fits.'

Pollution. Female testicles. Mother fits. The words dance in front of me. Mary's eyes widen and her bottom lip falls in wonder.

I struggle to understand in case Jane asks me later. How will I find the words? Bessie, I know, is listening too, though not in the same intent way Mary is. Bessie stares straight ahead, stroking the wood of the bench we sit upon, one finger seeking a small inscription scratched there.

'My examination was thorough and you will not find a doctor in all of the country who is as knowledgeable about the ways in which women's bodies and spirits affect their already weak chamber of wisdom, but I can truly say that it is not a frenzy of the womb that is the cause of her ailments. You will need to look elsewhere for the cause.'

Doctor Butler finishes his ale with a slurping sound and a flourish of his sleeve as he lifts the glass, then burps loudly. His housekeeper with the fat backside reappears, bringing a fresh bottle of the ale.

'I sell this,' the doctor says happily, 'should you want to take any home with you.'

The master's shoulders slump and he shakes his head.

'Doctor Barrough is right. Sorcery is the only explanation!' pronounces the doctor, so loudly that the master jumps. He waits for his words to take effect, then carries on: 'Think again, man. Did your maid refuse some neighbour a pot of herbs? Did one of your daughters let a dog loose among her hens? You never know with an old hag. Even the smallest thing might do it.'

'I cannot think of anyone,' my master repeats stubbornly.

Bessie wriggles in her seat. Mary and Jane put their heads together, whispering, and then it is Bessie, the boldest, who protests, 'But, Father, what about that nasty old woman? The one who brought the rye bread? She looks *exactly* like a witch – and Jane did say so!'

The master shakes his head quickly. 'No, no. We hardly know her,' he says, with great force.

Doctor Butler seems amused. 'It seems your daughters are more intelligent to these things than you are. You followed the trial of the witches of Chelmsford? It is not merely in Europe that witches abound.'

'You are the second person to mention it. I did, but this woman, this neighbour, has no reason to want to harm me or my daughter. We hardly know her – we've been in Warboys only since Michaelmas. And Jane had her first fit *before* the woman came to the house.'

My master stands up abruptly and signals to the house-keeper to fetch our cloaks: we must leave. It is puzzling to me why he is so adamant that it cannot possibly be Alice Samuel when she has some reputation for sorcery, and the reverend, too, suggested it. As we are all wrapping ourselves in our cloaks and money is changing hands, the doctor says, marvel-lous cruel, 'So not a soul in Warboys wishes you ill. You are the most popular new squire who ever existed, despite you being the greatest of friends with their landlord the Golden Knight, despite your grace-and-favour home? And sharing the name Throckmorton with a man who betrayed Crown and country?'

My master's face is stricken, all colour draining from it. 'This woman has no reason to intend malice on the family.' Then, in lower voice, 'And if she did, what would I gain by angering her further?'

The roguish doctor takes a last swig of his foul drink and nods. 'Ah, now I understand all. She *is* an old witch and you are afraid of her.'

'Of course not!' There is a pause, and then my master guffaws loudly, taking this remark as if it were meant in sport, although I feel angry on his behalf, and certain sure it is not.

'I'm in the best position to know what is right for my daughters. We plan to live quietly, without spectacle or scandal in Warboys. That is my aim.'

'Of course, of course,' the doctor says. Such a rude fellow! The two men are in good spirits again, as we bustle out of the door, the doctor leaning in with his sarsaparilla breath to pat Bessie's head and say to my master, 'Marry them all off as soon as you are able! You know that their sex is frail and subject to ruin.'

We bid the doctor goodbye.

Once outside again in the blue moonlight of the Cambridge alleyway, my master looks for Crabbie in a nearby alehouse while we wait in darkness in the cold wooden carriage. Our poor lively Jane, normally as cheeky as any kitten, can hardly walk at all. I wonder if my master, stroking his beard and no doubt missing the counsel of my mistress, guesses at the source of his daughter's misery. As with most men, the indignities girls suffer are surely a mystery to him. But then I remember the shocking remark the doctor made about Jane's most privy places and feel myself flush red once more from head to toe. If any could see me they would think a beetroot grew in the dark here. How can a man speak of such a thing with ease? I close my eyes, longing for my bed, and wish to forget all that has happened today.

But it is not to be. That night after visiting Doctor Butler we stay at an inn – a little excitement for us all, who have never done so before. Master says we cannot risk the treacherous dark watery route home (now black and icy too) and I am relieved to hear it. I picture for a moment us slipping into the water and all of us – the carriage and horse and Crabbie – disappearing with the will-o'-the-wisps and other phantoms.

Jane gives little heed to her usual pleasures of a good meal and a novel adventure. Instead she is quiet and not the same girl at all. She allows me to tuck her into the bed and the master to sit with her for a moment, kissing her cheek, stroking her hair and blowing out the candle. There is a notice on the wall of the inn, advertising Doctor Butler's Ale – *Famous throughout all of England and the cure of all ills*. 'Such a knave,' my master mutters, and then I know that he shared my misgivings. I am comforted some.

I sleep with the girls – me on the floor on a straw pallet, Bessie, Jane and Mary in the bed. Mary lights herself a candle from some embers in the fire, then reads a long time and has to be told to blow it out. She wants to ask me things that the doctor said: what is this 'weak chamber of wisdom' that we women and girls possess? What is a 'frenzy of the womb'? I tell her to sleep and stop disturbing poor Jane, who is exhausted. My master sleeps next door in a small room alone.

And in the night he taps on the door and opens it, putting his head around to say, in a whisper loud enough for my benefit, 'Martha? Are you awake? Come – put your shoes on, let's take a walk. I need to talk.'

I am awake, wide awake, still smarting over the doctor's insolence to me about my lack of a husband and his remark that there is still time to find one. My master's arrival – his face around the bedchamber door – causes my breath to catch in my throat. For the strangest moment it is exactly as he appeared in my dream, the one I had after we moved. A thought flares: do I have powers of premonition? Immediately I squash the thought and mutter a quick prayer. Sister Dorothy dreamed things that oft-times came true and it always made me afraid.

Bessie stirs in her sleep, opens her eyes and, sensing me not lying in my bed but standing up and some light coming from the door ajar, murmurs, 'Mama! Don't leave us.' Then, when I say nothing but pull on my cloak and boots, she gives me a hard look in the semi-dark, and says, 'I thought you were Mama,' and turns on her side, in some sort of bad humour.

The master is full of questions about my visits to towns before and discovers that I have only been to Huntingdon once and Cambridge never. And I have never yet walked the streets of any town in darkness. At first it feels marvellous strange to be walking now with him, and the sound of my boots on stones startles me so that I keep turning my head, with the sense that we are being followed. For a moment I have a notion that one of the girls – Bessie – has come running after us. (Sister Dorothy would have words to say about me, walking alone with a man at night-time, too. No wonder I feel followed: it is probably Our Lady Mary herself, come to chide me.)

My master knows the town well from his years studying in Cambridge and walks with confidence, once or twice reaching out a hand to me to hurry me along a wooden plank thrown over a deep puddle, or steer us away from a heap of dung, or straw. We are neither of us the slightest bit sleepy. He pauses beside me while I idle under his lantern to stare into a store full of books and pamphlets of every kind, then puts his hand under my elbow to direct me gently down an alley that looks dark and forbidding. A little tremor runs from my elbow to my breast at being touched – such a new thing.

We pass two scholars, flapping their gowns like dark crows, strutting, giggling and cawing. A smell of ale clings to them. I'm surprised how many alehouses and hostelries are open at so late an hour, smoke and voices reaching us from inside the mysterious, darkly lit rooms. My master says we are heading towards the river.

'What did you think, Martha? You may speak freely.'

Think about what? Doctor Butler? I hardly know where to begin. Am I to mention what he said about Jane losing her maidenhead? Or witchcraft?

'Since we came to Warboys, there has been nothing but trouble. Jane's fits are vexing and the last one worse than ever. Elizabeth – you can hardly have failed to notice – Elizabeth suffers. Is it her age, Martha? You are only a few years younger . . . Women of a certain age, when there is no longer the possibility of more children, they grow bitter. Lately she has mentioned the infants we lost – John and the first infant Mary. We named our dear Mary for her and I thought that might be balm enough. Is that a cold thing to say? What I mean is, we have not mentioned the lost babies these many long years and then of late their names are on her tongue night and day. She pines for Gabriel in an unnatural way – a young man must be allowed to leave home and go out into the world, however undignified the occasion that prompts it – and all her fears for Jane, for her health, consume her. I can only imagine that it is something to do with . . . women's troubles.'

I open my mouth, to venture some soothing remark, but, fast in step beside me, the master is like a riverbank breaking and all the words flowing out.

'And other things! The things she accuses me of! I do not know what to make of it. And Gabriel! Such shocking mischief there!'

At last I might learn what has happened, but no, he rushes on: 'One can hardly blame a father for being protective of his daughters. Is that not the God-given responsibility of a father? And yet to hear Elizabeth speak . . .'

I nod quickly. Whether he is a fond father, or too zealous in his care for his daughters, what do I know of that – I who only had a dear foster mother to care for me? His drinking, his brooding moods, is it my place to speak of them?

He runs on: 'That woman. The neighbour. What need is there to enrage her further? Am I wrong in that? In not want-ing – the moment we arrive – to make every tongue in Warboys wag? I learned that my wife believed her a cunning woman with some medicine that might help her, and an intention to consult with her – I think you knew of this, did you not, Martha?'

He stops for a moment, I open my mouth, but he smiles then. 'Ah, who can blame her? Jane's suffering is awful to witness. And Elizabeth drew back from that path, so there was no harm done, nothing we can be accused of, no papism or consorting with witches. I had an uneasy feeling when I met the neighbour. She has a curious look about her . . . Sir Henry had told me about the husband, John Samuel. He is rumoured to have had a role in the Muchwood riots – a brute, by all accounts – and yet he's popular in Warboys, popular in *some* quarters. One must be careful. Sir Henry was not able to find a man to stand against him on a jury so he has to watch and wait. He had some bad report of the wife from his spies in Warboys but did not know who she was. There is a daughter, pretty and quick – I think we saw her early this morning. Not a family to make enemies of. Why accuse the old woman of witchcraft? It will bring more unhappiness to our door.'

So far, I have not uttered a word. I am only walking beside the master, being sure to have my good ear beside him, and wondering at the frenzy in his voice, the worry and the scandal and agreeing in silence that, yes, Alice Samuel did have a curious look about her and it was a frightening moment, the time when Jane accused her. Weighing the matter, I agree, yes, invaded by so many fears and worries, there is much wisdom in not courting further griefs.

We stop to watch the boats on the river, the torches flickering on the black water, the smell of tallow and rotting reeds in the night air. A town – my first night in a town. This is what a town smells like.

'And then there are Elizabeth's brothers. The younger one, Henry. He is enthusiastic indeed about witches! He is here in Cambridge studying divinity.'

He gestures across the river to the white stone building glowing in the moonlight and, for a moment, I expect to see him: the lanky Henry Pickering, younger brother of my mistress, red-cheeked and quick to temper, emerging in his black robes, rowing across the water to us.

'They are coming next week, Henry and his friend Thomas Cakebread. I cannot deter them and Elizabeth will not try.

They are *much exercised* by the discovery that their own sister lives close to a woman accused by his niece of being a witch! Excited to see a reputed witch for themselves. After these trials at Chelmsford – did you hear of them, Martha? Three women hanged, condemned by their own children. And all three of the witches called Joan!'

This last remark is somehow funny. We look at one another, and before I know it, we are laughing.

'There is a ballad,' my master says, recovering himself first. 'No doubt Crabbie would know it.'

We walk onto a little bridge and a great wonder rises in me as we watch a boat slide under us and lift our eyes to the moon-lit buildings beyond. To think that man built such marvels! And me, all of us, but a speck in comparison: like a duck on the river, passing time, busy with its grubbings and peckings, but soon to be forgotten. Oh my life has been small! My first visit to Cambridge and such a sad occasion to prompt it. My master turns his face to me. A searching look. My heart swells with all that I dare not speak, longings and wishes I never knew lived in me. It is something about this rare moment of being *looked at*. I feel myself taking shape in front of his eyes: my hair, my brow, my nose, my mouth become true to me as he stares at me. Sometimes I have wondered, my life lived in the corners of theirs, if I exist for the Throckmortons. If I exist at all. His intense gaze makes me sure of it for the first time.

My mind returns to my anger at Doctor Butler. His rude questions. Yes, I long ago accepted myself as a spinster. Not because of my deafness or any other affliction, but by inclina-tion. My heart has belonged to the Throckmorton family since the first day I entered their home, swollen with gratitude, and I feel safe within their care. This has been enough for me.

The master drops his gaze and a light on the river goes out.

He takes my arm and we walk now with greater ease, retracing our path towards the inn. I hope that unburdening himself to me has helped him. Our steps fall into a sweet rhythm beside one another. His face is in profile, his trimmed beard, his fine nose, his height and his masterful step. His love for his daughters has always been much in evidence: many are the times I've heard him giving strict instruction for their care, or their education, or even how they should dress. He is the most doting father and always seen in sweet play with his girls, or moved to pity by their small woes, though I know that my mistress has sometimes spoken harshly of his concern, considering it at times too fervent

It is true I have noted my mistress's melancholy mood since arriving in Warboys, and grieved it. Dottie would sometimes say to me in Brampton (and not in jest) that I was deaf, dumb and *blind*, and that there was something very wrong indeed between mistress and master, but loving the family as I did, why would I want to know such a thing? In their new manor at Warboys they have an enormous bedchamber where so few sleep (unlike in the old house where there were guests on truckle beds, the oldest girls Johanne and Bessie, sometimes Jane, sometimes other relatives), but I have observed that my mistress now arranges to sleep with a thin blanket on a window seat, alone. In the old house the master would sleep clamped to her, with his arms around her middle. He was always restless at night, more often awake than asleep and sometimes, after much prowling, he liked to seek out her calm and solid form and soak up some of it for himself. He must feel her new coldness keenly.

'Poor dear Jane,' I say, at last finding my tongue. 'But let us pray she grows out of it. I will tell Mistress Elizabeth about the

Butler's Ale. Perhaps we should buy a bottle before we leave and say no more about his . . . other suggestion.'

He smiles, and sighs and turns to me, his face so close I can feel his breath on mine and smell the aniseed on it.

'Thank you, dear sweet Martha. Let us say nothing about his – diagnosis, or anything else. Anything he might have said about Jane's condition. Perhaps you will ask the girls to do the same. I'd rather not have Elizabeth worrying about witches, or have our family the talk of the neighbourhood. Her brothers will soon ignite that particular fire and no doubt my brother-in-law Francis will, too, but we might at least have a reprieve for now. Butler's Ale it is. And if not Butler, I hope God sees fit to cure Jane with it.'

I wonder then if my master guesses about the uncouth doctor's examination of Jane. I nod again, meeting my master's eyes with my own beseeching ones. I imagine him reaching out a hand to touch my face. But he only smiles his familiar smile and steps towards the door of our lodgings.

On our return I abide by my promise and mention neither witches nor privy things about Jane's little body to my mistress – after all, the doctor said such things were commonplace in girls from riding a horse or suchlike, and Jane has been ever lively and loved to ride since infanthood. Why concern my troubled mistress further with such delicate matters when the doctor has told me they have no import? The days in Warboys go by in peace for a while, with only my memory of a secret moonlit town and a walk like no other trembling like a new bird in my breast. I try to pour some cold water on the children's love of pamphlets because my master has his reasonable concern that such poor halfpenny literature might be firing their imaginations.

One day I find them huddled over the very one he spoke of, the one about the Chelmsford witches. They are in their bedchamber, a late afternoon when a fire is lit and the night has drawn in. Bessie picks up her bible on seeing me and pretends to read it. Johanne sits in her armchair, flicking through the pamphlet. Hob hides behind a curtain, peeping out periodically to shout, 'Whoo-hoo!'

'Churching, churching, churching, churching,' complains Hob, bitterly, when I say that they must come downstairs presently because not only is the vicar, their uncle Francis, staying for dinner but their other uncle, Henry, will be there with his young scholar friend.

Johanne glances up. 'Is it Thomas Cakebread?' she asks, and seems pleased with my answer.

I bustle around the room, picking up their discarded clothing, books, cushions and toys, keeping one eye on Jane. Our hope – mine and the master's – is that the Butler's Ale or Mother Caterill's fine cooking will help her and this will be the end of it.

'But what does it *mean*?' Bessie wails, flinging her bible onto the floor. 'I wish it had remained in Latin and none of my business!'

'Hush! Uncle Francis will hear you!' her sister Mary says at once, in great fear.

Johanne reads the pamphlet in her hand in silence and flicks it away from me when I put out my hand for it.

'You could ask Uncle Henry to explain the Bible to you. He would know,' Johanne suggests, with a smile. Being the eldest, she likes to have the young men in the house and finds them a welcome distraction from her Bible studies. '"The Apprehension and Confession of Three Notorious Witches, 1589",' Johanne says loudly, in theatrical tones.

I begin, 'Now, Johanne, your father has said to me that he is not happy—'

Johanne waves me away and makes a 'Pouf!' sound. Jane and Mary run to sit on the floor beside their sister, Grace and Bessie too. Only Hob stays in his place half behind and half out of the curtain.

I have always had this motley place in their hearts. Sometime mother, sometime sister, sometime governess, sometime maid. Sometime – like now – a tapestry on the wall or a cushion on the bed.

'Is it Joan Cunny's story?' Jane asks. So it is clear they already know the pamphlet and no comment from me will deter them. 'Read that one, my favourite!' They chuckle, move their heads closer together, and Bessie carefully places the bible on the armrest of the chair, the better to hide the pamphlet should their father enter the room.

The fire in the grate crackles and the children are giggly and alert. Festive, a little like a birthday.

' "Joan Cunny confessed that she sent her said spirits to *hurt* Master Kitchin, minister of the said town, and also to one George Coe of the said town, shoe-maker, to hurt *him* like-wise," ' Johanne reads.

'Oh, the shoe-maker – they're always such horrid men!' Hob says.

' "But the spirits could not hurt him, and the cause why they could not, as the said spirits told her, was because they had a strong faith in God, and had in-in-vocated and called upon Him, that they could do them no harm." '

'Ugh,' says Hob. 'God stopped them! Tell us about the imps!'

'Shush! Don't keep interrupting!' Grace reaches over Mary's legs to slap at her brother.

I try again: 'Really, I think the Bible is better reading.'

'Oh, Martha, we'll stop right away if Father comes,' Mary says.

'"The witch had nine spirits,"' continues Johanne. '"Two of them were like a black dog, having the faces of toads."'

'A black dog with the face of a toad! Ooooh!' Hob squeals, forgetting his instruction, and all five sisters fall on him, shrieking and snuffling as they fight to suppress him.

I glance anxiously towards the closed door and make a new attempt to scold them.

'Martha, do some dusting and pretend you can't hear us,' Johanne instructs tartly and, stung, I turn to my task, picking up things from the floor and replacing them in blanket boxes, and on shelves.

Johanne hushes the others so that she can go on: '"These spirits belonged to this witch, who allowed them to suck commonly on her sore leg, which this Mother Cunny had—"'

At this there is another roar from Hob. 'Ugh! Sucking on her sore leg!' Hob's screams and the girls' shrieks bring Dottie rushing into the room. Her apron is stuffed full of the chestnuts she had been about to roast and it is clear the noise could be heard from downstairs.

'What is it? Where's the mistress?' Dottie asks, looking at me. I shake my head, taking up the ruse that Johanne had suggested, pretending I had heard nothing of the shouting and laughter in the room, having my back to the children. I know Dottie is not fooled but she stands awhile, listening.

'"Mother Cunny had four main spirits,"' Johanne read out. '"The first was Jack. The second was Jill. The third was Nicholas and the fourth was Ned. Jack killed mankind. Jill killed womankind. Nicholas killed horses. Ned killed cattle."'

73

'Mother *Cunny*? What *is* this?' Dottie asks, astonished. The children ignore her.

'Jill killed womankind!' Bessie murmurs wonderingly.

'It is almost time for dinner,' I try again. 'Isn't that what you came up to say, Dottie?'

'I came up to find out what the to-do was! But, yes, the young masters are here. Make yourselves presentable.'

'So many witches, naughty witches and all of them hanged! They have imps to do their bidding!' Jane tells Dottie, taking her hand.

'Where is Chelmsford?' Mary asks. 'Is it far from here?'

Dottie tells her there is a good long way between them – seventy miles, she'd guess.

Finally Johanne tires of her tale and unfolds herself from the chair to bury the pamphlet back in the blanket box. She catches my eye and puts a hand to her lips. She knows I won't tell: 'My favourite is the Most Cruel and Bloody Murder – Hob likes that one, don't you? About the witch serving the fellow in the alehouse?' she says, brushing her long dark hair and smoothing down her dress.

She reaches inside the pamphlet to produce another, better hidden. Hob leaps up, flinging and twirling himself about the room like a sycamore leafstalk falling to the ground while Johanne begins reading: ' "There was a fellow, dwelling in Royston, one who loved the pot with the long neck as well as his prayers. This fuddle cap was playing cards with four malt-worms like himself in an alehouse—" '

'Maltworms! Maltworms!' cries Hob.

'Should we not go downstairs now, as Dottie bids us?' asks Mary, a little nervously, as the only one of the children with an ounce of obedience in her. But Jane's eyes are wide.

'". . . when a witch came in and stood gloating. Now this fellow could not abide looking upon a bad face (his own in the mirror was bad enough, when he was in his cups) so he shouted out to the old woman: 'Hey, witch! Look the other way! I cannot abide a nose of that fashion! Or else turn your face the wrong side out – it looks like raw flesh to blow the maggots in!'"'

'Raw flesh to blow the maggots in!' Hob giggles.

'"His fellow fuddle caps all laughed but, as we know, the end of all drunkards is to ming or to sleep, so he went outside and drew his gentleman's usher—"'

'What's ming?' asks Hob.

'We must go downstairs now,' I say.

'What's a gentleman's *usher*?' Hob persists.

'A doorman!' Bessie shouts.

Now Dottie joins the children in laughing.

'. . . and then suddenly, breaking from his ming, he finds he has a lump as big as a cherry on it!' Johanne shrieks. The girls' laughter and shrieking become thunderous. In no time the door to their bedchamber is flung open and here, of course, is my mistress. No one – least of all me – could have heard her quick light tread on the stair.

'Hush now, I came to tell you that dinner is almost ready,' Dottie says, springing from Johanne's side.

'Martha?' the mistress says, with a fierce look towards me. I am too slow to hide my guilt and make no defence of myself.

'You mustn't tire Jane. Look at the shadows under her eyes,' my mistress says crossly to Johanne. 'Uncle Henry is here and another divinity scholar from Cambridge. They are in need of supper and some distraction from their only subject of conversation.'

'What is that?' Johanne asks. My mistress rolls her eyes.

'But *where* did the witch give him a lump as big as a cherry?' Hob shouts.

Once more the room is all disorder, and this time even my mistress – after drawing a deep gasp of shock – joins in. Johanne gives her brother a tweak of the ear and leans in to say, 'On his pillicock, silly. Imagine all those imps she has, Hob, with the black bodies of dogs and faces like toads . . .'

'Pillicock!' Hob shouts. He runs to hide behind Grace. The two of them look much aggrieved.

'I know what a gentleman's usher is,' says Jane, very softly, slipping her hand into mine.

Dottie joins me in the dining room to try to assemble the children and get them to their seats. Mary sits down and looks sweetly at her uncle. Bessie and Johanne are all smiles, seeing that, for once, some young men are at table: their uncle Henry Pickering, with his high colouring and his plump chest, sits bursting out of his doublet and his friend Thomas Cakebread, beside him, quieter and more thoughtful with a shock of hair that puts me in mind of a corn dolly. I busy myself with retying the ribbon in Grace's hair, and nudging each child to take their seats beside Mary.

'"In the beginning was the Word, and the Word was with God, and the Word was God. The same was in the beginning with God. All things were made by Him; and without Him was not anything made that was made."'

The Reverend Francis Dorrington booms the prayer from the head of the table and Aunt Rosemary sits beside him, looking smaller than ever, and she, too, in her way has a shock of hair, only this time fine and pale grey, standing out all around her head in the candlelit room, like a dandelion clock. The two young men are at the other end, heads becked, ready for the victuals. Dottie nudges me, wanting me to see her saucy look towards the young man, to which I give little heed . If Thomas Cakebread is handsome, why should a woman of my age care for such a thing? And only handsome in the way of a boy, not a man, like Master Throckmorton, with command and great stature.

I sneak a look at my master from between my fingers, head bowed dutifully, and see that he has – to my mind – a look of worry and great care. I remember for a moment our walk along the Cambridge streets, the sight of the river, the taste of the strange sarsaparilla ale . . . but now, even as prayers and grace continue, Mother Caterill and Popsie have interrupted by bringing in some dishes, and my mistress has to shake her head at them, and the two young men eagerly put their hands down, only to realise that prayers are still coming. I stand behind the children, hands folded. My place has always been closest to them, no matter how Mother Caterill – who has not understood it – might chide me for it.

Bessie, Mary, Grace, Jane and Hob all have their chairs tucked in neatly, eyes fixed on the plates of food arriving and leaving. Johanne sneaks a look at Thomas Cakebread. The praying continues and the room grows stale and weary once more, with hunger and waiting.

At last the dishes are brought to the table and the family begin to eat. But the gaiety of earlier in the bedchamber is sadly missing. Thomas Cakebread ventures a few compliments to the cook in a surprisingly deep voice for one so young. Henry Pickering tries to engage my mistress, his big sister, in their previous discussion, a point of divinity. Their talk soon seems to roll across the empty table, like a marble, and all fall at last to eating in silence and the melancholy mood that the vicar prefers.

After supper, after the table has been cleared, we maids are running round the kitchen and outdoors, fetching water from the well, washing the pots, feeding the slops to the sow, and catching a bite to eat ourselves, when a message comes: more prayers. Uncle Francis has enquired about Jane's health, been told she has had no fits since the visit to Doctor Butler, and thinks that further prayers to thank God for that are needed.

'Servants too. Assemble the room, Throckmorton.'

I glance at my master, to see if he would dare contradict the vicar, but I see that he will not. He contents himself with a look, which speaks (to me at least) of his contempt for his brother-in-law but that he, as Squire of Warboys, must rise above it. He exchanges a smile with his sister Rosemary; she gives him the doting smile of a younger sister, apologising for her pompous husband. And yet, in Brampton, he would have said something, done something more.

The children are called. The mistress appears. We are to assemble in the big hall – the vicar likes this room, I suspect, for the grand sense it gives him and the way his voice bounces off the walls. The two young divinity scholars seem chastened. I wonder if they have been arguing points of scripture and this is the vicar's way to prove his point.

I long for the master to speak. Since coming to Warboys his moments of melancholia seem to take longer to shift, his glum moods to last longer. The mistress, too. Only the children feel lively in this atmosphere that the vicar rules.

'Let us all kneel, in front of the fire,' the vicar says, commanding the children to line up beside him. Bessie quickly arranges herself next to Thomas Cakebread. Johanne hardly troubles to hide her dismay. I thank the Lord that I remembered to sweep the floor today. And then the vicar commands us servants too: 'Come on, girls. Kneel and pray.'

Rosemary kneels creakily beside her husband. The vicar's knees snap loudly as he labours to the task but, of course, the children, especially Grace and Robert, flatten like frogs. Mother Caterill wears a face like thunder and struggles in her crippled way to lower herself to the floor.

The vicar picks up his bible. 'Almighty and most merciful Father, we have erred and strayed from thy ways like lost sheep . . .'

Bessie, nearest to the fire, sneezes explosively. Thomas Cakebread starts, then puts a hand over his mouth. Once, twice, then three sneezes.

The vicar raises his voice a little: 'Dear Lord our Father, watch over our dear little Jane and bring her no more fits, protect us from bewitchments and sorcery, and cleanse our hearts . . .'

Bessie sneezes again. No one says, 'Bless you.' The vicar falters. Suddenly Johanne sneezes too – dust from the fire, perhaps. But soon Grace joins her, Mary and Jane, too, and the room is filled with the girls' sneezes, their yesking. A swishing sound like a brush sweeping the stair, back and forth with increasing violence.

Thomas Cakebread and Henry Pickering glance at each other, their eyes alight. This is what they came for, no doubt. I cannot see my mistress or master, only their shoulders in the row along from me. No one speaks to scold the children.

The vicar, taken aback, pauses in his praying, as if in experiment. When he stops, the sneezing does too.

'We have offended against thy holy laws,' the vicar begins again, less booming. My knees ache and Mother Caterill is loudly groaning about hers. The tension in the room holds us in its grip but a giggle is bubbling up in me. The vicar starts up: 'And we know, dear heavenly Father . . .' And then Jane sneezes. Hers is the loudest of all, like a scream. *Aaaachoooooooooooo.*

And as she does, she keels over, first onto her head, with a loud crack on the floor near the fire and then at once, over to one side, fitting and jerking, and immediately, to my astonishment, Mary, then Bessie, then Grace follow her, and Johanne leaps up to cry, 'Mother!' and Hob bursts into tears. Mother Caterill, I notice, out of the corner of my eye, struggles to her feet and takes her leave of us.

'Oh, my word!' squeals Aunt Rosemary. The young men stand up, staring in bewilderment at the four girls in their fits in front of them. Only my master and mistress seem to know what to do. They gesture to Dottie, Popsie and me to hold the girls' arms and legs, stop them banging their heads on the bricks near the fire and pull down their skirts for decency. My heart is pounding but I rush to their aid, choosing little Grace – nearest to me – to hold tight.

'Lord, Our Heavenly Father . . .' booms the vicar.

'Were we best not to go any further, my dear?' Rosemary has stood up and now pulls on his arm.

My efforts to hold little Grace in my arms are not quieting her. The room is filled with sweat and crying and frantic girls. I glance up to see the vicar – his expression is frightened – climbing up from his knees and putting the bible to one side. Thomas and Henry are helping my mistress with Bessie, trying to hold her head, where already a bump as big as a walnut is emerging and she is in danger of knocking herself senseless on the firegrate.

Bessie's loud moans are a terror to behold. Once she starts, Mary and Jane join their voices to hers. The scene is noisier and more disturbed than anything we have witnessed yet. I cannot think where Hob is – perhaps hiding behind a large velvet drape. Sneezing, squealing, groaning, the girls' feet in shoes drumming against the hard tiles, their heads knocking this way and that, and all of us doing our best— 'Henry, would you try to take Bessie to the bedchamber, please?' my mistress instructs her brother with loud speeches. The young man seems affronted by the struggle Bessie puts up as he tries to lift her – she is like a tumbler, arching her back, her eyes rolling and unseeing in her head. Thomas Cakebread rushes to his assistance. It takes the two of them to carry her out and up the stairs.

'Go with them, Johanne, and sit beside your sister,' my mistress instructs.

Dottie, kneeling beside me and trying to join me in holding Grace, cries, 'She has the strength of five girls, in this state!' Dottie has no composure and begins weeping. 'Maybe it will be us next. Oh, what *is* it, Mistress? Has the old witch cast her glamour over the whole house? Oh, what if—'

'When you hold your peace, Francis, the girls might resume theirs,' Aunt Rosemary pipes up. She is delicately nudging her husband out of the hall and towards the front door. The scholars are struggling with Bessie and the master with Jane, when suddenly a scream from Grace – in my arms – almost rends the room.

Bessie has been taken upstairs by the scholars, Jane and Mary by their father. Johanne has gone to join them, Popsie to take them a green fairy drink. Hob is hiding. There is only Grace. She sits up. All fits are gone. Her little face is serene and her eyes open.

The two young men have returned to the hall. I imagine they did not feel at ease sitting in a young woman's bedchamber and seeing the girls in their frenzy. But they arrive, like an audience at a play, just as the curtain is rising.

'I see her. I see her here in this room!' Grace says, in a voice unlike her own. A cold trickle of fear runs down my spine. We all turn to the window, where Grace is staring. A candle burns there. And beyond – the house of Alice Samuel.

'She has an imp on her shoulder,' Grace says. Her voice is cold and gravelly. She does not sound like a child of eight. I hold my breath at the horror of that voice, because something evil does seem to tremble there. 'There she is! She has an imp. A chicken – it is a chicken. Oh, now she has also a . . . toad, sitting on her shoulder,' Grace says.

A toad. A chicken. Imps. The black dog with the toad's face, working its evil and sending old Mother Cunny to the gallows. A candle dances and a long shadow flies up and down the curtain.

'Who? Who, child? Who is it that has an imp on her shoulder?' Aunt Rosemary dares.

The vicar, the scholars seem to hold their breath to hear her answer.

'Why, our neighbour Mother Samuel, of course!'

Henry Pickering is about to burst forth with something, but a hand on his arm from his friend stops him.

No one touches Grace. She is very still now. I sit back on my heels, aware of a strange smell in the room. Grace blinks and smooths her silky grey ribbon with her hands. She looks around. 'What is it?' she says.

'Oh, Lord preserve us! We must go, *please*, Francis,' Aunt Rosemary says. She is ushering her husband towards the door. The feeling in the room changes, as the vicar goes to find my master and take his leave of us. My mistress recovers herself a little and looks around the room at the sweeping mass of soot on the tiled floor in front of the fire where the girls lay and kicked and drummed in their fits.

Henry Pickering steps towards Grace and asks excitedly, 'You saw Alice Samuel, the same woman Jane accused? You saw her with an imp, a spirit to do her bidding? A chicken, was it, and with a toad sitting on her shoulder?'

'Did I say that?' Grace says.

My mistress sighs. 'Henry, she's just a child,' she says sharply. The two young men are despatched to bring brushes to sweep the floor, to find Hob and carry him to bed. My master moves to comfort his wife but she steps free of him. Her voice is firm, a little like that of her old self. For now shame replaces fear in the room as we all look around us, as if waking from a dream.

She claps her hands and says all must leave. Only I am to remain: she wants to talk with me. Alone.

'Come, let's walk in the garden. There are too many people here.' She fetches a fur and I bring a blanket, for the evening is cold and the ground hard underfoot. We slip out past the spindly fruit trees and the holly, and open the wooden gate that takes us to the church of Saint Mary Magdalene. The vicar's church, of course, though he will be warming his feet by the fire across the road in the vicarage by now.

I am heartsore, wondering if the girls have worsened. What is it she so wants to confide?

The moment we have sat upon a bench, my mistress begins. 'What did Doctor Butler say about Jane?'

I spread the blanket over my shoulders, shivering. 'The girls are resting now? They are not still suffering?'

'Bessie and Grace are recovering. Mary looks glassy and still, and Jane – Jane I worry most about. Robert has said barely a word since coming back from Cambridge. Just that unpleasant Butler's Ale, which has not effected much of a cure – as we saw this evening!'

She speaks a little loud, for my benefit.

God alone is the searcher of the heart. I wonder what I must say. My master told me to say nothing. He did not want his wife to be fearful. But after this evening . . .

'Martha, you must have noticed. Jane. At around the same time her fits began. She – she made a very strange statement and it has been vexing us both ever since. I hardly know how to repeat it.'

The darkness seems to creep closer to us. I can make out the shaggy weeping willow in the corner of the graveyard, and all the sleeping headstones, laced with lichen, leaning with the weight of years, like biscuits sunk in a cake badly, as if one push would topple them all. I wait, wanting to bind my ears and hear nothing of what she is about to say, but knowing I must.

'Jane says a man touched her. Lay with her and touched her. Since coming here. We . . . You can imagine our distress. We could not think who it might be. So Gabriel—'

'Jane said it was Gabriel?'

Here my mistress pulls her fur up to her face and begins weeping. 'My dear boy! I cannot believe it. I would not believe it. Robert insists that we must – of course – mention it to no one. And it is so unthinkable that I had hoped it was simply . . . that Jane might be mistaken. '

I hardly know what to say, what to think. I sit for a moment, and my mistress weeps further. The doctor's strange comment on examining Jane looms in my mind and a huge fear rises in me. Such an unthinkable evil thing! A child so young. And Gabriel, sweet loping lad of seventeen, only ever kind and fond. What must I say? What should I say?

'It is impossible to think something so foul of your dear son, Mistress.' Floundering, struggling to find words, my eyes land on an angel atop a gravestone, lit up by moonlight, a trumpet in her mouth, and in sudden brightness she looks as if the instrument is choking her.

'The doctor did mention, he did say, on examining her . . .'

My mistress gives me such a beseeching, heart-struck look that I turn to her and whisper in her ear and she lets out a little scream.

'But he said not to mention it to her father, so I did not! And that it might have – innocent causes, riding, playing hobby horse . . .'

My mistress puts her face in her hands and sobs quietly.

'Did Jane *accuse* Gabriel?' I ask again.

'No. After her first strange speeches, she would say no more.'

'Could it be someone else? Crabbie? Our terrible neighbour, the man Samuel, crept into the house somehow? Another man we have not thought of?'

'I don't know. It is as if, having told us, and witnessed our shock, Jane wishes to draw the words back into her mouth, which is now sealed tight as a mussel shell. And then her fits began and they have become our concern, and the Lord knows we have had much else to vex us. It was Robert who suspected

Gabriel. I cannot. And now the girls! The others are in their fits too! It's as if they are contagious, like a plague . . .'

A barn owl sweeps into view, as if a phantom: heart-shaped face, long loping wings, like ears. My mistress crosses herself at the sight of it, and remembers her question to me.

'So, is there anything else Robert didn't tell me? Did Doctor Butler make any further suggestion? Did he say that the fits might *spread* like this, if left untreated?'

'He— he did mention . . . The doctor spoke of witchcraft, Mistress. That was his explanation. And it seemed tonight from what Grace said . . . it did seem true, didn't it? He asked if we had reason to – if anyone ill-wished us.'

'And what did Robert say to that? Did he speak of Alice Samuel?'

'He seems . . . he does not want to make enemies in Warboys. I think he said that John Samuel – Alice's husband – is a seditious man, powerful in his way . . .'

'Powerful! Ha. Yes, Robert is much exercised by the idea that Sir Henry has set him up as squire here and he must make his mark, he must win favour. Oh, I don't know, I can't understand it. Politics. He must make sure Warboys village is brought to heel, after Muchwood. This business with Mother Samuel is very unfortunate. But now, well after this evening's dreadful, *dreadful* events, after little Grace who is too young to be counterfeit, after that terrifying moment . . .'

Again, she puts her face into her hands and weeps, and I find tears coursing down my cheeks, too. After a moment, my mistress takes up my hand and sniffs loudly, searching for a handkerchief. 'Oh, you are kind, Martha. I'm so glad of you. Please don't let Robert know that I ever thought to consult Alice as a cunning woman.'

'But he suspects it already, Mistress.'

'Too late, then. I propose we let the vicar and God guide us. And my brothers! If they think Alice wishes some evil upon us, if the girls – even good, honest Grace – say it is so, then perhaps Alice *is* the source of all this misery. She might even have cast some kind of evil bewitchment on Gabriel to behave in a lewd way, or on Jane, or sent a spirit . . . Oh, this seems so fanciful, so wicked – could it really be so?'

My mistress's words drive a spike into my breast. Fear flows from it. Fear at the ungodly things I am hearing. That a child might be touched so by a man. That men – some men – have vile intentions towards one so little and innocent. That evil has taken a foul shape and entered our home. And then, a curious one, something else, a feeling as if a hand is over my mouth.

Is Alice a witch, as my mistress suggests? And what do *I* know of that? I know I cannot speak my heart to my mistress. If Alice is one, if I allow this fear to take a solid form, what do I make of my years with Sister Dorothy, the whispers and rumours I heard as a girl? She who managed to cure dropsy in our neighbour Mary Chapell and chilblains in old man Hobson, and save many a woman in childbirth, and oft-times told when a crop would be good or where a lost purse might be found, and yet when *another* had this skill she was quick to name it devilment. What to think of all of that, my childhood, my life with her until the age of thirteen, if in an ordinary place like Warboys a neighbour might also be in league with the devil?

Once, in our old home at Brampton, the housekeeper, a grumpy old hag called Mother Borrow, had hit me over the head with a plate and pronounced me a deaf-lugs, and a short while later, Dottie, coming across me red and shaking with rage in the scullery, asked me, 'Why are you all wax and honey? We can see you're angry but you won't come out with it, will you? You will never loose your tongue! Do you believe yourself better than the rest of us, is that it?' and flounced out, leaving me to contain the sobs that heaved up from my chest and mull anew the question for which I never did have answer: if it's not a true affliction, why am I so often struck dumb?

My mistress recovers herself and stands up, folding her handkerchief and dabbing at her eyes.

'Now if it were *Johanne*! Ha! We might not so readily believe her, is that not so? I oft notice how she loves to control the other children, to bait them and tease them. What is the matter with Johanne, do you think, Martha? Is it just her age? She has become thin. She is of bad temper and sulky. Sometimes I catch her staring at me with a look so dark I might fear my own daughter is a—'

She doesn't utter it. She draws her coney fur up to her neck and we walk back towards the house together. The word itself is a spell, a curse, a ghostly portent, like the barn owl. It is too perilous to say such a word in jest.

Part Two

The Confession

The next morning a feeling of shame and shock still hangs over the house. There are no sounds of children laughing or scampering feet. Only Bessie comes downstairs, bold, and dressed in a fine tight bodie laced with velvet, a silk ribbon in her hair.

My mistress has said to me that her brother and his friend Thomas were 'aghast' at what they saw, but I stay firm in my observation that they seemed as if they were at a theatre show. (I do not mention this to my mistress.) They were not so much aghast as thrilled. The scenes in the great hall, the feminine yesking and fitting and stamping of feet and flying up of dust and skirts, the strange smells, the absolute want of decorum or even normal relations . . .

Bessie preens while I am sweeping and cleaning the hearth. I glance at her, wondering at the fancy way she has turned herself out. I have no chance to question her about the Sunday clothes as Henry and Thomas appear behind her.

Thomas Cakebread enquires politely as to her sisters' health.

'This morning Grace is in good spirits and Jane too. And I am – thank you for asking.'

Thomas Cakebread is about to say more, but Bessie bursts out with 'Did you ever see a witch trial? What is it like? Will they put them in the stocks or—'

'I have,' Henry interrupts. 'I have seen several. When you are scholars of divinity, as we are, your own eyes and ears are needed to seek out witches, aided by the *Malleus Maleficarum*.'

'*Male* . . .' Bessie falters.

'It's a book,' Henry says. '*Maleficarum* means inflicting harm using magic. Casting spells over animals or crops or children, as your neighbour has done. It sets out procedures allowing us to discover and convict witches, under the 1563 Act.'

I am sweeping, sweeping, swishing as loudly as I can.

Thomas coughs. 'It has been used a great deal in *Europe*, Bessie. Whereas here, we do not burn witches and there are dissenting voices—'

'Reginald Scot? You're not bringing *him* up again?' Henry says, with a laugh, as if this is a familiar argument between the two, much played out, and now they have an audience a greater performance than ever. Henry smiles at his niece. 'Scot was sent down from Oxford, Bessie. His book was so bad he had to publish it himself. He attends trials, too, and only to dispute the evidence put before the learned men. And yet our friend Thomas here has been to hear him speak and even listens.'

'What is it that he says that is so . . .' I am sure Bessie does not know the word she seeks but is merely happy to be included, to wallow in the back and forth of their lively argument.

'Scot suggests that God alone can bring pestilence and disease, that witches have no such power, and that the great excitement in pursuing them has arisen because the Queen herself was ill advised as to the number of witches in England,' Thomas Cakebread says, seizing his opportunity, eyes blazing with earnestness.

I have swept all the soot into the pan and now would be the moment to leave, but I stand up and simply soften myself into the wall, like ivy or a moth, to watch the scene unfolding.

'Poppycock! As if there are no witches in England when last night little Grace, a child of what – six? How old is my niece, Bessie?' Henry bursts in.

'Grace is eight, Uncle, though small for her age.'

'Eight, then. A child that young cannot dissemble. Where would she get such a tale? She described her for us, with a black toad – an imp – on her shoulder! You must admit that was a most fearful . . . well, what a moment that was!'

Thomas agrees that it was fearful. Indeed, the memory of it produces a shudder as if Grace, witch and imp are in front of their eyes again.

'And in many trials, well, the one at Chelmsford I attended,' Henry says, 'it was brave children – a ten-year-old boy, I remember, who accused his grandmother. A terrible old woman. Imagine the courage, a poor ignorant country boy! To stand up to her! And the young woman, the youngest witch, Joan Cunny's daughter, had a child, which stayed her execution but now it is born, punishment is due, a hanging . . .'

I step out from my position. None has acknowledged me, or tempered their conversation, so I know that, as usual, I am invisible to them. I take stock of Bessie's pink cheeks and wide eyes and wonder how I might interrupt, to direct her to go upstairs. Bessie at last allows her eyes to land on mine. No doubt she has been delighted at the freedom with which the two young men speak in front of her and she now frowns crossly at me, as if to say: Don't chide me!

I am still struggling to find a way to interrupt and brushing the soot from my skirt as my mistress appears, with her nose for danger in relation to this particular daughter (the dangers of Bessie's own character, also a shapeliness suggesting a maturity she doesn't possess).

'Bessie! Go and sit with Mary and Jane. They are in their fits again,' my mistress says, and I wish I had known so that I could have said the same.

'I'm sorry to hear they are not well,' Henry says, his voice at once betraying him. He does not sound sorry to me.

'Yes, Mary is— Well, could you do a great favour for me, Henry? I need to find Robert, to help me. He might be in the White Hart in the village. On the way to the village pond. Turn left as you leave the house . . .'

I imagine that my mistress has reasoned that a tavern will keep them occupied for a while. I follow Bessie as she trudges upstairs to the bedchamber, noting her glance or two over her shoulder, down towards Thomas, who pushes his hair away from his eyes, the better to return her gaze.

My mistress claps her hands together. 'The White Hart! The tavern!' she says to her brother. The two young men go to fetch their hats, Henry loudly adding, 'We should not leave it to that imbecile the vicar! This is our chance, Thomas. On our own doorstep! The old crone needs bringing to justice.'

Thomas is saying something measured and quiet, which I cannot catch as they close the door behind them.

***

At the pond, Alice is collecting teasels. She is bent upon her task, regretting that she forgot to bring gloves, her hands snagging on the sharp thorns in the crisp stalks. But how many there are – queens, kings, all the best ones. She is pleased with her find, so late in the year. She had wanted some to make a tea for John's liverishness (his drinking has given him a yellow look, as if he is jaundiced), and some for her own warts, of course. The rest will fetch a good price from Florrie Caterill, Mother Caterill's daughter, as carding combs. If it weren't so late, she would have looked for borage too: she needs courage, after the shock of the Throckmorton girl and her accusation. She is still smarting over that.

The man approaching the pond is a little excited, Alice notices. His eyes glitter. He is shadowed by another man, equally overdressed for the country air, with a great shock of hair and slim as a stick of celery. She recognises the first: he has a look of his sister, Mistress Throckmorton, she can see that, with his florid cheeks and the colouring of a rosehip, bright among winter hedgerows. She straightens from her task. A friend of John, fishing at the edge of the pond, mutters, 'Well met, Mother Samuel,' to her, and she could snap off his tongue. Why, now the young rogues will know who she is. She gathers up her basket and takes a step forward.

'Alice Samuel? I am the brother of Elizabeth Throckmorton. Would you come to the house, Mother Samuel? Grace, the young daughter, cried out of you, and before that, a doctor, a fellow of Cambridge, confirmed that *witchcraft—*'

'No, I won't,' Alice says, and makes to continue on her way.

The brother looks astonished, but stands firm in front of her. The other hangs back a little, his arms dropping to his sides, his manner uncertain.

'My name is Henry Pickering. I am a scholar of Cambridge. I am here to tell you that – that you might release the girls from their torments,' the man says, pulling himself up to his full height, arms folded.

Alice glances at the spiky heads of the teasels in her basket. Will there be enough? She laments that their stalks are crisp: if there was any precious juice they could make dye too, the blue dye for which Florrie would have given her a penny more. But they will do for the tea for John, and the combs for the wool: yes, they will be good. It's a plentiful haul, she can stop now.

'I am not the cause of their torments, and well they know it,' she says, lifting the basket closer to her.

There is a moment when Alice wonders what would happen if she put out a hand and pushed the man, but she does not dare and instead contents herself with a loud protest: 'Let me on my way. I'm going home, I'm tired, and my husband will want his dinner.'

'We will walk with you. We're going the same way,' the second young man says.

She gives him a quick stare. His manner, she notes, is surprisingly polite.

There is little Alice can say to prevent the two young men falling into step beside her. They are wary of her. If she is afraid to touch them, it's clear from their awkwardness that they share the fear, Henry Pickering scuffing his heels like a schoolboy and muttering to his friend, as if Alice were deaf, that 'her loud speeches' are 'quite shocking'. The other one, he didn't give her his name, is silent, and watchful.

'I'm Thomas Cakebread,' he suddenly offers. 'Let me carry your basket, Mother Samuel. If you are any cause of the children's trouble, we only hope it might be amended.'

'Visit the squire's house again? So that another child can point at me and call me names?' Alice shouts, refusing his offer and clasping her basket of teasels to her. She strides ahead of the men, covering the ground surprisingly fast, anxious to get to her own front door where, she hopes, John will help her to bar them from it.

Henry Pickering catches up with her. Breathless and standing a little distance to the side of her, he gathers his confidence and threatens: 'I have the authority to command you! If you refuse, I am authorised by God and – and the University of Cambridge!' His red colouring now flies up to the roots of his hair.

Thomas Cakebread seems taken aback by this new stance, this declared authority and, putting a hand on Henry's arm, murmurs something. The distance from the pond to the manor house is but a short walk. The Samuels' thatched and lowly cottage is on the squire's land, a stone's throw from the manor house, so they are quickly close to Alice's own front door: the smell of peat burning in the hearth rises and, from the sound of girlish voices inside, it's clear that her daughter is at home.

'Nessie! Nessie, let me in. Don't let these curs in!' Alice drops the basket beside her and lifts the latch, barging in, then turning to try to bar the young men's way, shouting, 'Be sure to say nothing!'

Of course, she is not strong or quick enough. And, short of shoving them out of the way and smashing the door in their faces, such banishment cannot be achieved. They step inside.

Nessie and her friend Cicely Burder are attending to the bread in the oven. Nessie holds a long-handled bread pan with a loaf on it, bending by the fire, her rump towards the door. Startled, she and Cicely straighten and turn to face their guests. Henry seems taken aback at the sight of Nessie, and as Alice watches his expression she is certain she understands perfectly the incomprehension on his face: this beauty could be a daughter of *yours*? She puts a hand to her thrumbed cap and acknowledges that that's why she rarely takes the damn thing off: she feels a mixture of shame and vanity at her fading red hair, threaded with grey now. (If she lets it down at night, John in playful mood will whisper to her that it's not grey at all but the colour of apple cider – what a thought to enter her head now!)

The girls' faces are pink; the room is stiflingly hot. The men must crane their heads and stand like bent hairpins under the low ceiling. The air is full of a foetid smell, feline and heated, some barm foamy in its tankard, the yeast in the loaves, rising in the room. She sees them glance nervously around at her home: the tiny room, a cot in one corner with a flock mattress, a fire, a wooden table, a stand of uneven shelves, a blanket box and a solitary chair. Above it a loft, with straw sticking out: Nessie's bed. Henry and Thomas blink in some embarrassment. Evidently this is the first occasion they have seen a home such as hers.

Cicely drops the turf of peat she is holding onto the fire and attempts a curtsy. Nessie takes her lead from her mother and only stares rudely.

Henry turns to Alice. 'You naughty woman!' he says, a little breathless. 'We only ask that you come to the house. No one will touch you, we only request—'

'No one will touch me? Is that so? No one will scratch me or stick pins in me?'

Alice is rubbing at her hands, already a little sore from the teasel thorns.

Henry glances at them. '*Scratch* you?' he says.

Alice wishes she had never mentioned it. The word is out and with it the idea, and it seems to sizzle in the air, an alarming prickle to it.

Henry exhales loudly, as if the air in the room is choking him, and continues, 'What use are these loud speeches and tarrying? Why not come willingly to the house, speak to the girls and all will be well? Your daughter and her friend can come too.'

Nessie has shoved the bread on its long pallet back in the oven. 'Scratching to test for witchcraft is unlawful, isn't it?' she says defiantly.

Thomas is the one who replies: 'It is, and we only want to see if your mother can help the girls.'

'Rogues. Rascals. Say nothing, Nessie!' Alice repeats. There is a long, odd pause in the smoky little room. Then suddenly, rewrapping her shawl, Alice turns around and opens her front door. Let it be over, then. Let no one say she didn't offer to help. Why, if they'd asked her, she might have suggested an infusion of mistletoe, if it is the falling sickness the daughter suffers from. Why do they not simply ask her counsel and be done with it?

She is off and across the land between their houses, striding towards the front door of the Throckmortons' manor, gratified that the fools are slow to gather their wits and understand that, at last, she has decided to comply.

Over her shoulder, Alice catches sight of Henry, scrambling to escape the airless house and accidentally kicking over the basket of teasels left by the front door. She pauses, seeing him hop and crush underfoot at least one of the precious bristly brown seed heads. She opens her mouth to scold him fiercely but sees that, behind him, Thomas has stopped to pick up the teasels. Cicely and Nessie are helping him.

The early-evening sky has turned mottled yellow and brown, the colour of frog skin, as Alice knocks and waits at her neighbour's door.

They are admitted into the great hall, where Robert Throckmorton hides his surprise and thanks Alice Samuel warmly for agreeing to come and concern herself with the well-being of his daughters. He greets Cicely and Nessie without introducing himself, forgetting his manners, and taking several steps backwards to hold on to a dresser. The wife joins him.

'I must not tarry long. My husband will be home and want his supper,' Alice says. She removes her cap, holding it in her hand, feeling herself as exposed as a mushroom in grass with its top kicked off but determined, too, that there should be no repeat of the events of her first visit to the house.

The older girls, the dark one, Johanne – was that her name? – and Bessie are sitting by the fire eating oysters. Bessie leaps up at once and greets Thomas and Henry, seizing her uncle's arm to whisper, 'How did you get her to come?'

Nessie and Cicely stand blinking in the great hall, taking in the Turkish carpet, the tapestries of blue and gold, the inglenook with the enormous amount of turves stacked up in the fireplace, the room full of the strong smell of peaty soil.

Alice takes a step towards the two Throckmorton girls and her voice is not unkind. 'Now, girls, you seem in good health to me, so I'll be on my way,' she says.

'Oh, we are well enough, just now,' says Johanne, in her cold voice, 'but the same can't be said for the littlest ones. They are abed and it might be better for you to go up and see them there.'

Alice looks at the mistress, begging permission to make free in the house. The kind mistress glances at her husband, then at her brother, and last at Alice. 'Yes, as you are here, we are grateful and we— How worried we are. Mary has had many fits today. Grace was very bad yesterday evening. Jane has become silent and . . . not herself. They are all resting now.'

The mistress rubs at a frown-line between her eyes and adds quietly, 'I'm at my wit's end with worry, we'd be so truly grateful—'

'I'll come up too,' Henry Pickering says. 'And Thomas here. We will ensure that things are done properly.'

What these things are, no one says. The mistress, Alice and the scholars troop upstairs. Nessie and Cicely are encouraged by Throckmorton, recovering himself and addressing them respectfully, to do the same and following them with his daughters. Alice hears them behind her, Bessie in great eagerness, two steps at a time.

'Their fits come on much the worse at supper or at prayer,' the mistress confides, and Alice is gratified and relieved to discover she is to be treated as an honoured guest in the Throckmorton home, as befits one of her age. The younger girl, she notices – Bessie – is less respectful, staring agog at her and digging the other sister in the ribs to say, as if Alice is deaf, 'The smell! She smells like a coney!' Alice knows the yeast smell clings to her clothes from the brewing and baking.

'You might ask whether they *want* to pray?' Alice replies, stung by Bessie's words, that no one reprimanded her.

'Whether they would rather play the wanton?' Nessie, hearing her, stifles a laugh and nudges Cicely. Bessie bites her lip and tries to catch Johanne's eye, but fails.

Henry is quick to say: 'Before moving here they were little angels in perfect health. Mary is most devout,' he says pointedly, to Alice.

In the bedchamber, Mary, Jane and Grace are lying on the bed, the wool curtains tied back with cord, their bonnets off, nightgowns tied at the neck, all looking peaceful, as if sleeping, but with eyes wide open. Bessie throws herself down on the bed next to her quiet sisters, while Johanne stands silently by the window. Alice glances at the bed and turns as if to leave.

'They seem well to me. Now, I have come and now I should *like* to go home. Who will get my husband's supper? Who will fetch tomorrow's barm for the bread? It's a different matter for those with servants . . .'

'Yesterday Grace saw you here. You cursed her with an imp on your shoulder and her fits were powerful indeed,' Henry says.

He stands, arms folded, barring her way. Alice turns back into the bedchamber towards the bed, seeing that Bessie is gazing at her uncle admiringly. The church bell next door tolls loudly and everyone starts, Bessie giving a shriek and putting both hands to her mouth. At this, Jane begins moving, first slowly, then more jerkily, like a pickerel taken newly from the water.

'Jane, Jane dear . . .' The mistress says, going at once to her side.

Jane's arm shoots out of the bedcovers, stiff and with her nails ready, clawlike. 'Oh, that I had her . . .' Jane says.

Alice's heart leaps in her breast.

Henry glares at her, triumphant. 'She means you, Mother Samuel! Go and sit beside her.'

Alice looks imploringly at him and then at her daughter, who assures her: 'Mother, you came here to help. Sit beside her. The squire will see we mean them only goodwill and neighbourliness. And then we can go home.' Nessie holds out her hand for the thrumbed cap and nods reassuringly.

So Alice steps forward towards the child, and she is aware that Henry does too. He picks up Jane's stiff, clawlike hand and scratches the back of Alice's hand with it. The mistress says, 'Oh!' and turns in horror towards her younger brother. Alice leaps back, almost falling into Nessie and snatching back her hand to suck at it.

'You said there would be no scratching!' Nessie cries hotly, to Henry. 'You promised. You agreed it was unlawful.'

Bessie has the expression of one who is affronted that a girl of such lowly stock dare to speak to her uncle so, but the mistress and master only look anxiously from Alice to Jane, to see how their daughter now fares.

'But it was an experiment only. You saw how the child *wanted* to do it. If your mother is not a witch, it matters nothing. If she *is*, we all know it will lessen her powers. This way we shall discover which it is.' Henry leans forward to study Jane, who is still twitching, and then to stare at Alice, who is holding her scratched hand to her mouth. Bessie tries to stroke her sister's arm, but the wild and stiff movement soon shakes her off. Grace has leaped into her mother's arms.

'There, there,' the mistress says. She gently unlaces herself from Grace's grip. Bessie kisses her sister Jane, once, on her warm cheek.

Henry steps forward again. 'Scratch *me*, dear Jane,' he says, offering his niece the back of his hand. Her arm is flying up and down, her eyes unseeing, but she does not take up the offer, only turns her glassy gaze towards the three strangers in the room: Alice, Nessie and Cicely.

'Why have you brought her to me? The witch!' Jane cries, and points at Alice. Alice moves closer to Nessie, who clutches her mother's arm.

'Let us go now,' Nessie says. 'The girls can do their play-acting without us.' Nessie tries to nudge her mother and Cicely out of the room, but Alice shakes her off, staring back at the bed. Jane is making a repeated squeak, like the sound an otter makes, a signal of alarm or joy, Alice has never known which. She would like to push the bedevilled child onto the floor and *then* run out of the room, shouting, but that would never do, that is the worst thing she could do, so she stands, a little dazed, aware of the stinging pain on the back of her hand, Nessie whispering in her ear, 'Say nothing, Mother. Hold your tongue, for God's sake!'

The servant Martha appears in front of them then, carrying a tray with the green fairy drinks on it. She moves into the chamber wordlessly to sit on a stool by the bed beside Jane, the mistress and master, trying to still her by clinging to her flying arms.

'You see how she did not scratch *me*?' Henry says, turning to his brother-in-law to repeat his discovery. 'It might be unlawful to use the test, but did you see how much the child wanted to do it? And, yes, Mother Samuel appears to feel pain but we know that witches do not, so . . . is she play-acting? The scratching may reduce her powers in time and that is all to the good. But for the proof we have the fact of Jane's desire to do it. Why don't you go now to Sir Henry? We surely have the evidence we need.'

'We need more than this, and you know it.' Throckmorton, who has been much occupied with Jane, now steps up to command the situation. 'Henry, Thomas, I thank you, but the girls need to be alone now. And, Mother Samuel, young ladies, thank you for coming.' He gestures towards Bessie and Johanne, indicating that they should also leave.

'I came willingly, as a good neighbour, and see where it landed me!' Alice shouts, stroking her scratched hand and stamping one boot, twisting herself away from Nessie's grip. To be treated so! When she came to help! To offer some suggestions of remedy!

The mistress offers her a handkerchief and nods to her husband. Alice, Nessie and Cicely hurry downstairs, hastening away from the room where Jane's fits are lessening, subsiding to quiet cries and smaller movements.

'A naughty way to treat a neighbour!' Alice shouts from downstairs. Nessie gives her back her cap and attempts to help her fix it on but Alice angrily shakes her off. Cicely giggles again, more frightened than amused, but unable to stop herself.

'I came in good faith! The child is still in her fits so what proof is that?'

Blood, in five bright spots, springs out on the bony surface of Alice's hand as she slams the door to the manor house behind her.

***

I'm in the garden with the sow, and the ungodly creature is running away from me to the other side of her pen, ears

105

flapping in the wind, tail bouncing, so that I have to chase her, and then the beast is growling and will not let me near her to determine if the boar we borrowed last month from Crabbie's grandfather went about his business successfully. Just as Bertha turns, planting her feet to give me the hard stare that means she's about to bite me, I see the mistress hurrying from the back door of the house, again wrapped in her furs, come to find me. I am too clever for Bertha and nip over the fence marvellous swift, tipping out the bucket of slops for her and leaving her distractedly munching while I wave at the mistress and wait for her approach.

Mistress Elizabeth stops as the thick mud worsens, and instead we go to walk in the orchard, where the ground is hard and skimmed with ice, but not so deep and rutted.

In seeking me out here, I know my mistress wants to tell me something privily so I wait. The back window of the house is an inch open and we hear a loud shriek of laughter from Bessie, followed by the warm deep roll of the young man's voice. Thomas Cakebread.

'We're sending Bessie away. To Titchmarsh, to stay with my brother Gilbert.'

'Mistress?'

'I want you to go with her, Martha. Keep your eye on her.'

I nod. She wriggles her hands inside her coney fur muffler. (I wish I had brought myself a blanket, but had not realised I would be required to stay outside so long.) More shrieks and giggles from Bessie and a pained expression on the mistress's face. She gives a quick glance towards the cottage of Alice Samuel and her family. The door there is firmly closed but smoke rises from the chimney and the usual smell of rye bread and yeast tells us that the women are at home.

'Isn't Titchmarsh where Gabriel is staying?' I venture.

'Not any longer. My brother Gilbert has found him a position somewhere nearby. And . . .' here my mistress takes my arm, wrapping her fur with her other hand against the chill of the air, steering me further away from the house '. . . we asked Jane again about her accusation, but she – she didn't seem to know what Robert and I were talking about. She said nothing had happened to her and what could we mean? She didn't remember. It was all a misunderstanding. Robert has forbidden me to write to Gabriel but if I did see him – if you saw him – I would like you to let him know a mother's sorrow for wronging him so . . .'

'Of course, Mistress.'

She bends to pick a very old, hardened medlar from the ground, examining its wizened shape, and smiling, saying, 'Gabriel had a naughty name for these.'

Dog's arses. They look like it, too.

'Oh, Martha! These fits are so tormenting. It is unbearable to watch my daughters suffer so. And if it were *only* that! As well as their physical torments they seem . . . I am dealing with . . . I don't know, all is changed since we came here. Johanne is melancholy. Bessie speaks out of turn and will not be made to sit at Bible study either, and wants to spend all her time with Henry and his friends. I do not remember being wilful at their age! I only did what my parents bade me. The green sickness? Will they grow out of it? Jane seemed to start it and now they all follow. Sometimes I have the most awful fear that I cannot share with Robert, only with you, Martha . . .'

As she says it, the trees seem to reach their thin arms to the sky, like skeletons stretching bony arms from a grave. I know what she means. I see it for a moment: Grace, Mary and Jane in bed, lying very still, and instead of eyes open, their eyes are closed, their faces pale, their little spirits fled. I have feared it too, watching their fits. A fear that opens like a cavern, or dark water full of snakes, ready to swallow you.

My mistress stops as we near Alice Samuel's house. The cold is gripping me by the throat. I can see my breath in front of me.

'Why would the old woman want to hurt the girls? Did one of them anger her – Jane, Mary, Bessie? Did they throw a stone at her door or tweak the tail of her cat?'

'She doesn't have a cat. Only hens,' I say.

My mistress moves close so that I might hear her better. 'That day she first came to the house, did you think her strange? Even before Jane spoke, accusing her, I felt – something curious happened that I could not name . . .'

I cast my mind back. I hop from foot to foot to keep warm. My first sight of Alice Samuel that day in the manor house: I thought her low-bred, rude and loud. She kept her woolly hat on in the house. She has a saggy old woman's body, a gobber tooth, a shuffling gait. That is all I remember. And yesterday those spots of blood on the back of her hand, and her hard speeches as she left. If she didn't mean the girls harm that first day, it would be impossible to believe she didn't now.

'Robert says we should befriend her. Invite Alice and her daughter to stay. He's convinced that appeasing is better than angering her – he seems to have a great fear of her but I cannot fault his logic. Henry, of course, thinks we should present her at once to the vicar for a confession, to be whipped or put in stocks. The idea of a witch on his doorstep! He is writing to friends in Cambridge about it. More scholars and young men will no doubt come. That is another reason Bessie should be away, Martha. She is the most . . . impressionable. The one I fear for most. Her age. She grasps at things with such open arms! Her very openness is her vulnerability. Not to mention her . . . comeliness. When I was her age . . . Well, we do not need to go into that. Johanne will fare better with her closed manner. I know you understand and I thank you, Martha, for your help and your advice . . . So many things that I cannot speak of, to anyone. Oh, what would I do without you?'

Of course I haven't opened my mouth, but I do not mention this. It is just as that day in Cambridge with the master, walking by the river. Mistress and master both like to thank me for my wise counsel, whereas I know it is only my one good listening ear that they seek out.

'Are your brother and his friend staying much longer?' I ask, and the mistress sighs.

'Yes. Best to get Bessie to Titchmarsh by tomorrow evening – it's a day's ride and it will be harsh weather. Tomorrow is St Thomas's Day – Bessie will be sorry to miss Christmas here but it's for the best. Do go and let Crabbie know to ready the horses. And may I charge you with telling Bessie? She will not be pleased and I cannot bear an occasion for her to weep and carry on so.'

We are now closer to the manor house and the pig pen, to the sound of Bertha grunting and growling. As we approach her, the sow chooses that moment to widen her back legs, in a gesture I well know. I steer my mistress towards the kitchen, hoping to avert her eyes from the sight of Bertha directing a long jet of water thumping to the mud, in her marvellous rude way.

***

Alice is gathering kindling in the woods behind the manor, grumbling to herself – where is Nessie when she needs her for this most hated of tasks, which always causes her back to ache from bending and will make her already sore hands worse?

She hears a horse go by and sees a flash of grand livery through trees and she knows with absolute certainty that it is him.

So. At last. It has happened. He has come to Warboys: the Golden Knight. She is full of a prickling, stinging fire. Her fingers stroke the scabs on the back of her hand. He is no doubt here to visit the Squire of Warboys, or the family.

She hurries towards him, not stopping to marvel at her own foolishness, or recklessness, or think anything at all of what Nessie would say, or John: she is now snapping and blistering, a blaze raging in her. She is running, then draws to a sudden halt, to find him towering on his horse in front of her, an expression of amazement and disdain on his face.

That face. The long nose, the mouth. Eyes.

She hears her own voice but hardly makes sense of what she is saying: her tongue, lashing out like a flame, like a salting whip, again and again, phrases she didn't know she knew, curses and oaths, fouler than any she has ever heard. She feels in the grip of something dangerous and huge, the wind catching fire.

The Golden Knight – Sir Henry – with his pale eyelashes, his beady eyes, a dull green, the colour of the pond, only stares at her, bewildered, tugging at his greying beard, as if she were a dying vixen and he surveying her with his hounds. She reads only affront in his countenance, not recognition or fear.

110

'You are mistaken, Old Mother, in these strange words. I bid you hold your tongue!'

'Old Mother! My maiden name was Yibbot. Alice Yibbot! I have a *name*!'

He seems to be considering, taking in what and who she is, what he has been told, before speaking again.

'Mother Samuel, compose yourself. What you say makes no sense to me. I have rarely been in Warboys before now. You are a woman of turbulent and unquiet spirit. I understand that you are much vexed by accusations and events of recent days. They have reached my ears. Although I am a just and kind man, with some sympathy for women such as yourself, given the seriousness of your current case, speaking to me in this way will scarcely help you.'

A door opens, the kitchen door to Warboys Manor, and is quickly closed again. Alice thinks she sees a face at the kitchen window. One of the servants! The servants, the household, the girls, how she hates them, *hates* them, what spoiling and havoc they cause her.

Alice spits then and raises the largest stick from her basket of twigs. Sir Henry's horse rears up a little and without another word, and no sign of fear, or even acknowledgement, he turns the animal with skill and pointed leisure away from her, in the direction of the track back to Ramsey.

***

We arrive at Titchmarsh, tired and saddle-sore, as the sky is gathering pink. Bessie has been silent, not her customary cheery self, throughout the journey, asking me only once, 'Is it to get me away from Mother Samuel? Or Uncle Henry and Thomas Cakebread?'

To which I have no answer. It's true that we found Henry reading Bessie a pamphlet about Alice Milne, a girl of twelve who could cast herself upwards in the shape of a hoop. 'Oh, Henry . . .' my mistress said, and shooed Bessie upstairs, whispering to me: 'Titchmarsh cannot come soon enough.' At least this is a journey on dry land, away from the treacherous ague-ridden Fens, and I do not spend it thinking about snails and vipers, only more earthly fears, closer to home.

The church bell is ringing God's glory as we arrive and on the little pinchbeck that runs behind the main street we see five cormorants with sharp white beaks sitting like watchful priests. My heart gives its first little burst of hope that perhaps the children in Warboys *will* recover and that, here, Bessie will too. There are some Christmas mummers out begging in a street where the sky has turned rapidly from pink to violet, lit by a fingernail of moon. They go from door to door, holding up their torches, calling, 'Holler, holler, make the bells ring!' and banging with wooden spoons. Bessie laughs and says, 'Will there be Christmas singers and plays?' and brightens a little at the thought. She laughs at the names of the places in Titchmarsh too: 'Polopit' and 'Plum Pudding Lane'. She has not been to visit since she was but a little girl of five.

Titchmarsh Grove is a grand house beside the church, and Bessie's uncle, Gilbert Pickering, appears outside the door now to greet us and to help Bessie down, bringing his stable boy to show Crabbie where to take the horses. Master

Pickering is the older brother of my mistress and young Henry – he has the look of them both. The same colouring, quickness to redden, dark eyes and rather large forehead. Beside him is a servant, a severe-looking woman with a face almost hidden by a huge raised scar (from a burn, for sure, poor soul), and behind, a wet-nurse with an infant. And then two small children – freckle-faced, pink-cheeked little things – appear, followed by Lizzie Pickering, the mistress of the house. I knew she was a sober wife but I had forgotten she is from a Puritan family. Here she is, with her dark dress and apron and wearing the Puritan coif on her hair, and Bessie almost takes a step back at the sight of her. I'm behind her and have to reach out a hand to press Bessie forward in politeness.

'Aunt Lizzie,' Bessie says. The mistress has an expression so fierce that I do not open my mouth. Crabbie, passing behind us, leading the horse, is singing a little tune. 'The Puritan wife, the Puritan wife,' he observes, his head jerking. I am glad he is soon out of earshot.

Bessie sinks to her knees to embrace the children: Jonnie, a little younger than her brother Hob and a girl introduced as Mary, pretty and quick, with a big bow in her hair.

The church bell ceases pealing. Bessie surprises us all by asking after her brother Gabriel. The master tells her, as we step into the house, that he has been found a position, but hopes we might see him, perhaps on St Stephen's Day. Suddenly, overwhelmingly, I feel Bessie's misery. How long are we to be here? Her parents did not give instruction for when we might return. Perhaps Bessie was hoping to enjoy being encircled by some attention, forgetting that her aunt and uncle have children of their own. Or, more likely, has she been harbouring a secret hope in her heart to see her brother?

I wonder how much she understands about Gabriel's banishment. I feel it weighs heavy with her.

'My dears . . .' Master Pickering begins, guiding us in towards the parlour.

'Here it comes!' screams Bessie, throwing herself backwards as if hit by some invisible force.

Mistress Pickering's face crumples in horror, like paper crushed in a hand. She leaps forward towards her niece, but fails to catch her. I start, stretching an arm towards Bessie, but it is too late: she is already lying on the floor, rolling and thrashing, churning up the rush from the mat.

The wet-nurse, the fire-burned servant, the mistress and the children look on aghast. What has become customary to me, stripped of its shock, is in these new surroundings a lamentable sight. I bend to Bessie, doing what my mistress always does: stroking her hand, or trying to hold her thrashing legs.

The baby in the arms of her nurse sets up a shrieking and cringing.

'O Lord, preserve us, dear God!' Lizzie Pickering stares at us both in horror. Master Pickering, so commanding when we arrived, now appears at a loss.

'Where is your stable boy? Shall we call him? Does she need a man of great strength to try to still her?' he asks. Bessie continues twitching and bending, like someone struggling between death and life. The servant woman catches my eye and drops to her knees on the other side of Bessie. She sensibly tries to lift Bessie's head onto her lap – Bessie's skull thrashing and cracking on the earthen floor is a frightful sound – but Bessie's strength is unrivalled once she is in her fits: she snatches her hand from mine and heaves up her belly, arching her spine. Yes, her spine bending like a *hoop*: when was it I heard it described so?

The wet-nurse has quickly swept the children somewhere and the mistress follows them, covering her eyes, the baby's wails trailing her.

At last the master recovers and begins reciting prayers, dropping to the floor to help me and the servant – Susan – to hold Bessie. His eyes catch mine and I know he is afraid. He had imagined it, yes, when his sister described the girls' fits to him, but not quite like this. Bessie is like a pike taken from the river, so clever is she at dodging us, flipping away from us. For ten minutes – oh, for how long – we struggle, Bessie making tiny mewing sounds, her eyes rolling horribly in her head.

And suddenly she is tranquil and lies still, the storm passed. I smooth hair away from her face where it has caught in her mouth, picking off the pieces of rush; from her dress too. Her eyes are open.

'Bessie, dear . . .' Master Pickering says.

Bessie, in an icy voice, quite unlike herself, interrupts him: 'She popped a mouse in my mouth.'

I feel a cold chill run down my spine as if icy water trickled there.

'Who did?' Master Pickering's voice trembles. The servant is flattening Bessie's dress for her, unfolding one of her legs and straightening it. Now Bessie is as a doll, floppy and biddable. She sits up, breathes out loudly: some dust and rush scatters. The smell of the disturbed wormwood and catnip rises from the mats.

'Mother Samuel, our neighbour,' Bessie says, in the same deep voice. I sit back on my heels beside her. Susan has gone to fetch Bessie's leather case, set down somewhere in a hurry.

Master Pickering appears stuck to the spot, like a melted candle, his eyes bulging and fixed on Bessie. She gazes in wonder at the house, at the dresser with its garnish of pewter, at some kind of dole cupboard, at the dark wooden beams of the ceiling, as if only just finding herself here.

'I felt a little mouse,' Bessie says. 'Johanne told me I would. Oh, a warm, furry small thing – in any case, a small, horrible, live thing – dropped into my mouth!'

'When?'

'Before we left the house. Grace saw the black toad on the old woman's shoulder . . . But this was a yellow-necked mouse, with huge black eyes. Mother Samuel slipped it in my mouth. It is her imp. So that she can still work her magic here.'

'Oh!' cries Susan, returning with the case, and hearing her.

Master Pickering whispers a prayer to himself. 'Imps . . . How do you know these things?' he asks Bessie.

'Oh, Johanne has read about them. We all know. This mouse has a name. Mother Samuel called it Catch, Johanne says. Johanne says we are not welcome in Warboys, that the Samuels hate our family . . . It is something to do with Sir Henry. Or with Father. Or him being the squire,' she murmurs.

The master fixes his gaze on her. 'I have heard as much,' he says to me. 'Your uncle Henry wrote to me and told me of this witch, Alice Samuel. I had not thought Satan's reach was quite this far . . .'

To Bessie he extends a hand and invites her to stand up. 'It is over now, my dear. Perhaps a walk or a lie-down upstairs will refresh you.'

'Why *do* our neighbours hate Father?' Bessie asks, standing up and blinking innocently.

116

Master Pickering glances at me and coughs. 'The riots at Sir Henry's woods. What do you know of them?' he asks her.

'Nothing. Except that Sir Henry is kind and gives coins to strangers, and that's why he's called the Golden Knight. Father says we are not to mention Muchwood.'

'My brother writes that your neighbour, John Samuel, is popular in Warboys. Violent. No one would want to cross him. And here we have your unfortunate father, given the manor by Sir Henry, the same landlord who tried to bring a case against Samuel for sedition but could not find a juror in Warboys or Ramsey to speak against him.'

Bessie, I see, does not understand what John Samuel's sedition has to do with her situation: the mouse she finds in her mouth. I have heard that my master must bring Alice Samuel's husband to heel in some way but it is rare for anyone to speak so openly of Muchwood.

Finally, Master Pickering seems to remember I am standing there, along with Susan.

'Martha, do help Bessie up to her bedchamber. Susan will show you. Perhaps you ought to sleep there, too, on a truckle bed to watch her in the night.'

I nod to the master, and Susan leads us upstairs.

The Muchwood riots. Five years ago now: a party cutting the spinas in Sir Henry's oak woods surrounding Ramsey, damaging the cover for his coneys and fawns, so that their own animals might graze there. I remember Dottie saying afterwards, with a very red face, to any who would listen, 'It's common land, not his! My family has grazed their sheep in those woods since the days of my great-great-grandfather!'

'But what does he mean – what does Muchwood have to do with Alice sending a mouse to bewitch me?' Bessie whispers, after Susan has left us, with a bowl and jug of water to wash with and pillow covers to put on the beds. She dances a little around the room, delighted and much impressed to have a room of such riches for herself. The truckle-bed for me is found and we tug it out between us.

'Only that your father and Sir Henry being long-standing friends and John Samuel Sir Henry's enemy, he might set his wife to ill-wish you,' I suggest.

'Jane said Mama told Mother Samuel that Father and Sir Henry were *not* long-standing friends. That it was a distant acquaintance. Why did she say that if it's not true?'

'Oh, just a small untruth,' I quickly say. 'Your mother would not want Alice – Mother Samuel – to make too strong an association perhaps with Sir Henry, who is not always a popular man.'

'Mother Samuel did *seem* to dislike us, whatever Mama said, did she not? Even that very first time we saw her, when Jane told her to take off her thrumbed cap, I was scared of her, weren't you, Martha?'

'But, Bessie, you weren't in the room that day!' I reply, astonished.

She giggles and rushes forward to kiss me. 'Oh, dear Martha! Will we see Gabriel, do you think? We are here for Christmas. I do hope so!'

Bessie's cheeks are glowing again. She seems scarcely to remember her torments of but a few moments ago. I find myself breathing out: a huge sigh of relief. Whatever mouse was in her mouth has run off.

Dear Lord of Heaven, I pray, *please let Master Pickering be wrong, and grant that Satan's reach now fails him.*

*

Weeks pass before the day arrives, the longed-for day, of seeing Gabriel again.

'Oh, Master Gabriel, my, how you have grown! And a beard too. It suits you.' I take him in my arms and where once he would have dipped his head for me to kiss it, he now stands firm, allowing my arms to circle his warm chest. We are outside in the garden near the herber. Christmas and St Stephen's Day came and went, Plough Monday too: that promise was never fulfilled. Here we are in late January before we see him.

My heart leaps in my chest at the firm embrace of this taller, older Gabriel. I reach a hand to touch his jaw, his beard. Where is the little boy who snuggled onto my lap the way Hob does now? (Oh, how much longer must I be away from Warboys, from the children, the only true source of my joy?)

'We've missed you! When will you come home?' Bessie, sharp as the point of a knife, says to her brother.

Here Gabriel looks pained and does not meet our eyes.

'A young man must have a position, Bessie! He can't be kept at home with his sisters, like kittens in a basket!' I tell her.

'Pouf! Here no one gets a Christmas box! Can you imagine how serious Aunt Lizzie is?' is Gabriel's retort.

'I can!' Bessie answers.

'I was here alone for many weeks before my position was found.'

My mistress's words are hammering at me. I am her proxy, here. *If you see him, Martha, do let him know a mother's sorrow for wronging him so . . .*

But melancholy thoughts never last long with Gabriel. He and Bessie are alike in that way, have always been so. His big brown eyes are like hers, full of light, all feelings writ there, passing with lightning speed and always the drift towards laughter. Now, his sister so close again, his cheeks are rosy like hers and he cannot keep from smiling. He and Bessie link arms: he wishes to show her the herber.

'And are you now well?' he asks her, and Bessie says gravely that she is *not*, she has been in her fits many times since arriving, then chats happily about the mouse, the imps that Mother Samuel sent, the wonderful things that Thomas Cakebread told her, whispering that 'Uncle Henry was bent on bringing Mother Samuel to confession, to make his name among the scholars in Cambridge by proving there lives a witch in Warboys.'

I walk at some distance, understanding that sister and brother would like their privacy but wondering at my task of carrying the message to Gabriel from his mother. Gossips are frogs: they drink and talk. It must not be done anywhere near Mistress Pickering, or the wet-nurse, or the servant Susan.

'Oh, *why*? Why can't you come home? Is – was there some sort of row, with Papa and with Jane? Or was it Johanne, she can be so— Oh, why will no one tell us?'

I step further away, away from Bessie's plaintive cry. He will never be allowed home, no matter that Jane now withdraws what she said. Or, rather, points the finger elsewhere. Gabriel's banishment had such secrecy and shame attached, like a bucket of stones at the bottom of a well that cannot be dragged to the surface. I find myself wondering what was told to the Pickerings when they accepted him so speedily.

'The garden at Titchmarsh Grove is a fine one,' I say, hoping to divert Bessie from her talk of witches and enchantments towards fragrant, healthier considerations.

Here is a vegetable patch of skirrets and chickweed. Here are spring signs: the dancing heads of snowdrops. Gabriel crouches beside them to lift their little heads, and I crouch beside *him* – here is my moment, here, here, I must tell him, but I can only whisper, 'Gabriel, your mother wanted me to send you her love,' and he nods, his face stony for a second, stretching, rubbing his back, standing up.

So clumsy! That isn't quite it, it didn't include the apology, but now I've missed my chance. And my throat aches to say: Gabriel, I believe you! You have been wronged. Jane has wished to withdraw her accusation. There is something – a dark heart beating in the house in Warboys – but, I feel sure, you are no part of it.

And then: 'Oh I've missed you!' Gabriel says, flinging his arms around me, catching me by surprise, swooping back to say, close to my face, 'Martha – I have dwelled here in this sweet country air but I've missed you, with your smell of the kitchen and the fireplace!' It is as if he understands me. As if words passed between us, though not aloud. The child I've raised from boy to man . . . as if he were my own beloved. I could not be wrong, surely, about his goodness. I stand up from the herber, brushing some strands of grass from my skirt.

Gabriel names the plants for us, and takes us to see the bees overwintering in their hives, showing himself remarkably knowledgeable.

'This Thomas Cakebread,' he asks me, when Bessie is skipping off to pick some leaves of tansy and lemon balm. 'Bessie speaks of him a great deal. Do you admire him, Martha?'

'He has hair that's marvellous strange!' I answer, surprised. He has caught me unprepared with an opinion. I have not given Thomas Cakebread consideration.

'He sounds very clever. And to think – to imagine – that one day I had assumed myself to be a scholar at Cambridge. And now . . .' He looks down at his feet.

Here is my chance, here my occasion to tell the tender boy I love of how wronged his mother now feels him to be.

'Am I a man, now, Martha? Is this my – my life?'

Seventeen. Yes, of course, in the eyes of the world. He towers above me: handsome and commanding like his father, but in his smile, in his long eyelashes, in his soft beard . . . Oh, how my heart twists. No mother could love him more. A gusty wind surrounds us. With my bad hearing, it sounds like a fire crackling, or a great rise of water, threatening to drown us all. 'You are, my dear boy, but your mother wanted me to tell you . . .'

And then, striding towards us, Uncle Gilbert. He claps his hands, he shouts (for my benefit): 'Time for prayers! Bessie. Gabriel. Servants too. Join us in the study before dinner.'

Bessie is beside us, a smear of green across her cheek. 'Uncle is keener on prayers even than Uncle Francis in Warboys,' Bessie says to her brother, none too quietly. She is twirling a piece of honeycomb the beekeeper – appearing in his ghostly veil – gave her, and all of a sudden darts forward to bury it in my apron, before someone can take it from her.

'Oh, Bessie!' I scold. (I have some ground ivy there, picked from the herber to make a good flavouring for ale-hoof, for next time any of the children start their sneezes. Now it will simply stick to the cone . . .) Bessie licks her fingers.

Using a corner of my apron, I wipe a strand of honey from Bessie's face. Gabriel seems to think I am about to do the same for him and, laughing, ducks away from me. In his eyes and movements the boy I loved appears. His aunt arrives just as he does so and gives both children a face to chill the blood. Both fall at once into a sober manner and step into the house, towards the study to do as bade.

The study is grand indeed, warm and smoky from the fire, with the strangest charts and globes and maps on the walls and a powerful smell of beeswax: two large candles burn hard. The Puritan ways of Aunt Lizzie seem not to extend to her household: no tallow used here, every candle is beeswax, and always two lit where one would surely do. In the kitchen the glut of rabbits and pheasants hung in a huge sort of ventilated cupboard has astounded me, the flagons and glasses of wine, the size of the pewter porringer, but I've learned to say nothing to any of it because Susan's only answer is 'Mistress likes it so.'

Bessie dances alongside the shelves, cocking her head on one side to read the spines of the books aloud: '*On the Tricks of Devils* . . . *The Discovery of Witchcraft. De la démonomanie des sorciers* by Jean Bodin . . .'

Susan and the other servants crowd into the room. Mistress Lizzie kneels and, with a look, directs Gabriel and Bessie to do the same. Bessie ceases her chatter, knowing well how her aunt disapproves of it. The mistress and master are kneeling on a fine rug that in Warboys we would have thought too good for the floor and hung on the wall away from muddy boots. (These small considerations – the want of wisdom in the housekeeping – have begun to occupy me these last few days. One more reason to long to return home.)

Bessie and Gabriel, then the rows of servants kneel upon the floor. No sign of the younger children to lighten the mood. The wet-nurse must be readying them for supper and bed.

Master Pickering is soon off, praying and sermonising up a storm. He has chosen for his text Deuteronomy, no accidental choice: it is his nightly favourite. Chapter eighteen, warnings against: '"There shall not be found among you anyone

123

who makes his son or his daughter to pass through the fire, or that uses divination, or an observer of times, or an enchanter, a witch, or a charmer, or a consulter with familiar spirits, or a wizard or a necromancer . . ."'

It is easy enough not to listen, a trick I have now of almost closing off the good ear if I choose to, and with a hand in front of my face, inhale the smell of the ground ivy and honey.

But Bessie interrupts with the loudest of noises. She parts her buttocks and farts: a great fat rolling sound. She is next to Gabriel who wriggles with surprise. I can hardly breathe with embarrassment. And now a bad odour fills the room. Worse, I can see from the shaking of Bessie's shoulders that she has been seized by laughter, now spreading to Gabriel beside her, and my own bubbling up instantly.

I try to concentrate on what Master Pickering is saying to stop the laughter shaking my ribs.

"'For all who do these things are an abomination unto the Lord,'" he says, "'for those nations harkened unto diviners, but as for thee, the Lord thy God hath not suffered thee to do so . . .'"

Bessie just can't help herself, egged on by her brother. She farts again.

The mistress makes an utterance of disgust or dismay. My shoulders shake with the realisation that the mistress cannot reprimand her: what word can she possibly utter to name the crime? Gabriel has probably come to the same conclusion. He peeps out from between his fingers and laughs openly.

Somewhere in the house is the wail of a baby crying, far away, as if gulls over the sea are calling.

'Lord preserve us! This household is open to Satan's messengers!' Aunt Lizzie shrieks, losing all restraint and shouting at her husband. 'Surely you rue the day you intro-duced your sister to that friend of yours – *Throckmorton*!' At that same instant, Bessie gives a ferocious sneeze, and a second, louder than the first. Then she simply falls to one side, as if she were but a nine-pin in a game of kayles and a wooden ball had just felled her.

All laughter flees. Tears fill my eyes at the familiar sight: Bessie shaking and twitching.

'Bessie! Bessie!' Gabriel rushes to her side as the servants scatter, as Mistress Lizzie runs from the room, with only the strong one, Susan, coming to help us.

'Get her upstairs!' Master Pickering commands. Gabriel and I move to lift Bessie, but Gabriel is there first. He does not need my help. With his new strength he lifts his sister so tenderly, scooping her up as if she were but a small baby. It hurts my heart to see it. I push the study door wider for him so that he might pass through it. Her eyes are closed, her skin as pale as milk, her feet thrusting and thrashing, strange moans coming from her. Her skirts are damp, and where she lay on the beautiful rug there is a dark patch and an unmistakable smell.

'When you have settled her with the servants, you may return to *your* new home, Gabriel,' his uncle tells him. 'Your presence here has not helped your sister.'

Gabriel gives me such a beseeching look – but there is noth-ing for me to do except follow him and Bessie to the bedcham-ber and wait for the storm to pass.

'Bessie's symptoms arrive much worse when the name of the Lord is invoked,' Master Pickering says, later that evening, as we sit at dinner. 'This can only be a proof that witchcraft and necromancy are involved. I intend to write to my brother-in-law in Warboys and find out what progress has been made in making your neighbourhood witch confess.' He does not look up to see if we have absorbed his words. His large forehead is as wide and blank as a sheet of paper.

That night, Bessie wakes me from her bed, crying: 'My belly hurts! Oh, Martha, come in here with me, my belly is heaving!'

I pull back the curtain from her bed, climbing in beside her in its great height. The bed feels wet. Bessie's nightdress, too, is wet and clings to her legs. 'Oh, my belly, my belly, it hurts so much.' She is soon sobbing. I know this is not wanton but a very real pain.

'Do you think it's Mother Samuel, as Uncle says? Has she now put a spirit in my belly to lap at the milk there?' Bessie asks me in the darkness, her breath hot on my face, and still smelling of honey. 'Oh, do look, Martha, what on earth is all this wetness?' And she bids me put a hand to the bedclothes beneath her and fetch a candle.

I light it with a tinder from the fire and return. In the candle-light the bedsheets do indeed appear horrifying, black and wet. I move away at once to sit on the edge of the bed.

'Oh, Mistress Bessie,' I say.

'What? What is it? What has she done to me?'

'No, no, this is not the work of Mother Samuel. This is . . . this . . .' How in God's name to tell her what Sister Dorothy explained to me, what all women must learn one way or another?

The wet blackness is on my hands, smelling of iron and salt. I instruct Bessie to lie still and wait for me. She does so, softly crying. I take the candle downstairs in search of fresh linen, a bowl and a jug of water.

'It is nothing,' I say, returning from downstairs, where I had found a pail of water by the door, meant for mopping the kitchen floor in the morning. 'It will happen every month. Did not your mother tell you? Or your sister Johanne ... or perhaps the dairymaid might have mentioned it. Why do you think Popsie is not allowed into the dairy for four days every month?'

Bessie's eyes are wide. No sneezing or shrieking, all sobbing ceased. 'Shall I tell Uncle? What is this – blood? Am I dying? My belly hurts so much, I must be—'

'No, you are not dying. I'll make you a spencer belt. Do not mention it to Uncle. Better if men know nothing – they have horror enough of our womanly bodies. Give me a moment, the linen here is fine quality and stiff. Place this folded here . . . We will scrub the sheets tomorrow. The servant Susan will help us.'

'Oh, no! Don't tell Susan. Won't she think me even more cursed? She already hates me and so does Aunt Lizzie. I want to go home, oh, please, I want to go home!'

'Don't be silly. Susan doesn't hate you. She knows all about it.'

'She does? How does she know about this?'

'Because she would have been wearing flaps about the same age as you. Just as I did. Just as all girls do . . .' I try to explain then but stop short of telling her of coupling and childbed because Bessie's astonishment is already at a pitch that will mean no sleep this night. Hadn't she ever noticed back in Brampton, the bitch that was always being chased?

Bessie shakes her head. 'So animals, too, have this horrible thing? Of bleeding but not dying. Are they magic then, that they can survive this bleeding and live?'

'No,' I say, 'it is part of God's design for womankind, not witchery.'

'Do men have it?'

'No, only women, and female animals,' I tell her.

'What about Johanne?' she asks, astonished. 'Why didn't Johanne tell me?'

Here I answer cautiously. Has she not noticed that Johanne, even though older, is less . . . womanish than her? Straight up and down like a stalk of grass? Well, some girls develop differently, only God knows why . . .

'So a girl who is not comely or plump does not bleed like this? I should stop eating!'

'No, they all do, in God's time, but the boyish ones start later.'

'We are foul indeed,' is her reply. 'Oh, my belly hurts so much,' she wails again. I put the flat of my hand against the cotton of her nightdress, knowing well the pain she means. She puts her own hand over mine, saying, 'Can you feel how big my belly is? There's something in there, surely, Martha. An animal, a spirit lapping at some milk, a horrible spirit that Mother Samuel put there . . . I think it must be a little mouse. Put your ear to my belly – can't you hear it?'

'No, don't be silly. Women have swollen bellies, it's just how it is. This one cannot be blamed on Alice.'

A new thought then crosses her mind. 'You won't take me to that doctor, will you? The one who— Did you see what he did to poor Jane?'

'Let us never speak of it!'

I remember the doctor's frank question to Bessie about her monthly courses and her bewilderment.

She nods. Her eyelids are drooping, her face close to mine, and her warm breath starting to slow, as if readying for sleep, turning her back to me. Then flinging herself towards me again, sudden quick, asking: 'Is *this* the reason for the fits? Not Mother Samuel at all?'

'No,' I answer patiently. 'Your fits are not because of this mother sickness. The two doctors, Doctor Barrough and Doctor Butler, both said witchcraft, and bade your father to look for the cause.'

'But what is this *green* sickness? I heard Mother say it once, about Jane.'

'Green sickness is just a blood sickness. It comes after copious bleeding. It can make a girl very weak. The cure is red meat and red wine. Or spinach. But not everyone suffers from it. I never have.'

Bessie nestles close then, her warm form pressing against me. 'Oh, dear Martha! What would I do without you?' and at last she allows me to pull the sheets from under her, to help her into a clean nightdress, remake the bed and heap the soiled linen into a basket, to launder in the morning.

As a watery light creeps in from under the curtain, a cockerel somewhere and other noisily peeping birds wake us, the room appears in all its disorder, and with a sigh I set at once to tidying it.

By breakfast, Bessie has caught a new antic. She does not want to eat, but sits at the table giggling and saying that Mother Samuel has tied up her mouth. Her aunt gives a gasp at the mention of the name, as if the same old woman is in the room. The master fetches a letter from his brother Henry and begins reading it, nodding and murmuring to his wife: They tried a scratching test to reduce her powers but the true proof is that the Holy Name of Our Lord sets her off the worst . . .'

Bessie's eyes land on the letter, and I know that, like me, she is thinking, What would it take to return home now?

'I cannot even drink milk!' Bessie moans, her hand over her mouth.

'You could drink milk through a quill if your mouth is tied,' the mistress suggests. She orders Susan to fetch a quill. It is brought, and dipped in the glass of milk. We all watch and wait.

Bessie puts her mouth to it but only splutters and pulls away, splashing milk onto the table and squealing in despair.

The mistress jumps, and looks in fear towards her husband. I am awaiting instruction, standing by the dresser with the breakfast dishes on it. It is not my place to scold Bessie in front of the master. Would that I could.

'Let us try the same experiment as yesterday,' Master Pickering says. 'We shall take you out into the garden near the church to eat and see if we can shake old Mother Samuel off in that way . . .'

'She has sent a toad this time! I feel it!' Bessie screams, running from the breakfast table. The children begin to smile and then, glancing at their mother, fall to crying instead. Mistress Pickering rises from the table. I follow Bessie, meaning to chastise her, but discovering the master right behind me, I remain mute.

Bessie is hopping on one foot. 'Oh, she has tied up my leg now!' she cries, clinging to the other foot. She wants her uncle to carry her. Her feet are bare and I note him glance down at them. I had expected to see kindness there, or perhaps indulgence of Bessie's silliness. But there is something else.

One of the children – the little boy Jonnie – appears in the hall, the way Hob sometimes does, leaping from nowhere and hopping from one leg to the other (in perfect mimicry of Bessie), then just as swiftly disappears back into the scullery, where his nursemaid draws him, as if on a string.

I fetch Bessie's cloak and prepare to follow her and the master outside. Bessie is bobbing and hopping on the path, like a little robin, and in becking her head so low, she hits herself once on the wooden arch over the church path and makes a dramatic fall – almost a swoon. We both run to her. I reach her first. I expected to see her in her fits but instead she merely opens her eyes to me, the master and – standing at some distance – the mistress. She simply puts her hand to her head and starts giggling.

'I will carry you,' the master says, bending his old stiff knees to put his hands beneath her. His wife, still at the door to the house, takes a step back. She opens the door. For some reason I feel she would like me to step away, too, to fade into the house with her, inside the servants' rooms, the kitchen and the scullery, like a shadow, not remain out here in the chilly sunshine with the master. But my loyalty to Bessie, to my mistress and the charge I have, of the children, makes me determined to stay. I hold out the cloak for Bessie. The master waves, bidding me stay away. 'I will try prayer, first,' he says. He is sweating and there is a strange mood around him, a sort of urgency to be gone and to be rid of us.

'Away with your toad, Mother Samuel!' Bessie cries, loud enough for the whole of Titchmarsh to hear.

Alice's imp is a toad now, then, is it, no longer a mouse? My mind flashes to the toad I saw once, the one gorging on fire-flies and glowing alight in the darkness as I stepped on it, like an ugly fat lamp. Have I ever told Bessie about it? That toad was fearful indeed. Then I remember the black dogs with faces like toads in the stories of Joan Cunny. How Hob did shriek about them! Enough for the vision to plant itself, like a nightmare, and inflame the mind.

Bessie and the master move away from me without accepting the offer of a cloak. Behind me I hear the door to the house open and close again. Susan stands where the mistress was.

'Master and Mistress are not used to her mischievous ways,' she says.

Even though I have been thinking something similar, my ire rises at once and I feel strong speeches forming in Bessie's defence. Susan's eyes, behind the terrible burn that snakes across her brow and nose, are hard to read. She might have been a handsome woman once, or a wise one. I wonder what she thinks, really, about this home with the severe mistress and the bookish master, alone in his study, the infant always crying somewhere, the wet-nurse and the children usually kept out of sight?

Bessie's giggling and shouting can be heard all the way to the door of the church. Loud bells ring out. Whatever her uncle, carrying her like a bride in his arms, is saying, is lost beneath them, as the bells call to God, singing His praises and begging for His mercy.

'Oh, when can we go home, Martha?' Bessie cries, stretching her arms and throwing back her long hair, on waking in her feather bed.

She has grown thin and pale, her hair lank and all its curly lively beauty gone. She pines for her brother, her sisters and her own dear parents. The hopping from foot to foot, and her poor, sorry mouth, one minute a pocket for toads and mice, the next minute sewn up by Alice, has left her unable to eat a morsel and she has indeed succeeded in making her shape less comely, and more like her sister Johanne's.

'It is not my place, a servant, to petition your uncle,' I tell her. She asked me yesterday to comb her hair and look for nits and, hoping to make her prettier, I am searching for the nit comb and the lavender oil. The little red devils are visible now that her hair is so lank and greasy, making my job a little easier. I comb diligently, and throw them onto the fire.

'Is it not strange that Aunt Lizzie's children have the names of my dead brother and sister?'

'*What?*'

'John and Mary. Mother often speaks of them. Curious to think they would be older than Gabriel. Where do dead children go, Martha? And why does Mother have so many of them?'

'They are in God's Heaven, of course. Have you learned nothing from the Bible?' I cross myself, then return to the combing, not knowing what to say, as Bessie tries to tug her hair away from me.

'Why does Aunt Lizzie have a new infant, when she is as old as Mother?'

'Questions, questions!' I rap Bessie's head lightly with the comb, and find myself blushing. I had thought something similar, and marvelled at relations between the master and mistress, which do not seem in the least warm. 'Your sister Johanne never asks me such things!'

Bessie snatches her head away and runs from me. She is smiling but her eyes flash. I dread another day of hopping, screaming, bobbing, Bessie being carried in and out, the master and mistress discussing her and arguing and – usually – at the end of the day, exhaustion and fits.

'Why does no one tell me *anything*?' Bessie cries. 'Why can we not speak of things? Why is there *so much* we are not told, we can't understand, so many privy things and secrets? Poor Gabriel, will I ever see him again? My mouth *is* tied up – and yours. You know it is! And Mama's and my aunt's. Is this Mother Samuel's doing or someone else's? Oh, our house – and this one – is one big beehive, and all of them swarming *inside* my head, worse than these nits.'

A horrible image indeed. Gabriel and Bessie at the beehives, his sweet, handsome, kind face, in all its hurt and bewilderment. Tears spring to my eyes.

'Shall I write to Mother? Beg her to call me home?' Bessie asks, and then, collapsing a little to a stool by the window and staring out hungrily, 'But it will be Uncle Gilbert who decides. You must ask him for me, Martha. You must say that the only thing that will lift Mother Samuel's bewitchment is to make her confess to it. Uncle Henry told me that's what happens. A witch must confess. In front of others, the whole village. Then she will be – oh, whipped or something. Then it will end. We will be happy again. Thomas was not so sure that would end the fits, but Uncle Henry had a book that told him what to do, and he was.'

'I hope it is that simple. I will petition your uncle, yes. Let me finish with your hair and we will go to him together,' I say, trying to seize some stout courage. Bessie, for all her youth, has plenty.

Bolstered with her plan, she asks me to help her lace up her bodie and goes to find her uncle in his study. I follow, head bowed, expecting to be exiled from the discussion.

134

The master is in his chair, reading by the window, and looks up with a smile as we enter. 'You are well, Bessie? You are rather thin – your mother will be much aggrieved.'

'Yes, and I should like to return to Warboys, Uncle.' Bessie casts about for some reason that does not sound ungrateful. Some of her fine courage fails her now, I see.

The master lays down the book he is reading, and arises to close his study door, ushering us further into the room. We breathe in the masculine smell, his pipe, a glass of strong liquor and the smell of his books warmed in the sunshine.

'We must find a way to defeat Mother Samuel,' he says gravely.

Bessie says: 'Today I feel no harm in my body, Uncle, but if I return home and we try your test on Mother Samuel – saying the Lord's Prayer and asking her to repeat it . . . Uncle Henry said we must bring her to confess and repent.'

The master nods and tugs at his pipe, wafting the smoke away from us. It is a sweet plum smell but I fear my head is swimming with it.

'I believe they tried a scratching test on her . . . It may be too late for repentance. We cannot allow her to continue her foul work in our midst . . . *Thou shalt not suffer a witch to live* . . .'

I stand silently behind Bessie, still as her shadow, willing myself to invisibility. The nit-comb, abandoned upstairs, heaving with little creatures and their eggs, flashes into my mind, and Bessie's curious remarks about the brother and sister who died before she was born. I had not known their ghosts to hover like that.

Master Pickering reaches up to his shelves seeking a book to show us. '*Malleus Maleficarum*. Henry has drawn it to my attention, Bessie. An old book, but a truly important one. Every good Christian should possess a copy. The power of witches is great indeed but, of course, the power of God to discover them and snuff out their evil works is greater.'

Bessie nods soberly. 'Oh, yes,' she says. 'Thomas Cakebread discussed that book with me . . . *Malleus Malefic* . . .' She falters a little, seeing that her uncle's attention is not on her. He looks over her head then, at me, and shocks me out of my reverie by directing a remark to me.

'*You* are not convinced? I have not heard you say that you believe Mother Samuel to be a witch. Perhaps you share Robert Throckmorton's doubts. Perhaps you have some knowledge – some village gossip – to counter this claim? You know of other witches?'

'No, Master,' I stumble.

He takes his pipe from his mouth and starts digging at the contents with a sharp knife. The smoke has gone out. He throws the heavy book down upon a little leather side table and bids Bessie leave the room. 'I will consider your request, my dear,' he says. He opens the door for her, shows her out and closes it behind her. Now it is just him and me, the strong plum smoke smell lingering. He seems unsure what to say to me. I am close enough to see the large forehead like a field, with every furrow showing there. Have I angered him in some way? I search my heart but find no answer.

He listens at the door and returns to me. 'You can read, Martha?'

'Yes, sir. My . . . mother – she was a nun – taught me.'

'A nun who had a child?'

'She adopted me, I should say.'

He raises his eyebrows at this, furrowing the great brow again, his hairline rising. He seems angry. I should not have mentioned nuns in a Puritan house. Nuns, nuns, he probably already has us cursed as pope-lovers. His breath is coming a little short. He has rather fat cheeks above his beard and large eyes, which seem to be swimming, or glazed.

'And you never married? You are a spinster?'

'I am, sir.'

He ponders this. I wonder if he is considering, as Doctor Butler did, whether I am still serviceable as a wife at thirty-four, and who might have me. I brace myself for such a suggestion.

'This book!' he cries, sudden indeed. 'You would be surprised what filthy deeds the women in it are capable of and which part of men's bodies they seek to control.'

I would not at all be surprised, I think, seeing at once the direction his thinking is going in, but of course I say nothing, and he begins reading, softly, but standing very close to me, so that I see his chest straining inside the silk buttons of his doublet and smell his plum-tobacco breath on my face.

'"A certain young man who had an intrigue with a girl" – you know what "intrigue" means, Martha?'

I nod, miserable.

'"Wishing to leave this girl, he lost his member. That is to say, some glamour was cast over it so that it would not stand up" – you know how a member stands up, Martha?'

'Master, I should go.'

'"When the man put his hand down to his" – feel, here, *here* is where I mean – "his member had gone. He could touch nothing but his smooth body."'

He is still reading, but now his voice comes more breathless still and ragged, and hot. '"The young man went to a tavern to drink wine, and got into conversation with another woman who was there, demonstrating in his body by taking her hand *here* – again, I ask you – "and the woman was astute, and asked whether he suspected anyone, and he named such a one, the witch of his undoing."'

I gaze longingly towards the door, my heart thumping, prayers rising, *Dear Holy Mother, what to do? What speeches to make, what to do, to make him release me?*

'"If persuasion is not enough, you must use some violence with this witch, to restore to you your health." That's what she told him. Some violence.'

'Master, I beg you—'

'"So the young man watched the way the witch was in the habit of going, and found her. And when she maintained that she was innocent and knew nothing about his sorry member, he fell upon her, and winding a towel tightly about her neck, choked her, saying, 'Unless you give me back my health, you shall die at my hands.' Then she, being unable to cry out, and growing black, said, 'Let me go, and I will heal you.' He then relaxed the pressure of the towel."'

Here he puts his hands to my throat, very lightly, and although I am afraid to touch him, I cannot help but put my own hands there. And so we remain, his hands, mine on top, feeling his warm clammy skin and wishing that I were anywhere but here, touching him. I feel that indeed inside my throat is some ghastly thing – a mouse, a frog, a toad – longing to leap out and jump from my mouth and, yes, smite him.

'"And so the witch touched him with her hand between the thighs, saying, 'Now you have what you desire.' And the young man plainly felt, before he had verified it by looking or touching, that his member had been restored to him by the mere touch of the witch."'

138

He takes his hand from my throat and places mine firmly where he wants it. His hand is over mine, hard and pressing. The room is stifling, my face aflame and my breathing caught in my breast.

'Please, Master,' I whisper. *Please, God*, I pray. Please, *Holy Mother – anyone – help me!*

A child sets up a scream, a wail, a siren, outside the door.

The master leaps, as if burned, and drops my hand.

'He had a towel around her neck while she reached for him,' he says, quietly. 'Do you think the young witch *liked* that, Martha?'

The master's eyes are boring into me. I have been holding my breath and am still unable to let it out, a choking feeling squeezing at my lungs.

'*Well*, Martha?'

The room – the tiny smoky leather-filled room – closes in on me and I still hold my breath and dare not let it out. I fear I might be sick. The horror of it all: suddenly Master Pickering's fat belly in his doublet puts me in mind of the viper swallowing a fat snail and my arms feel light and full of air, a rising feeling and a black tunnel travelling towards me. His eyes marvellous strange (the baby still wails, and there are footsteps arriving, oh, let it be the mistress, *please, Lord*) and then, in perfect mimicry of Bessie and Jane and Grace and Mary – the Lord knows I've seen it enough times – I drop to the floor and fall, knees to the rug, not quite in a faint, but remembering to cry out, 'Oh, Master, Alice Samuel has reached me even here. She must have cast a spell on me, sending her imps in the form of – *lice*! The lice in Bessie's hair!'

His revulsion is immediate. He steps away, backs against the book-lined shelves. His eyes are wide, frightened and shocked.

'Get up, get up – get out of here! Get up, woman! May God have mercy on you!'

He grabs my arm and heaves me to my feet. All sickness has left me. I smooth down my dress, my bonnet – all of me is dishevelled – struggling to cool the heat in my face by taking breaths, deep and slow. *My prayers*, I keep thinking. Yes, I prayed to God, but I also prayed to the Holy Mother, to the Virgin, and that is now forbidden.

'Who schooled you in this? I will give you the best counsel: you are lucky indeed that only God and I witnessed it, Martha. I will write to my sister and send you and Bessie home, and we will not speak of your wanton performance again.'

The master – first straightening himself – opens the door to his study, puts his head out, then gives me a push between the shoulders. The wet-nurse sits opposite, on a fine settle, feeding the baby. She nods her head to me in some kind of recognition. I wonder how I must appear to her: pink, disordered, angry.

The baby, full and sleepy, slides from her breast and the woman, a fine country girl with long thick hair the colour of straw, simply sits there, buttoning herself up and staring at me. I'm struck that she does not seem the least surprised to see me emerge from the master's study with my bonnet undone and my eyes full of tears.

That night, in my truckle-bed, I listen to Bessie snoring, happy as she is with the news that we are at last going home to Warboys. My face grows hot remembering how Master Pickering looked at me, and afterwards how he rebuked me. And his story, his filthy story, about the young witch and the way he told it with such godly zeal. Now the tears turn to sobs.

The bed itself seems to shake, the moonlight in our room to shimmer and tremble. I feel as if I might be on a boat, at sea. Some kind of late shock grips me, in my little bed.

But the shock soon turns to fury. A high-minded man dressed in fine clothes, and behaving no better than the pigs in the yard. I might have suspected a rough man, like John Samuel or Crabbie, but Master Pickering! He holds himself so far above us. And if he could act so lewd with me, what did it mean for others in the household? For the wet-nurse or his wife? Was he godly with them and only filthy with me? What did I do to provoke it?

Then the shaking turns to marvelling. What had possessed me to fall on the floor like that and affect a swoon? I had surely saved myself so. Or – dreadful thought. My ribs contract in fear as if someone just put their hand around them: I had prayed to the Holy Virgin. I had beseeched the world at large to help me: did some person – some *thing* – in fact stretch out their hand and strike me to the ground? Was it the reach of Alice Samuel, her long bony arm catching me even here at Titchmarsh?

Now I am wide awake, my heart cantering fast. I examine my conscience as Sister Dorothy taught me to do. To pretend like that – yes, I was tormented by fear, and the thought to do it, to fall on the floor, had come unbidden (is that how the devil works?) and now I am struck for the very first time: is Bessie doing the same thing? I had several times suspected her of counterfeiting but then, when her fits are upon her, it is hard to see how any child could grieve herself so and for so long.

And the other children. Jane is so young, nine years old and the sweetest of natures: how could a girl of nine act the wanton? Many times we have seen Jane in her fits doing things no child would do if she could control herself. Her face, her manner, the strength of her fits . . . And little Mary, so bookish and good, a child such as she could not keep up such a performance, as Master Pickering had called it. And then Grace, Grace only eight years old. A girl of eight could not keep up such an act and persuade so many sober men and women, doctors and pastors, and God, too, looking on.

My straw mattress on the truckle on the floor beneath Bessie's feather one makes an awful crackling noise. I fear I must wake her with my upheaval so I creep out of bed to sit by the window.

I lift the curtain to look at the moon, a little half-moon, like a speckled egg sitting inside a blue basket. I wish – not for the first time – to be able to ask someone about these matters. My master or my mistress. Sometimes, back in Brampton, Dottie would speak freely to me, and assume an intimacy that I did not find easy to share, with my silent ways, my eyes cast inwards. Dottie would comment freely about the master and mistress, the bad relations in the household: why was the master abroad so often? Why did rumours of his carousing with Sir Henry reach us in Brampton, a full twelve miles from Ramsey? What was wrong with the oldest daughter, Johanne, become so downcast and silent? I would shut my ears to them, banish her ideas as ungodly thoughts that a loyal servant should not entertain. My fidelity to the family who saved me from ruin – Sister Dorothy dying the year my service with the family began – how could it be questioned?

Bessie is right: our mouths are sewn up. I picture mine like a little purse, the stitches drawn together. And where there are secrets, where there are things hidden and impossible to bring to light, there the devil must live.

I could hardly suggest to my mistress that her own daughters were deceivers. What cruelty. And she already mourning her son and with her own privations and fears. My mind turns with longing to picture myself at Warboys, but I am staring at the moon and something ghastly happens.

On the speckled-egg shape, first a dark, shadowy hare, and then the outline, the form of the bent old hag Alice Samuel, her hair loosened into long grey plaits, appears there. I gasp and, fearing to wake Bessie, put a hand to my mouth and press down my terror.

It must be *she* – Alice Samuel – who made me act so. She who saw into my bad heart and gave me a fancy and, also, a solution. One so bad it would never otherwise have occurred to me. It is she who brings all this badness to us. Who else could it be? To drop to the floor, to affect a few spasms (I did feel dizzy, I did feel sick, I did feel as if someone was squeezing my lungs – even my neck! – and I didn't know where the idea came from, so *surely* it must have been she, the old witch, who sent it to me). Or the devil himself, so subtle, full of craft and sleight.

A great grief rises in me then, all the sorrows of the world pouring into me, right up to the brim, and I feel such pity for myself. I arrived in this world without father or mother and now – as others are at pains to draw to my attention – I have left it very late to find a husband. I have been happily occupied with the task God gave me of loving the Throckmorton children with all of my breath and being, but now it seems hollow work, because so many afflictions hold them in their grasp and I am powerless to save them.

Why am I even here on earth? Has God Himself forgotten me? (And then I remember my shameful prayers, to our Holy

Mother, to *anyone* – and I shudder, pressing the thoughts away from me, digging them out, like cutters in pastry.)

I must plead with Alice Samuel, seek remedy. I will beg her to release us all from her bewitchments.

Time drags on and we are not permitted to leave immediately: Uncle must write letters and confirm with his sister. By the time we leave Titchmarsh, daffodils are sprouting full yellow under the trees, the hares playing in the fields. When we stop for docky we watch a game – four golden hares racing to the centre, their tails a-flying, then leaping in surprise as if they suddenly spy each other in a mirror. Bessie laughs aloud as they make their high jinks – 'Oh, look at them, Martha, it's like a country dance,' she says. We sit on a log, on higher ground, eating the bread and apples Mistress Pickering packed for us and watching the hares on the fields below.

'What are they doing now?' Bessie asks, in her cheeky, knowing way.

'Them sallies scream like witches,' Crabbie says, kicking his heels beside us. 'Scream like witches. You laugh to hear it but you don't laugh long if you're out at night alone.'

He is feeding the horse one of the apples, patting its nose. The only time he is free of his twitching is when he talks to his horse.

'Witches turn themselves into hares and race each other across the fen. That's why a sally screams. Screams like a witch. Even your old dog will creep close to you in fear then.'

Bessie glances at me and back at Crabbie, her mouth wide, the apple still in her mouth, unbitten.

'Oh, Crabbie! You're scaring the child,' I say, with a mouth full of bread. Bessie is watching the hares, rapt.

'You cannot think of a single alehouse in the fens called the Hare and Hounds, can you now? A fenman would rather go without his beer than drink in a house with that name.'

He wanders off then, his crablike walk, ducking his head and muttering, towards a tree. I see him undo his breeches, his back to us. Just in time I shift on the log to block him from Bessie's view. She is now quietly munching, but her eyes are on the distant hares.

'Can witches turn into hares, then?'

'So they say. Sister Dorothy did tell me she once saw – one night, by moonlight – twelve of them in a circle. Hares, I mean. With one in the centre.'

Why did I tell her that? It scared me almost out of my skin when Sister Dorothy told me. And that night, when I saw the shape of Alice in the moon, it stirred again an uncomfortable memory. How did Sister Dorothy know so much? Why did she consort with witches if she was devout?

'What are they doing *now*?' Bessie repeats. The hares have sprung apart, turned to face each other again, and are now up on their strong hind legs, boxing.

'When I was a child I thought they were fighting. The males for the female. Now I know better,' I say. 'The female is defending herself. She's trying to fight him off.'

I shouldn't tell. It will prompt questions. But Crabbie has moved away from us, the mistress and master are not here to silence me, and somehow I feel such a pinch in my heart for poor Bessie. Why are girls kept in such ignorance? How does it help them? She is such a quick, pretty girl. So open, as the mistress herself said. The reason for sending her away from the household full of scholars. Would it not be a kindness to furnish her with some greater wisdom? My mind goes to

Master Pickering. What saved me there? Not boxing, standing on my hind legs with fists. Not ignorance. The vision I had of Alice comes back to me, her shape in the moon, appearing at the window, had she truly sent me the fits as a solution, a way to keep me from harm?

'The sally – she's outnumbered,' Bessie says wonderingly. She stands up, losing interest, and gives her apple core to the horse. The hares, huge ears a-twitching, have capered away.

But why, I ask myself – why would a woman like Alice care for a woman like me? No, in the cold light of day, witchcraft, sorcery at a distance, did not seem to be what saved me. Perhaps, after all, God had been watching over me.

But even that did not strike me as true. No, it was my marvellous quick wits and my knowledge of pigs saved me most.

The greatest of surprises greets us in Warboys. We arrive by late afternoon. There are some brief speeches of joy as Bessie is embraced by her mother, her sisters and her brother – Hob flinging himself into her arms, kissing her and crying for how much he had missed her – and my mistress saying in an anxious voice how wasted poor Bessie looked. Hadn't her brother Gilbert and his wretched burned old servant been feeding her? My master appears and lifts her off her feet. 'Lighter than a feather,' he declares, and 'a pretty quick girl'. All agree on how much they have missed her.

Bessie asks if Thomas Cakebread is still here and is told, 'No,' and her mother pinches her cheek fondly.

'Henry and Thomas are back in Cambridge. But the girls have been well and the reason is—'

And then we see them: Alice and her daughter, seated in the inglenook by the fire with Mary and Jane, who are reading to them! The old woman has taken off her cap, and her hair – that strange colour, not grey exactly but the colour of a faded redhead, rather a sour colour – is woven high upon her head, and she has a tankard of ale in her hand. The daughter, Nessie, with the slim shape and the bold gaze, looks up at my arrival and nods a greeting.

I hardly know what to say.

'Come outside, Martha, and walk with me,' the mistress says. 'Bertha has had her piglets, six of them! Let's go and see.'

Bertha has had her piglets. Without my help. So we have been gone a whole three months. And in that time . . .

'I know it is a little strange,' Mistress says confidingly, as we step outside the kitchen door.

'Marvellous strange,' I reply.

'It was the suggestion of Sir Henry. He thought it would be better to appease our two neighbours, treat them kindly and hope that their wish to cause us harm ceases. He has been to see Robert and they were in consultation for a long time. Robert seemed . . . rather shaken afterwards. You know he has always been so excessively . . . afraid of witches, has he not? Do you remember when that old Mother Gibson was accused at Brampton and Robert carried a witch-guard at all times in case he came across her in the street?'

I do remember, although until now I'd forgotten it. My master, usually so manly and commanding, had seemed cowed, a little like a child, like his own son Hob, in his fear of witches. Of course, witches are fearful creatures and it is right to be afraid of them, but at the time we – the servants – all thought it extreme. I remember now that Doctor Butler accused him of it: *Ah, now I understand all. She is an old witch and you are afraid of her.*

My mistress is still talking: '. . . Robert asked them and has insisted they are treated kindly. And since the two women came the girls have not been in their fits! Or, well, that's not quite true, but only once or twice. And nothing like such bad fits as before. If they do fall into fits, Robert makes Alice repeat the Lord's Prayer and she does it, even cheerfully (I would say she finds it amusing and silly, but she does it), and the fits seem to disappear.'

'And why the daughter? Why *both*?'

'Well, Jane did once accuse *her*, too, of being a witch, so Robert felt we should include her in the experiment. There's no keeping it private – we are the talk of Warboys and further. The curious part, the part I don't understand – it was something in Robert's demeanour after the counsel with Sir Henry. Martha, he was very altered. I would say . . . Well, I wish I knew what Sir Henry said to him. He seemed . . . quite afraid.'

'It seems an extraordinary thing for Alice to agree to,' I mutter.

'Money is involved, too, and that seems to have sealed it.'

Bertha, exhausted, gives a sudden loud grunt, flinging back her ears and rolling on her side, where five of her piglets are snuffling and sucking. The sixth – a little runt – strays to the corner of the pen, as if expelled.

'He will not last long, poor fellow, unless we get him suckling,' I say, stepping over the wooden fence. Bertha immediately growls at me as I pick up the piglet – his backside is grey, the rest of him pink, as if he were dipped in the inkpot – and try to push his nose towards her teats, displacing one of the other piglets, which runs off squealing. Bertha gives me a look of recognition and I pat her muddy flank and turn again to the mistress. 'So they stay here, mother and daughter? They sleep in the house?'

'Well, while you were away we needed someone to look after the younger children and we'd lost a servant and Robert felt—'

'And the husband allows it? He didn't complain?'

'Oh, he did indeed complain! Hard speeches. He is a frightening man when angered. But . . .' here she drops her voice '. . . Robert offered him ten pounds. And that settled it.'

Our presence so close to Bertha's babies is unsettling the old sow and she keeps trying to get up and attack me. My boots are already covered with mud. Mistress has stayed sensibly outside the fence. We leave the pigs and walk together towards the fruit trees. Blossom has appeared like a great white and pink storm, and bees buzz around our heads.

'It is curious, Mistress . . . If Alice agrees to repeat the Lord's Prayer to try to stop the girls' fits, has she confessed to being a witch? If so, shouldn't she be arrested and put before the judge?'

Here my mistress sighs, and stops. 'She still denies she is a witch. I feel sure Robert is – I have never known him to be so . . .'

'What, Mistress?'

'Oh, Martha! He wishes to placate her. He thinks this way is best. Paying the husband money. Keeping her in high style. And the daughter too! He does not wish to anger her. I know he has had some . . . curious and changeable moods over the years but I have never seen him quite this . . . cringing, *frightened*, even . . .'

At this I gaze at her, astonished. 'How does Alice respond to this treatment?'

'Oh, you know, she is greedy, like Jane. She loves her food! She accepts the feather mattress and the rosewater biscuits. I'd say she was indulging him, playing along. Ten pounds is probably a great sum to the family.'

'Mistress, do *you* think she is a cause of the girls' afflictions?'

My mistress stops, looks thoughtful. 'I do not know what to think. They do still have the fits sometimes, but it is true that since the arrival of the two women they come out of them more easily. And more significantly, their mood and the feeling in the household are . . . what shall I call it? . . . happier. Not melancholy. They enjoy the heed the two women pay them. Yes. It is indeed as if something – a spell – has been lifted.'

I return in my thoughts to my own questions, in Titchmarsh, about Alice and whether she is the cause of these enchantments and of my own. My mistress has said something I did not hear. She sees my incomprehension and repeats a little of it.

'Mother Samuel sometimes seems only to be a bad-tempered neighbour, a scold, a foolish woman who is too outspoken, but is she a witch? I find it hard to believe, except, except . . . well, Dottie told me, just before you went to Titchmarsh, she saw Mother Samuel talking to Sir Henry on his horse in the woods behind the house. The woman was shouting and waving a stick! I know Dottie exaggerates and has a terrible habit of eavesdropping and concocting stories, but it's very troubling to imagine a woman of Mother Samuel's standing speaking to Sir Henry in such a manner.'

I am about to ask more of this, such a curious encounter, and how was it that Dottie was there (how was Dottie always there?), but my mistress suddenly turns to the subject of Gabriel, asking if I passed on her message. I say hesitantly that I told him how much he was loved, but had not time or occasion to say more.

'But you told him, you said I was sorry?'

'I gave him your love.'

'Did you tell him that we felt Jane was mistaken and he had been wronged?'

'I— There was not the occasion for such honesty. I simply told him you loved him.'

She accepts this, linking her arm in mine. 'I'm so glad you're back,' she says, and as we walk into the house, the sweet scent of cherry blossom clings to her. Still, something troubles me. Her arm feels but a twig in mine. She is not as she was when I left. These new concerns about Robert and his intrigue with Sir Henry, something has changed.

In the kitchen, Dottie hugs me and asks after Gabriel.

'Oh, he is so grown! So tall! In only a matter of months,' I say.

'But when might he come home? What is he doing there?'

I don't like to admit that I don't know, so I say, 'Oh, I believe he is apprenticed to a fine gentleman and will soon begin his work.'

Popsie arrives in the kitchen then, pulls her mouth into a pucker, a habit she has. 'But Bessie, poor little Bessie. She is shocking thin! Did no one feed her?'

'The fits did not leave her. And – Bessie said, even in Titchmarsh, Alice sent her imps to tie up her mouth.'

Dottie and Popsie glance at one another, grasping this new detail. I wonder that they are not more shocked, for now the witch in question lives under their own roof. My fears of Alice do not seem to extend to them, and I seek Dottie's opinion (she being usually so quick to venture one): 'Why is she here, Dottie? And the daughter? Am I the only one who thinks it strange?'

Dottie brushes some hair inside her coif and nods. At least she acknowledges it is a curious turn of events. Then she shrugs. 'The master wanted it. He said we were a servant short, with you gone. They sit at his board, you know, like honoured guests! He seems . . . Oh, I cannot say. The household is lightened, though. There is laughter again. I even think that the younger ones have grown to *like* them being in the house. It's not so strained and stuffy. Not so much churching!'

'And no fits?'

'Oh, fits a-plenty. But not as often and not as powerful.' Popsie fetches the elderberry wine from the pantry and some sweetmeats for Bessie: marchpane, her favourite.

As she is about to go upstairs to take them to Bessie, she says, 'I'm glad you're back, Martha. *More* visitors are coming. Lady Cromwell and her daughter-in-law. Come to see the old witch for herself.'

'She's like the Queen – you have to curtsy,' Dottie says.

'I didn't see the Golden Knight last time he was here. Maybe I'll be luckier this time and catch a coin as he throws it out of the carriage!' Popsie laughs, taking the tray once more and leaving us to our tasks.

Dottie picks up a broom, muttering, 'You'd be luckier to land a fish,' and then mouthing to me, 'Or a *disease*!'

Dottie has always made clear her feelings about Sir Henry Cromwell, despite his being our landlord in Brampton, as here.

But then, owning as much land as he does, it would be hard to escape him as landlord, wherever we might live. I know Dottie was on the side of the Muchwood rioters, though she was not reckless enough to take part herself. It's known that it was mainly wives and children sent to do the men's dirty work, as it would have been harder to prove their intentions. It might have looked as if they had made innocent errors in destroying vegetation meant for Sir Henry's fawns. The men followed later under cover of dark.

'He's even talking of draining the fens at Cloughs Cross and depriving us all of our ducks and eels,' I remember Dottie saying, flushed with anger. She had come back from the old Black Bull at Brampton where ale and perry and hot rages had been flowing like lava.

The Lady Cromwell is a rather fat lady, with many skirts and a very stiff ruff and fine kirtle. We all dread what Crabbie might say, watching him as he opens the carriage door and she waddles out with her large backside, but though he twitches and ducks his head, thankfully he then steps to one side and buries his comments in his hands, like a sneeze, as his mother taught him. The younger lady follows, emerging from the carriage with much difficulty, arriving like a plum hanging on a tree, with the weight of the child she carries.

The ladies sweep in and kiss my mistress. We have been watching them through the open door, lined up in the hall to greet them. The younger Lady Cromwell is fair and pretty, standing beside her mother-in-law with rather laboured breathing on account of the size of her, but a blank face.

Sir Henry is not with them. He has ridden his horse from Ramsey and is in the churchyard with the master, discussing business.

Greetings and formalities over, the ladies are shown into the parlour.

Lady Cromwell can barely disguise her excitement, chattering loudly to our mistress. 'And why does Robert keep her here and the daughter too? Is it to test her? Is that what the Reverend Doctor Dorrington advises?'

I make haste to the kitchen to help Dottie fetch the best silver goblets of wine and some dainties Mother Caterill has prepared. On our return to the parlour what a scene greets us!

Alice and her daughter are seated in the inglenook with the children. She sits marvellous happy, with her betters, eating their food and burping. There is a feeling as if we were at some sort of party, the children chattering and gay – they had been reading to Alice and now, I notice, are not in haste to leave the room. Dottie is right: they do seem to like her, and her daughter.

Lady Cromwell is huffing with the effort of trying to gain a proper look at Alice, blocked as she is by the bodies of the children. Her daughter-in-law is quickly brought a chair and both women sit heavily, while Dottie moves a little table beside them to place the goblets on.

'How do all our good friends?' Lady Cromwell asks nervously. She cannot take her eyes from the scene surrounding Alice, and her open desire to see her.

'We're all well met but so much the better for the return of Bessie – we missed her!' the mistress says. The children are invited to step forward and greet their guests.

'Now, let me acquaint myself again. Grace, she is your youngest daughter here – and, Mary, you are very devout. I hear you read very well for your eleven years of age. Now

Jane . . . is this Jane? Or Bessie? Oh, Bessie, you are lively and jumpy, are you not? You are the eldest – Johanne? Oh, you look like your father. And oh! My goodness! What a start you gave me, little boy.' Each child curtsies in front of her, but Lady Cromwell hardly hides her true interest, craning to see the face of the neighbours who sit in the inglenook.

'And the fits and trances, the afflictions, they have ceased?' enquires Lady Cromwell.

'No, my lady, but they are much improved,' Mary says, ever the most polite child, with a curtsy.

'They have lessened in severity, since our guests have joined us,' Mistress is saying, and now Lady Cromwell is staring boldly at the woman and her daughter, not troubling to drop her eyes.

'So – it is *you*!' Lady Cromwell mouths.

I am the only one to see it. It is not spoken aloud. But to me – accustomed to reading lips and looks – there is no question: the two old women recognise one another, and it is not a friendly greeting. We are all standing, awaiting our instruction. Popsie is all of a twitter, like a robin flitting from place to place, anxious to please the two grand ladies and not spill or drop something.

Alice returns to her eating, and nodding, and picking crumbs from her bodie.

Then the most shocking thing happens. Moments after my mistress has said their afflictions are lessening, Bessie makes a terrible sound and drops to the floor, strangely handled in her fits. And then two others: Jane and Mary sit stiff in their chairs like puppets, arms and legs jerking, eyes unseeing. Grace runs to hide behind a curtain. Johanne remains still. My mistress runs to her daughters.

Alice and Nessie gaze about them. They seem accustomed now to the fits but wary of how this will turn out for them.

Lady Cromwell rises in alarm, and her daughter-in-law looks as if she has turned to stone, holding one hand on her belly.

Popsie drops beside the girls in an instant, trying to soothe them, muttering kind speeches, and I on the other side do the same, trying to soothe the moaning coming from Bessie.

'Oh, do help them, help them, the poor things,' Lady Cromwell cries. 'Oh, it is worse, worse even than I heard.'

I flee the room to find the master, discovering him returning without Sir Henry and quickly whisper what is needed. He and another man – Sir Henry's servant – soon carry the three sorrowful girls upstairs to continue their fitting out of sight. I do not go with them because there is an upturned tankard on the floor and I must fetch a cloth to wipe the spill. As I return to the room Grace reappears from behind the curtain, pointing and staring at her remaining sister, Johanne.

Johanne has, until now, been sitting very quiet by the fire with a cushion on her lap, sulky and silent, as is her way. Now she stands up. 'I feel strange,' she says. Lady Cromwell gives a strangled gasp.

Then Johanne says, in a high, terrifying voice, 'I heard it in my ear. Did none of you hear it? A voice saying that Mother Samuel has sent her spirit and bewitched us all!'

Alice stands up then, a face like thunder and about to make some very hard speeches, but Johanne drops to the floor, twitching and jerking her grieved limbs as if she has the palsy, as bad as any of her sisters. Little Grace runs to her, upsetting a stool and crying, for Johanne has never been in her fits. My heart plummets: so now it is Johanne, too.

The two Lady Cromwells look on with wide, frightened eyes. Still, it is hard not to think that this uncouth adventure is what they came for.

'Oh, so grievously tormented. Elizabeth, how do you bear it?' Lady Cromwell wails.

The mistress is pale and has tears in her eyes. I am much grieved for her, and together we sit either side of Johanne, trying to soothe her, awaiting the return of the master, to carry her upstairs like her sisters.

'It passes, it passes in time,' my mistress replies. 'Johanne has been free of the fits until now. I know no cause why . . .'

Johanne has dropped to the floor in unseemly manner. It is clear to me and Popsie that it would be better if the two visitors would leave and allow us to arrange things a little better but how to say this while at the same time trying to stop Johanne smashing her head against a chair leg. The master reappears from upstairs, nods to the two ladies though makes no gesture to Alice or Nessie, and struggles to pick Johanne up. Johanne is striving and kicking, and crying out, 'She has sent her imp – a nasty toad – to do her bidding!'

'Oh, my Lord, preserve us!' screams Lady Cromwell, and slumps back in the settle as if about to faint.

At this Alice loses her temper. She steps forward and Lady Cromwell shrinks back into her seat. 'Why do you accuse me? You do me a great wrong to blame me!' Alice shouts, bold-faced, making to leave. Nessie gives her mother a beseeching look but, like the young Lady Cromwell, seems rooted to the spot.

I cannot think what to do, or say, or how to help.

Alice moves towards the door. 'I want to go home. I'll not watch more of this wanton performance,' she says angrily, and clicks fingers at her daughter to join her. The girl stands up, uncertain.

My master hastily lifts Johanne and carries her from the room. We all hear Johanne shouting, from the stairs, 'Oh, now she sends her cat to do it! Can no one else hear it? The cat is yowling in my ears!'

Alice throws her shawl over her head and steps towards the door. To our astonished eyes, the stout Lady Cromwell shows herself spry and determined and is suddenly beside her, seemingly very vexed. The two women glare at each other.

In that moment, I understand: not only was their greeting unfriendly, they are old adversaries. Lady Cromwell is breathing heavily, her bosom rising and falling. She makes a faint growling sound – like the warning noise Bertha made when I approached her piglets. The air in the room is hot, the smell overpowering.

'Mother . . .' the young Lady Cromwell begins.

'You've bewitched them! You old witch! I knew it!' the old Lady Cromwell shouts, undeterred.

Alice takes a step towards her, shouting back: 'They are very wanton girls to accuse me. And you, too.'

'*I* do not accuse you, only the girls themselves! Innocent children – you see how afflicted they are!'

'Let me pass,' Alice says, with a voice full of menace. My blood leaps in fear but whether it is fear for Alice – for her boldness – or for my mistress, for the shame of the scene, or for some other reason, I do not know. Mistress has her hands over her face. The young Lady Cromwell remains dumbstruck.

'You are a very wicked woman! You know my husband is the Sheriff of Ramsey and Justice of the Peace – you would do well to tell the truth and remove the spell you've cast,' Lady Cromwell booms.

Alice makes a derisive sound, a cross between a jeer and a shriek. Now it is not Bertha they put me in mind of but two hissing geese guarding the path with fearsome rage. 'Calling me a witch. You old trull! I never did you any harm yet.' And Alice tries again to pass her

The room seems to open in a wide gasp and close again, Alice calling Lady Cromwell a trull. I feel an odd clap of laughter rising: this is very wrong of me, as a godly woman. At the utterance of the word, Lady Cromwell startles us by uttering a scream, hot and fierce.

There is more: she rummages in her bag, then pulls out a pair of shears. In one movement, showing herself to be of stout courage, she snips off a piece of Alice's hair and some of her braid, her hair-lace, too.

Now we all look about us in fair astonishment.

'You wicked whore! Your fundament is as big as a mousehole!' Alice bellows.

The mistress almost faints in shock. The two younger women – Nessie and young Lady Cromwell – are both on their feet, trying to hold the two old crones apart, like men at a yard fight.

'I'll fix you! A witch can't cast a spell when her hair is burned!' Lady Cromwell threatens.

She has the piece of hair-lace and snipped-off lock of hair in her fist and rushes towards the fire, while Grace and Hob cower there, watching in amazement as she tosses in the pieces. We all stare towards the flames. Presently, there is an offensive stink in the room: the smell of burning hair.

At last my mistress rallies. Dazed, deprived of her senses for a moment by the foul words said in the room, she gathers the youngest children and bids them leave. Then: 'Martha, show our neighbours out,' my mistress murmurs, and I go to do her bidding.

As if in a trance, I accompany the two women to the front door, unlocking it for Alice, permitting her at last to leave. Her daughter follows her, shaking her head in disbelief. But Alice still has spots of anger on her cheeks.

'As big as a mousehole,' the daughter is saying. 'Mother, how could you?'

But as the door closes, the sound is unmistakable, even to a deaf-lugs like me. The two women let out peals of laughter.

Lady Cromwell is still in her hard speeches, as I return to the parlour. She is panting, a little. Her round face is very pink and her eyes glitter. She smooths down her skirts, pats her coif, putting the shears back in her bag and sinking down into her chair.

'Martha, please fetch our guests some more wine,' my mistress asks, very faint. A little pulse quivers in her throat. The young Lady Cromwell closes her eyes, resting herself in seeming shock, her hand rising and falling on her large belly.

The smell of burning hair and fabric lingers, and Popsie drops a curtsy; we are glad indeed to leave them there.

'That's done it. They'll arrest her now,' Popsie squeaks excitedly, in the kitchen, carrying back the trays and beginning to wash them in a bowl by the window.

'What, for calling Lady Cromwell an old trull?' Dottie asks. She has heard already then. She struts among the pots and plates, pretending to be Crabbie, muttering: 'Your fundament's as big as a mousehole!' Soon even Mother Caterill is laughing, and scolding at the same time.

'No, not for that. But Johanne – Johanne was in her fits! Even Johanne, now! She named her a witch and said she'd – what was it? – sent another imp, a toad or a cat, I think.'

'She won't be arrested on a girl's word,' Mother Caterill says. She likes putting us to rights. 'They'll want her to confess. They'll want her to do it in front of the whole of Warboys so that *they* don't look bad, the vicar and the master and all. So it looks like all of Warboys took part, not just the Throckmortons. And then she'll get a whipping or a time in the stocks or a few weeks in gaol and we can go back to our lives.'

'Oh, but – *confess*!' says Dottie, pausing her antics to be serious for a moment. 'Did you *hear* her in there?' (I realise that Dottie must have listened outside the parlour to every word since it was only me and Popsie who were there.) 'She is such a scold and as rude as Bertha for grunting and growling. She will *never* be brought to confession – nor the hot-headed daughter neither!'

'The mother is rude, but the daughter . . .' The daughter interests me more than I can explain. She has such outstanding long and ungodly coloured hair. Fine eyebrows and a bold stare, a little chin that tilts to let you know how defiant she is, whatever her silence. And stranger still is the way she walks, tall and firm, proud, even, as if she were a lady. This causes the greatest astonishment to me.

'Alice doesn't help herself. Who has schooled her to say such naughty things?' Dottie says, addressing herself to Mother Caterill, who after all, has known Alice a long while.

'Naughty things,' repeats Popsie, giggling. She has finished washing the goblets and tankards and is making warming pans to take up to the bedchambers, struggling with a big pan of boiling water on the fire. I rush to help her as her flimsy wrists look about to snap.

'No doubt the husband,' Mother Caterill says. She heaves herself onto a stool, the better to direct us in our tasks and warm to her subject: Alice Samuel and her naughty marriage. 'John Samuel is a knave, but he loves her—' she begins, but Dottie cuts in with a sudden thought: 'Did you think the women knew each other? Martha – did you think it?'

I did think it. Old adversaries, I thought. 'But how did *you* gather such a thing, listening outside the door?' I ask Dottie.

'Oh, I heard more than that. I heard the master and Sir Henry talking outside, in the churchyard earlier. Sir Henry said that John Samuel's wife was a woman they *hoped* they would never meet again! And the master was strange and anxious – don't you think he is always so these days? Hard speeches. And asked, "How can you be sure?" And "Why did you send me here, to live near to the old bitch?" And then Sir Henry was all putting up his hands as if – you know, as if they were fighting and telling the master to calm himself and saying how could he have known John Samuel was married to one such as she? What do you make of *that*? They knew Alice to be a witch long ago? That she had bewitched them before? Was she known to be one, Mother Caterill? I'm sure Sir Henry said, "so long ago".'

'Oh, Alice, as a girl she was a beauty. She looked like her daughter ... trouble. She was known to have the skills of a cunning woman. The same skills Martha here has, or so I've heard, in assisting at childbed and, you know, herbs and cures. Didn't Alice help your mother bring you into the world, Popsie?'

'She did,' Popsie says cheerfully. Spry and simple, she never seems to notice a shift in mood or in a countenance. Nonetheless, I hide mine from her, turning away to busy myself with the stove.

I feel a tremor here. *The same skills Martha has.* When did the skills of a cunning woman become witchcraft? When did Elizabeth Mortlock, with her magic girdle and prayers that so helped women in childbed, become *wicked* – when did that change, and admiration and trust in the secret knowledge of women in their great sufferings turn to fear and arrests? Sister Dorothy had tried to hide the news of the trial of Elizabeth Mortlock from me but I heard of it by and by.

I remember, too, the day in Cambridge with Doctor Butler when he asked if I could read and how he stared at me as I proudly stated my skills in midwifery and medicine. He looked at me as if to say, 'This is *my* world. I'm the one who has concocted Butler's Ale. What could an ignorant woman like you possibly know?'

Something has changed, and it has happened slowly, little by little. It has happened outside our household. It has happened because the new religion must be obeyed, and we must attend church or be fined, and learn our bibles in English so all can read them, but neighbours do not know from one minute to the next what new rules have been created overnight, whether we will be blamed as Papists or as Protestants, what mysterious new rules we might have transgressed.

'But how on earth could a grand lady from Ramsey know Alice Samuel?' Popsie asks, chewing still on the encounter between Lady Cromwell and Alice. Thankfully, she has been thinking about that. My midwifery skills have been forgotten.

'Lady Cromwell only married Sir Henry a few years ago. The summer of the Muchwood riots. She was common enough before then! She and Alice might have run into each other – they're the same age. I don't know. If Alice ever went to Ramsey or Susan Weeks – Lady Cromwell – came to Warboys, it's not *impossible*,' Dottie says. She's swigging some elderberry wine from one of the silver goblets before plunging it into the bowl to wash.

Mother Caterill rubs her gnarled old back and stretches her swollen ankles out in front of her, her backside on a stool, and chuckles. 'Susan Weeks . . . it's a common name, true enough.'

'We saw her once or twice when we lived in Brampton, didn't we, Martha?' Dottie muses. 'But back then we weren't grand enough for a *visit*. The servants used to laugh about her. Not you, Martha. You were always too virtuous. We'd laugh that she'd tried to catch Sir Henry while he was still married to the first Lady Cromwell, Lady Joan. Dragon's blood sprinkled in milk to bind him to her, but that didn't work. She needed to be with child. She needed to use a stronger charm. A curly golden hair from Sir Henry's privy parts—'

Popsie gasps and Mother Caterill says, 'Oh, Dottie!'

'She sewed the hairs into a fur tippet and wore it in his company.'

'How can you know such things?' Popsie says. Then, 'Was she blessed with children?'

'No. Sir Henry, though, sired two more by a third mistress. Seven or eight children he has, and not one of them hers. Still, I'm sure she judged the charm a success. The first wife died promptly and Susan Weeks married him within the year. '

Dottie is enjoying Popsie's giggles and – no doubt – the look on my face.

'How do you know all this?' Popsie repeats, and this time

Dottie answers her: 'Oh, Brampton is not so far from Ramsey. You Warboys folk know *nothing* about *anything*!'

This is aimed at Mother Caterill for chiding her. Dottie takes great pride in her talents as a storyteller and gossip, and since arriving in Warboys has been at pains to prove her superiority to Mother Caterill at every opportunity and chafed at the older woman's scolding of her. 'Sir Henry, the golden cockerel. He and Master Throckmorton are like thieves at a fair. Have been since boyhood,' Dottie adds, with a flourish.

I think again of the mistress telling Alice the two men were only of distant acquaintance, and wonder if the mistress wishes it were so. 'Thieves at a fair' has a very bad odour to it.

'Alice is lost if Susan Weeks tells Sir Henry. I remember Sir Henry searching a house in Stukeley – a Catholic house – to discover a Jesuit hiding there. He was relentless. A terrier shaking a coney. He never lets anything drop,' Dottie says.

The voice of the mistress cuts into her story, arriving among us and calling sharply, 'Dottie! Are drinks taken to the girls? Popsie, are the beds warmed? Martha . . .'

I flush red to be so caught, gossiping with the servants, when my position in the household is closer to the hearts of Master and Mistress. My face so aflame and my conflicted loyalties do not escape Dottie: she sets her mouth in a hard line and tosses her head a little, returning to the stove to prepare the wormwood drinks.

Popsie and me wrap the warming pans in linen. We move in silence to take them to the children's bedchamber. But on the stairs Popsie turns to me and says, 'I heard Lady Cromwell as they were leaving. In her carriage. Crying that Alice would now send an imp. She sounded . . . frightened, Martha.'

*

My sleep is fitful. Dottie's snoring is more like a pig's than a human soul's and my trick of putting my bad ear upwards and my good one against the pillow isn't working tonight. I have to leave the bed and take my blanket to the warm hearth in the kitchen and lay it in front of the fire. The rush-mat is scratchy but smells of comforting tansy and wormwood, yet still I am awake at first light, as the cocks are crowing, still picking over the day's events, the terrible affliction of the girls and what can be done to help them.

I pick up my brush and set to sweeping, while the rosy blush flows in through the leaded glass panes in the great hall, making the prettiest of patterns.

My mistress appears then, raised from her bed, in her night-gown, her hair tumbling from her nightcap.

'Martha! Did you not hear that commotion? Horses? Go and see who it is!'

I prop the broom against the settle and rush to throw my coat over my nightdress, but I answer the door in my bare feet. It is a man with a black cap: he looks like a reed bunting atop a stick of sedge.

He hands me a letter and says something. I take it, close the door and give it to the mistress. I see that it has a seal on it – the coat of arms of Sir Henry Cromwell: three swords, three fleurs-de-lis, a white lion with outstretched tongue and claws, and beneath that another one, black but otherwise the same and equally fearful.

My mistress takes the letter from me and begins reading.

'Oh, Martha! A letter from Lady Cromwell. She is afflicted, and has been all night long. She is horribly ill. She is certain that Alice has sent her imp to bewitch her. A cat! A cat clawing at her. A dreadful message, she wants me to tell the vicar.'

166

'Is it the same sickness as the girls?' I ask. The letter makes me tremble: the beasts on it look like devils to me and I have the feeling that something awful has been allowed into our house.

'Yes, it seems so . . . like the palsy, she says, and shaking, and stiff limbs that she cannot control. A cat sent to her in a dream to claw her skin off.'

As we both stand there, in the hallway, our feet bare, shivering a little in our cotton gowns, my fear creeps upon me: this sickness that stalks us, stretching out its long tongue and claws, where will it strike next? A breeze rattles the door and my heart quickens. I fear for a moment that the beasts, the white one and the black one, claws splayed, are shaking it, trying to enter. A trembling spreads from my knees to my breast. The mistress begins weeping.

'Is it Johanne? How are the girls this morning?' I ask.

'I don't know, I don't know – oh, Martha! What has happened? Was it coming to Warboys? First Gabriel, then these fits, then Jane accusing Alice . . . What should we have done differently?'

I move to comfort her, fetching a shawl to put upon her shoulders and steering her towards the inglenook where I lit a fire earlier and the peat turves are piled high.

'I do feel it,' I say quietly, not knowing any other way to answer her. 'But we must pray to God to deliver us, as He has always done, and if the source of our misery is Alice Samuel or her daughter, to bring them to justice, too.'

She nods, but she does not answer me. I cannot read her expression. She reaches out her hand, 'Stay awhile, Martha,' and I pull up a stool beside her. We sit together by the fire, breathing in the deep peat smell, not as mistress and maid, but two women. We share one heart when it comes to our love for the children. My mouth might be sewn up, but my mistress has always known it.

Johanne will not leave the bedchamber and it has been three days now. She is not in her fits but she lies with her back to any who enter. The mistress has tried to talk to her. Now it is my turn.

'You feel ill?'

I tie back the curtain to the bed and sit beside her, creakily. The warm lump of her remains still, so I lean over and start smoothing her hair away from her face.

'I brought you some eggs in moonshine, I know how much you like rosewater . . .'

I put the dish on a blanket box at the bottom of the bed, since she shows no interest. She does not move. I stare around the room, then place myself beside her on the bed once more, careful not to sit on her legs.

'The neighbours, Mother Samuel and Nessie, have gone home. The vicar says that the time has come for Alice to confess before the village, and be done with it,' I tell her.

At this a flicker of interest. A small sound from her: 'Huh!'

I lean in. 'You are certain sure it is Alice – Mother Samuel – who is the cause of . . . your affliction?'

At last. She sits up slowly and looks around her for the plate of eggs, which I bring to her. Her tongue comes out, a little slow, as she tastes the rosewater and nods. 'Of course! Didn't Jane call her a witch? Didn't Bessie? Why does everyone suddenly doubt *my* word?'

'They don't! No one doubts you.'

'Are you calling me wanton? Mother Samuel did! A liar! No one believes me, nothing I say is heeded.'

'Now, Johanne, that is not true.'

And suddenly, pushing the plate of wobbling eggs into my hand, she tosses herself face first onto the bed, sobbing. She lifts her head to cry, 'I hate it here! Don't you hate it, Martha? I wish we had stayed at home. I hate those women! I hate the fens! I hate all of Warboys! I hate all this churching and the bells tolling all day long! I hate it, hate it, hate it!'

She is weeping furiously while I place the plate back on the blanket box and turn to her. I put my arm around her, but she stiffens and shrugs me off.

'No one believes me. No one *listens* to me!'

'But we do.' I am shocked by the strength of her emotion, as if a storm has whipped around the room, lifting up blankets and tossing us hither and thither.

'I told Mother. I told her some . . . important things when we first arrived, and she only said—'

'What important things? About Alice?'

'No, they were . . . It was to do with Jane.'

'What? What was it? *Tell me.*'

'Mother did not believe me and you won't either – I won't *ever* repeat it.'

'Was it . . . something about Jane and your brother?' I ask, as delicately as I can.

Johanne flings her face to the wall, shouting, 'No! Not at all. No one pays me any heed! I won't tell! All I know is this house is *bewitched.*'

'But, Johanne, if you are mistaken about Mother Samuel, if any of you are mistaken, you must say so now, before it is too late!'

'Why do you doubt me? From the day we moved here, we were shaken like dolls and shamed in front of visitors

– Mother fading, Gabriel sent away, Bessie turned into a simpleton! Father never here, but always "at business" with Sir Henry! Everything is wrong – and – and— Why are you blaming *me*? Lady Cromwell could see that the horrible old woman, and worse, *worse*, her wicked daughter are to blame for all of it!'

The vehemence of her words. I study her face: the dark eyes, the large, angry mouth, the red spots on her cheeks. But she has not finished.

'Father is never here but when he is . . . Did you see that he walked in the orchard with that – witch and talked to her as if she was not low-born but his equal?'

I feel my face colour. The master walk in the orchard with – with Alice? Or Nessie? Why on earth would he? 'You must be mistaken,' I say.

'I am *not*! I watched them from my window. That horrible girl. He was *talking* to her. Oh, they thought no one could see them.'

'I am sure your father had his reasons. Perhaps to beg her to lift the spell, if it were she who—'

'And while you were away, Martha, one night when Mother Samuel was staying with us, she – old witch! – came running out of my parents' room in the dead of night saying that her belly hurt and making all kinds of lamentations.'

'Yes, but I don't understand! All guests must sleep on the truckle-bed in your parents' room and a woman her age, well, her belly might indeed pain her. An old woman is beset with misery.'

'You used to be the only person I could talk to but now even you, even you, Martha . . .'

'You are invaded by many fears and worries.'

Her eyes seem wide and glittery, and I feel her forehead, anxious that she might be running a fever. I am smarting with fears and worries of my own, begun in Titchmarsh weeks ago. Am I, too, bewitched by Alice Samuel? Why do I keep changing my mind on this matter, one minute fearing her a witch, the next that we are all cruelly resolute towards her and the real cause of our suffering lies elsewhere?

Johanne's comment about the master walking with Nessie in the orchard flickers into life, a vivid picture that I cannot shake away. A sense of secrets swelling, kept against me, secrets that cannot be unburdened but loom as large as clouds, filling the air we breathe. Johanne turns her face away from me with another loud 'Huh!' A signal to me to leave her be.

Outside a cockerel crows and the bells – the bells that Jane complains of – start their peal and remind me that I have duties in the kitchen. Fish to prepare and other children to soothe. Johanne is right on one thing: the household has not been happy since we arrived here. But were things better in our old manor cottage at Brampton, or just better hidden? This is a bigger house, with more spacious chambers, and it seems that some light or air has been let in. In Brampton Dottie used to speak of 'bad odour' between Mistress and Master. She was forever trying to prise open the drawers and unlock the boxes where secrets lived, but . . .

The locks remain fastened. Let me not delve further. I pray to God that Alice Samuel might be brought soon to confess, and with her confession our miseries and confusions might end.

In the night I am awoken by Dottie shoving me. She says she has heard a cry above, and pushes me, calling me as deaf as a white cat, and insisting, 'The children need you, Martha.' One of the children, in their chamber upstairs. I hurry from my bed and creak up the stairs, the warmth from the fire still in the air, letting me know it must only be about midnight and I've not been long in bed. At the top of the stair I stop, and so does my heart. A figure. Slender. A girl – it might be Johanne, but she seems thinner and older. Dark, with long hair sweeping her shoulders, and big dark eyes, in a red cloak or dress. She is mostly in shadow. I take a step towards her, uncertain. Is she coming down to the kitchen to ask for a drink of milk? Perhaps even walking in her sleep?

'Mistress . . . Johanne?' I whisper. And suddenly she is on me – just like a cat – pulling me, grabbing me, dark hands scratching and clawing at me, tugging me towards her, trying to topple me down the stairs. I know she wants to kill me, suck all the life from me, and my terror flares but so does my fighting spirit and before I know it I am screaming, and tearing back at her, aiming for her face, her hands, clawing the way that Jane clawed at Alice and blood springs out on her skin and I see it black and wet in darkness on my hands and under my nails, but she is gripping me, firm and hard, shaking me, by the shoulder, shaking me marvellous fierce, her hands digging into my skin.

'Martha, Martha! Wake up!'

Hah!

Dottie is beside me on the straw mattress, tugging at my arm. A nightmare. She did not send me upstairs: that was part of the dream. *She* – Alice – must have sent me a nightmare, as she did Lady Cromwell. Lady Cromwell who is now so sick and taken to her bed. But who attacked me in my dream? I put my hand to my chest and feel my heart racing, as if a thousand footsteps patter there.

172

If only I had seen her face properly. The eyes were . . . familiar. My breathing – like the panting of a dog – becomes quieter and Dottie turns on her side on the mattress beside me, wafting up a smell of sleep and sweat, making hard speeches and cursing me for disturbing her.

So. The witch has let me know. She intends to hurt *me*, too. Was it Alice Samuel, taking her daughter's comelier form? But why did I think it Johanne at first? I must put some scissors under my bed so that she cannot reach me here again. But this is a warning. A witch bottle might not do it. A shudder runs through me. I had thought myself beloved until now. My arrival in the world was blessed. God had looked out for me, bringing me safe to Sister Dorothy, and finding me this post with the family. Why would He desert me? Some evil wishing, some curse has reached me.

Perhaps it was the day, that day when I had the dream about the master, and seemed to know something or understand something.

No. It was not that day. It could not be that.

I lie back down and try to return to sleep. A hard night ahead. A night of tossing, like being in the cradle of a boat.

And in the morning I discover that poor Bessie has been in her fits in the small hours – fits I did not attend – and surely Alice Samuel sent those too, and hopes to afflict the whole family.

The scholars are back: Thomas Cakebread with hair that reminds me of a straw bear or a corn dolly, young Henry and his books, and another friend, Edward Harkening, with a barrel chest, huge hands and a habit of nodding away, agreeing with everything Henry says. They have heard of Lady

Cromwell's suffering. They are certain sure now it will go to trial.

'Isn't Sir Henry a Justice of the Peace? And he has the ear of the Queen.' Young Henry is a little breathless at the thought of a trial – he speaks of little else. He is disappointed that my master is keener on a quieter route: the Reverend Doctor Dorrington bringing the witches to confession and local justice being served.

'Won't you take your arguments to the White Hart and get out from under our feet?' my mistress says to her brother. Bessie presents herself, ever helpful, with copies of papers and books they ask for, or fresh tankards. Thomas flashes her a smile here and there, blushing as he does so. He is unable to keep from glancing at her. Poor Johanne who as eldest had surely believed herself the likeliest daughter to catch his interest has fallen into further misery, as it is evident where his attention lies. Since being back at home Bessie with her curls and her curiosity, her liveliness and love of learning, has recovered some roses in her cheeks though she is still much thinner than before.

'Now that Lady Cromwell has accused her, they have to take it seriously,' Henry says, to his friend Edward.

'Oh, my testimony and my sisters' count for nothing?' Bessie tosses her hair, presumably trying to make her remark sound playful.

Thomas is not fooled. 'Of course your testimonies count! Most of the trials I've been to have brave children as the accusers, but children do not have the means to bring a case to the attention of Sir Henry.'

I leave them then, still in their excited speeches, on an errand to fetch duck eggs from the pond (an errand I fear, imagining the angry John Samuel might appear, and contest the master's fishing and eel rights, although all must know they were granted by Sir Henry). I walk fast, from the house down the high street past the mill, a ten-minute walk, no more, thinking of the eggs to be gathered, the floors to be swept and whether Popsie remembered to put a stone over the henhouse last night – might the fox have got in? A million tasks at the house; the scholars eat like field hands and make much work for us.

Soon I arrive at the pond's green edge, marvelling how the water at this time of year is so clear and teems and swarms with eels, snakes and fish. My eyes catch sight of a pretty ripple, a silver arrow showing the path of a fish, and then a bird flits in front of me landing on a fine green blade. A reed warbler, swaying the grass to and fro, like a child swinging on a wooden gate.

And as I'm watching it, Alice appears from the door of a house opposite the pond. The house of Anne Burder who, like Alice, brews ale and bakes rye bread. Alice is carrying a tankard, probably with the barm in it. She spies me and I, remembering the ill spirits in which she left our house a few days ago, do not know how to greet her. But a 'Well met, Mother Samuel' escapes me just the same. She grunts something and makes her way towards the pond.

And then from up the high street, near the White Hart, the three young scholars appear. They have taken the mistress's advice and are about to pass some time there, but now, recognising Alice, Henry changes his mind at once and strides over towards us at the pond. His friends follow him, two paces behind.

The reed warbler flies off. Alice stops for a moment, uncertain, and regards the three Cambridge men: well dressed, black hats, their approach determined. I hesitate, too, and freeze where I stand, my basket of eggs over my arm.

Alice draws in her head against her chest, cradling the tankard she carries, intending, I am sure, simply to pass the scholars and continue along the high street with no greeting.

I am slightly hidden behind the tall reeds, unsure whether Henry and his friends have spied me. A dragonfly, glinting blue, flits past my face. Circles appear in the pond, as if it is brimful and unable to settle.

'Here we are again. Stop here! I wish to talk to you.'

Henry. He does not bother to address her politely, so she stops, a little distance from the men, glances once over her shoulder at me, and sighs.

'Good day, Mother Samuel,' Thomas Cakebread says.

'You can see I'm busy. Say your piece and get away with you.'

'You know exactly what I'm here for.' Henry is hopping from foot to foot, his hands dancing a little at his sides. The early summer day is a warm one, blossom fluttering to the ground, like pale fingertips, the light clean and casting shadows. Soon some men have come out of the White Hart to position themselves on a wooden bench, as if to watch a puppet show.

Poor Thomas has the grace to look shamed. The other fellow, Edward, throws his legs wide, standing like a soldier at Henry's side.

I feel ready to walk past, back to the house, certain the mistress has need of me, but Henry stops me, with a gesture, addressing me and the two witnesses at the alehouse: 'How do, all our good friends. You know that Mother Samuel here is accused of making the Throckmorton children

suffer, and as they are my nieces, it is my solemn duty to . . .'
Here he looks about him at the company: at me and the two
old fellows on the bench, as if we were a grand jury, but he
doesn't finish whatever fine speech he is about to make as
Alice cuts in: '*Children!* They misuse me with their
wantonness.'

Henry, his colour very high, takes a step towards Alice. 'You
accuse the children? Innocent girls, of not telling the truth?'

'I do! And the master of the house, too! If they were my
children, I'd give them what-for.'

'You are shouting! Keep a woman's virtue and lower your
voice.'

'A woman's virtue? I was born in a mill, begot in a kiln – let
me past, you stupid man.'

Henry's two friends move as if to restrain her, but Thomas
lets his arms drop to his sides and instead puts a hand on
Henry's shoulder. I begin walking. I see that the men are not
willing to touch her, and they allow her to brush past them. I
must go home. I do not want to witness more.

'You nasty woman!' Henry shouts. 'You'll pay!'

My heart has quickened and lodges itself in my throat. I am
afraid, afraid for Alice, and I do not understand my feelings.
She is not my mother or aunt or godly neighbour. She *is* a
nasty woman who doesn't know how to hold her tongue. How
does my heart feel Christian pity towards her, one old and
wicked such as she?

They are now some distance from where I stand, all four of
them hurrying down the high street past the alehouse. I follow
them, nursing to myself my confusion, a few steps behind.

Alice turns back to the men, shouting, 'My God will deliver
me, my God will defend me!'

'Your God? *Your* God? Which God do you serve, then, Alice Samuel?' Henry shouts.

'The God of Heaven and Earth,' she snaps back, marching as fast as her twig-like legs will allow.

In a voice that the gaggle of drinkers – indeed the whole of Warboys – might hear and note keenly, he says: 'The vengeance of the Lord will find you, even in death. I'll see you burned at the stake.'

This time Alice lets out a sound: a sort of scream or whimper. Surely, surely Alice will be cowed now, run for her home, for her husband, run to escape them.

'I'll douse you head to toe in that pond if you come near me!' is Alice's reply.

Her figure – the black woollen cap that the girls had mocked, her cloak with its grey tassels, her solid backside, which does not wobble as she walks but looks as if it were carved out of hardened wood – elicits laughter from onlookers, astonished at her rudeness or daring.

Anne Burder and Master Whittle open their front doors. Tom Dibbert, a fisherman who works alongside Alice's husband, shakes his head at her, and at me as I pass him.

Henry is speechless. The colour flames in his face. His hair seems to stand on end, like a lit torch. The village folds its arms, widens its doors and waits for the next act in this theatre play.

It comes with an explosion from Henry. He lets Alice pass, then turns on his heel, screaming after her departing figure, 'You ugly old hag! I'll bring the wood myself for the fire!'

I put my head down and hurry farther from the scene. Behind me I'm aware of a commotion: Henry no longer sounding like a scholar, or even a man, but like a boy, mad with rage and humiliation, all dignity fled.

Now more people emerge from houses, opening doors and shutters to see what the noise might be. Florrie Caterill, daughter of Mother Caterill, appears, staring openly.

'Go your way home, Alice!' cries one, not unsympathetic.

'The children will blow the coals!' Henry screeches.

I glance back as Mistress Audley, a do-gooding sober wife, steps out of her front door and makes a move towards Alice, as if to advise her. Alice shrugs herself away, pausing for a moment to acknowledge her neighbours' stares. I glance once behind me and hurry on. The danger and the scorn intended for Alice are now sweeping me into their net. If I say nothing, perhaps people will mistake me for a friend. The whole of Warboys heard Henry's declaration. Until now accusations against Alice were made by Doctor Dorrington, or the girls themselves, and only the family and we servants knew it. Even Lady Cromwell had only accused her *inside* Warboys Manor. All at home. Now this is buzzing in the open, like bees swarming.

As I reach the house, I am panting. I feel tears rising and a wish not to go inside right away but to stay out here awhile, calm myself, so I sit down on a seat in the churchyard next to the house, placing my basket of eggs beside me, the better to catch my breath. And there I am sitting as Alice approaches, muttering, 'That family. Those girls. If they were mine they'd be given a beating!'

She has come right up to me and stands crossly staring, as if expecting me to reply, still clutching the tankard from her errand. Her shape now reminds me of a robin: fat body above, thin legs below. And angry, as a robin often is.

'My God will protect me,' she says, as if I had spoken.

'Why, Mother Samuel, I—'

'My God will defend me and take revenge on my enemies.'

The strange words rattle around me. I put my hand protectively over the duck eggs. I have not, until now, been alone with her or so close, and I do not know what she thinks of me: does she judge me her friend or enemy? Indeed, which am I? She seems to be watching my face for understanding, remembering perhaps that I don't always hear well. We gaze into each other's eyes and I have time only to note that hers are green in this light, whereas I'd thought them grey. Her expression is so fierce, so furious, so – *searching*. Words flee from me.

After a long minute, Alice says something more. I fail to catch it, so she says, louder, 'You want to try the gall of a hare, heated in a pan and melted down. You make a wax and clean the ears.'

'A hare!' It slips out. Alice sees her mistake and harrumphs.

'Keep your ears stuffed, then. It suits you to hear nothing in that naughty house, I can see that.'

She stamps away from my bench and, opening the wooden gate, heads towards her own house, banging the door behind her.

She lifted the words from my tongue. The very air around my bench seems to crackle as she leaves. There is a movement in a nearby sycamore tree. I let out a scream as something shadowy – a small form – leaps from it, and thuds to the ground.

I jump up, my heart thrashing.

'Hob! You will break your leg, jumping like that!' I scold.

He has been hiding in the tree. He runs inside the house, laughing and screeching, while I stand with my hand at my breast, trying to still my hammering heart.

She has ill-wished me, I think. I should have spoken out, defended her. A poor old woman against three learned men. Against the whole of Warboys. And I said nothing.

I look for a witch-guard, a stone with a hole in it, lying around the churchyard. I have one in the house, perhaps in the pocket of an apron. I must look for it. But I fear it is of no use. Nothing will save me. No good will come to me now. A witch has damned me and threatened me. I am cursed.

The house feels in an uproar. The scholars have returned and young Henry is booming, Thomas placating, and the kitchen, too, is all in upheaval – feathers flying from one end to the other from the plucking of a duck that arrived before my return from the pond – about Alice and her uncouth tongue and how it is time now, time to bring her to heel. Strangest of all, my master appears, with an expression of grave terror, tugging on my arm, wanting to take me aside.

He is very close, so close that I can see the sweat resting on his forehead, the new grey hairs in his beard.

'I saw you talking to her in the churchyard. What did she say to you?'

'Oh, it was – she was very angry. About the young scholars. She said God would protect her.'

'That's all?' My master has arranged to find a quiet space, between scullery and kitchen, where only mice scuttle on the floor, leaving their black droppings in corners for me to sweep every morning. He peers at me, his eyes betraying something hard for me to understand. Why does he care what Alice said to me?

'She said – she offered me a cure for deafness.'

'A cure? A witch's remedy?'

'No! It was a well-known cure, no more. She also said – God will take revenge on her enemies.'

I do not want to be the one to damn her with the mention of a hare, and I do not understand my reluctance, but there it is. I put my hands up to my face, expecting my master to comfort me in some way, to reassure me that the ill-wishing of a bitter old woman will not constitute a great terror, that God will protect us in this house, but he does not. My mistress is right: his fear of witches is deep and grave.

'She didn't say anything – about me?' he asks, in a voice very quiet, so quiet that I need to read his lips to be sure of what he says.

'No, no, your name was never mentioned!'

Since our walk together in Cambridge, I have longed for my master to share his intimate thoughts with me. But now I feel a welling of great fear. He is not reassuring. He is not the master of the house. My womanly nature makes me yearn to relieve him of his burden by admitting the same vulnerability. But I must tread carefully. I offer: 'I did feel some *fear* that Alice had . . . found me out in some way, some weakness or badness. That she had . . .' I struggle now, unaccustomed to confiding '. . . looked into my secret heart and found me wanting.'

'Yes!' Here he lets go my arm, taking a step back. 'Yes! Looking into your secret heart.'

I think he is about to say more, but he checks himself. 'Well, that's foolish, isn't it? Only God is the searcher of our hearts, not a witch. We are mistaken, both of us, as to the powers of Alice Samuel.' He is recovering himself. He brushes the front of his doublet, tugging it sharply, as if to straighten himself, offer himself some stronger support.

'Doctor Dorrington will deal with Alice. I have asked him. Better to keep things quiet. My wife's brother is thinking only of his university career, his reputation. The Church position he will one day hold. He would love to be part of a local witch trial. To write the account of it.' He permits himself a smile, takes a deep breath. 'But we – the family – we only want for the girls to be well again. And for the villagers to think favourably of us. The quickest way for that to happen will surely be for Mother Samuel to confess in public, be sorry, and for us then to forget these terrible months and continue in all neighbourliness.'

Continue in all neighbourliness. Hard to imagine how that might be achieved. But my master's speeches are now loud, as if for others to hear. The wild eyes of a moment ago are gone. I find myself standing alone, while he sweeps back to the parlour where the heated discussion with the scholars is taking place.

I stand very still, alone, closing my eyes. I do not know what he tried to ask me, or what he confessed.

A fear of Alice. A fear that she knows something about us? About *him*? I conjure again the searching glance Alice gave me in the churchyard, trying to summon her words. *My God will avenge me.* I feel for the witch-stone held in the pocket of my apron, and close my fingers around it.

The next day Mother Caterill arrives from her home in Warboys, and before she has put her basket on the tabletop, utters, 'Well, Alice is to confess, then.'

The church bells peal: Sunday. Dottie has already been out to milk the cow and is now churning butter in the shed out at the back, while I seem to run about between children and scholars demanding milk and butter pudding for breakfast. Snatches of conversation are all we can manage but, breathless, I do ask, 'How was Alice persuaded? She said she never would be!'

Mother Caterill sucks on an old pipe and begins unloading the linen in her basket: rhubarb, great fat sticks of it. 'The old vicar begged her, I suppose. They say that now Lady Cromwell is striving it would be better to make amends. From what Dottie said before, I doubt Lady Cromwell is a forgiving woman.'

'I didn't think Alice too concerned last time.' Dottie laughs, returning, pink-cheeked, to the kitchen, and no doubt remembering Alice's rude words.

This morning a quick scurry to their bedchamber reveals all the girls to be fine and healthy, none in their fits, though of course Johanne is as sullen as ever and Bessie still sadly thin, refusing breakfast and dreadful quiet. Fetching bonnets and boots, I hear Johanne saying to her uncle Henry that Mother Samuel keeps her chickens as imps and she'd seen her feed them blood from her own chin. These days Johanne enjoys a special closeness with her uncle and takes every opportunity to enchant him further. Young Henry is taking notes. He is writing a pamphlet, he says. He will ask his brother Gilbert to endorse it, and it will be a most strange and admirable discovery of witches.

'There is also a *Thing*,' Johanne adds. 'It skips and plays up and down, and runs beside her.'

I move away, shuddering at the mention of the chickens now as imps (first toads and mice, then cats and chickens – what next?) and seeing them in my mind: pinky-gold from early sunrise, nodding and trotting at the feet of Alice, while she scatters seeds at them, becking their heads in mimicry of her. I had barely slept from my restless thoughts about what my encounter in the churchyard with Alice meant and, further, my conversation with the master, a conversation full of unsaid things. It was curious to be reminded by my mistress of the master's great terror of witchcraft, and her hint that it was of a different hue or more sweeping than the dread that all God-fearing people feel. Was that time of great shame about the Throckmorton name, the execution of his cousin, still holding him in its clasp? Or were the afflictions of the daughters, his wife's unhappiness, or other tribulations shaking loose his reason?

No, I must not consider my master to be losing his reason. The thought is wrong and disloyal.

A peculiar dream had come to me in the night. In it my beloved Gabriel was returned to a little blond boy, capering and smiling and saying, 'Not today!' in the sweetest little singsong voice, like the angel he was named for, and then with light flowing all around him and pointing, he turned grave and said, in his deep grown-up voice, 'Martha, men *show* themselves. They do not change course.' But the dream was all mixed up with the green vipers raising their heads and the little jars of vipers' gloss and the drowned lands with horses tumbling into them. When I woke I felt shaky inside as if something was growing horrible large inside my breast.

The bells at the church next door are clanging loud – could it be such a short time, eighteen months, since we were living in Brampton with the bells pealing like this to celebrate the ditching of the Armada? It feels so long ago. Then the *dong, dong* had a happy sound, gathering us all in its embrace, but now the peal sounds thunderous, calling the whole of Warboys

185

to witness the confession of Alice Samuel. Oh, that I could stay at home! I sigh and go upstairs to find the children.

For once they do not seem unhappy with more churching, just ill prepared. We rush to seek their collar cuffs, some hose for Hob, his favourite felt hat, a doublet, a cloak, then a chemise, a bodie and bonnet, clean apron and wool stockings for Jane. The bedchamber looks as if a pirate has ransacked it. Only Mary helps, in her kind and mature fashion. Johanne and Bessie are already downstairs with their uncle and his friends. There is an excited air, as if we were on our way to Sturbridge Fair, not next door to church.

I do my best to make the little ones presentable, and my mistress sweeps in and nods and says, 'Will she really come? They must have threatened something – I cannot believe it would be her own choice.'

I glance at her in surprise. Openly expressing some pity for Alice. Some doubt. And yet everyone else – the scholars, the children, the vicar, the servants, even the master – is sure that she's a witch and deserves no such pity. All the learned ones, who know about such things. We are ignorant and sentimental. Perhaps we are under Alice's spell. Perhaps, as women, we have weak intellects to feel any hint of sympathy towards a woman who has made friends with the devil himself. Something flashes back to me then. Something that Master Gilbert Pickering said in that fearful encounter, reading from his great books to me. Women are more credulous, more impressionable, and they have slippery tongues. 'A woman either loves or hates. There is no third grade.' Well, it is certain sure that Alice has a talent for hating. Pity that she spoke with great passion to her enemy Lady Cromwell. If she could hold her tongue, she would not be in trouble now.

The family troop into the garden and stand a moment under the trees in the orchard, where blossom sprinkles the ground and the fruit is showing. There will be work in great plenty later, picking apples and medlars for jellies and jams and pickles. There is the feeling of a party, a curious air as if all the flowers and fruits are putting on their finest show, something playful, a festival, laid out in front of us, instead of what it really is: the day an old witch is brought to confession.

Crabbie, too, stands on the path, doing his little dance, his shoulders twitching every five minutes, bursting to shout something lewd. Perhaps the master will succeed in keeping him out of church today, sending him to tend the horses, to calm him. Although we know there is a halfpenny fine these days for non-attendance at church, so the master might think better of that idea.

I glance down the garden path towards the road and see that people are arriving, a stream of thrumbed bonnets, black jackets and frocks appearing between the yew trees, children running and leaping beside them.

This dread is in my stomach, as if a stone is lodged there. Alice is nothing to me! I should be glad that a witch be brought to confession, her witchcraft quenched, and any glamour she'd applied to any of us should now be lifted. I long to shake the picture in my mind of Alice's eyes, sudden deep green, young and pretty in her old face, and their fear, their questions, the way her gaze sought mine.

I peek at my mistress to see if she shares my misgivings and I'm shocked at the look she shoots me. She quickly stares back at the ground, her hair falling to hide her face. If you had not known the happiness of her life – seven living children and a handsome, well-appointed husband – you might feel a dread

187

certainty that she is without hope or joy: that her life is bleak despair.

The time comes to go next door to the church of Saint Mary Magdalene. The light, falling on its stumpy spire, seems clean and fresh – may some good come of it. All is poised: the very stones in the graveyard, laced with their lichen and bindweed, leaning in a little, as if listening, as if waiting. I cross myself, a tiny gesture, hidden, that none must see.

I sit beside the youngest children: Grace and Hob to my left, Mary and Jane to the right of me. Johanne and Bessie sit in the row in front of us, with their parents and the three scholars – the front row, as befits the squire and his family. Behind me are the servants: Dottie, Popsie, Mother Caterill, her daughter Florrie and Crabbie. Crabbie arrives with a woman, who must be his mother, thin and stripped of flesh, like a wishbone.

Outside a cockerel crows and a dog barks and I fix my attention on the stone pillars inside the church, on the roses and fleur-de-lis on the ancient stone font that so many children will have been baptised in, dust motes dancing above it. Years ago we would have sprinkled the children with holy water to cure them – Crabbie, too, for his afflictions. The vicar's smallpox must surely have been treated in such a way, or else how had he survived it, with only his pockmarked skin to show for it? I'm sure Sister Dorothy would have suggested it, and perhaps, once upon a time, we might have more openly sought help for the girls from cunning women, the old wives' wisdom we once thought to ask of Alice. I shudder to remember. We know all that is forbidden now, along with crossing ourselves, prayers to the Virgin, candles lit for saints and all the other

188

popish ways. We fear forgetting ourselves and slipping, as the mistress and I did at first over Jane. It is fortunate that only the master knew of it: we might have been accused of the same evil doings as Alice.

The wooden eagle hovers on the lectern on the brink of striking. I dare not catch the eye of any villagers, or look back towards the door. Hob is fidgeting; I put a hand on his to try to still him. The church has filled. Seems like the whole of Warboys is crammed into the little space, villagers trying to lower their heads and look pious.

The shift in movement, the noise and shufflings from the congregation, tell me the Samuel family is arriving. The pews fall deathly silent, heads are bowed in prayer, eyes peeping from between fingers. I permit myself to turn my head just once and see Alice, her husband John and her daughter, taking up a place near the back of the nave. My heart starts to drum fast, like anxious fingers upon a table. *She'll never confess.* And then: *Alice – don't say a word!*

I don't know where such thoughts come from. Sedition and witchery! I reach for Grace's hand, as if to comfort her but the better to steady myself. In front of me, Johanne leans back to say, 'I hope I never reach that horrible age!' She seeks my agreement.

'She's not so old,' I whisper back, then sit more upright in my pew. I know how girls dread age, of the ways bodies will wither. I notice that Henry is watching Johanne closely. He always seems to resent her great familiarity with me, a servant, and shoots us a look of disapproval.

Johanne sits back then, her arms folded across her chest.

'Ugly old witch!' shouts Crabbie, and several of the congregation titter, while the skinny wishbone mother puts a firm hand over his mouth. Thomas Cakebread permits himself a fleeting smile, then bows his head. There is movement and disturbance – surely this shout was overheard by Alice and her family? I look around: the husband's expression says he is ready to punch the first person to say it to his face.

Someone is knocking on the door of the church, which is jammed. I picture the black polished lion's head on the door knocker, angry at being rapped so hard. Doctor Dorrington nods and says something to his verger to go to it. The door opens with a burst and all crane their heads to look.

Cicely Burder, the young friend of Nessie. A terrified-looking girl, face scrubbed and eyes wide, but here defiant: breathless and determined to enter, seemingly too small to have made such a big noise. She scurries to a seat at the back, her face flushed but her head held high. The three scholars watch her keenly.

'Let us pray!'

All eyes turn to Doctor Dorrington, at the altar in his robes and booming out his text of repentance to comfort the sinner. We all beck our heads, hushing. I touch Hob's to make him do the same.

I put my palms together, breathing in their dust and fire smell, remembering then that I had not washed my hands before coming. I am worrying about Hob's leg in his black boot banging softly back and forth against the pew, not paying attention to the hearty prayer to God that the vicar is making, his loud speeches of great terror. 'If any witch will confess her ill-wishing and the harms she has brought, our Heavenly Father will forgive her and the joys of Heaven await her, once she has . . .'

Hob shifts suddenly, craning his head towards the rows behind him. I become aware that everyone seems to be responding to something, some sound, perhaps. The scholars are looking back towards the congregation. Thomas Cakebread has a distraught look in his eyes. I do not understand: what is everyone hearing that I am not?

'Mother Samuel is weeping.' Mary leans in to tell me.

It pinches my heart to discover it. I press my face inside my hands to stem my own tears, pretending to be praying harder still. I feel Mary's anxious eyes on me. I somehow can tell from the shoulders of my mistress in the row in front that her heart is stricken too.

Heads are turning. Johanne twists back to look. I glance back just once. Alice sits weeping beside her husband (stony-faced and staring ahead). Her daughter is on the other side, her expression defiant, not daring to comfort her mother but holding her hand tightly.

Doctor Dorrington claps his hands. 'Let us all rise and pray. Repeat after me: " Our Father, who art in Heaven . . . "'

There is the noise of pews scraping the floor, bibles being dropped and outside the dog barking again, and the people of Warboys begin to mumble the Lord's Prayer, with the voice of Henry Pickering the loudest, strong and confident, rising like a wave. It is the only prayer we all know. The one they say a witch can never utter without faltering.

Voices lift in a rumble: 'Thy kingdom come, thy will be done . . .'

But when we sit again in quiet, I risk another glance back at Alice, in the rows behind, and see a terrible thing. She has a large handkerchief up to her face, spattered clearly with blood. A nosebleed. Her daughter is fussing her, trying to get her to tip her head back, but Alice is pushing her help away, sobbing and hiccuping. Still the proud John Samuel stares ahead, defying us all to pity him.

The vicar looks angry. The people are turning and fidgeting. The three young men in the front row have their heads together, discussing something, so the vicar loudly claps his hands again and nods to his verger to bring him a folded sheet of white linen. We all know what this is.

'Come forward – Alice Samuel,' Master Dorrington booms, and the church sizzles and silences as if a hundred candles had been doused at once.

Alice stands up. She wipes again at her nose and, folding the handkerchief, puts it into her jacket. There is a smear of blood from nose to cheek, which gives her a ghoulish look, like one of the masks the children make at All Hallows. Her sobbing subsides into one long shuddering – a womanly sound, loud and ungodly in this place. I turn my face away from her towards the vicar at the altar, and bid Hob and Grace to do the same. The three young men have ceased their chatter, and turn to watch Alice.

The tick of Alice's boots on the stone floor of the church, like nails knocking into a coffin.

When she passes our row, little Grace grabs my hand. Alice's nose flows still, the odd stream of blood. She rubs it afresh with the handkerchief. The verger approaches her. He is a small man, a little like a weasel with his long bent neck. He opens out the sheet of white linen and a white wand and Alice, expressionless, takes both. She knows what to do. She envelops herself in the sheet – red spots immediately stain it where they fall from her nose. She seems not to care. She takes hold of the wand. We can all see her hands trembling.

It is as if the whole place breathes as one, holding its breath.

'Now, Alice, say after me, in front of the whole congregation: I acknowledge my sin unto Thee, O Lord, and mine iniquity I have not hid.'

There is a little cough from somewhere. A girlish cough. Cicely Burder?

Then Alice's voice, as harsh and angry as ever, repeating the reverend's words. '. . . and mine iniquity I have not hid,' she states gruffly.

Hard to detect repentance in her tones. I would say, if I dared, defiance. For a moment I think I see my mistress's shoulders shaking. And Henry seems outraged. Is Thomas Cakebread stifling laughter?

'I will confess my transgression unto the Lord, and beg forgiveness for the iniquity of my sin . . .'

Here Alice blurts a huge gasping sob so loud that several people jump.

'Transgression!' bellows Crabbie, leaping in his seat. His mother hushes him. Thomas Cakebread laughs aloud this time, then quickly claps a hand to his mouth.

Now Alice falls to lamentation. Her shoulders shaking, so many sundry emotions passing over her, she can barely repeat the words, her weeping growing louder beneath the white sheet. The vicar does not spare her, but reads the lines from Psalms again and asks her to face us all as she says it, to make her confession and repentance to the villagers, not just to the Throckmorton family. All her neighbours, and all her friends, need to know of her great wickedness and that she repents.

The bloodied sheet around her trembles, as Alice stumbles out her confession and begs the Lord and the congregation's forgiveness. 'Poor old lady,' Grace mouths to me. She begins quietly crying, too, and puts her head against my shoulder. Hob drops his bottom lip in wonder, kicking his legs against the pew. I feel fresh tears welling but have to stifle them, for fear others – the vicar, the family, the scholars – might take me for an accomplice. But I wonder if others feel some sympathy as I do. I felt sure moments ago that the mistress did. Mother Caterill? She has expressed some sympathy for Alice before now. Cicely is friend to daughter Nessie. Wasn't it Mistress Audrey who tried to give Alice good counsel, that day outside when the scholars chased her, near the White Hart tavern? But now, all of them, like me, fear the word attaching to us, too. Henry is nodding grimly throughout, but I am sure that Thomas with the straw-bear hair and easy laughing way holds a different view.

At last – *at last* – it is over.

People stand up, begin filing out. Alice walks back towards her seat, against the crowd. Not one person moves towards her or her family, the daughter and husband who remain seated. No friend says hello. They do not meet her eyes. Why must we shun what God has planted in our hearts: human sympathy? Because she is in league with the devil, comes back my answer. I try to accept it. I hesitate, standing behind the Throckmorton family, as Dottie and the other servants join me in shuffling towards the door. I hold Grace's hand on one side, Hob's on the other. Mary, concerned for me, keeps her eyes fixed on my face and I feel there would be a danger in letting my feelings of sympathy show. But I cannot help looking back, my eyes seeking Alice, sitting with bowed head, between husband and daughter, the penitent's sheet crumpled and stained on the pew beside her. I see the husband reach out his hand, and stroke his wife's face. They – everyone – say he is a brutish man. Solid as a bulldog and as violent. But I see something else. This gesture towards his wife.

The wood pigeon calls in its soft, lonely way, high in the grand yews of the churchyard.

I cry aloud with my voice, all praise be to the glorious God, reply the bells.

***

For Alice, the church is a terrible place. Scene of all her undoing, so many years ago. The creaking of the church door opening. Sudden cold light. Two boys, not much older than her sixteen years, rushing at her. They were still bedecked in ribbons and alleygags so that she couldn't recognise them: their faces were smeared with soot in disguise. She had gasped as the boys rushed at her and almost said something, some kind of greeting – 'Hello, well met' – but the words didn't have a chance to bloom. Then the third appeared.

This was the moment when she felt herself to be tossed on a coin, flung towards her terrible future.

***

The kitchen that evening is neither gay nor festive. We should feel relieved that the witch has confessed and the evil will now be at an end. But instead there is an intense feeling, a shame descending. We can none of us look at one another. The kitchen is hot because Dottie forgets to open the door. We are trapped as if in an oven or the fires of Hell. No one wants to speak first. Grace wanders in and buries her face in my skirts. After moments of her tugging I cease my striving at the stove and look down properly at her. Her face is wet with tears.

'Grace!'

'Her nose was bleeding!' Grace cries. She reaches for my hand.

Dottie turns from a pot she is tending. 'That was the devil leaving her. I heard her say: "Oh, sir, I have been the cause of all this trouble to your children! Good master, forgive me!"'

'When . . . when was this?' I ask.

Dottie sets her mouth.

Mother Caterill stirs herself, handing Dottie the pig bucket to take out to Bertha. 'It was wrested and wrung from her. What kind of confession is that?'

'Come to the bedchamber,' Grace whispers, pulling me down to her level to hear her, and taking my hand, she leads me from the kitchen upstairs to the children's room.

'They're writing it down and forgiving her. The master is forgiving her! I would not forgive an old hag for bewitching *my* children!' Dottie continues in her hard speeches while we walk upstairs. Dottie has such a heavy tread that I feel the vibration throughout my body, as if she wishes to hammer home her words. No one could doubt her sincere hatred for all the witches throughout the land.

In the bedchamber the children are huddled on the bed, the curtains half drawn around them, and many candles lit.

'Johanne is not well,' Grace says.

I step forward. 'Should I call your mother?'

Bessie says, 'Oh, don't trouble Mother! She is so anxious these days. Tarry with us, Martha. The fits will pass if we sit beside her and stroke her. I can't understand why she has them still now that Mother Samuel has confessed.'

Johanne's eyes are glassy in the candlelight. I see that the younger girls are huddling around her, trying to keep her calm; she is not fully in her fits, only beginning to jerk a little, like a puppet with strings jerked. Grace is crying, hiding a little behind my skirts, afraid to look at Johanne.

'We're all going to die,' Grace says to me. Mary sits the other side of her sister, quietly reading her words from the Bible.

Johanne's arm shoots up, stiff, as if wooden, and Mary falls silent at once. Johanne's finger points in front of her: 'There goes a green gown . . . I marvel how it goes alone.'

As she speaks, the candles gutter and the girls gasp. I do for a moment see it there, a long green dress, and there can be no doubt who wears a gown of such a colour: *Nessie*.

Mary, in fright, tries to lower her sister's arm, pulling on it.

'Now the mother has called off her imps, she sends *the daughter* to harm us!' Johanne says, in a low voice. 'The girl has a bat, a little foxy-faced bat, with folded wings, called . . . Patch.'

The girls are whimpering, and the door bursts open, as the three scholars enter the chamber without ceremony. Henry stares at Johanne and then at each girl in turn. He was clearly looking for the mistress, his sister.

'She is downstairs,' I tell him.

Henry flourishes a letter. 'Where is your father? There is news! Lady Cromwell is dead!'

Johanne drops to one side, like a nine-pin falling, almost tumbling from the bed, and Bessie leaps up, pulls the curtain around her sister and ushers the young men from the room.

'She blamed Alice Samuel right up to the end. It is now a hanging matter,' Henry says gravely to his friends.

I'll bring the wood myself for the fire! Henry's words, that day by the pond.

In Europe they burn witches at the stake. Not here. But perhaps it's only a matter of time.

Part Three

The Discovery

They arrest her a few days later. I'm at the well, pumping the handle, the bucket splashing and knocking, and I see men shouting at the door of her little cottage, but I cannot hear what is being said. Two constables with their black hats are thumping on the door, which is flung open. John Samuel appears, and has to be restrained by one of them. They venture into the house and drag out Alice and her daughter, weeping and clinging to her mother. Nessie is pushed back inside the house, John Samuel too, no doubt threatened with arrest. Then the men march down the road, Alice stumbling between them, like a doll, and then they are gone. I hurry to the kitchen to find out who knows what.

Mother Caterill carries a heavy porringer to the kitchen table and, for once, does not hold her tongue. 'They've treated her like a mule! As if she had a sign on her back: "Kick me!"'

I stare from her to Dottie, busy with the morning tasks, preparing some soldier's tea from horehound for the mistress. Dottie is not perturbed. She turns angrily to Mother Caterill, the great bulk of her as solid as any bull in the field when challenged.

'Now we might have peace. Did she really think she could curse Lady Cromwell and cause her to suffer so, and that lady would not go straight to her husband, as promised, and weigh the matter?'

'What will happen to her?' I had not noticed Grace creep into the kitchen. She shadows me these days, clinging to my skirts.

'You're to join the mistress in Ramsey. They need help with the funeral,' Mother Caterill instructs. This is me. It is me who is to go. Grace begins weeping again.

'Don't leave us, Martha! If Mother Samuel has sent her imps to kill that grand lady, won't she do the same to me and to Jane and to—'

I squat to her small form and sweep the hair from her eyes, smoothing her forehead. 'I won't be gone long, my love. Fetch Hob so I can cuddle him. I need to tell Crabbie to ready the horses.'

My master wishes to speak with me before we leave for Ramsey. It is as before: he seems much grieved, not relieved at all.

'The red-haired Samuel girl,' he asks, 'what do you think of her, Martha?'

'Nessie? I know no more than anyone.' We are outside, under the apple trees, bees buzzing and damp blossom under our feet. The truth is, I have grown tired of his need to seek my counsel yet withhold his private thoughts. I do not know what it is I am supposed to say, how I can offer comfort if I don't know for what.

'Does she – did either of them – ever speak of me to you?' he asks.

'You have asked me before, Master. And my answer is the same.'

'Yes, yes, but that was Alice Samuel. I wondered if she had . . . poisoned the *daughter*'s mind with some untruths about me.'

I remember then Johanne saying he had walked in the orchard with Nessie. He has spoken to her himself. Why does he hide this from me?

'I do not know Nessie Samuel. I have barely spoken to her. May I ask, what are these "untruths"?'

'Do not the servants talk? Popsie, she has lived here all her life, she must know her, or Mother Caterill. Has the girl a sweetheart? Someone she would confide in? That Cicely girl, the one who came late to church, the friend.'

'Nessie Samuel is much younger than me. She is the Samuels' daughter. I know no more than you do.'

If you would share what your concerns are, I might be able to assist you. Or if you could perhaps share them with God, in prayer, your mind might be soothed. I do not say this.

He sighs then, and an angry expression crosses his face. He flings his arms around his chest and shivers, perhaps aware suddenly of walking in the dew with a maid, dressed only in his black velvet nightshift. Such is his agitation that he had forgotten. A cabbage white butterfly flutters near a lavender bush; we both watch it land. A pause as it settles, and then: 'Well, Sir Henry will deal with her. Daughter, too, if need be. Johanne has given evidence of the daughter's witchery. She saw her – a visit in a gown. I believe you knew this, Martha?'

A flicker of fear then. It is true: I did not report it to the master and mistress as I should have done.

'Yes, Johanne did say, but I was going to—'

'Mary told me. She is very frightened. It is out of our hands, Martha, and God will prevail.'

He turns away from me, striding back towards the house, all the sweetness of years ago, and of our walk together in Cambridge, gone from him. *Out of our hands!* As if it was ever in mine. It is they – the master, young Henry, the vicar, the Cromwells – they whose hands hold the cards, the fate of Alice. (A little voice says then: *God, surely you mean God does.* But it falls in my deaf ear.) I stare after him, my thoughts trailing back to Michaelmas last year and our arrival here, our troubles arriving too, in great plenty.

And a question I ask myself: When did my own heart harden towards the master?

Mary wants to talk to me before I leave. She comes shyly to find me, out near the pigsty, helping to tip in the big bucket of slops. Mary is the quietest of the children, the one most devoted to her father, and at great pains to please and be clever, like him. I am not used to her being troubled, or seeking my counsel, though it is true she has been in her fits a few times, the last few months.

'What is it, my dear child?' I crouch closer to examine her face, her large eyes and gentle, concerned expression. She looks very like her mother.

'I wish you would not go, Martha.'

'It will not be for long, and there is nothing to fear, now that Alice – Mother Samuel – has been arrested.'

'What will happen to her?'

'She is . . . They have taken her to Huntingdon gaol, I believe.'

'But Nessie is still here! So close to us! And Johanne says she is a witch, too. She saw her figure in a gown going about the

204

house with nobody inside the gown. I mean, it was moving on its own! And she has an imp. And Uncle Henry says a witch might be *anywhere*. That any one of the neighbours, villagers, *servants* might be a witch.'

'Does he indeed?' I straighten up. Dangerous territory. If I now say something in support of Nessie – only recently included in the witchcraft accusations – will that somehow find its way back to Henry? And be used against me, if he is seeking out witches everywhere?

Mary's voice is rising in pitch: 'Why did Gabriel get sent away, Martha? Will they send me away too if I say a bad thing?'

'No, no, of course not, my love. Your brother . . . Well, that is a different matter. A matter for adults to decide. He needed a position in the world and, at seventeen, it was the right time. But you are just a child! No one will send you away. And what is this bad thing that you might say?'

Here her little mouth closes tight. She bites her lip and widens her eyes. She appears to be deciding, then suddenly flings her arms around me in a tight embrace. As I'm crouching near the pigsty she almost knocks me over. I feel her shoulders through her dress, like bony wings.

'I'll be back very soon,' I say, then add, to reassure her, 'Mother Samuel is now in Huntingdon gaol. That's all I know. Let us turn our minds to our prayers, and to more godly things, and put our full trust in the Lord.'

Advice that Sister Dorothy often gave to me. Of late, I'm finding myself struggling to follow it.

We are soon together, my mistress and I, in front of the manor house, near the apple trees. Crabbie approaches us, leading two horses, his head twitching as if he has a bee in his ear. He is hatless, his hair stiff and wiry: he looks like a teasel.

'Hang the witch!' he murmurs, in a voice without menace, the same kind tone he uses to settle the horses.

My mistress's health is not improved. Pale, thinner than ever, her age quickly upon her in lines and furrows. She is shrinking in front of our eyes. Worries for her children, and her husband, and her son Gabriel grieve her bitterly. Each morning I make her a tonic of sage tea, but she leaves it untouched. She says it is nothing but the natural trials of women in this time of life, and forbids me to mention it.

We will travel some of the way by flat-bottom boat, so Crabbie has another Warboys man with him, Jack Gotobed, who will carry us for that part of the journey.

It is a slow and solemn journey. We travel in silence, lost to our own thoughts. I am invaded by so many fears and worries, weighed down by the questions that the children asked me. Warboys feels cloaked in heavy gloom as we pass though.

As we reach Wistow Fen I spy a buzzard floating from tree to tree, just ahead of us, sitting there a while and eyeing us. He spreads his fine feathers like fingers at the bottom, and beckons us on with his harsh, insistent cry 'Kee-yaw!' drifting to the next perch.

'Lady Cromwell died in great despair,' my mistress begins. She has been very quiet up until now, but my habit of silence and waiting has unlocked her tongue.

'Her daughter-in-law claims she said all along it was Alice Samuel, after that day at our house. Alice who sent a cat to claw and attack her. Lady Cromwell was very much afraid of her. I don't quite understand it, but now I think, even that first time Alice arrived at the house, she was . . . unsettled, was she not? And why had Lady Cromwell come so prepared, with the shears?'

'Well, she had certainly heard we had a witch as a neighbour, Mistress!'

Crabbie says that here is a good place to rest. He helps my mistress dismount and brushes twigs from a log so that she might sit on it.

My mistress closes her eyes and sits heavily. We take out the buttered cakes that Mother Caterill prepared, but my appetite has gone. Jack Gotobed, the slodger, has set a small fire going, near the water. Reeds peep from the boggy waters. Fragrant smoke fills the air and the buzzard cries again, losing confidence this time, caught on the wind, vague and fading. A glance up and I see it fly over, its strained shape, striving. I think again of imps, Alice's imps, and wonder: Might it be birds next?

I breathe deeply and bite into my buttered cake, trying to calm myself. There are no imps here. The imps come only when the children bid them – they even have names for them: Pluck, Blue, Catch, Patch, Smack, White. Sometimes other names. Chickens, cats. Bats, toads, mice. My head spins.

'The girls . . . Mary wondered what happens next. I said that Alice was in gaol, but I knew no more.'

'Sir Henry has arranged it. Of course, he is the Sheriff of Ramsey as well as the chief justice. There will be a period of mourning. And then Alice will be brought to trial.'

She turns to me. 'My brother Henry will be thrilled. I imagine he is writing the preface to the book as we speak.' She says this with some bitterness. But Alice is an old woman. A wicked one. A *witch*. What matters her fate to me?

'What will happen to Alice?' The same question Grace and then Mary asked me. It has burned in my mouth.

'The confession she signed for Doctor Dorrington and my husband will be used in evidence at a trial. Unfortunate timing, for Alice. She confessed while Lady Cromwell was very much alive. Witchcraft – wishing harm to others – is one thing. Punishable by whipping, a year in prison or a time in the stocks. But causing *death* by witchcraft. To someone as eminent as Susan . . .'

'And what evidence will they use? Is it simply that Lady Cromwell fell ill, after they met?' I am fearful: Will I be called as a witness, will I need to tell my suspicion that Lady Cromwell and Alice had met before? That I read the lips of Lady Cromwell and felt sure she said, 'So it is *you*.'

My mistress says: 'The cursing of Lady Cromwell, we all heard Mother Samuel say it in the hall, "I never did you any harm *yet*." I think Susan took that as a threat of the strongest order.'

I wonder: Does my mistress feel as I do, that some other evil is abroad, that Alice and her witchcraft might not be the only harm in our household, that our troubles are not yet over?

'It would be a blessing indeed if the girls' fits now ceased,' is all I venture, to which my mistress counters quickly: 'And yet they *don't*! I would say that Johanne's are worse. Bessie's too. All is clouded in unhappiness and mystery. And I –' here she glances at the two men, sitting at the fire, a little distance from us '– I return to the night when Jane told me of that . . . terrible misfortune. Told me, then I told Robert. At first we could scarcely believe her.'

The horse gives a loud whinny, startling us.

'Mistress, I wonder why Doctor Butler told me not to mention Jane's . . . the fact of her . . . the *evidence* that she might have been interfered with. Why did he ask me not to mention it to the master?'

My face is aflame with this painful subject but my mistress looks up, much intrigued.

'I have pondered the same thing. Why do men feel that fathers will be too outraged or shocked to be told such simple truths? Robert . . .'

Here my mistress's expression is unreadable, as if some very dark thoughts are floating past her eyes, like clouds.

'My poor little girl. She did not dream it. But now she will tell me nothing more. She denies she spoke to me. Nor will she say if she knew – or saw – who it was.'

'Do the other girls know anything?'

She shakes her head. 'Johanne once said . . . But now she retracts. Mary is, as you know, ever silent, her nose in a book. Bessie is so terribly thin and not herself at all. If they do, they're also not saying. It is a house of secrets.'

Crabbie appears then, his boots scuffing the earth beside us with his curious shuffling sideways walk. He nods towards the water, says the time has come to leave the horses and go the rest of the way by boat. He will take the horses back, and the skilled boatman Jack Gotobed will take us the rest of the way. 'Skilled boatman. Skilled boatman.' He begins dousing the fire with leaves, then stamping on it.

A woodcutter somewhere close by raps a knotty tune. The mistress closes her mouth, leaving words unsaid. Jane. I feel she tried to tell the truth and had her mouth sewn up, and the truth has tried to burst out in a hundred different ways since.

I am not the same woman who arrived at Warboys. I cannot tell my mistress this, but I do think she senses it. So much has happened. It's as if the casket of secrets has been opened, but only a crack, allowing bats to fly out, swooping and diving back and forth, too fast for the human eye or ear to catch.

The lighterman slides us along the water, the moorhens puttering up towards the boat in great curiosity, then scurrying away. Jack Gotobed laughs that they are the stupidest creatures, 'who wish for their own end', and curses that he has no gun with him.

Do any of God's creatures *wish for their own end*? His comment disturbs me. The words of Mother Caterill float back, likening Alice to a mule. 'As if she had a sign on her back: "Kick me!"'

We pass the church and little town of Bury, oak woods in the background, before the grand town of Ramsey shows itself, the walled gardens of what used to be the monastery in the distance. Jack Gotobed is kindly and helps us from the boat to the walkway and then waves, delivering us to a manservant of Sir Henry Cromwell, who will take us to Sir Henry's fine house. This is his summer home, the man tells us. In winter, Sir Henry retires to an even bigger house in Hinchingbrooke because the water 'laps marvellous close' and Ramsey becomes cut off. Henry is a great man. He has entertained the Queen. He doesn't like to be stranded there, circled by water and the boggy fens with corn buntings atop reeds. Of course we know all this, but we listen politely, seeing that he is so proud of his information.

The talk of the water and the dangerous fens makes the vipers of my nightmares rear their heads, and I think about how deadly they are, lurking in the water we have just left, swallowing their snails. There's only one jar of vipers' gloss left, and as we walk through the town I wonder who cares for the church plate, these days, now that the abbey is all crumbled to the ground, the monks long gone, along with the old religion. I am glad that as we drew closer to Ramsey I kept myself from thinking these dreadful thoughts by counting the cranes and herons flying over in great plenty, or the godwits clustering, and singing a little song to myself so the mistress wouldn't think me cowardly. My fear is growing. I should be much relieved, now that Alice is arrested. I cannot explain the swelling dread.

As the manservant prattles and the mistress listens politely, my mind strays to dear Sister Dorothy, her stories of Ramsey and how it came to belong to Sir Henry Cromwell. The abbey all broken up and the stones taken to Trinity College and the gate carried to Huntingdon to become part of the grand house there. Sister Dorothy could never speak of him – Sir Henry's father – without spitting, because all the friars and monks and canons were given money and houses, but not the nuns. The nuns at Chatteris were told to marry, or go back to their families.

'Those are his beloved trees in the distance, Muchwood – Muchfoughtover, more like. Or Muchgood-it-does-us,' the manservant says. He stops quickly then, realising his error in front of the mistress, but she pretends not to have heard.

We arrive at the locked gate to sounds of workmen and horses and building. Sister Dorothy's name for Richard Cromwell was the 'Thief of Stone' and I hardly dare raise my eyes to the crumbled part of the wall, broken off like a new piece of bread, for fear that I might see the place as Sister Dorothy described it and as it had once been, long ago: the black-hooded monks in the garden, chanting and swinging their silver censers of incense, filling the whole town with the haunting smell.

A bell is ringing. I pull my coif tight against my ears. The church right next to the house of Sir Henry is the old abbey church, where my own story began.

My mistress is quickly taken to the house: servants with black aprons thrown hastily over dresses, and black bonnets and bodies, draw her inside the grieving home. I am being taken to a side door, to the kitchen, but on my way, through the very same walled garden (with crows aplenty up above, moaning and lamenting), the most dreaded thing awaits me: Sir Henry himself, standing, chatting to one of his gardeners.

I hope to pass him unnoticed, but he spies me at once. I am forced to drop a curtsy and respond to his beckoning.

I keep my eyes lowered, but am surprised indeed that the Golden Knight is not tall, as I always pictured him. He is older, and marvellous stout, too. He does not even have gold-coloured hair, as I had imagined. Beard and head are both grey, his cheeks are puffy, and his mouth has the look of a wizened medlar.

This is not a thought I would like him to know so, trembling, I put a hand to my mouth and compose myself.

'You came with Mistress Throckmorton? Are you the deaf woman?' He speaks very loudly, the little mouth growing large inside his beard.

'I am not deaf, sir. Only in one ear. The other compensates perfectly.'

'Are you simple?'

'No, my lord. It is something in my face makes people ask that.'

'Ah . . . Robert has often spoken of you. You have been with the family since a girl, is that right? More of a nursemaid to the children, and not simple at all. I remember he said you read well.'

The crows in the trees above us keep up their moaning and sawing, and I wonder at this shaking in me that Sir Henry has commanded. He takes a step towards me, as if to examine my face. He lifts my chin, and stares directly at me. Without meaning to, I take a step back. And, fearful of my error, I quickly remember my manners: 'I'm sorry for your great loss, my . . . sir.'

'Yes, yes,' he says, and continues staring. His eyes are green and his lashes pale. He finally drops my face from his grasp. The feel of his fingers on my chin lingers.

'You are a foundling, I have heard. As a babe, found right here in the abbey church. I was newly the sheriff of Huntingdon then. You were raised by an old nun?'

I gasp. I had no idea of the master speaking to Sir Henry of my beginnings. The great stork carrying me in a linen cloth and basket, wavering above fen waters. Being placed in the arms of dear Sister Dorothy and staring up into her kind old face, wrinkled as the softest old peach. I cannot think what to say: tears well in my eyes.

'Well, well. It all worked out, did it not? You are pretty, and quick. You have an excellent position with Squire Throckmorton. He and I, we spent many a youthful day hunting together. Robert has spoken of you. I have been interested to meet you.'

'You knew of my mother, sir? My parents? Might you give me any information?'

Here he looks angry: I have stepped over a boundary.

'Your mother must have been a very stupid woman, surely long dead. I know nothing of the circumstances of your arrival in the world beyond what I have said.'

I stand mute in my misery and shock.

'And how are the Throckmorton children? My wife was certain that Alice Samuel was the cause of her troubles, and the children's too, so have they ceased now that the old witch is slung in Huntingdon gaol?'

I think of Johanne, her pointing and her shaking. And the green gown that goes in front of her.

'They are not, sir. The older girl, Johanne, is still afflicted.'

He considers this. He pulls on his grey beard and, with a gesture, dismisses the gardener and the manservant, hovering nearby.

'I had thought that might be the end of it. There must be other witches at work, also. Oh, well, there will be a trial. Henry Pickering has written to the privy council of the university and promised one, and a publication too, and I have arranged it. Is there another witch we should know about?'

I shake my head. He tugs at the corner of his moustache, giving himself a curious air.

'Alice Samuel . . . I met her once, when visiting Warboys. The old crone threw words shocking and bold at me. I had not known she was wife to the seditious John Samuel. Learning it, I warned Throckmorton to be on his guard against the whole family. You confirm my fears. He mentioned that the woman had a daughter . . . Agnes, Ness?'

This. The crows creak like a rocking chair above, unending. *I have confirmed his fears: what have I said?* I think again of the black-hooded monks. I smell the incense. I feel a great welling around me. Someone is here in the garden with us, very close. The kindly face of my old adoptive mother, her skin like folded paper, her crinkly eyes. Her wisdom in great plenty. My terror rises, but stills, as I hear her voice, in my stuffed-up ear. *Martha. Say no more. Words have legs, and wings, and claws.*

'I know nothing of that, sir,' I say, and drop my eyes.

The bells of the abbey church, the very place where my little infant self was found – toll suddenly. The birds explode with the greatest of fuss, screaming and flapping.

Take Heed and Pray, For Ye Know Not When the Time Is.

Sir Henry nods at me. I am dismissed.

I am shown into the house, and to a little room with a truckle-bed where I will stay. I am expected downstairs in the kitchen to take up my place with the servants while my mistress comforts the young Lady Cromwell, newly delivered of her infant.

But I sit on the bed and find that the tears, long trembling like a pan on the boil, now spill.

Sister Dorothy. A poor old woman in a hovel much smaller than Alice Samuel's. God blessed her, she always said, in bringing her the gift of a child, so late in life, when she had been cast out of the nunnery, had nothing. And she opened her heart, and the rough place she had found to live in, and never burdened me with the story of my own beginning, with the feeling of being an orphan, unwanted, or lacking. My life has been for ever altered by her kindness. What confusion such half-knowledge of our own beginning makes. A stoppered-up feeling. The tears feel like relief, and I have a strange memory then: of myself with my fingers stretching and soothing the udder of our cow, Daisy, on a chilly morning, the smell of grass, the milk finally flowing. Memories roll themselves up and spring out.

Such a gift to be here on this earth.

Sir Henry's comments made me think of Dottie, saying that she had seen the master and Sir Henry in 'hard speeches' in the churchyard, the day that the Lady Cromwells visited us. Hard speeches about Alice.

And Alice waving her stick in anger at Sir Henry! That must have been the encounter in the woods before I went to Titchmarsh. My mistress had said Dottie witnessed it ... a meeting of the grand and the poor too extreme to imagine properly. The boldness of Alice – to throw words at him! Did she try to curse him, as she had Lady Cromwell? Would he mention this at her trial? I do not know why I would not speak of the daughter, only that Sister Dorothy begged me not to.

Voices on the stairway alarm me. I gather myself, swabbing my face with my apron, and stand up so as not to be found shirking. But the voices and steps pass my room so I venture out. The stairway is huge. I step down past the portrait of Sir Henry above it, in his white ruff collar and fine black clothes, one hand on his hip, his moustache tweaked up at the ends and his green eyes looking down at us. The manservant's comments float back to me about Sir Henry's forest, Muchwood. Muchfoughtover. He is surely as powerful as any king. And he has had power over my own life, a power I never knew until now. I trudge downstairs.

In the kitchen I am offered a cup of ale and a piece of bread. It is a noisy place, busy with preparation for the funeral. There is a fat matron – the cook – her daughter, Maggie, and another girl with a limp, whose name I do not catch. They show great curiosity in me, the story of the Throckmorton home and the fate of the witch living close to the squire.

This is a hot kitchen, full of gossip and liberty. None are sealing up their tongues here.

I sit in silence for a while, then feel obliged to ask what I might do to help and am given a jar of chestnuts from last year: 'You could make up the laundry liquid.' When I am slow to the task, the old matron changes her mind and says, 'Are you a good seamstress?'

'Oh, yes, Mother, my stitches are neat and true.' A memory, then: of a beautiful baby's blanket that I'd stitched and embroidered for our dear Gabriel, an infant born with a full head of fair hair like a corn dolly.

'Did you know her? This Alice Samuel?' The matron's eyes are red and still wet from much lamentation. She sits herself on a stool at the table beside me to enquire.

'She was our neighbour, yes. I knew her only since we moved to Warboys.'

'A cat sent to scratch my poor mistress! Striving and suffering and now this! What a wicked thing ... My mistress touched the old witch's hair-lace and threw the lace and hair on the fire and the witch said to her: "I never harmed you *yet*." She struck her a deep, deep blow and sent her imp to do it.'

Maggie, with a small cry, crosses herself, then gasps in case I might consider her popish. 'Lord protect us!' she adds quickly.

She is excitable with all this calamity, as if a party is unfolding.

'I wonder what this Alice had against our poor old mistress. Did she once live in Ramsey or Bury? Did she know Sir Henry? There's many a wench round here who did. Is that it?' the daughter asks.

I shake my head. They met only the once, he told me, and that was but recently, though I do not repeat this.

'They say her daughter is a witch too. The Throckmorton children will be witnesses at the trial,' Maggie says, a little breathless.

'Yes,' I say primly, not wanting to share details of my girls, either.

The matron is biting on a stick of liquorice and now leaves off to sit herself down on a stool and say to her daughter, 'Of *course* they knew one another. Didn't Alice Samuel call my lady a naughty name? My mistress,' sniffing loudly, 'was not a happy soul, God rest her. Her marriage was a short one, but five years, and she feared she had never truly won Sir Henry's heart.'

'He was still in love with his first wife, then,' the daughter says, wanting to be at the centre of the storytelling, 'Lady Joan, mother of his children.' She has a tankard in one hand that she is wiping with a cloth and presumably waiting to be told she can help herself to ale.

But the matron interrupts, batting her comments away. 'No, no, not her, not his old wife Joan, you fool.'

I wait. The fat matron wipes some tears and gets up for more ale, refilling my glass and hers and offering none to her daughter.

'The man was bewitched, since youth. My mistress confided in me. His pizzle would never stand properly, except when he thought of a young red-haired maiden he had once loved . . .'

I do not like to think of Sir Henry's pizzle, standing or not standing, and squirm.

'Was it the mother of one of Sir Henry's brats caused trouble to his pillicock?' Maggie asks. She finally stops her frenetic wiping and shoves the tankard pointedly in front of the jug her mother safeguards.

The matron's arm sneaks out to wrap around the jug of ale. 'No! He never found her again. My mistress never told me more, but many a night I heard her weep over it.'

218

'She died of a broken heart, then,' Maggie says. At this the fat matron stands up and, in her haste or anger, overturns the jug. I rush to find a cloth and help her, sopping up the ale spreading across the wooden table.

'What a waste!' Maggie cries.

'She didn't die of a broken heart, you stupid girl! She was never the same after Warboys. You saw her! A headache, a fever, a sickness. Wailing, weeping, stiffness, twitching. A pain in her stomach . . .'

'The fen ague, then,' the daughter says. She seems to be quite slow and unable to follow her mother's thinking.

'Not the ague! *Witchcraft.*' The matron sighs dramatically, fetching more ale from a big flagon, finally pouring a small tankard for Maggie, and one for each of us. She sits herself back down, waits until she has my full attention, then announces: 'She died of the evil that Alice Samuel wished on her. The old bitch will hang for it – and good riddance!'

I breathe out so loudly I might be a horse, panting in the room. I did not realise I've been holding my breath, the matron's hard speeches making me anxious. I feel a shudder and sickness at the remarks about Sir Henry and his pizzle. They echo the story Master Gilbert Pickering told me in his study: of the witch who put a glamour on a young man's member. Is this truly what Sir Henry claims? I'd like to snort aloud! The spell must surely have been lifted, or how had he sired so many children? (Were all the mothers redheads then?) Of course, these mocking thoughts are not to be shared. Oh, Dottie would have seen the humour in it – I can see her now, saying it, with her arms folded and that expression she has, 'Men!' – but, these days, things that might once have been laughed at in the Black Bull in Brampton appear in a more dangerous light.

The other servant girl with the limp appears and, after some words, goes away carrying heavy swathes of black fabric over her arm, for the curtains in the great hall. My thoughts are elsewhere: *What is it to me if Alice hangs? Or her daughter with her? Again I wonder, why should it trouble me so?*

'You are not a friend of the witch, are you?' the matron suddenly asks, moving closer to peer at me, so that I can smell the beer on her breath.

'No, no, not a friend, not I.'

'I wish all the witches in the land were hanged, and their spirits with them,' says the matron, glaring.

'Yes,' I say swiftly. I long for the day when the funeral is over, and we might return to Warboys.

'They're scratching her!' Dottie says excitedly. 'They're taking away her powers!'

We tarried longer at Ramsey than we expected and we have been away almost a fortnight. Our arrival home in the Warboys kitchen is not the peaceful one we'd hoped for. My mistress and I both, we are weary and travel-sore yet there are visitors and noise in great plenty, and the children are not in bed, and we soon discover that the arrest of Alice has not soothed their fits at all.

Dottie is listening outside the parlour door. She straightens on seeing us, and makes to go back to the kitchen, but my mistress stops her and says, 'Who are they scratching?'

'Nessie, Mistress.'

'Nessie is in the house?'

'The master fetched her. I heard him outside in hard speeches. "Nessie, your old witch of a mother has done untold harm to my family. *Tell me what you know!*"'

220

'Were you hiding, Dottie, when this was said? Eavesdropping is a sin,' my mistress says. Her face is thunderous, a look I cannot quite understand. Dottie colours and returns to the kitchen, her mouth set in a line.

The scene in the parlour is as a nightmare. Chairs and furniture are pushed back, men ring the edges as if at a cockfight. My mistress stands for a moment, observing the heads: young Henry, Thomas Cakebread, Edward Harkening, her husband, the Reverend Doctor Dorrington are all there and another man – one I gasp to see – her older brother, Gilbert Pickering.

We step closer and I try to look over the shoulder of the shortest man, the barrel-chested Master Harkening. Nessie is sitting on the Turkey carpet, her face streaked with blood. Her arms are bare and she wears no hat, and her white skin shows scratch marks and bleeding too. Johanne sits some distance from her, her fingers covered with blood, paring her nails with scissors in a clumsy way. Some splotches have stained the beautiful scarlet and blue carpet. All around is a charged feeling, as if twigs snapped and crackled. The air is thick with it, the smell of the men's sweat rising to fill the room, mixing with the peat from the fire to make a very potent smell: a room full of imps, strong and troubling.

'Let me at her, let me!' Johanne suddenly screams, lunging at Nessie.

Nessie is sobbing and puts her head down, but does not pull away. 'O Lord, do please save me,' she says.

The vicar leans forward: 'Charge the spirit to depart, Nessie. Show those here assembled how it is done, Nessie. Repeat after me the Lord's Prayer and Creed.'

The girl begins, but stumbling over her words, while Johanne sits transfixed. The other girls are there, around the edges of the room, sitting quietly. Bessie, Jane, Grace, gentle Mary. Not in their fits, but their faces closed and dreamy, as if they are not quite here.

A horror rises in me and I dare not even glance at my mistress. I hear her panting beside me, and reaching for the arm of her husband: 'Robert! *Stop this . . .*'

My master turns towards us and I expect him to do as she begs. But his countenance is stern and his eyes – everything about him – start up a further fear in me. Is he under some glamour now? His cheeks are suffused with red, his eyes a little bleary. A look of a man with a great amount of wine inside him.

He makes to steer us out of the room. 'God would not allow any of this if she were not guilty of witchcraft,' he says, and the Reverend Doctor Dorrington, on seeing the mistress has joined the room, adds, 'Anyone unable to finish a prayer is surely in the palm of the devil himself.'

'Why did you fetch her? Have there been further accusations against her?' my mistress asks, her eyes falling on Johanne, the daughter 'of bad temper and sulky', the one she accused of trying to control the other girls, of baiting and teasing.

Her husband has one hand on her arm, and the other on mine, saying, 'Elizabeth. Let God and the reverend do His work and then Nessie will be . . . There will be no need for her to join her mother at trial.'

Master Gilbert Pickering is staring at me and I am only too glad to leave.

Days pass. More fits, more scratching tests and beseeching for repentance, more visitors. More tests for Nessie, always with the master in charge, and always with the promise that if she will confess to being a witch they will not send her to trial at Huntingdon to join her mother. But she will *not* confess.

Johanne is always at the centre, taking part in the scratching or accusing, or sometimes Bessie or Jane. Mary sits still and watchful, sometimes with a book, sometimes sewing. Occasionally Mary also falls into a fit, which passes swiftly, and seems to shake through her like a mild shower of rain. Grace takes no part, seeking out her brother Hob and often hiding, or crying, in some corner or behind a curtain.

We servants are in a fever of industry: brewing beer, feeding animals, running back and forth to neighbours for bread or a peck of apples and always a new man arriving.

After that first time, my mistress shrinks from it. 'Poor young woman,' is all she says to me, but she makes no further attempt to stop it. She accepts only the smallest morsels of food. More and different men arrive, drinking the master's wine and coming to see the young woman of such bad fame and making their pronouncements, droning their prayers. Hob runs from the parlour one day, calling, 'Blue! Drew! Catch and Smack!' one minute and the next: 'My delicate firebrand darlings!'

Who is saying such things?

'She's made of sterner stuff. She'll never confess,' Mother Caterill pronounces.

And another time: 'That Johanne! I'd give her a whipping if she were mine.'

Grace comes to find me, crying. 'Why do they scratch her? Why is she bleeding so much?'

She flies at me, burying herself in my apron, nearly bowling me over. I take her in my arms and flop down on a stool by the fire, nearly a-toppling it. Popsie and Dottie, much aggrieved by the work they are doing, start huffing and puffing to be sure

I know it, so I take Grace by the hand and usher her towards the front door, past the great hall where the sudden screams and the men's deep voices continue.

'Will she die?' Grace mouths to me.

Thinking she means Nessie, I begin some kind speeches but she shakes her head. 'Mother. Why does Mother stay so unhappy always in her chamber?' For this I am unprepared, and the question quivers between us. Why indeed?

I think I must ask Dottie about the conversation she heard, between the master and Nessie, which, if she was spying, must have taken place at the front door of the Samuel family, while Dottie hid behind a tree nearby.

'How did he get her to come here?' I ask.

'Well, of course, if she would confess to being a witch, she will not be arrested . . . he said.'

'If she is *not* a witch, there is nothing for her to confess to!'

'But she is, she is, and I heard the master press her.'

'How?'

'He said, as I already told you, "Nessie, tell me what you know!" And something like "You and your mother will not ruin me – or my family – with your wantonness and lies," and maybe he said "witchery" or "sorcery". I don't know, I don't know *quite* what he said. Surely I was wrong to be there, so I went back to my work.'

Dottie, though younger than me, is solid and well built. I'm sure she knows that, when she chooses, the heft of her feels threatening. She draws herself up to her full height to stare at me, and my courage fails me.

I leave her then and attend to Grace, talking tenderly to her and saying, 'Let us tarry outside a while, to escape this – these things.'

Her eyes are wide and her little body shakes, like a candle guttering. Fear swoops in and out between us, looping from one to the other.

Outside, I unlatch the gate to the churchyard next door and we sit upon a bench. Grace creeps onto my lap, like she used to when she was but a babe, still with her downy hair and newly sewn hare lip. The air has a chill, and we nestle together, I stroking her thin shoulders.

'Are they lying, as Nessie says?' Grace blurts. 'Are my sisters wicked?' When I say nothing, she asks: 'If she *is* a witch, what will she do to us?'

Her father should not have permitted Nessie to stay. The parlour smelt of iron and peat and blood, Bessie and Johanne shining with sweat, their hair straggling their faces, and Nessie in their centre, a vixen trapped by baying dogs. A wicked thought but I cannot snuff it. Jane and Bessie so grieving themselves and the learned men in the room acting as if they are deprived of their senses at the possibility of finding another witch in their midst and this time a pretty one. I had succeeded in avoiding Master Pickering but his presence glowered. He and his younger brother spend much time with heads bent together, poring over the Bible and various documents. Only young Thomas has any shadow of sympathy in his eyes. I hear him once again speaking of this Scot fellow he has seen give a lecture, telling of his doubts and dissenting views. He is mostly shouted down by the louder Edward Harkening and Henry.

All is inflamed, as if rage and revenge never rest. What to tell her? The churchyard is quiet. I feel as though even the birds are poised and waiting.

Grace lies across me, face down, my hand on her warm head. The bench faces the gravestones with their trumpets and angels laced with lichen. A little plaque to the glory of the old parson, the one before Doctor Dorrington, Gregorious Garth. I'm staring at the church wall and the bosky grounds behind it, thinking of this and that, woe and sorrow and nothing, then slowly, slowly I become aware that I am not alone. A woman with better hearing would surely have heard their voices before now. My master and Sir Henry, on the other side of the church wall, standing in private counsel, their heads together in urgent speeches.

Sir Henry – *here?* With his wife newly in the ground . . . and that dreadful penny show going on in the parlour of our house? My master, I see, is agitated, arms flying, holding his hat in his hand, sweeping it back and forth and then flapping it in his palm. I hear the words 'Plough Monday'. My master is shouting but Sir Henry has loud, clear tones, and it is *his* words that reach me: 'For God's sake, Robert, who would believe her?'

As I cannot make out my master's words, I wonder at his *tone*. He does not sound angry. He sounds . . . Again, I fear he has taken leave of his senses. I think of how he looked in the house, and the times I've seen him of late, swaying in the hall as he enters and righting himself, seemingly trying to straighten himself, as if forcing a stick down his spine. He has always been able to carry the strong drink he takes very well. This is a new trouble.

Dusk is falling. A bat sweeps around us on our little bench as I consider how to make our way quietly into the house, without the two men spying us. I try to signal to Grace to lift her head and make no sound, tapping her and whispering in her ear. But I feel the warmth and the heaviness, the rise and fall of her: she has sunk into sleep.

The wind hisses through the apple trees in the orchard. If we are found sitting here my master will be angry indeed. Eavesdropping is a sin, though the Lord knows Dottie indulges in it frequently. I stare out at the ivy-tangled bedheads of the long dead.

'Sssh,' I murmur to Grace, as she stirs. The bat flits close and flees from us. A bird somewhere peeps a startled sound. My heart is ticking.

And then something happens to me, something marvellous strange. Sometimes my poor deaf ear sounds a note – a high note and my skull seems to open up, like the shell of a walnut. I feel it now. And although Grace remains on the bench sleeping, I sense myself leaving the spot, as if in a dream. Weightless, my hair flying, my skirts upturning like a black flower, soaring above the bench, and looking down at the two men in the churchyard, the child curled, sleeping. The house, its chimneys spouting smoke, and its awful antics – all far, far beneath me.

With my splendid eye I see and hear all, like the Holy Mother herself. Water moving and retreating, the trees standing within it, reed warblers swaying atop a willow; a streak of turquoise; snakes making their zigzag shape on the surface. The Muchwood riots, the clearing of the brush, the women and children running, the way coneys scatter in a field. A hare springing from its sighting of another hare, as if spying itself in a mirror. Its white tail, its golden form, racing faster than any living creature.

Sister Dorothy had a treasured statue, a tiny figure of Our Lady the Virgin carved and painted in wood, hidden in the pocket of her apron. She showed me many times this cherished possession. She told me to think of the Holy Mother, and pray to her sometimes, no matter what we were told, no matter how it was forbidden. When she said such things I used to tremble with fear. I never knew where that statue ended up, after Sister Dorothy died, or where she had rescued it from. But sometimes, it is true, when I kneel and pray to God it is not the Lord my Father I see but instead a womanly form, the Holy Mother, who looms in my mind, or even sometimes Sister Dorothy herself smiling down at me, a blue robe sheltering her face, touching my head.

And in this strange moment, I believe she has been there all along, and now I have found her again, and become her true daughter and disciple. I know all and understand all. Nothing is hidden from me. The pictures of the Virgin and Child might be whitewashed in the churches, her eyes dug out with knives or head lopped off but she is speaking to me. *I am still here. I never left you.*

I see the church next door surrounded by water, and green vipers swimming on its skin, raising their heads.

I see the time before my birth and after it. I hang there in a cradle, above that abyss, but I am like all the daughters of the house: my mouth is sewn up. *Give thanks for the Bread of Life*, says one of the gravestones. *Who would believe her?* Sir Henry asks, of a woman who means nothing to him, less than a pebble dropped in a pond.

What has *my* life been? A foundling. A kindly mother who had so few worldly goods but opened her heart to step in and protect me always from the feeling of being unwanted, the knowledge that I am the daughter of a wanton desire that never took a godly shape. I have loved the Throckmorton children with everything I have in me to give, and I do not feel regret. But I have been foolish where the master is concerned, loyal to those who do not deserve it. And with each year passing, I grow further and further from the chance to have children myself: what will I leave on this earth behind me?

I peer down. A shaggy weeping willow bows its head. I see in my mind's eye a distant town – Huntingdon – more water, a brick alley, a wooden beam, with crowds surging to see a show. The light makes me squint. A bird peeps its fierce tune – a robin – piercing the veil. And then I drop like a stone, the way a kestrel drops to the earth, and at last I rejoin myself and Grace on the wooden bench.

My breath comes marvellous hard, as if I have been running or truly swept myself into the skies with my arms.

Grace wakes easily this time when I shake her. The master and Sir Henry are gone, as if they, too, were part of the dream, or the enchantment. We stand up and open the little wooden gate from the churchyard to the garden of the manor house. These days, the church is named after Saint Mary Magdalene but I remember suddenly that long ago this church in Warboys was named for the Holy Mother. *I am here. I never left you.* Yes.

The door to Alice's house is opening.

Here is her husband, John Samuel, with his goggle eyes and his rough hands, wearing an old pair of breeches, a man roaring, angry, stamping from his house to ours. Like a wild boar in the brush. Grace clutches at me as if a dog had bared its teeth to her.

'Throckmorton! For the last time! Bring my daughter outside!' he rages. This has been his pattern since we returned, and probably while we were away. In his rage he is impotent. He comes to the house and thumps on the door with his fist. One of the men inside – a guard, one of the scholars – is despatched by Master Gilbert Pickering or my master to threaten him with arrest and he is soon seen off, to drink and strive and suffer alone for a day or two, only to return like an angry stray dog when the drink wears off. He might have fallen silent when his wife was first arrested, believing that his best course of action. But now he is relentless in his fury. Banging at the door, like a Plough Boy, with his stick, a rascal, a knave, a scoundrel.

A Plough Boy. Why was my master speaking of Plough Monday? In other villages I've heard it called Naughty Night and I know that many a wife has come to dread it. People even spoke of a 'Plough baby' born nine months later, as every year they appeared in great number. There must be those who look forward to it, too: the men disguised and dressed up as Plough Boys, threatening to rough up your land and your yard if you don't pay, always returning drunk and with the loot they have begged from households too scared to refuse them. Why would the master be speaking of it to Sir Henry? I have never known a high-born gentleman to join the village Plough Boys. The words snag and catch at me, like a hook in wool. They will not let go.

Then I remember something. Who was it who mentioned Plough Monday, when we first came to Warboys? It was Mother Caterill. In the kitchen. A muttered thing about Alice.

I creep with Grace to the back door of the house, past Bertha in the pigsty, lying on her side, tiny eyes closed, all eight of her piglets clambering over her, squeaking. We enter that way. In the kitchen there is a lull, Mother Caterill with her pipe in and her shoes off; our entrance startles her awake and the clay pipe clatters to the floor.

'What is happening now?' I whisper.

'Oh, the same, the same. They are trying to make Nessie say the Lord's Prayer again. Sign of a witch if she can't utter it.'

'And does she?'

'The girl does not know if she is coming or going. She does her best.'

Grace scampers away to find her brother Hob, and I help myself to a cup of soup from a pot on the stove. We can hear the hard speeches of John Samuel continue in the hall outside: 'You've locked up my wife and stolen my daughter . . .'

'Mother Caterill,' I ask, 'you once told Dottie something about Mother Samuel. When Jane first accused her. You mentioned a Plough Monday. What was it about?'

'Oh, it was a tale from long, long ago. I was in my cups that day in the kitchen. I should never have told. The secret was not mine to tell.'

The house has its strange smell that the male visitors bring, the sense of something bristling like a hog in the corner, and for a moment my legs feel weak and I must collapse to a stool. Mother Caterill is looking at me fearfully. Stories told freely in the early days of arriving in Warboys have taken on a different hue. She gets up and sees that neither Dottie nor Popsie is about and Grace has gone. For now the shouting seems to have stopped. She closes the door between the kitchen and the scullery so that we are closed in together. She seems to make up her mind.

Then she takes a curious action: she steps closely towards me, examining my face.

'Will you run straight to the mistress with the tale?' she asks plainly. 'Will you swear to keep it to yourself?'

I nod, hoping to convey that I *am* to be trusted. There are moments in which we stare at one another. I lower my eyes first, to stare at her brown-spotted skin, her gnarled fingers. I am waiting.

'It was three men. Ravished her. Here in Warboys in the church. She was but a girl. They were Plough Boys,' she says.

I must have misheard her. *'Three?'*

She nods. 'They had faces blackened the Plough Boy way, of course. Disguised. Two held her. Each took a turn, one after the other. Maybe she said the third were interrupted – didn't get his full chance.'

In the *church*.

Mother Caterill glances fearfully at the closed scullery door, beckons me to come closer and watch her lips so she can lower her voice.

'She said she was certain who one of them was. She knew. She "unpicked the knot", unravelled it.'

I have never been this close to Mother Caterill. I can smell her ale-breath on my face. The terrible pictures are flying at me – of Alice, young Alice, bundled like a chicken in a sack between three men, and I would like them to stop.

'Who was it?' I squeak out.

Mother Caterill shakes her head and here she relaxes, rubbing at her aching back and making to open the door.

'Was it the brutish husband, John Samuel? Did he have to marry her then?' I ask.

Mother Caterill scoffs at this. 'Not John Samuel! My, what a foolish question! The man is rough and a drinker but he loves Alice. She never told me the name, she just said she'd "unpicked the knot" of who the devil was. And she hoped he would burn in Hell.'

'You said there were *three*?'

'She did not know the names of all of them. She seemed certain, though, of the leader. But she did not tell me.' Mother Caterill stares at me for a moment, then closes her mouth, as if done with me. She barges past, into the scullery.

I put up a hand to my ears and find them red hot, throbbing. My breath comes quickened and the knowledge is beating at me. *Who?* Who did insult Alice all those years ago? And if she has harboured such rage and sorrow in her heart, what witch would not use all in her power to gain her revenge?'

Outside the kitchen, all is commotion and storming.

John Samuel has somehow managed to free himself from the man who held him and bellows, 'You're a rogue and a papist and a lecherous bastard – you and fucking Sir Henry Cromwell too. And any who say it are charged a witch and that's the end of all dissent!'

The names he calls out are so uncouth that I put my hands over my ears. His blue eyes are burning bright as the two Pickering brothers, Henry and Gilbert, wrestle him to the ground and fold his arm in a lock behind him. He continues his roaring as two of the young scholars rush to help, and the vicar stands mopping his brow, saying, 'Oh dear, oh dear . . .'

'Men must – consider – the high sovereignty of God – over all things . . .' Henry pants, endeavouring to pin John Samuel to the floor. Now there are four of them piling atop him. I look around for Sir Henry. It can only be minutes since I saw him with the master outside in great agitation behind the church wall. But he is nowhere here, and while the master joins the others grappling with John Samuel along with the guards, Master Gilbert Pickering stands a little to one side, issuing orders, telling me and Thomas Cakebread to remove the children from the scene.

'Make haste!' bellows Master Pickering. 'Arrest the young witch too! What a family! And may God protect us from the evil of witches.'

I run upstairs, two steps at a time, shooing the children in front of me, like chickens.

John Samuel was correct then, in his augury. He will be charged with witchcraft now, too.

'The girls must travel to Huntingdon as witnesses, and you must go with them, Martha,' my mistress says. I am in her bedchamber, where I have brought her sage tea, and soldier's tea, hoping one or the other will provide the tonic she needs. She is, she says, too tired and low to accompany us.

'Mistress, you are certain you need no doctor?'

'Oh, Martha. We both know this is a time in a woman's life that no doctor can cure. It will come to you, too – the cessation of monthly troubles. Mine is just a little earlier than some. Robert . . . Men do not wish to hear of such things. They feel horror of it. And we know, too, that privations of the spirit accompany this stage.'

'Will all the girls attend the trial, Mistress? Even little Grace? She is very frightened.'

'Grace may stay. First Alice and Nessie must appear before the bishop in Buckden for some further confession. The trial of the three will be at Huntingdon Assizes. The older girls only: they must be part of the trial and give their account and have their afflictions witnessed.'

I stand close to her, rubbing and pulling at my ear, not knowing how to respond. I indicate the cups of tea, urging her to drink.

'Johanne will enjoy it,' she says wryly, sitting up in bed, sipping the soldier's tea. Her eyes meet mine. It is not a sweet look that passes between us.

'I wish my Gabriel would come home. I wrote to Gilbert but he said nothing of it when he arrived. I don't suppose he even passed on my letter. I am now more certain than ever that our beloved boy did no wrong,' she says, keeping her eyes fixed on mine.

I say nothing.

'As a child Gabriel was the sweetest, was he not? Thomas Cakebread puts me in mind of him. So eager and open. Ever crouching to look at a moth, a butterfly. He loves to explain things to Bessie, and he seems to have some tender-hearted-ness. Whereas others – *some men* – show us from the start their true hearts, do they not?'

My dream, the one I had of Gabriel as a little blond capering boy. He spoke as my mistress does now: *Men show themselves. We do not change course.* I am disturbed by the similarity in the words. Once again my dreams feel full of prophecy.

From Gabriel my thoughts shift to my mistress's brother, Master Gilbert Pickering. How he revealed his true nature to me. Such lechery is more commonplace than I imagined, and now I have learned where it might lead: to the sort of men who attacked Alice. But nothing can prepare me for what she says next.

'Robert. When we first met. He told me. His early hunting days with Sir Henry. They would go carousing, join the village men, black their faces to be disguised along with those revellers. Sometimes with my eldest brother. Plough Monday celebrations. So that they might have some sport.'

Words are rising in my chest, travelling up my throat. I feel full of them, yet taut, and frightened, and I tremble, wishing to hear no more.

'Robert used to laugh about it. About his "carousing days" with Sir Henry. Thirty years ago or more. I did not think it was a concern of mine. I barely even remembered it. I did not fear that he would ever forget himself and bring such – lewdness so close to home . . . Sir Henry and Robert have been in secret consultation all day long. Their Plough Monday tales came back to me.'

Why now? Why is she speaking of this *now*? More than thirty years. From what she just said, is it possible she heard the master and Sir Henry mention it, as I did, earlier in the churchyard? They did not trouble to lower their voices, and if I with my imperfect hearing could pick out the words 'Plough Boys' . . . I close my eyes and the images, the terrible thoughts that have begun since Mother Caterill told me – no, before that, since I saw my master and Sir Henry in their agitated counsel – now flood my mind. High-born men disguised as Plough Boys. Is it possible it was a common game among grand gentlemen? Is it possible that the ones in Alice's case were *other* gentlemen, were *not* my master and Sir Henry and, it seems, Master Pickering too? What is it my mistress knows? What is she trying to confide in me? *Dear Mary, Mother of God . . . Our Father, who art in Heaven . . .*

I take my mistress's hand in mine and it is icy cold. She feels skin and bone, her back through her nightdress a ribbed washboard. Her long hair hangs loosely and her eyes, they search mine, as if for knowledge or corroboration.

'Did you hear something? Did you?' she asks.

I do not know how to reply: why do you tell me of the master's antics as a Plough Boy *now*? 'Oh, Mistress, it is better not to remember such things, from so long ago,' I say, but she shakes her head.

236

'I feel sure you know something, Martha, that you are perhaps sworn to keep to yourself.'

So now I am most caught, like an eel in a trap. A ghastly consideration. Was it not my master that the mistress heard, but *me*, that is, myself and Mother Caterill? Is *that* why she asks? A thought too terrible to contemplate. I *cannot* tell the mistress what I know, the story I heard from Mother Caterill about Alice. I have a lifetime's habit of tying up my tongue. How would it help my poor mistress to know the *extent* of her husband's wickedness and lechery, which she describes as 'sport', when she is already sick and grieving her son's banishment, struggling to comprehend? And her brother, too, was one of them? It makes sense, I realise, of my own horrible understanding of the man, as someone lewd and incapable of self-restraint. And, of course, all those years ago, my mistress was introduced to her husband by her older brother. The families are very tight. My discovery threatens to choke the air we are trying to breathe, and my mistress's eyes fill with tears. Placing the tea down, she lies back against her pillow, sighing. She is very frail. I take her hand. We sit in weighty silence.

I picture purses, sewn up. I remember Johanne wailing, 'Why are you blaming *me*? Lady Cromwell says that horrible woman and worse, *worse*, her daughter are to blame for all of it!'

I see those same purses, velvet, gathered, puckered, with the stitches now unravelling, opening their mouths, and then all the wild, ungodly things, bats, moths, devils, *words*, flying out.

Part Four

The Trial

The sun is lowering as Alice and Nessie arrive in Buckden at the palace of the Bishop of Lincoln. The light strikes the gold tips of the spiked gates and the building – a great tower, a castle, Alice has never seen the like, with its diamond-patterned bricks and its moat of sailing swans. It looms more frightening and glittering than ever as they hurtle in the strange contraption towards its thundering gates.

Her joy at her daughter joining her in her dank cell last night soon turned to despair when she examined Nessie's arms and hands – scratches, some very raw, some already dark and scabbing. Alice's tears flowed: 'Did you confess? Is that why they brought you?'

'Mother, you look smaller than a mouse! Do they feed you nothing at all?'

The two women examined one another in bleak despair and fell quickly to silence. In the morning they heard that John Samuel would stay another day in his cell in the men's gaol, chained to a pillar after blacking the eye of a guard. (Alice pictures him like a bear she once saw at Sturbridge Fair, shuffling its great feet and raising itself up, like a man, to sniff the air.)

This visit to the Bishop of Buckden is the Church part of their trial. The criminal part will follow at Huntingdon Assizes.

'What should I confess to?' Nessie says miserably, in answer to her mother. 'And that Squire of Throckmorton, he asked me over and over, out of the sight of the others, what did I know, and what had I told? And I kept answering, "Nothing, my lord," but he did not seem to believe me.'

At this, Alice hangs her head. That shameful day.

It *was* him. That day when she first saw him in the manor at Warboys had stirred a terror, like something floating up from a pond. She had known one of them to be Sir Henry – she had long ago unravelled that. But who the other two had been, the first man, the last, the one who hung back: that she had never known.

Sir Henry: his name could never be mentioned without the same sharp pain, as if someone turned a knife in her ribs, followed by the surge of rage that made her feel that things around her, twigs, logs, might burst into flames. It had been a flickering thought, in the manor house on her first visit. She had wondered, fleetingly, if the two men were friends, and then Mistress Throckmorton had assured her that they were but a *distant* association. A lie. A lie no doubt to protect Elizabeth Throckmorton's husband from association with a landlord whom many in the village of Warboys – her own husband included – loathed.

Still, that first day in the manor house, she *had* feared it. For so long she had both avoided and dreaded ever meeting Sir Henry again, and yet in some small pocket of her heart (the part of her that cut spinas at Muchwood), she had also cherished a desire to *destroy* him and destroy his property, burn and slash the things he possessed. If she had brought such a memory into the parlour that day, the day when Jane first accused her, it was only a glimmer, hardly formed. Yes, over many years she had sometimes permitted herself to wonder who the other men were who had accompanied Sir Henry. Then she had seen Sir Henry and Robert Throckmorton together, giving her a new anxiety that it was not *such* a distant acquaintance at all. Finally, with Throckmorton's insistence, his *guilty panic*, his great terror of witchcraft and retribution, his need to snuff out her entire family, he had fanned that tiny spark into certainty.

The strange cart they are brought in shakes and rumbles, the horses' tails flying up in front of them. They trundle along rutted paths, like eggs tossed in a basin, hardly sighting the receding waters of the fens, full of godwits and giant sweeping herons.

'If I confess I will surely hang,' Nessie whispers miserably. 'When I denied it they scratched me further. *Those girls!* Oh, those daughters of the house. Why do they hate us so?'

Alice has no answer for this except an irrational one, or an unlikely one. Could the girls have felt such strong instincts, such instant hatred of the old woman and her daughter because they perceived something bad the moment they saw her? Something evil that she brought back into their home? (*Am I a witch?*) *How can things that were unknown, that were secret, be known at last, and no one said a word?*

The wheels of the cart slide over damp leaves and stones laced with lichen and slippery with rain and come to a halt at the bishop's gatehouse. The men accompanying them are speaking to an official at the gatehouse, showing papers, muttering. Next door a church bell tolls. Alice cranes her neck to glance up at the pink sky and sees a golden cockerel twisting in the wind – a weathervane – looking one minute like a spear, a golden sheaf of wheat, the next like her own brown chicken.

Alice hears her name spoken by the men, Nessie's name too. There is some mumbling and even a burst of laughter – shocking, cruel. Then the gates are opened and they are admitted.

Ahead of them on the damp grass a squirrel darts, tail flat behind it, then whisks along the rim of the walled garden, fleeing into the twilight. Sounds of sheep bleating, axes chopping, men's voices from the cottages dotted around the grounds, and they pass a gardener with a wheelbarrow full of herbs: the smells of lavender, rosemary, tansy rise up, and for a moment Alice is startled by the vivid yellow of a pot of marigolds, their colour a stab to her heart in this bleak place.

They approach a bridge, curved and small, spanning a moat of brown water, thick as gravy, the swans like pieces of snowy bread drifting in it. They rattle across it and Alice peeps over the side, seeing feathers floating and swans drifting, one with its leg cradled oddly under its wing, as if it carries a long ladle. Craning further, Alice spies a strange oversized fish with gaping mouth, and closes her eyes. If only she might topple into the water, sink beneath the swan's black feet, let it rake over her . . .

She shifts position, her ankles feeling swollen, but the chain cuts into them and does not permit movement. *As I am a witch* . . . Of course, Nessie is right. The confession was a grave mistake. She had only been confessing to bewitching those naughty girls! Or, rather, the occasion had dragged it from her: the shame and humiliation, the whole of Warboys turned out to watch as if she were a performing bear with chains around her feet.

She had believed she would be whipped or put in stocks, and the matter would at last be ended, her family kept out of it, and she could return to her life baking bread and drinking beer. How could she have known that trull Susan Weeks would die within the blink of an eye and of nothing, nothing as far as she could tell, apart from bad timing?

Such a blessing, such relief it had been, *Oh, it's over, at last, all of it, it's over*, made more joyous later, when she heard that the girls were asking for her, wishing to share a little cake they had made with her. A cake! Made for her! An apple cake with medlar jam inside it!

Now they are travelling on the wooden bridge over the moat, the horses stepping carefully, fearful of the moss and the wet gloss of the rain that hangs soft and drizzling in the air.

The bishop's coat of arms is above the door to his quarters: white rosettes, gold and black chevrons. Alice remembers that when the good queen, Katharine, was banished here, her people knew that she complained bitterly of the cold and damp, of the fenland bogs that circled the towers, with the trees peeping out of the watery lands, of the fen ague that moans in every aching bone, and she feels it too, the creep of cold and damp and misery here that no fire will warm.

The diamond patterns in the brickwork of this building, grey and black and red, are dazzling and shining wet but make Alice think of a theatre, of the fair, of puppets and players, acrobats and tumblers and (though she would not wish it) of those long-ago Plough Boys.

The shame of it flames in her again, the memory and shame worse than any pain. The back of her head smashing hard on the stones as if it might crack and the two boys so silent, only grunting, that she had wondered for a second if both were dumb or if it were not really happening but only a nightmare from which she might soon wake. One held her, the other laboured. And then a third boy appeared inside the church, also with soot-blackened face. She had not heard any door open. He was obviously known to the first two, and she had the sense that they were preparing her for him, like a chicken trussed for a meal. A meal fit for a lord.

Foolish, craven Robert Throckmorton. Doesn't the imbecile know that a woman would rather die than tell her daughter or husband such a shameful thing? That he had no fear of her *telling*? Such tales are to be shared only between women friends, who can be trusted to have a tale or two of their own. His anxiety in asking Nessie what the girl knew only confirmed his own guilt – although she suspected he had some other shade of interest in Nessie too, a kind of sickness, that made it impossible for him to stay away from her. Yes, while at the manor house she had soon observed many hints, a sort of miasma that hung about him, that struck her as foul and intense. It was he himself who allowed the doubts and suspicions that she had tried to keep at bay to take hold.

She had worked so diligently her lifetime to forget: she had buried the day so far inside herself, like cloth pushed deep into the back of the fireplace, there to lie blackening, turning to ashes. She had kept it from her family. She had never intended to confront Sir Henry. But that day, that sudden moment when he appeared on his horse, from out of the trees, how startling he had been. There he was and she was no longer in control of herself, shaken as if some devil did indeed have her in his grip. Her fate was sealed, then, perhaps. She should have kept her mouth closed, kept a 'women's virtue' as the other Henry, the young knave, had once urged her.

But knowledge had come to her in its own devilish way. *As I am a witch . . .*

Who was the third, the one who held back, the man who had the lesser part? Dressed like the others and hidden behind his blackened mask, but also a wide-brimmed, feather-trimmed hat. He might have been the Bishop of Lincoln himself for all she knew.

Her eyes stray then to the terrible building they are about to enter. To a plaque with the names of previous bishops upon it. John Langland. Sweat springs, pooling in her back, dampening her bodie. The constables shout, tug and pull the women from the carriage, where they at once tumble on the grass until keys are produced and ankle chains undone. Soon mother and daughter will be led down some stone steps and along dark, cavernous corridors, then shaken out and tossed at the feet of the bishop, like teasels tipped from a basket. Who knows what fresh sorrow awaits them?

The theatre continues. The bishop, in his robes and his pointed cap, is a small and spry man, like an elf or a scamp, or a fool in a travelling show. Mild-mannered, red tufts of hair explode above his ears, he is not at all the terrifying figure Alice expected. She and Nessie are herded to the front of the grand hall, then the constables step back, disappearing through a small wooden door hung with curtains. The vast room has a fireplace, lit and glowing red, but giving no warmth. Above it are grand portraits, gold-framed, and tapestries of Bible scenes line the walls, along with coats of arms. Alice's eyes fix on a painting of a fine gentleman in fur and robes with golden goblets and bowls of fruit and a black servant behind him, like a shadow. When she squints the blackamoor seems to step back, disappear. When she opens her eyes wider, he reappears, staring at her.

They shuffle, unable to walk freely, although they are now unchained.

The bishop sits in the grand chair, lost inside it, like a child. Church officials are seated at desks to either side of him. This is a court, an ecclesiastical court, but nothing like Alice expected.

To Alice's great surprise she and Nessie are offered refreshment, and stools brought for them to sit on, placed on a magenta rug on the stone floor in front of the bishop.

'I am the Bishop of Lincoln,' he pronounces, in a squeaky voice, 'William Wickham.'

Alice refuses the stool, 'for after that wretched journey my backside pains me', and the court erupts in titters. Nessie sinks to the other, lowering her head.

'You may well act ashamed, young lady,' squeaks the bishop. 'I have heard your mother will not hold her tongue, and that is no doubt the cause of much of your trouble.'

Nessie keeps her eyes lowered, but accepts the little silver tankard of ale from the tray, sips and looks around for somewhere to replace it. A footman takes the tray away.

Alice stares at the bishop, taking in his silly pointed hat, his richly embroidered cloak and the old, wizened figure of him inside it. What had she expected when told she was being sent to an ecclesiastical court? She hadn't understood the word, but she knew – or did Robert Throckmorton say? – that it had great power and could deal swiftly with the most serious of crimes. She had not expected the drink brought on a tray for her, or the stools, or the cold, cold stony castle room with its curiously lavish furnishings, the smell of burning incense. Her breathing quietens and the feeling of nausea ebbs.

The bishop sits a little straighter in his chair, raises his height, to peer at her daughter. There is a fringed velvet cushion under him and he adjusts this. His gaze rests on the girl. It is a look Alice knows well: Nessie always provokes it.

'You are Agnes Samuel, nineteen years, known as Nessie, daughter of Alice and John Samuel, yeoman of Warboys?'

'Yes, sir,' Nessie says quietly.

He turns to Alice. 'And you are Alice Samuel, fifty-one years, of Warboys, wife of yeoman John Samuel?'

'I am.'

'You must lift your chin when you speak, Mother Samuel. And call me "my lord bishop".'

'I am, my lord bishop.'

To the man seated at a desk to his right he says: 'Write this down. The examination of Alice Samuel of Warboys, in the county of Huntingdonshire, taken at Buckden before the Right Reverend Father in God, William Wickham, by God's permission Bishop of Lincoln, 1590.'

Ink is dipped, scratching of a quill: Alice's soft breathing fills the silence.

'Now, Mother Samuel,' says the bishop, 'you have confessed to the Reverend Doctor Dorrington and Master Throckmorton, Squire of Warboys, of your witchcraft, and that you did curse and bewitch their children, sending your imps to do it, likewise sending your imps to bewitch Lady Cromwell of Huntingdon, wife of Sir Henry Cromwell, residing in Ramsey and Hinchingbrooke House, who has now died of a lingering illness. How do you plead?'

249

'My lord bishop?'

'You confessed, I believe, to the vicar of Saint Mary Magdalene church in Warboys, in front of witnesses?'

'Yes, I did, my lord. But to the children – to the *sickness* – not to hurts to Lady Cromwell. I did not confess to that.'

'Note that down. She claims she did not hurt Lady Cromwell but confesses to being a witch and hurting the Throckmorton children. And who does this work for you?'

'Huh?'

'I asked you to address me properly, Mother Samuel. Do you have imps to do this work for you?'

'My dun chicken, my lord.'

'Is it a natural chicken?'

'No, it is not.'

'How do you know this?'

'Because it suckles on my chin, my lord, and when I wipe it off, though I feel nothing, there is blood there. And in church it sent me a nosebleed. And the harm that came to the children has come by means of this chicken.'

Nessie sighs, as loudly as she dares, and lifts her head a little, to try to catch her mother's eye. Now she has mentioned her dun chicken Alice feels comforted. Oh, she can say what she likes now, what does it matter? Alice pulls the stool a little towards herself, remarking chattily, 'Ooh, I think I'll have a sit now, sore backside or no.'

Again, titters.

'The dun chicken is now in the bottom of my belly,' Alice says. 'It makes me so full I'm likely to burst. This morning I could scarcely lace my coat. When they wanted me to get on a horse it was so heavy it pulled me off. They had to bring that – thing instead to carry me here.'

'And was it your imp, the dun chicken, that cursed Lady Cromwell? Did you send it to her?'

Here Alice pauses, takes a sip of her ale. She crosses her legs, glances around the room, trying to remember. Didn't she say a moment ago that she had never cursed Lady Cromwell? Nessie tries with eyes ablaze to convey to her mother to hold her tongue. Alice feels the look, but shakes it off. That old bitch Susan Weeks. She was glad she was dead, glad, *glad*, whatever or whoever the cause of it.

'Well, my lord, Lady Cromwell did cut my hair and my hair-lace and throw them on the fire. I said to her that I had never harmed her yet. But I believe she did tell one of the maids, or was it her daughter? Anyway, she told someone that I sent a cat to claw at her in her sleep.'

'And *did* you?'

Nessie makes a sound, a loud breathing sound, staring at her mother as hard as she can, but there's no stopping Alice.

'No, my lord bishop. The ill and trouble that came to the children, that came because of the dun chicken. And that has now gone from them.'

'Who gave you this gift of the familiars?'

'My lord?'

'Was it a man? Who sent the dun chicken to do this work for you?'

Ah. This is what they want. Men's names. She had not reckoned on that. She is feeling dizzy, with the drama and the tension of it all. Perhaps there is something in that ale. Stronger than the sort she might brew herself. A feeling of nausea welling . . . Well, as long as she keeps Nessie and John out of the tale. That is what she must remember. She glances at her daughter.

'It's all in the confession, my lord, that Doctor Dorrington – the vicar I mean – he did write down. You can read it there.'

'I'd like you to say it here, Mother Samuel, for the court, and we can then write it and I will be able to decide what next steps to take. Was there a man who gave you the gift of the spirits?'

Nessie blurts: 'My lord bishop! My mother has suffered much already at the hands of our neighbours and is but a simple woman whose tongue is prone—'

At this, a guard steps forward. He has been standing behind them. Neither woman had noticed or feared him, but as he looms in front of them, his sudden and deliberate step quells them both. Alice has a fit of dry retching, as if something is trying to escape her. The sound sputters weakly in the huge hall.

Nessie lowers her eyes once more, quivering, her hands folded in her lap, their scars and scabs such a pitiful sight, glowing darkly.

'Our Lord guide and preserve us,' the bishop says, drawing his hands together in prayer for a moment, then raising his eyes above them. 'Let us turn to you, Nessie Samuel. What is your part in this?'

'None, sir.'

'Then why are you sent to me?'

'I do not know, sir – my lord bishop.'

He begins reading the dispensation on his desk. 'It seems that it was the fifteen . . . oh, she is sixteen years old now . . . the daughter, Johanne Throckmorton, of Robert and Elizabeth Throckmorton, who accuses you. She says the spirit came to her at night – the Thing – and brought news. It claimed she would now have extreme fits and this came to pass. And she saw your figure in ghostly form, a green gown moving on its own. And during these torments, Doctor Dorrington writes, the spirit, which was called Blue, made her nose to bleed copiously and other parts of her, and when asked why, this spirit said: "I have been sent, not by Mother Samuel, but by Nessie. For she too is a young witch."'

'No, sir!'

'You deny it?'

'I do . . . I do not confess to it. I beg you, my lord, to believe me.'

Nessie begins crying and Alice's trial of coughing gathers pace again, rising to a squawk: 'You must believe her, my lord! She is innocent, she . . . Why, the imps come only to me and their names are – what is it? – Pluck, Catch and Smack, and this one, Blue, well, who is he? I've never heard of him!'

A burst of laughter then from one of the officials somewhere in the room. The bishop silences him with a wave of his hand. 'Blue, Catch, Pluck and Smack. This is not a matter for mirth. My judgment is this: you, Mother Samuel, will be taken to a room in the palace with the guards, where you will give the name of the man who sent you these spirits and tell if he had carnal knowledge of you. You are fit to stand trial at Huntingdon along with your daughter and husband. You have confessed yourself a witch, and if the others do not confess we may yet discover evidence to find them guilty.'

'They have never done hurt to any!' Alice cries, leaping up. Nessie begins quietly weeping. Alice is shouting, her words tumbling over themselves, as two guards step up and try, with arms under her elbows, to escort her from the room.

'It's the children!' Alice wails. 'Aren't they well now, apart from Johanne? She was always wanton! She is a wicked girl, foul-tempered. Someone else could have sent this imp Blue! He might be acting for another!'

The bishop leaves his seat and steps forward. 'You acknowledge you know him, then?'

'I've told you, 'tis the first I heard his name!'

'You would do well not to curse the daughters of Robert Throckmorton. This Blue, he is not the brown chicken that lives in your belly? Or a mouse, perhaps, for it is written that you also sent a mouse to appear in the mouth of another daughter, Bessie Throckmorton, and a cat to visit Lady Cromwell.'

At last the room gathers heat. The fire seems to be rising, flames shooting from it. Alice, dazed, looks about her, as if she herself caused the flames to leap. There is laughter and the sound of stools tumbling over and the bishop is up and standing and directing his men to march Alice Samuel from the room, she loudly protesting, the fire roaring in its high golden vigour, Nessie trying to stifle her sobbing, as she sinks back to her stool, seeing her mother escorted away.

The bishop steps forward. 'You, my dear, may wait. When we have finished recording your mother's words, we will send you back to the gaol at Huntingdon. Your trial is set for the twentieth. By confessing, as your mother has done, you may be able to offer balm to the family and help the children to leave their fits.'

Alice hears Nessie protest: 'But, my lord, my mother. Her mind is beset by devils but not true ones . . .'

'That is not for you to say, young lady. The secular court will decide. Your mother has confessed to Doctor Dorrington some things that perhaps you did not hear tell of. She will tell my men privately in an anteroom. It is not for a daughter's ears. A wise woman is the ornament of her house – I bid you be silent.'

Over her shoulder Alice sees Nessie pull her thrumbed cap around her face and hears her sob afresh.

In the small room, it is the face of Johanne that flares in Alice's mind, with her big dark eyes and her sulky mouth. And the little one – the first to accuse her. Jane. That girl has a look of her older sister: spiteful, determined. Cicely Burder told her she disliked the girls, those two in particular. Nessie had asked her, when they stayed at the house, what was the wrongness that hung everywhere, like a miasma, something that wasn't about illness, but about spirit? Why was the lady of the house so downcast? Why were there such hard speeches, shouting to be heard at times, and not from servants, such endless churching, such a curious feeling of – *what?* – in the air at the manor house? The dumb maid who swooned around the master and the son who was sent away . . . Grace, Mary and the boy Hob having a lightness to them, an unspoiled nature, which Jane, Bessie and Johanne seemed not to possess. Not quite the pall of misery, it sizzled: almost a smell, like a will-o'-the-wisp over the fen, the bad gases twitching.

Alice had not wanted to reply, but only thought, Yes, Nessie is right about this miasma, this foulness of the soul, of the spirit, not a sickness quite, that hangs in the house. If only she could *understand* it, name it, it might save her. Was it the nature of the master that had brought it about? A naughty house, she once said.

Alice cannot speak, while two men stare at her like that. They are too close. It is making her sweat and a great fear arise in her, and it draws a memory to her, too. The men have parchment and one holds a quill, dripping a blot of ink. They need names, they say.

The room is cramped, the furnishings dark, a green curtain drawn across the wooden door. A coldness creeps in with her as if something else is in the closeted space with them, beating its wings.

Fingers on her face. The taste of soot. The smell of terror and the fire and the flapping and fighting and tumbling and she struggling to exist, but cleaving in two, trying to kick but one of the boys holding her legs, and pulling up her skirt.

The bishop's men's words confuse her. She feels hungry, hollow, like a blown eggshell, its contents spattered; her legs ache, so old she feels. Where is her spirited self now, the girl who fought like that? Seeing how the world shapes itself around her, wanting it to be over, now.

'Is there a man who bedevils you? Whose bidding do you do, old woman?' the bishop's guards ask her. Again she is bewildered, as if they are speaking in French, in Latin, although dimly, somewhere, she believes they are not.

The three faces, blackened with soot. The churchyard. Plough Monday, the Plough Boys.

'Did he have carnal knowledge of you, this devil?'

She remembers what she is always trying not to remember. The thing that makes her feel foolish and girlish and ugly and wrong. Her hand goes to her chin. She wants to sit but the men are now pacing around her. Sweat trickles icily down her spine. She must stand, they say. She will be asked these questions in court, so it is better that she tell *them*, now, under the ears and eyes of God, in the bishop's house. It will be better, they say.

And in that little dark room, a confessional, her lungs are squeezed and thoughts are tumbling: the men who roughly handled her, the Plough Boys who changed her life, who set this in motion – and she shakes her head, sickened and confused. Her grey plait has come undone and, under the scrutiny of the men, she feels as she did then: naked.

The terrible smeary soot-blackened face of the biggest boy. A man, really. She told herself she would never forget him if she survived. And yet she had tried with equal strength *to* forget. His eyes, the colour of pond-water. His long nose. His complete silence, except for his breathing, and his grunts. He did not even curse her. And until that day, the day she had seen him again upon his horse, she had wished never to see him again and hoped him dead.

Struggling with the man's weight on her, on the cold stone of the church floor, she had seen an eagle carved in wood, atop the lectern, talons poised to strike and she prayed with all her blood and terror pounding, *Oh, help me help me please help me, dear God, thank you for loving me and giving me all that I need and now in my darkest hour, please . . .*

And moving her eyes from the eagle, she had seen something else, a little face, carved in the biscuit-coloured stone, the strangest of faces, the size of a vixen's face, or a little cat's, low in the interior wall, made by the stone mason for *what?* To ward off evil? To amuse the parishioners? Its mouth was open in alarm, she felt, blunt stone shock at what it was seeing. And so she found herself praying to the little ugly open-mouthed face, *Oh, help me help me please help me,* and then – miraculous, indeed! – she had heard something, a door opening, and her prayers had been answered, in the shape of God's servant, the vicar she thought it was, though she hadn't dared to look at first, such was the shame of how she was: so tumbled and so disturbed.

The Plough Boys had instantly released her. They were standing, adjusting their clothing, hardly even hurrying, sliding out of the church and somehow disappearing like the mischief-makers they were dressed up to be, into the bosky lands beyond the church wall. The leader, the man, had managed to climb off her, reorder himself. He was dressed in a labourer's hose and shirt but he had a small purse, tied with a belt, and it was that, that which had alerted her. She had stared at it, trying to make sense of the thoughts churning inside her. Thoughts about the fine shoes that the Plough Boys wore, not the poor boots of labouring men, and the feeling of a ring, a ring on one of his fingers digging into her skin, a ring such as no poor boy would possess. Of course Plough Boys might carry purses to keep safe their gathered loot, but this was of a different order. Silken, it was of a good material, and his gesture, that arrogant, deliberate, gesture. Still he did not speak. As he turned, he *had dropped some coins on her*, with a glance and nod at the vicar.

The Golden Knight. When she heard his name later, she knew.

The man, the vicar, had reached out a hand to her to offer his handkerchief to wipe the charred black from her face and her throat and her apron. She had stood up, her knees feeling like marrow-bone jelly, thinking about their silence. Why had none uttered a word? It must have been because they were high-born and all the soot in the world could not disguise it. She was thinking about those coins: should she pick them up? In the end, she only pulled down her skirts and pushed the filthy handkerchief back into the vicar's hand, thanking God for answering her prayers and saying to herself: *It is over and I am alive, I am blessed, truly blessed, and I must be grateful and good for evermore and surely nothing bad can now happen to me after this, because didn't I come near to being a tiny vole in the talons of that eagle and God Himself delivered me from danger?*

But it was not over, as she discovered.

The bishop's men are waiting. They have not been patient while her mind drifted and they are calling her name, ordering her to attend to their questions, to give them an answer. Her mind returns to the stone face the mason had carved inside the church. Whenever she had attended church she had looked for it. But it was cleverly disguised among all the interior stones, the colour of toasted bread. It was low down – you might only see it if you were on the ground. She could not remember *exactly* where it was. She felt it must have been a fancy, because it was nowhere to be found. And then that day, the day of her confession, just before her nosebleed, she had glimpsed it again. Who on earth was it, looking out at her from deep within the church? Was it an imp, a devil? Was it God, or the Holy Mother, directly staring at her, its mouth open, its expression ancient, all-seeing, all-knowing, curious, amused, angry, shocked?

'We need his name, Mother Samuel. Repeat after me: "O Devil, I charge thee in the name of the Father, the Son and the Holy Ghost, tell me the name of the stranger which gave me the spirits."'

These guards are insistent. It was not God who had delivered her that day. It was surely the devil. In the shape of an imp. Or sending his right-hand men to labour for him. Her mind is drifting again and she wonders at their forms: dogs, was it? Or eagles ... descending on her ... She remembers talons, tense, huge wings. And three fleur-de-lis, three swords, chevrons, two lions with claws outstretched. Oh, those dun chickens, the blood coming from her nose, the pain in her belly, day after day, all of it welling up. What must she say, what must she tell them, for it to be over?

'Give us the devil's *name*, Mother Samuel. It will go better for you, and for your daughter, if you do.'

Of course they had names, those three Plough Boys, lives that continued. They were upright men. The hints, the discoveries and suspicions that came later to her, she had swiftly buried them again. The vicar who had helped her, she discovered he was the Reverend Master Garth, and Sir Henry – the Golden Knight with his habit of throwing coins wherever he went – well, he was the grandest of men for miles: she could not have failed to hear of him. It seems that Sir Henry had possession of a ring, a diamond ring that had been given to his father by the King for skills at jousting – there was much talk of it. The ring she had felt digging into her flesh when he had put a hand over her mouth. She was certain. That day when she finally saw him at Warboys, when the rage in her had burst into flames: although she had accosted him with loud speeches, waved a stick at him – how clear it was that he had forgotten her, given her life not a moment's thought – she was as nothing to him.

The first devil, she had learned his name too. Yes, he was not a *distant acquaintance* of Sir Henry. He was another well-born man. The first to defile her. The one who had held her legs.

The face of the bishop's guard looms for a moment, close to hers. The eyes seem red-rimmed. Oh, yes, she knew their names. Two of them. But she must never say them. It would link her to them. It would give her a motive for her cursing. It

260

would be worse for her daughter, for her husband, if she did. If she says nothing, Nessie and John will have a chance. Anyway, who would believe her? Sir Henry made that clear. *As I am a witch* . . . She smells them again, and the terror that was in her that night. She remembers stones, and moss curling like hair, wretched, twisted angels and, again, an eagle ready to strike, talons clenched. The feel of fingers painfully probing her undergarments, her shock and shame . . .

'His name is John Langland,' she says. 'The devil tells me.' She does not know where this comes from: it appears in her mouth. Has she ever heard the name before? No, she thinks not. (Or did she but read it earlier?) Never mind, it is a man's name, it will do, it is a good one, it has arrived, and the effect of it is startling.

They step back affrighted, checking over their shoulders. The one with the quill brings up his knee to lean his parchment upon it, a curious young gesture, Alice thinks, in order to write the name down.

'And where does he live?' he asks. His eyes sharpen, waiting.

Alice says she does not know. 'There is more . . .' she says.

A swelling feeling in her heart. She is enjoying it, she realises. Oh, why hold back a secret rising, like yeast, for thirty-five years? It feels good to let it out, a boil lanced.

'There were three men sent to me by the devil to do his work. The worst of these was a gentleman. His face was black and I could not know him, or the one who stood beside him. There was a third. He aided the other two. His name was John Langland. I do not know where he lives, or even *if* he lives.'

The two guards shudder. 'His face was black' – ah, yes, just as they expected. One twitches at a green velvet curtain beside him as if to shake out any devils hiding there.

'Did these servants of Satan visit you in your bedchamber, old lady?' The fatter, balder guard leans in, his eyes a little watery.

'No.'

'But you met with them for lechery, conjuration and magic? Did they have use of your body?'

'They did,' Alice says, and the little space in which they are confined seems to breathe in softly and contract. The quill scratches on the page, recording her shame.

'Did they leave their marks on you? Marks of Satan – do you have them?'

'I do,' she says, very soft.

'And afterwards where did these servants of Lucifer go?'

'We stole two bushels of malt and rode together, high and low, into the night,' Alice says, swaying slightly, in a singsong voice.

The one with the bald pate says: 'Repeat after me: I charge thee, be gone, old devil, in the name of the Father, the Son and the Holy Ghost . . .'

Alice begins repeating, relieved, exhausted. She'd like to sink to her knees, but she knows they will only haul her up again. Her fate is decided: she will soon be on her way back to the gaol and then to court in Huntingdon, and what then? Nessie and John will return home, surely, now that she has confessed. Who knows who will believe what? She can scarcely keep a thought safe in her head. But as she is praying and repeating after them a strange smell arises in the room, like the reek of a pyre. Sulphur, like the worst fen rotting gases on a dark night or the stink of burning Hell. No smoke – the two men do not interrupt their prayers so she feels sure it is only she who smells it.

She opens her eyes. This secret has been with her, like hands pressing on her chest. The devil must have sent her to the squire's house, to see for herself the man and to understand the part he played in her life and how she would never be free of him. Her own guilt. A woman singled out in such a way, a woman who gave away a child, is wicked indeed and must burn in Hell for it. She thought the name-callings by the children were her punishment and suffered them willingly (though not in silence), but now she sees that is not enough. She must be reminded of how whorish, how bad a witch she truly is.

Alice repeats the prayers, but inside her thoughts are calming and taking an honest shape. She thinks, I hope it was this new spirit, this one in the kindly pecking shape of a brown chicken, the one they call Blue, who brought me to the house in Warboys and to this knowledge. She thanks him, under her prayers . . . *as I am a witch* . . . and asks him to deliver her to her fate.

***

Walking past the flickering ripples of the pond at Ramsey is a girl, newly delivered. A harsh winter is almost come: hard rosehips bud on branches. A young Alice carries the child in a blanket, and the babe – a girl – sleeps peacefully, sheltered close to her bosom, under her shawl. An autumn day, leaves soft and limp underfoot. A little golden mouse sprints from the cover of one heap of leaves to another, and Alice starts, almost steps on it, stumbles. She can barely walk, the ache in her womb so heavy and the bleeding so copious. Ten days it has been, and Elizabeth Mortlock, who helped to deliver her, has returned to her home. Alice forgot to ask this one who knew everything if the bleeding would ever end. She has bound her breasts, and Elizabeth said the milk would cease in a day or two but would be painful fit to burst before it did.

If she does not live, the infant must, she decides. *By grace are you saved and through faith and not of yourselves: it is the gift of God.* The gravestones topple with their curling ivy, with their messages. The monks are long gone, and she wonders who will discover her little child, the girl with her blue-white skin, the great round moon of her face, the eyes tightly sealed as if in death. Alice had felt sure for a moment that the babe was deaf, so silent and still was she. And then a crow squawked and the baby's tiny eyes followed the sound, and then her mouth opened and a weak wail came, like the mewing of a kitten. Not deaf then, just mild in nature. Contented.

If she cries, how will I hide her? I will be found: I will be undone. I cannot care for her. I must give her up.

The door to the church is closed but not locked. She steps inside, into the cold stone entranceway where another small blackened wooden door beckons. Alice puts her face to the door. She listens: she can hear someone moving inside. She sniffs the air: a fire burning, incense mingling with onions, with tallow, with the smell of candles and cooking.

She draws the babe out from inside her wrap where the little heart has been beating next to hers. The girl's warmth leaves her. One eye opens, the other is crusted and sealed with milk. In answer, Alice's breasts ache and her nipples draw tight, readying themselves. She licks her finger, rubs it on the eyelid until it opens. Now the babe seems to be considering her, a very piercing stare, two slanting eyes, bright as tiny pieces of green glass. Alice wraps the blanket tighter, tears away her glance. She bends to place the child on the step, at the doorway. It is cold but Alice feels sure that the instant the parson steps out he will see her. The church is next door to the house of Sir Henry Cromwell and to the old abbey. Someone there will know what to do. What need does this babe have of a mother with no husband, an orphan, and penniless?

Alice does not kiss the child. She does not look back. As she steps out from the church into daylight, the milk in her breasts bursts forth as if from a dam, soaking the laced bodie of her dress. The church gardens smell of lady's bedstraw, camomile, dying and wizened, and yarrow. On the road she can hear horse's hoofs, and in front of her a bare tree mocks her with its one lonely leaf dangling, clinging to the last. Her womb aches, lying like a low-hanging fruit, deep and bruised inside her. Elizabeth Mortlock did not mention how long this pain would last; using the magic girdle and the charm to invoke the Five Wounds of Christ, during the labour, should she pray again, now? In the height of the pain, when Alice thought she might die and hoped bitterly for it, clutching at Elizabeth's hand and hearing those chants, well, yes, she was sure the words had saved her because words can do that.

Weary, bleeding into the linen she has fashioned for herself, she starts the four-mile walk to Warboys before winter floods the fens. Since her mother died in the early months of her discovery and she was left alone she has been staying with the nuns cast out by Cromwell – not Sir Henry, his father – to live in the cottages near the old nunnery. Now she must get far, far from Ramsey, far from the seat of Sir Henry, as far as her legs can carry her. Far enough that none will have heard her tale. Sister Dorothy has been kind. She told her what to do with the baby: leave it in the abbey church. Then go your way. The babe will be well looked after: it will find its way back to me, or one of the other nuns.

She does not expect to survive this walk. She cannot think what to do beyond escaping. She is weak. The bleeding, the heaviness, the aching in her buttocks, her lower body: she feels an exhaustion unlike anything she has ever felt, and at Wistow Fen a light pattering rain begins and she stands for a moment to watch it glossing the purple-black sloes, washing their dusty lustre until it gleams. One minute she is staring at the berries, holding out her apron; the next she is on the ground, and remembers nothing.

It is a man who wakes her. He is crouching by her, laughing for no reason. He has blue eyes, of the most pale and unusual colour, just like the sloes she was moments ago thinking of gathering, and he has a black beard and coarse hair and a bag of rabbits beside him.

'Was thinking I might have to carry you,' he says. His voice is loud, and full of vigour. She feels it bounce from the little canopy of trees and opens her eyes wide, to get a better look.

He already has his hand out, his fingers circling her wrist, like a bracelet. Young Alice thinks she would like to call him a cheeky rascal but is too tired. She staggers to her feet, and he helps her. He ties the bloodied cloth bag of rabbits, so that it hangs around his neck, and then, with a gesture quick and nimble, hoists her with one arm, onto his back. She winces, a pain leaping. But she is grateful, and rests her cheek against the rough male stink of his neck. He makes no gesture to hurt her or rummage her person. He holds one arm firm under her backside and begins walking.

She feels, as she bounces on his back, that she might be one of his rabbits, or a sally perhaps, done for, half alive, half dead. She closes her eyes, abandoning herself to the rhythm of his swift walk and the feeling of surrender. As night falls she opens them and sees the stumpy spire of the church of Saint Mary Magdalene and knows they are arriving at Warboys. She thumps at his back and he sets her down and she asks if he lives here, and what is his name?

'John Samuels,' he says, 'trapper, eeler and fisherman, at your service.'

They have approached the village of Warboys from the direction of Wistow Fen and she has not spied the pond, or the alehouse, only the church, looming like a bad dream in her vision.

'Where is your home? Is it to your people you were headed?' he asks, adding, 'I thought you a stranger here, left for dead by some knave . . .'

His assessment of her condition then: he had thought her ravished or attacked, dumped on the muddied path. She does not correct him, but as for her people, she shakes her head. Her sister and mother died this last year of plague. Her father many years dead. She is alone. She says nothing about the babe, for what is there to say?

'Can you walk a little now?' he says, and she falls into a stumble beside him.

By the end of the journey, his sloe-blue eyes have a better colour, darker, like the berry when the rain glosses it, and she marvels at this. There is something of wonder about him. He is ready to bid her come and live with him. 'You have no one else,' he says, and it is the truth. He is proud of his quick fingers, his skilful way with a punt gun.

He kicks open the door to his cottage. He shows her a pallet on the floor and a blanket. He shows her the bread oven, and the well. He has a pig – Donald! – and hens that he is proud to call his own. It is a house a little bigger than the one she grew up in, and there is an upstairs, of sorts, a loft room, with a ladder where his old mother lives, half blind. The old woman peeps out from a straw bed with the same startling blue eyes and nods at Alice, opening her toothless mouth, pointing at and rubbing her stomach.

Alice sets to work and finds his larder well stocked, his guns lined up orderly, the rabbits soon skinned and hanging in a big vat of stew.

At night she thinks: Does a man, a young man, does he know if a maid has had an infant? He already believes her sullied, the victim of an insult to her person, and seems to welcome her just the same, so she has some hope. The poultice and the bandages Elizabeth Mortlock bade her wear have made her breasts harden and the milk retreat, and if she does not think of the baby's mouth, no tingle erupts there.

The night falls after a good supper of the rich rabbit stew and John Samuel lies beside her on the pallet. His hand reaches for her, warm fingers lifting her nightdress. She pulls the garment down, says, 'I'm ill at ease.'

When he blinks in the darkness, and moves closer to her, his nose the only part of him she can make out, she touches it and says, 'I'm wearing flaps.' Still he reaches out his hand, persists and seems not to understand.

Didn't his mother ever tell him about monthly courses? She feels rather than sees his confusion. He remains still for a moment. Then: 'I had no sisters', he says. 'And you saw my mother, she doesn't say much.' She puts his hand to her waist to show him the spencer belt she wears, whispers in his ear. He grunts, groans, puts his hand to his member and turns his back to her. The mattress shakes for a while and then subsides, like a boat in a storm.

In a month or two, he tries again.

The first time he takes her is robust, as he is in all things: rough and quick but there is kissing first and much fondling and rubbing her with his big hands, as if he is trying to start up a fire, and somehow, with his calloused hands, he succeeds. She is surprised by the warmth he stokes in her. His energy, the way he tears at her, his warm mouth: she welcomes them all. She stifles a cry as he enters her and he mistakes it for joy; she puts a hand to his belly to keep him better at arm's length and he grins in the candlelight, supporting himself on his elbows, and saying, 'Go slow, eh, is that it?'

And so it is a silken back and forth – she marvels at the slipperiness her own body can produce to oil his movements, something she knew nothing about – and it is not as bad as she thought and even, she'll admit, has something good, some sweetness to recommend it. She thinks she will try again later, and might well grow to like it.

John Samuel himself is a wonder to her. His silence, his independence, and his sudden warm bursts. The blasts of laughter that come for no reason. He is often in good humour. He is proud. He tells her that for many a year he has been chosen by the village to be the annual Straw Bear, so skilled is he at dancing and his fiddling (he demonstrates and, as in most things with John Samuel, it ends up in drinking and in no time at all in a spirited game on the mattress) and, yes, he makes a handsome dancer and a lively fiddler, she tells him, giggling into his ears, her hand over his mouth to silence him so that his old lady in the loft above might sleep soundly.

She loves to walk behind him on his fishing trips out to the duck-filled waters, watching the length of his stride and the pumping swing of his arms. She can barely keep up. She marvels at the dark growth of his beard, the top of his lip showing like a blue shadow within hours of a morning's shave. He is vigour, growth, youth; he is like a sapling that astonishes with its speed. And health and joy: she feels both creeping back to her and begins her new life with gratitude – cooking, baking bread, fetching flour from the old mill, keeping the fire stoked, carrying water, feeding and tending Donald the hog, the chickens and also the old lady, with a spoon, bathing her, growing fond of her, with her long plaited hair, the same sharp blue eyes and deep gruff voice as her son. Alice loves sweeping the little cottage, taking the clothes to the pond to launder them, bartering with the other women in Warboys. She believes herself accepted – she even believes herself befriended, to have a place with her neighbours, coming to her for their cures for dropsy and the fen ague.

She listens for stories of her baby daughter from Chatteris or Ramsey, but none reaches her. She is aware that the task of finding the child a home would fall to the Sheriff of Ramsey but thinks nothing of it, or of him. She tries her best to banish all thoughts of him. One day, she does not remember how, or who, someone mentions that the old nun Sister Dorothy had died, and Alice blurts out: 'Didn't the nun care for a foundling?'

'Oh, that child . . . I heard she died, too,' came the answer, and that was that.

*

That God chose to save Alice but not her baby broke her heart. John Samuel never asked her about the circumstances he found her in. When something troubled him, he put a cap on it, pulled it down low and did not look out from it. Or else he picked up his fiddle and played a nonsense tune, and danced a silly dance, and tried to make her smile.

Then there was that other thing. The small discovery a few months after being with John Samuel as his wife (and before the vicar blessed them, or God did, some good many years later, with the arrival of their daughter) that her lower body, the inside of her thighs and secret parts and her fundament: all was now covered with little growths, small seeded things that looked like a crop of warts. She did not dare show them to John Samuel (she had now learned that in between his dancing and good humour there were bouts of roaring and blows that rained down on her). She bathed them in vinegar and tried rubbing an onion on them or a piece of meat to bury in the backyard, and sometimes they seemed to be leaving, only to reappear in summer nights when the light was better, or when she held a candle there, and felt for them. They never really left her, and she grew accustomed to them, small as they were; they did not pain her. But only now, today, at Buckden, does she feel again the wonder at them, and fear the discovery of what they are. Marks of Satan. Were they seeds planted by the first men or by John Samuel? She has never known. They came, they went, in her long life, no cures – meat, string, onion, prayer – could rid her of them. But now she fears that they will be, like her, uncovered.

So long since she has thought of John Samuel saving her, finding her, rescuing her. And now it is as they are saying. It was not God but the devil she had contracted with all along.

She had thought Satan to be in the Plough Boys, their faces now fading from memory (but not the feel of them, the fear). She is weary. *As I am a witch* . . . Her life has been fuelled by rage with but rare occasion to vent it. She has longed to confess and to be absolved. She was used in the most wicked and whorish way. She abandoned a child. She kept secrets from all. If not absolved, then let it be punishment. What she cannot bear is nothing.

Muchwood, 1585, the summer. John Samuel had woken her early, and Nessie too, with only a small cup of caudel to line their stomachs: the walk to the huge woods on the outskirts of Ramsey is dark, their skirts soaking up dew, their two burning torches after a time joined by those of others – women, maid-servants, daughters, carrying baskets of victuals and a few innocent tools. Just a mattock for slicing the brush.

The men keep out of sight. They know what to do – many a long night well met at the alehouse, discussing and drinking – yes, Sir Henry has now submitted his complaint to the Star Chamber and has the ear of the Queen herself, accusing them of taking his private hunting park for their own! Common land, commonly owned, they say: land that they have farmed, rivers and ponds they have fished, and wood they have made use of for longer than anyone can remember, hares and coneys and ducks that have fed their families since the days when fires in the abbey windows burned bright and the dark figures of monks and nuns went about everywhere, and Sir Henry Cromwell, the Golden Knight, was but a twinkle in his grand-father's eye.

The men had settled it: it would be in the early hours of the morning and they would send in the women first. That way Sir

Henry and his men would not be alerted until it was too late, and the land cleared. That they would be children and maids and old women meant they would not, John Samuel claimed, be taken for a mob. Just womenfolk going about their business, gathering willow for weaving, spindle-twigs for making their pegs and needles.

As they arrive at the edges of the disputed woods, the land Sir Henry claims as his hunting grounds, a cockerel in the distance can be heard, announcing the dawn. A surge goes through the women and they lay down their torches, dousing them in the nearby river, where the mussels glint in the dawn light, open palms, just as the otters left them. Trees are dark skeletons, the ground grey and only the rosy light starting to awaken it. The women, with little gasps and shouts, pick up their tools, their hooks, their pickaxes, their mattocks – Nessie has a scythe – and they kneel and crouch at the underbrush, fences and thistles, flushing out a long-legged hare, whisking across the woodland floor away from them, as they begin to cut at the bushes.

Alice feels tired, and not a little afraid, wary. She has not the young bones and the fearlessness of her daughter beside her. She hears and sees the women ahead of her, cutting and slicing the brush at the edge of the forest. Yes, of course she agrees with the men, with John, that it is wrong, *wrong* of Sir Henry to want to ban them from land that has been commonly held for hundreds of years, but she has her own feelings about Sir Henry to master. Her hatred and long-held desire to avoid him wars with another more powerful wish: to take her opportunity to spoil something that belongs to him.

She trembles at the thought that she might encounter the man himself. There is so much danger here, so much to fear.

John Samuel, his position. He might cover his face all he likes but it would take only a rumour to reach Sir Henry and the excuse or proof that their landlord has long sought to punish him would be achieved. There is great risk in angering a man who must be every Warboys' family's landlord.

She tries to keep her mind to the task, the cutting and the gathering, and the clearing, her hands already a little scratched, and she does not look up, trying to suppress her awareness of being so close, so close now to Ramsey, to the little abbey church where she once left something precious and has tried never to remember it, her heart pattering so fast, racing like the feet of the hare they flush out, her head bowed, unaware of the other women moving ahead of her, at the other side of the pingle, until it is too late.

The woman towers over her, and at last, hearing the breath of the horse and smelling it, Alice looks up. The woman sits, gazing down at her.

'What is it that you women are doing here? On my husband's land?'

'Your husband?' Alice is confused, for this woman, not a young woman, not a pretty one, but stout and puffed up, stuffed inside her riding jacket, is speaking not in the voice of a sober matron but a common woman like herself.

Alice straightens, her hand to her aching back, to regard her. 'I'm Alice Yibbot, ma'am, and I'm clearing the spinas – the thistles – so that our animals might graze here.'

Alice, quick-thinking, using her maiden name, so that no blame will attach to the leader of the rebellion, her John Samuel.

'You have no right to do it! I shall tell my husband at once!'

274

Alice can hardly believe her ears, the way this old trull is speaking to her! It's true that, now she looks properly at her, the woman is wearing fine boots and a bodie of some good material and carrying a rather grand whip, and now that she is assessing her she spies a coat of arms on her livery that is familiar: two beasts, three fleur-de-lis, three swords, three chevrons.

The woman draws herself up straight, then leans to put one hand on the horse's muzzle, speaking slowly, as if Alice is an imbecile. 'My husband is Sir Henry Cromwell. The owner of Muchwood. My *new* husband. I will forgive you for not knowing me, but not for your rudeness. And this assault on his land. He will be much angered.'

Sir Henry Cromwell. This fat whore is his new wife. Alice feels her belly plummet and nausea swim over her. She cannot find her tongue: it has grown thick.

The coins he dropped, with such disdain. She sees them now, the Golden Knight, scattering them over the church floor.

All these years. Anger rises in her. Hatred. A pounding in her temples. She feels her face glowing red. The man had simply lived his life, even marrying again, and all this time he but seven miles away, swiving and tupping to his heart's content.

'You old bitch,' Alice says, and spits.

'*What?* What did you say to me?'

'You heard me.'

Lady Cromwell steps down from her horse. Her polished boot steps in the soft soil of a recently erupted molehill, distracting her. She shakes her foot and fumbles in the pocket of her jacket, lifts her hand. Alice fears for a moment that she is about to strike her, but instead Lady Cromwell takes a step back, crosses herself, hesitates. Then Lady Cromwell starts and points her whip: 'Who is *that*?'

Nessie has arrived.

Alice tries with her eyes to convey to Nessie to keep tongue still, but it is not necessary: she sees at once that Nessie has some measure of the scene unfolding.

Lady Cromwell puts a hand to her mouth and makes a queer sound. 'Is this girl with you? Another seditious bitch from Warboys? Your daughter, perhaps?'

'We will leave now, quietly, if you permit us to,' Alice says.

She is expecting more anger from Lady Cromwell, more outrage. She expects punishment and threats. She is astonished when the woman finally pulls out of her pocket a little bottle, which she sniffs and then scatters its contents on the ground in front of her. The old trull is flustered, almost weeping in the most astonishing way as she puts a hand on the flank of her horse to steady herself, saying, 'The words you spoke to me! Do not come, you or your daughter, anywhere near me or my husband!'

The women stare at one another.

'We are going, ma'am,' Alice says, her hand on Nessie, who looks in bewilderment from her mother to the grand lady now climbing upon the horse.

Once remounted, Lady Cromwell regains some composure, though she is trembling. 'I hope never to see you again.'

The blood is pounding in Alice's ears and sweat springing all over her body.

Lady Cromwell, with a great whip at the horse's flank, takes off. Nessie stares after her, astonished.

Alice would like to weep, to throw herself on the ground, kick something, scream. She does not want to look at Nessie.

Her face blazes. 'I am . . . I might stand in need of some medicine.'

'What is it, Mother? Are we now to be whipped?'

'No – the old trull will never mention it. She – you saw her – she was afraid of *us*.'

Nessie takes her hand, amazed. 'Why should she fear us? What harm could we do her?'

'Oh, she did not like my temper or my words. She's one of those who feel great spite in their hearts and believe they see it in others. You saw her. She took out a witch-guard!' Alice says, taking a deep breath, steadying her breathing. So Sir Henry has married a superstitious country woman, evidently the most passionately witch-fearing sort, finding them under every bush and spina.

'Lucky it was not Sir Henry who saw us,' Nessie said. 'I doubt he would be so easily seen off. Hurry up – say nothing but success in our task to Father!'

Muchwood had added a handful of rue to her bitter cup. She had prayed it would be the last occasion she would ever meet Lady Cromwell. It was unfortunate that this particular prayer was not answered. She might have lost her temper that day when she spied Sir Henry on his horse in the woods of the manor, but she had believed herself in possession of it again by the time she had met Lady Cromwell in the Warboys manor, right up until the moment the old bitch had come at her with the shears. (As Nessie had pointed out, she concedes, it would have been better to hold her tongue, but that is easy for those to say whose words do not burst out of them the way Alice's do.)

All the times she tried *not* to think of it, *not* to remember that Plough Monday.

And when she had told Margery Caterill, not the names of any of the men, only that it had happened, all Margery had said was 'What were you doing in the church on your own?' and then, after a pause, 'What happened to the child?'

'I left her in a church doorway. I heard years later she died.'

Margery Caterill let out a shocked sound, like the hiss of a goose, and crossed herself. 'Well, you were blessed to have Nessie then. I'd keep that Plough Monday tale to yourself and count yourself lucky to be alive.'

Yes. She used to count herself lucky. She had tried to keep it to herself. Her God had saved her, up until now. She did wonder, increasingly, as Henry Pickering once had, whether her God was the same one that others worshipped or if she was indebted to someone else.

What does it matter if she has conjured the third name from thin air? Let the last be William Langley or John Langford or the bishop himself. Who cares, now? Her God has supplied her with two names out of the three.

***

The morning of the trial: the girls are ready to leave Warboys at first light. Bessie appears beside me downstairs, where I am packing away my straw mattress in the kitchen, dressed in her bonnet and already laced into boots, looking sober, with her hair all tucked away. Jane is standing beside her, knitting her fingers together anxiously, and then, appearing like a shadow, Johanne. Who can say what thoughts pass through Johanne's mind? Her dark eyes and her plain expression speak nothing.

My mistress has asked for the girls to come and say farewell in her bedchamber as she is too weak to bid them goodbye outside. She embraces each in turn. 'Martha will take good care of you. Be a lady and speak up loudly and don't be afraid. As long as you tell the truth, God will protect you.'

The girls troop out of the room, Jane snivelling a little, but my mistress calls me back.

'I am so glad it is you going with them. It is such a strange thing, to make children the chief witness at a trial.'

'I have heard it is common, Mistress, throughout Essex. Children do not lie, they say.'

'They say that, do they? Fine men who see them only at prayers with all their ribbons tied, or running in the fields picking daisies, might believe it.'

She pauses then, struggling to sit up. I rush to put a pillow behind her, stroking her hair away from her cheeks while she grabs my hand and presses it. 'If Jane or Bessie should be in her fits, do get Robert or Henry to carry them away to a quiet room, away from the . . . from society, if that's possible . . .'

'Yes, Mistress.' Her dark hair has more grey than ever, as if someone has tipped a sack of flour on her head. The worry is in her eyes.

She leans back against the pillow, bids me sit. 'We have known each other many years, have we not? You were the same age as Bessie when you came to us – is that right, Martha?'

'A little younger, Mistress.'

She sighs. I am conscious that the family wait for me down-stairs, and Crabbie has the horses stamping outside in the fresh early air.

'And how we did hate and fear old women like Alice!' she says. 'How fearful we were of their horrible bent bodies, their missing teeth, the ghastly shape of them, knowing, I suppose, that our own beauty was but a brief gift from God.' She gives a feeble laugh, which soon turns into a cough.

'Mistress . . .' I am picturing Sister Dorothy, old indeed, the veins knotted around her legs, but thinking, I never did hate or fear her. I always knew how much she had to teach me and how big her heart was in taking me in.

'Why is that, do you think? Why do girls in particular feel so strangely handled? And now we have become old ourselves—'

'You are not yet forty, Mistress!'

'But I fear—' Here she starts coughing again, and I run to fetch her the horehound, the soldier's tea, a cold cup of it left on the washstand by the window, to try to help her swallow.

'Oh, Mistress, I wonder why you are so convinced it is only the natural tribulations of women at this time and there is no cure for your ailments.'

'If Robert were here, he might say Mother Samuel had bewitched me too,' she splutters. I know this remark needs no reply. She does not believe it. When her expulsions have passed, her big eyes – dark eyes, like Johanne's – swim with tears, and she says, 'Oh, why did I ever believe him?'

'Mistress?'

'Robert. Why was I so willing to believe him when he pointed the finger at Gabriel? Now that I think of it, I do not remember Jane saying anything at all against her brother . . .'

Again and again she returns to this. I lift the tea to her lips once more, but she shakes her head, she wants to talk:

'Robert took up the cause at once, and insisted it was Gabriel, and of course, he said, who else could it be? How could another man gain entry to the house without us knowing? I did not *want* to believe it of my son but I thought I *ought* to believe it, I must believe it. If I was a good mother then I must take my daughter's part, and that God was testing me. *Brothers* – brothers cannot be ruled out, I said to myself. I thought I was being brave! It was all done with such shame and hurry, and such insistence from Robert that we acted promptly and never again discussed it. I did not think to challenge him. My son, my son . . .'

A memory then. Gabriel, five or six, blond curls, the perfect cherub. Stamping little feet in fury at being accused of breaking a wooden doll belonging to his baby sister. 'Why does no one believe me? I could never do such a thing.'

Her hands in mine are icy cold. The saddest of thoughts washes through me: a deep stretch of water, the yellow marsh marigolds atop, the children and I running alone, *alone*, chattering like chiffchaffs in the reed beds, while she floats somewhere else.

She gathers herself and seems to see the thoughts drifting through my mind.

'Thank you, Martha, and take care of the children for me. And Thomas Cakebread. He might make a reasonable suitor for Bessie in a year or two. Please make sure that our dear Gabriel knows how loved he is, by both of us, and that I never . . . believed it.'

'Oh, Mistress . . .'

I beck my head, trembling, for I know she is speaking not only of these days ahead of us, but of a much longer stretch than that.

***

Alice, Nessie and John are ushered in to stand in the wooden dock. William Wickham, the Bishop of Lincoln, is here again, also Judge Jenner, a tall man, very thin, with an even taller hat, making him look like a stick of sedge. Another name Alice trembles to hear: Francis Cromwell. The brother of Sir Henry. Indeed, for a moment, she had thought it *was* Sir Henry as he strode into the small courtroom, stuffed with people, then realises her mistake. This man is younger, thinner and some-how but a shadow of Sir Henry.

Sir Henry enters a moment later, taking his seat beside his brother. Huge starched ruff, standing out like a halo around this throat. Very calm, she notes. Nodding to one or two men he knows. Composed. And then another man. A man she has not seen before but recognises: he must be the eldest brother of Mistress Throckmorton, the one who lives in the village of Titchmarsh. He has the colouring of his sister and younger brother but a very large head, like a pumpkin. His expression is grim.

The Throckmorton girls are brought in, the moon-faced maid shepherding them, to sit on the witness bench in a row close to Alice, Nessie and John Samuel.

Judge Jenner clears his throat and reads the indictment: 'Against Father Samuel, Old Mother Samuel and Nessie, their daughter, for bewitching unto death the Lady Cromwell, late wife of Sir Henry Cromwell of Hinchingbrooke in the county of Huntingdon, knight, and for bewitching Mistress Johanne Throckmorton, Mistress Jane Throckmorton and others, contrary to the statute made in the fifteenth year of the Queen Majesty's reign. Brought by Gilbert Pickering of Titchmarsh in the county of Northamptonshire and Robert Throckmorton Esquire, father of the said children. The grand jury will hear evidence first from Doctor Francis Dorrington, vicar of Warboys aforesaid . . .'

She can hardly follow but she understands this. Her confession. They will begin with Alice's confession. Sleepless, starved, Alice has wits enough to know that this is a very bad place to start.

The confession is read, and the courtroom hushes to hear it. 'Alice Samuel was asked about her spirits and admitted to a dun chicken, which she fed from the blood on her chin and from her nose. I did then ask, "What about a mouse, a toad with a black face, a cat: did you have other puckerels?" And her reply was "They changed their forms, sir."'

A little ripple of sound and excitement travels around those standing at the back of the court as the Reverend Doctor Dorrington in booming voice reads out his lengthy report of Alice's confession. A chicken, a mouse, a toad with a black face, a cat. All the details are there. Yes, they have seen old women talking to such creatures. How old crones love their cats!

And then their names: 'Blue, Catch, Pluck and Smack . . .'

After the confession is read, a very long time that the vicar enjoys as much as in any pulpit, he returns to his seat next to Master Throckmorton and the judge asks a guard to bring Alice forward. Her daughter darts the quickest of movements, a sharp squeeze to her mother's shoulder, before a guard steps in. Alice knows what it means: an attempt to silence her. But she shakes her head defiantly. She has already confessed and these men want details. The room is entranced. Why should she hold her tongue now? Alice is marched to the front of the court and turned to face the jury, and the row of children.

'Do you swear to tell the truth before God?' the judge asks her.

'I do, sir.'

Master Throckmorton shifts a little, next to the reverend. Sir Henry – Alice dare not raise her eyes to look on him, yet she cannot help but be aware of his presence. She senses rather than sees him leaning forward, with interest.

'In front of the Bishop of Lincoln at Buckden you did admit that a devil had carnal knowledge of you and directed you in your necromancy – *three* devils, you said.'

'Yes, sirs. I did meet a man who bedevilled me. His name was John Langland.'

This causes a stir. Those assembled do not dare laugh, but the name is shocking.

'Where does he live, this John Langland?'

'I do not know, sir.'

'Are you suggesting he is related to John Langland, the former Bishop of Lincoln?'

The bishop who had examined her at Buckden is conferring with the men beside him. She sees his expression and he is not amused.

'You know this man is not here living, and yet you sully his name?' Judge Jenner asks.

'I did not know that, sirs.' Alice glances around and this time spies Throckmorton. His expression – she is gratified to see it – is tense. Even at this distance she can see he is sweating, his forehead shining. She glances at the man she thinks is the mistress's older brother from Titchmarsh. His face sickens her. His brow dominates his small mouth and nose; she thinks it is as if his brains were swelling out of the top of his face. She draws her eyes away, pulls herself upright, attends to the question.

'I think I spoke in error, my lord. It was many a long year, sirs. His name was William Langley. I beg your forgiveness, I have never done hurt to any—'

'Except the children in question! You were taught by this man, this William Langley?'

'William Langley?'

'The man you said bedevilled you. You gave entertainment to him? He lay with you as a man and sent his spirits to you?'

'I named him – I said, I think, his name was John, sirs. John Lang . . . Langland.'

'John Langland? A moment ago you said William! You must make up your mind. And now, what are the names of these other *servants of Satan* who came to you?'

Alice stares wildly out at the court. Her eyes land on Gilbert Pickering again and quickly take flight. What matters it if she never discovered the third persecutor's true name or character and calls him by an invented one? (And her misfortune to pick such a name!) None of the three had sought to learn *her* name, these good many years, so that seems fair.

She cannot help but dwell on the figure of Robert Throckmorton, dressed handsomely, but his shoulders slumping, his posture craven, staring down at his hands, as if in prayer. Then she slowly turns her gaze to Sir Henry. Here there is no sign at all of concern. Even of a husband's to find out who bewitched his wife. She wonders what to say, what she might say, her tongue growing thick in her mouth. What would bring the outcome she wants? To go home. To sit at her own fireside, with her husband: knitting. For Nessie and John to go free. Surely there is still time for that.

Her husband sits in the dock staring ahead, his face suffused with rage. Nessie is white with fear beside him. Now Alice's eyes stray to the Throckmorton girls and their maid. The maid's face is as wide and blank as the moon. She and Alice lock eyes for a moment. Should she open her mouth into a little round o shape, like the carved face in the church at Warboys and call out? Is now the moment to spill all? Still the names tremble on her lips.

Words wait in the wings, up high among the rafters, threatening to swoop down and scream in their ears. Alice notes that the children, Bessie, Jane and Johanne, seek the eyes of their father for comfort, but he avoids their glances: he is tugging at the ruff at his throat. His face is blanched, pale. Sir Henry leans in towards his brother, whispers a remark and the brother smiles, as if it were something amusing.

Slowly, suddenly, Johanne stands up. 'Oh, dear God, please deliver me!' she cries, and her scream makes those in the courtroom first leap in fear, then fall into enthralled silence.

She tumbles at once towards the maid beside her, jerking and twitching, and with one arm shooting out, stiffly pointing. Her sisters rush to attend her, trying to hold down her shaking limbs and also to hide her from the room. But Johanne shakes them off, screaming, like a polecat.

The first man to move is Doctor Dorrington. Alice stands uncertain in her dock, while he hastens to the children, and the master soon follows. He speaks a little to the maid. The judge asks if any have need of a glass of ale. Johanne gives a great groan and Alice sees how the crowded room sways as one towards them, captivated.

'The Thing has spoken to me,' Johanne says, standing up. She seems nervous, the rising and falling of her chest in her bodie is visible, but bold, too, and determined. Alice wonders if she might step down, now, return to the bench next to John or Nessie, but the guards either side of her, their hands under each elbow, make it clear she is to remain standing.

'The Thing? What is the Thing, my dear?' the judge says, inviting Johanne with a beckoning hand to step into the witness box.

All shaking has gone from Johanne, her face white. She walks to the box.

'God is above the devil, my lord, but the Thing has been sent to all my sisters, and that is why we are handled like this . . .' Johanne is firm, and loud, and all hear her well.

'Who has sent it?' the judge asks.

'These three members of the Samuel family,' Johanne says, with a gesture. Alice's knees pain her and she sags suddenly, the guards holding her up. The maid sitting with the girls on the witness bench makes an odd, wordless noise – the strange sound that the deaf make sometimes.

Alice's ears ring from the screaming in the courtroom. *That girl!* When will she give up this wantonness?

Her mind is beset by devils. All her life, she has struggled to hold her tongue. It was surely her rudeness to Lady Cromwell or her cursing of Sir Henry that has brought her to this – and now, *now*, should she learn continence at long last?

'The Thing is sent from Alice Samuel to do this harm to you? And by John Samuel, her husband, here also charged? And by Nessie Samuel, their daughter?' the judge asks Johanne.

'Nan, we call her, the young witch. *Nessie* Samuel. Yes. The Thing tells me she is his dame and he must do as she commands and punish me. He says he was sent to bewitch Lady Cromwell by Alice. And he handles my sisters again in the same way, especially little Jane, his most beloved.'

Nessie! The courtroom turns to poor Nessie. She has not moved or spoken, but her face alters. Her skin has the grey pallor of a death mask. She is a shocking sight to see. The sleeves of her dress are torn and along her forearms a pattern of scratches, scabs and old scars leap, dark against the white, as if she now wears the skin of an exotic animal, a tiger, seen only in paintings. Alice's heart contracts to see her. The judge is asking that she step forward, to stand next to her mother and face the charges. The smell in the room, of sweat, of excitement, intensifies. Rain begins pattering on the roof of the building.

Two guards bring Nessie to join Alice at the front of the courtroom.

The Reverend Doctor Dorrington jiggles a little in his seat alongside Throckmorton, puffing up like a cock in the yard, now that the witnesses and jury can see what the family is up against. From his seat the vicar half stands and calls to Nessie, as if he is speaking from the pulpit: 'The child charges you with command of the Thing. You must call it off!'

'Stuff and nonsense,' Nessie snaps back tartly, and Alice lifts her head to nod to her daughter. The assembled gasp and – Henry Pickering leading them – shake their heads reprovingly. The rain pounds a little more heavily.

Nessie stands tall but shaking, and says, 'I have no command of this Thing. The girl is – it is *counterfeit*.'

Oh, Nessie. Alice feels a stab of pride: her daughter has spirit indeed, to say such a thing to a room full of accusers, but for a maid, a low-born girl like Nessie to accuse the master's children of lying . . . A shock whips around the room, like the tail of a viper. Under her breath Alice bids her daughter be silent, as her daughter, her entire life, bade her.

Jane screams and falls sideways on the bench. The maid – Martha – holds the child and smooths her brow, while those assembled stretch to get a better look. And then a dreadful new turn of events: Johanne's nose begins to pour blood.

'The Thing is inside her and trying to escape!' calls one.

The room first rapt now unsettles, like the contents of a button box scattering, as people stand and lean forward, provoking Judge Jenner, in his great black hat, to stand up himself, to try to tower over them.

'Order. This is a courtroom. I must have order!'

Alice feels dizzy. The sight of blood pouring from Johanne frightens her. Of course, of course, the girl is faking, she tells herself. Then she remembers her own nosebleed. Her confession in the church at Warboys, the penitent linen sheet splattered with red. She didn't fake that. It isn't possible. Some devil *must* be inside, trying to flee.

Johanne speaks then, and the chills in the room deepen. The hair stands up on Alice's neck and on her arms to hear it.

'What is this in God's name that comes tumbling to me? It tumbles like a football. I think it must be some puppet player . . .'

Johanne is glaring at a bloodied handkerchief rolled into a sodden ball in her hand. Then, slowly, she raises her eyes and fixes them elsewhere. All follow her gaze. Alice watches the entire room crane to where Johanne is looking, at some point in front of her, as if she is drawing their eyes on fine thread. Finally, Alice, too, turns to gaze at the same space.

And she sees it. *All* in the courtroom see it, she thinks: the bloodied handkerchief rising and floating, hanging in the air like a giant puffball, full of evil breath and evil intent, spores of words, large and round, tumbling and foul. The evil that has burned in Alice's heart, the secrets she has kept, all that she has longed to reveal and say, the devils in her mind and in her dreams, the wickedness she did, the child she abandoned, all those secrets are surely here, in the courtroom with her, now, for all to see.

Nessie begins to crumble. Her knees buckle and she stumbles a little and rights herself just in time. Alice turns towards her daughter but feels the restraint from the man at her arm, preventing her from moving.

Johanne sits, on a stool that the guard has fetched her. The bloodied handkerchief drops to her lap.

Judge Jenner asks Nessie, 'Do you confess, here before God and your neighbours, Agnes, Nessie Samuel, to the witchcraft here charged? Repeat after me, if you do: "As I am a witch . . ."'

'I do not confess,' she whispers weakly. Oh, the girl is strong. She is a true daughter, Alice thinks. They will surely have to reprieve her and send only *me* to the gallows.

Still the Throckmorton daughter persists. 'Oh, it is not a puppet-player,' Johanne says, in the same low voice, the voice of the Thing. And now she is turning to John, still sitting on the bench. 'I see what it is. It is Alice Samuel's thrumbed cap. Do you remember, Jane? The cap you saw that let us know her true nature.'

Jane cannot speak: her own trance has sewn up her mouth.

'What is your name? I pray you?' Johanne continues. She is holding the bloodied handkerchief in front of her, addressing herself to it. None in the room venture to silence her. Even the judge and the Reverend Doctor Dorrington are rendered speechless, riveted to the spectacle unfolding. None has felt evil breathing so close to them. A woman in the public area drops to the floor in a faint.

Sir Henry. Does Alice dare now to glance at Sir Henry? She raises her eyes to his, and as she does so, he stands up, bending to say something in the ear of his brother, then turning his back as he shuffles across the row of people to leave the room. His gesture has spoken to her directly: he need not trouble himself to remain in court, so certain is he of the outcome. Just like the day she confronted him at Warboys. The same heedlessness. How he had merely turned his horse, with skill and pointed leisure, away from her, in the direction of the track back to Ramsey. To show her how he would always do exactly as he pleases, because he has the means to.

The vicar clears his throat, standing up, calling to address Johanne as a witness.

'What is its name? Is it a spirit sent from Alice Samuel? Or her daughter?'

Johanne is smiling. 'Oh, it is Master Blue. Master Blue, you are welcome. I care not for you – do your worst!'

As she speaks, more blood pours from her nose. And now finally she stops staring at the handkerchief – in her lap once more – and instead her eyes scan the room.

They fall again on John Samuel. His gaze is defiant. *A girl* . . .

'Blue tells me you have all spun a fine thread but from this day on your devils will no longer be at your command. It will be no better with us until all of you, all three of you, are hanged.'

She sits down again. John Samuel has not spoken and something about him is altered. Alice has always thought of him as more alive than other men, his beard, his vivid blue eyes, his strength: alive, bristling with it, with vigour, with something burning, the very force that makes trees grow and shoots push through hard earth. And in that instant some light in him goes out. He looks uncertainly around the room. A child's word. A girl's say-so. Surely, this will not . . .

But a hush has fallen. The room remains enthralled. The rain has ceased and the wooden courtroom feels like the interior of a boat: damp, dark, retreating and shivering, as if after a storm. Johanne stares glassily ahead, and the maid puts an arm around her.

Judge Jenner scans the room and nods, as if someone asked him something. To Martha, he says, 'Take her from the room, dear, and her sister. We will pray that she now makes a full recovery, the other girls too. They have done well. We do not need names if Mother Samuel will not give them. Her silence will be another strike against her. No need for the Throckmorton girls to hear the other witnesses. We have many. I now call Martin O'Chappel. You did claim that John Samuel once assaulted you in the White Hart tavern and bewitched you later that same day when your only cow died.'

Martin O'Chappel stands up. He has a face like a terrier. There is a line of them. Friends and enemies both. Those who rioted alongside John Samuel at Muchwood and had sent their wives and daughters, but who later had had their pay docked and regretted it. They would not stand against him then. But witchcraft is a different thing. The louder they are in accusing, the less likely they, too, will ever be named a witch. Alice knows that is their logic. And more than that: while the Samuels are in the dock, every grudge, every petty neighbour's quarrel, every gripe might be aired and given its due. The times when Alice made them a thorn apple soporific for their pains, or goose grease for their breathing troubles, or a cake of hemp seed and rhubarb root for their pain in childbed, indeed the many children she had helped to see into this world, oh, all of *those* are long forgotten.

Instead it is the times she scolded their children, drove them from her house for chasing her hens, or refused a neighbour bread or barm when she had little herself or was not in the mood to be generous. It is the times John roared at them in the alehouse over some card game or led them towards sedition. The times her prideful daughter tossed her head at their young sons. Whatever their reasons (and she was not certain they even needed reasons, such is the way that wickedness gathers once it has been fanned into life), the people of Warboys line up.

After hours, many hours, of these dispensations, Judge Jenner bids all to be seated, except for those three now charged.

'You have heard the charges here today. And the witnesses and we have seen for ourselves the spell you have cast on that young girl. How do you plead? Do you confess yourselves witches and ask for God's forgiveness?'

'I do not,' Nessie says, in small voice. Her thin body in her ragged dress sways between the guards, like a straw doll, all pride tossed from her.

Once again, absorption in the room gathers. All faces rapt, directed at the young woman standing before them.

'Is there any reason you should not be hanged?'

The matrons in the room look at one another knowingly. They will be called upon to verify the fact, if Nessie should claim it as a means of evading the noose.

'No, my lord. As I am not a witch, neither am I a whore.'

John Samuel makes a shout, half laughter, half bellow.

Now the judge turns to him. 'Do you confess to witchcraft, John Samuel?'

'I do not,' says John Samuel, loudly, his tone bitter.

All eyes now land on Alice. She stands in the middle, a shoulder smaller than the daughter and husband, with the guards flanking the family, like yew trees in a graveyard. How brave they are, she thinks, how brave. She must sacrifice herself so Nessie and John will be saved. That is what she will do. Alice's spine, growing daily more bent, is driving her neck forward, and the way she becks her head gives her the look of a snail tentatively appearing from its shell.

'And what of you, Alice Samuel? You have already confessed to the bewitching of the children. We have that document here. How do you confess to the charge that you did send a cat to do your bidding: the bewitching of Lady Cromwell, leading to her death?'

The bewitching of that old trull? The bitch who waved her whip at her, who looked down her nose at her, after all her filthy husband had done to her with his pillicock?

Someone scrapes their chair on the wooden floor and coughs, and her mutterings, her curses are lost.

'Louder, for the jury,' Judge Jenner says, his hand reaching for the gavel. 'How do you plead?'

'Guilty, my lord. As I am a witch, so shall it be . . .'

'"*As I am a witch!*" She is confessing!' flies around the court-room. An uproar. The people erupt like a pot of soup boiling over.

'Praise be,' Bessie says, the only sister left on the bench. 'Farewell and be hanged.'

The jury makes no great delay – the trial has been but a matter of hours – and finds the three members of the Samuel family guilty as charged. The sentence is to be hanged by the neck until they are dead.

***

In the anteroom, while the business of the trial is concluded, we wait. Jane eats some rye bread I brought her and swings her legs. Bessie has joined us and is one moment full of shock and dismay – 'They will hang now, the entire family?' – and the next running to the window, turning to her sisters and saying with delight, 'Now Mother will be well again, and we will none of us be in our fits, and Father will be at home more, and Gabriel – Gabriel can come home!'

I do not like to tell her that I believe not one of those things will happen.

Johanne is quiet, spent. Her face is very flat, and white, and I worry for her. She does not seem well at all and will not eat the docky of bread and cheese I offer. We have mopped up her bloodied face and her nose, left the dark scabs intact in case we dislodge the blood flow again, and suddenly, she turns over the handkerchief in her lap and says: 'Why is it so bloodied?'

'You do not remember the nosebleed you had?'

She shakes her head. Bessie comes to her side. 'Johanne! You had a very bad nosebleed! And you – you said that Master Blue was in the room with us, and he was, we all felt him and feared him and—'

'You do not remember what you said, about it looking like a puppet-player?' I ask.

Again, she shakes her head. She eyes the handkerchief suspiciously, then says, 'Did someone take it from me and bloody it?'

A shudder runs through me.

'You think I'm counterfeiting – you think I'm lying, as that witch said – and not in my fits at all?' Johanne says, angry now. Bessie opens her mouth to answer her, then sees that the question carries great weight and has been directed to me.

'No, I . . .' What do I think? 'God alone is the searcher of the heart,' I try, but Johanne leaps up, furious, raging: 'That's not a reply! Do you believe me a liar? Do you think those three innocent, not witches, and all our fits are pretence?'

Johanne has never addressed me with quite so much fury before. I do not know how to answer her. I struggle, wanting to tell the truth as she demands, to search my own heart, but finding my hands come up empty.

'I believe the fits are an affliction, of course. You are all strangely handled and not pretending. But the *cause* of them—'

'It's not a bewitching? You disagree with the court? With Judge Jenner? With Father and Uncle Henry and Uncle Gilbert, and Uncle Francis, too, and Sir Henry Cromwell, oh, yes, and many other learned men – and *what*, you, Martha, idiot maid, think you know better than *all of them*?' She is almost spitting now, her eyes huge, her face angrier than I have ever seen it.

The hurt leaps in me at her terrible words and I tremble. Whatever I was striving to utter, striving indeed to *think*, flies from me.

'No, no, Johanne, of course I don't think I know better than those learned men. I only—'

'Maybe you're no better than a *witch* yourself, Martha.'

With that she sits down again and allows the word to settle, beating its wings.

'I am so very sorry,' I say quietly. 'I did not doubt you. I did not believe you a liar.'

Only perhaps *mistaken*. Misdirected, perhaps. I will not speak of it again.

The master arrives to join us then, to begin the journey home.

***

Huntingdon is a town atop water. The morning has a dark brown and red tint, strange before it even begins. Alice has never been to Huntingdon and cannot make sense of what she sees. Surging, the river has swelled its banks and now flows in a sepia colour, tipping itself up to the doors of the houses and other buildings, flowing under the wet stones of the bridges, the arches dark and glowering, the swans bobbing hopelessly in the swirl. She has barely slept. She is wearier than ever in her life and can barely put one foot in front of the other.

She, John and Nessie, chained, are marched from the gaol at Orchard Lane down the piss-scented alley and past the hotel and the grand horses and coaches and onwards, over the little bridge, over the water a-bobbing and throbbing, a sulphurous colour and odour, towards Mill Common, dotted everywhere with yellow flag, the mound with the wooden structures, towards Hell itself. They do not speak. There is nothing now to be said. No prayers, no sorriness more than she has ever felt. Nothing will undo what has been done.

There are onlookers a-plenty, dancing around them, throwing stones, hissing, pulling scarves and hats over faces: *Witch!* A spectacle, something to brighten this watery day. Alice stumbles against slippery stones; the guards hold her up. John and Nessie are marched ahead. Doors open and close. *A hanging!* The air sizzles – a street seller offering pies, jugs of ale, while the birds make themselves scarce. A rat swims under the bridge and the sky sags, a great weight of rain threatening.

Alice had not understood – oh, she had already been tired, she had been confused, weary, her mind had been leaving her – she had not for one moment imagined that in her own confession she was damning her daughter and her husband. She could not unpick their rules: they had told her it would be better if she confessed. If she confessed, she would be hanged. But still, they said, it would be better to confess. She had not named names. Throckmorton or Sir Henry, even that last man she had recognised, she had not named them. She thought she had done the right thing by keeping her secrets and accepting her guilt, and yet, how wrong she had been.

How could she imagine it, her own death, *the end of me?* Last night in her cell, closing her eyes, she knew herself to be about to go to sleep for a thousand years, and tried to stay awake. She wanted to think of everything she had experienced, everyone she had loved. The feel of John's beard in her hands when he kissed her. His sloe-blue eyes darkening sometimes in play, sometimes in anger. How he was always a man quick and strong. Nessie . . . Nessie climbing upon her knee as a girl, or sleeping on her chest at bedtime, a warm lump, like a loaf of bread. And then that other child . . . the babe with the very still, quiet quality, the one she had suspected was deaf. The first baby she has tried so hard to forget, the one she knew she wronged because she forbade her even that: to climb upon her true mother's knee. The girl with her blue-white skin, the great round moon of her face. She thinks of her young self, sixteen, and all the lively dreams she'd had. She had felt herself special, singled out for something, more than the life of a poor fen girl – what had it been? The events of her life seemed to turn on a penny, and the penny she knew was that golden one, tossed on her that day in the church, that Plough Monday, so many years ago. The rage had been seeded that day, had swelled in her. And how could it be, as if that wasn't insult enough, that one of the perpetrators of her sorrows should one day move in so close to her, with his scar, the moon neither waning nor waxing from that day to this?

And his daughters hale and living, and her baby girl gone, who knew where?

Oh, the anger surges then and feels good to her: it's a friend, a familiar, a lifelong friend, a balm.

There was something that came to her mind in that courtroom. Among the long speeches, the great flurry and rise and fall of interest and attention, there had been a moment when she had caught the eyes of the maid, Martha. She struggles now to understand what it was that passed through her mind. She knew Martha. She had seen her many times since the Throckmortons had moved in. She had spoken to her only that one time privately, when she had mentioned the gall of a hare, melted, for clearing ears of wax.

'Keep your ears stuffed then. It suits you to hear nothing in that naughty house, I can see that,' was what she'd said to her.

There are now some steps to walk up and a field of eyes to stare down, but she says to herself: Out of the ashes I rise with my red hair, *I curse you all*, lifting her head a little, to see the folk of Huntingdon, decked out to watch the spectacle. *May your children die young, your wives grow old and ugly. May your husband lie abed with another, just like Lady Cromwell's did.* She does not look to left or right, but she hears her husband and daughter step onto the wooden platform beside her. The voice of the vicar, droning, and asking them again to beg God's forgiveness. The hangman slips the rope around her neck. She inhales the smell of hemp, the knowledge that others have worn it and breathed their last in it. She makes a swift prayer. Not a prayer for forgiveness. No, not that at all. A prayer only for the birds.

***

And thus ye have the story of the three witches of Warboys. If any be desirous to know the present state of the children, how they are and how they have been since the death of these parties, you shall understand that not any of them have had any fit at all, but have all of the them been in as perfect health as ever from their birth. God's blessed name be evermore praised for the same. Amen.

Part Five

The Dream

It is not the whole truth, what the pamphlet says. I'm reading it now, from our new home, in Ellington. *Not one of them have had any fit at all* . . . in perfect health . . . No, this is not the truth. Bessie is still very thin and not the same lively girl: her fits happen less often but they have not ceased entirely. Johanne has not been in her fits, she is the one most improved, but not little Jane: she is still sometimes afflicted. The same is true for Grace. Worse is Mary. Mary, who strove to be invisible and cause no alarm to any, these days she is a sickly child, meeker than a mouse, lost always in her bible and trying ever more to please and slip unseen into any room. But what do the writers of the pamphlet care for that?

After my mistress died – a year, I think it was, after the trial – we moved from Warboys to Ellington. In Ellington, there have been some small improvements: we have left behind the poor rye bread that came from Warboys and the fen air that carried so many ticks in its marshy waters. The fits and antics have been less dramatic: the girls have not struggled between life and death but, as I have said, only in Johanne have they disappeared entirely. The younger children seem to be recovering their spirits little by little, though, of course, much grieved by the loss of their mother.

My master surprised us on our settling into Ellington by taking a new wife – and her name being Alice, and she being so much younger than him, and the marriage a little sudden. The girls were much disturbed, and heartsore, but of course they did not trouble their father with that, only me.

Privately, I understand my master now. I intend to stay here with the family in Ellington until Grace and Hob are old enough to have no need of my care and supervision, then join the new household of Bessie or whichever daughter marries first, to care for *their* children. Even Gabriel, one day, perhaps, in the future.

At my mistress's bedside as she lay dying, and I held her hand and wept over her, my master only stared at her and muttered – he was much the worse for drinking, 'Martha, is her reach beyond the grave? Am I being punished even now?'

Though I did not answer, I knew exactly whom he meant.

The vicar and the judge had both said that a witch's power is entirely ended by hanging, but I did not feel like consoling my master with this fact. I should say that I intend never again to make efforts to console my master. I might even add a wicked thing: that I was *glad* he suffered so from his own fears and fancies that had long claimed his reason. But my task here is to care for the children, biding my time, as I have said, until I can leave.

The day of my mistress's death I concerned myself with little Hob, weeping in my skirts, and the other children's shock and dismay, and with making sure that a letter my mistress wrote to her son Gabriel some days earlier might find a secret way to reach him. In the envelope, I included a curl of his blond baby hair I had once kept for a love token and remembering his childhood self, small and sweet. I wrote: *One day I would like to come and visit. Send word. Your loving servant, Martha.* I hoped that Gabriel might see my heart beating there on the paper, and understand all that I ached to say.

It felt a strange coincidence that the master's new wife was called Alice, and an ill-starred one.

Sir Henry sold off the Samuels' house and belongings and with the money from the sale – forty pounds – a goodly sum, he paid for a sermon to be given in the church next door about the evils that dwell in every village and town, and how to root them out.

Before we left, only Mother Caterill mourned the passing of the three Samuels. Or, rather, she was the only one to dare speak it. 'Some girls who know no better,' she said, once, and Dottie squealed and cried that she would tell the master that Mother Caterill was ill-wishing his daughters.

Dottie said, 'When the gaoler came to cut down their bodies, Alice had little lumps of flesh, like warts, adjoining so secret a place it was not decent to be seen. The gaoler said that's all the proof needed that the devil had had his way with her.' Mother Caterill put her apron up to her face. She did not want us to see the tears still flowing.

In our new home, I no longer dream of vipers. Instead, as I fall asleep – I have a feather mattress, in Ellington – I smell peaty soil, the flicker of camomile tickling my nose. I feel the shadow of a kestrel turn above me, like a sundial, and see the three shapes, dangling there.

My longings, my life before I came into being, my life afterwards. The mothering of the Throckmorton children, my life of service. A life of waiting and waiting. My naughty arrival on this earth, a naughty beginning, and never to know – only in dreams – where I came from and what naughtiness seeded me.

In bed, I feel my spine stretch and uncurl from my form. My long ears are dark at the tips – they twitch and flicker like corn in the field. At last! I have perfect hearing and perfect understanding; I am no longer afraid to speak. I hold out my hand in front of my face: my paw is furred, my eyes are golden; I am bounding over the fen, down through time, legs strong and huge – I feel their power, bouncing up behind me. I'm swifter than a deer, a fox, a greyhound. I'm the fastest creature in England. And at last I am together with my true mother, all my mothers, a long legged stubble-stag, a wood-cat, a jill, a hedge-springer. The jumper, the rascal, the racer. The sudden start, the shake-the-heart. The creature bearing all men's scorn. The creature no one dares to name. Quicker than a spell, a curse, a wish. Quicker than truth or memory.

Acknowledgements

For information on the case here described, I used a pamphlet published soon afterwards, in 1593: *The Most Strange and Admirable Discoverie of the Three Witches of Warboys Arraigned, Convicted, and Executed at the Last Assises at Huntington, for the Bewitching of the Five Daughters of Robert Trockmorton Esquire, and Other Persons.* The pamphlet is 'anonymous' but believed to have been written by the Reverend Francis Dorrington, Robert Throckmorton and his brother-in-law Gilbert Pickering (who became a witch-finder in other cases in Northampton, years later), so not exactly unbiased. (I am grateful to *my* brother-in-law Francis Bowles for sourcing other historical documents for me at the University Library, Cambridge.)

I first came across the story of the Samuel and Throckmorton families when I moved here to the Cambridgeshire fens in 2003 and discovered a subversive and fresh take on it – a contemporary story where a Samuel witch comes back to the village of Warboys to haunt its residents – in the novel *Weird Sister* written by Kate Pullinger (Weidenfeld & Nicolson, 1999). I am lucky that Kate is both a friend and a novelist whose work I admire. Lucky, too, that she was so generous and open – I would like to express my heartfelt thanks to her for that and for those early conversations here.

I am grateful to the librarian at Warboys and to Rosie Vietch, Cambridgeshire librarian, who sourced for me the book by Moira Tatem, *Witches of Warboys* (Cambridgeshire Libraries Publications, 1993), and also *The Witches of Warboys: An Extraordinary Story of Sorcery, Sadism and Satanic Possession in Elizabethan England* by Philip C. Almond (I.B. Tauris, 2007), a rich and entertaining account of the case.

I'd like to thank the historian Clive Carter, who provided me with some fascinating research (particularly about Titchmarsh and the Pickering family) and exposed some factual errors in other accounts, which I was very glad to learn so as not to repeat them. Also my thanks to Malcolm Gaskill, a leading expert in the history of witchcraft, for his advice and help. (I take full responsibility for details I have deliberately changed or any factual mistakes made.) For knowledge of plants and herbs and local or rude names for them I am indebted to Sonia Lewis.

For information about the Golden Knight and the Muchwood riots I am indebted to Anne Reiber DeWindt and Edwin Brezette DeWindt for their study *Ramsey: The Lives of an English Fenland Town, 1200–1600* (Catholic University of America Press, 2006).

I am blessed with the most brilliant agent and would like to take the opportunity here to express gratitude for the impact Caroline Dawnay has had on my writing life, for her continued support and guidance, perception and kindness, and many other attributes besides. Also to the fabulous team at United Agents, including Kat Aitken and Christian Ogunbanjo.

Sophie Scard deserves a special thank-you for providing probably the best email I'll ever receive on finishing a book, and for her impeccable timing, as does my friend Sarah Ninot for her expertise and advice on Elizabethan clothing, and also Sally Cline for her kindness and support.

The other great good fortune in my writing life was meeting my editor, Carole Welch, so early in my career (she published my first novel, and every other novel since). Her input is incalculable. It's good to have the opportunity to thank her again for everything she brings to my novels. I am indebted too to her assistant, Irene Rolleston, and to my copyeditor Hazel Orme for preventing untold bloopers from occurring in the text.

I would like to thank my son Felix Dawson for inspiring the character of Thomas Cakebread and for answering any question any time on any plant or bird or otter and for his description of the sound a buzzard makes.

Meredith Bowles is my first and best reader. For those long lockdown walks and talks about witchcraft and everything else, I'm more grateful than I can ever say.